SWEAR ON MY LIFE

S.L. SCOTT

S.L. SCOTT

ALSO BY S.L. SCOTT

To keep up to date with her writing and more, visit her website: www.slscottauthor.com

To receive the scoop about all of her publishing adventures, free books, giveaways, steals and more:

Visit www.slscottauthor.com

Join S.L.'s Facebook group here: S.L. Scott Books

Read the Bestselling Book that's been called **"The Most Romantic Book Ever"** by readers and have them raving. We Were Once is now available and FREE in Kindle Unlimited.

We Were Once

You do not want to miss the international sensation, **Best I Ever Had**. This book has won readers over with its emotion and soul deep love. **Best I Ever Had** is now available in ebook, audio, and paperback, and is Free in Kindle Unlimited.

Best I Ever Had

Audiobooks on Audible - CLICK HERE

New York Love Stories (Stand-Alones)

Never Got Over You

The One I Want

Crazy in Love

Head Over Feels

It Started with a Kiss

The Everest Brothers (Stand-Alones)

Everest - Ethan Everest

Bad Reputation - Hutton Everest

Force of Nature - Bennett Everest

The Everest Brothers Box Set

Hard to Resist Series (Stand-Alones)

The Resistance

The Reckoning

The Redemption

The Revolution

The Rebellion

The Crow Brothers (Stand-Alones)

Spark

Tulsa

Rivers

Ridge

The Crow Brothers Box Set

DARE - A Rock Star Hero (Stand-Alone)

The Kingwood Series

SAVAGE

SAVIOR

SACRED

FINDING SOLACE - Stand-Alone

The Kingwood Series Box Set

Playboy in Paradise Series

Falling for the Playboy

Redeeming the Playboy

Loving the Playboy

Playboy in Paradise Box Set

Talk to Me Duet (Stand-Alones)

Sweet Talk

Dirty Talk

Stand-Alone Books

Best I Ever Had

We Were Once

Missing Grace

Finding Solace

Until I Met You

Drunk on Love

Naturally, Charlie

A Prior Engagement

Lost in Translation

Sleeping with Mr. Sexy

Morning Glory

You are not a drop in the ocean;
you are the entire ocean in a drop.

~ Rumi

PROLOGUE

Numbness beats the pain I endured, but I realize the next stage is death.

I close my eyes, too tired to hold them open any longer. *So tired . . .* I just need to rest to save my energy. My breath stalls in my throat as darkness takes hold. Despite what you hear, there is no light to guide your soul.

There's music.

My breath returns as a melody calls me back. I open my eyes to a cloud-laden sky and trees that bend to the will of the stronger winds. Roots creep over the edge of the cliff above me while a bird sings from a low-hanging branch.

Broken, I lie there, captivated by the brown-feathered bird and its yellow mask keeping me company. I grin, but the pain that has returned is too much to maintain, so I listen for hours, waiting for my date with destiny.

An ambulance shows up instead.

1

Harbor Westcott

Room 156.

   Row 14.

   Seat 20.

I recognize her the second I see the back of her head. *I should.* I've stared at it enough to memorize every subtle strand of brown and golden blond that weaves through it, even when it's pulled and twisted on top of her head like it is now.

She's a nice reprieve from the memories that haunt me, like sunshine shining through a crack in the blinds and the first warm spring day after a long, dreary winter.

As I walk toward her, this is the first time I've been this close. She's five-three, maybe five-four on a good day, though I would have guessed a little shorter, sizing her up in the auditorium.

Usually, I see her dressed in a pair of faded exercise pants with a baggy T-shirt hanging over her waist. Today, she's looking damn good in the denim cutoffs hanging on the swell of her hips, and the shortened shirt doesn't dare brush against the top of the shorts, leaving the slope of her waist exposed.

Though, I'd always wondered what color her eyes were, I'm now given the privilege as she looks up as if caught in a thought. Green and bright despite the shadows of her dark lashes under the fluorescent lights of the convenience store. Her sneakers have hit the pavement a few times, judging by the scuffs and black asphalt staining the bottoms that leave the slightest of prints on the white linoleum.

I've always thought she might be a runner by how toned her legs are and her chosen wardrobe in the past. I like that they're not sticks and hold strength in muscle.

It's not that I'm *not* a tits man, but I do love a great ass. *Hers has been noted.*

I move down the aisle from her, eyeing the groceries lining the shelves. There's nothing I need here, but her sweet scent and my deep-seated hunger to be near her draws me closer.

What am I doing?

Why am I acting like a fucking idiot?

I see her in class all the time, at least on the days I go. But I've never craved her company, not like I do now. Sure, she caught my eye. Lots of chicks do. She's different though . . . seemingly oblivious to my existence inside—and apparently, outside—the classroom, judging by her lack of awareness of my presence.

My ego isn't fragile.

I like a challenge, but I *love* the taste of victory.

My life's been boring walking a straight line for too long. This woman is just the detour I'm looking for. *At least for a night or two.*

I imagine she has a boyfriend, probably some schmuck

back home, wherever she calls home, who's waiting for her to return after graduation. I'd bet a day's work that doting middle-class parents who saved every penny to send their only daughter to an East Coast university are a part of her story, along with a hand-me-down Subaru with another good fifty-thousand miles before the odometer rolls over for the third time.

Such a charmed life she must lead.

My assumptions don't do her any favors, but I never claimed I wasn't an asshole. I was never good at balancing bad deeds while looking the part of an altar boy. Not like Lucas was. My cousin is probably laughing beyond the grave, watching me act like a nervous pre-teen having a brush with a middle school crush.

He might have laughed, but he'd also know that hitting on girls isn't my usual MO . . . Opportunity usually presents itself and hits on me first. We never had trouble turning the heads of the fairer sex.

My innuendoes aren't subtle. She's either playing hard to get or is wholly consumed by the can of Beans & Franks in her hand. I'll assume the latter and make the effort. "Don't get hurt," I say. Not my best work, but we're in a convenience store, so I'm certain the bar is already pretty fucking low. When I latch my gaze onto the pale-pink hem of her shirt, a flash of skin is given when she moves. But I catch her gaze just in time to see it sliding up my chest until her eyes meet mine.

Tilting her head up, she studies me in silence, making it hard to read her thoughts. *Did I screw up?* Is she going to give me the time of day or a tongue lashing . . . must rid that wicked thought from my mind or start praying she's into that kind of play. I straighten my shoulders, debating if I should grab the requested diet soda and move on.

But then a half-hearted smile graces her lips. "Is that a warning?" She furrows her brow as her eyes narrow in the slightest. "Have we met?"

I shove my hands in my pockets, eyeing the full package. *She's cute. Innocent, like prey that doesn't recognize the danger around her.* Not sure she would stand out in a crowd, but she stood out to me prior, even in an auditorium full of people.

"No."

"Are you sure?"

"I'd remember." I'm too quick with a response. If I'm not careful, I'll show my cards, and I'd rather her reveal her thoughts first.

Her expression eases, soaking in the compliment. "You would, huh?"

"Absolutely. I'd never forget you."

She laughs, the sound ringing in the air. "Very charming." Her gaze slides down my chest and back to the can as if it's much more interesting.

"I try."

Sighing, she does the slightest of eye rolls before I'm on the receiving end of her glare. "I have a feeling you don't have to try at all when it comes to girls."

Not seeming to break through her cooler composure, I finally realize I have no game with this girl.

"It was a warning," I reply with full intention.

"For you?" She holds up the small can with an all-knowing grin and sees right through me. "Or this?"

This girl.

Fuck me.

What was I thinking? I just hit on her in a gas station convenience store in the middle of the day like she'd fall at my feet. *What did I expect, for fuck's sake?*

I'm arrogant enough to believe I'm worthy of her attention, so I keep my eyes on her. "If you're wise."

"What happens if I'm not wise?" Her voice is as steady as her eyes are on me, which are locked in place.

Call me impressed. The girl can stand her ground, but I'm also starting to think she might be into me. "You might get hurt."

Her gaze shifts, lengthening to a back corner of the store before she looks at me again. "Sometimes the pain is worth the risk." Her body fills with attitude, shoulders straightening and chin held high. "Don't you think?"

"Guess it depends on the risk."

Biting her lip, she smiles to herself and looks back down at the can in her hands. "You're probably right, but I'll take my chances."

Rubbing the pad of my thumb across my lower lip, I then say, "Don't say I didn't warn you."

"Don't worry. You won't be held liable for any damage in the aftermath." She starts to leave but turns back a few feet away. "We're talking about the beans, right? Like, this isn't our meet cute?"

This girl. *Fuck*. She's got my full attention and couldn't care less. "I don't know what a meet cute is."

"It's how they meet in the movies."

"Who's *they*?"

"The main characters," she replies like everyone knows what she's talking about.

I'm still staring at her, trying to figure out what the fuck we're going on about when I realize what she means. "You're really into movies, aren't you?"

"I am. It's a nice escape."

"From what?"

"Life."

That has to be one of the most honest answers I've ever been given, and I've never felt more understood before.

With straightforward honesty like that, I'm determined to find out why this fascinating woman needs an escape from life. "I get that." There's a pause as her eyes look into mine, seeming to search for answers to questions she hasn't asked.

The last thing I want to do is pour out my heart under the stench of gas or show that side of myself that I've worked fucking hard to bury. I need to get over it. I need to get on with life.

I say, "Did we ever decide what you wanted to discuss? The frank and beans or how we met?"

"Quite frankly, pun intended," she says, laughing lightly, "I'm not sure." I have a feeling that's the only thing she's ever been uncertain about.

She has me competing with beans, for Christ's sake. I'll do it if it gets me closer to her. "How about we find out? You can eat that alone, or we can discuss the virtuous qualities of canned meat and beans versus our meet cute over something we didn't heat in the microwave. What do you think?"

She takes me in unabashedly, not seeming the least displeased with what she sees, but then says, "I'm good," and walks away.

Damn.

I played this all wrong . . . *I played her all wrong.*

But when she starts back to me like she's on a mission to settle a score, I know I've gotten to her. Guess I played this right, after all. She holds the can up and waggles it in the air. "And who said I'll be eating this alone?" Cocking an eyebrow in challenge, she knows she scored the winning point. The rubber bottoms of her sneakers squeak against the linoleum tiles as she heads to the register.

I cover my wounded heart. Okay, not really, but I fucking hate to lose. Throwing my arms out to the sides, I ask, "So is that a yes?"

Shooting me a glare that buries any chance of redemption I thought I might have, she says, "It's a no."

They say you can't win them all, but my record remained undefeated until now. I look around, glad there are no witnesses.

I grab the soda for Marina, almost forgetting the reason I came in here, and head to the counter.

"Hey, how are ya?" the guy asks my current fixation . . . *Is that what she is?* Am I fixated or fascinated? I might side with fascination more than fixated, which borders on obsession. Though by how I've watched her over the last month in class, obsession might not be far off.

I don't like the way he's staring at her with his smarmy smile after a quick rattle of his fingers across the register keys. He dips down on one elbow and smacks his lips together. "I get off in an hour if you wanna . . ." Clicking his tongue, he continues, "You know. I'll even let you come behind the counter. There's lots of room down here."

What the fuck? I move to her side, staring the fucker in the face. "What'd you say?"

"Mind your own fucking business, kid," he snaps.

Kid? He's what? A few years older than I am? *He's got some fucking nerve.*

As if I'm the one in need of defending, she edges her shoulder in front of mine. "First of all, you must be new here." Can't say I'm not impressed and a lot amused. The girl's got bite.

He replies, "Just started Thursday."

Leaning closer, she says, "Secondly, ever talk to me or any woman like that again, and you'll be looking for work elsewhere. I know TJ doesn't take kindly to creeps working his counter." She slaps her money on the counter. "And for the record, I am his 'fucking business,' and I want my change for the soda and beans." Turning to me, she adds, "You good, babe?"

I chuckle under my breath. "Yeah, all good, sweet cheeks." I lean in for a kiss because I'm a fucker like that, but I'm met with her middle finger pressed to my lips.

Tugging me by the beltloop of my jeans, she pulls me close, our bodies pressed together, and whispers, "Save it for later. When we're alone."

Fuck. I think I'm in love.

The change clangs against the counter, all twenty-three cents of it. She slides it into the palm of her hand, skipping the tip jar, before taking the bean can from the counter and walking to the door.

Just outside, the door closes, and I say, "I take it you're not friends with that guy?"

She bursts out laughing as we clear ourselves away from the entrance. Eyeing me, she grins. "Can't say we are."

I shove my free hand in my pocket and look at her as if I'm seeing someone entirely different than the girl inside the convenience store. "It's too bad you have to deal with shit like that."

"Part of being a girl." She tries to shrug it off like it was nothing. It was something and made me want to punch his fucking face.

Although I have no doubt she can take care of herself, a vulnerability entangled in her strength causes my chest to tighten. "He was out of line," I say, keeping my voice low between us.

"It is what it is." She starts to back away. "Enjoy the soda."

The soda reminds me of Marina, who's sitting in the car waiting on me. I can barely make out her silhouette behind the tinted window, but I'm really hoping she can't make me out at all, or I'll be hearing about this over the dinner table at every major holiday meal and then some.

"Hey," I say just to the beauty in front of me. "I owe you for the soda."

"My treat." Her shoulders pop up and then down before I'm met with her back as she nears the corner of the building.

I don't go after her, but I make a last-ditch effort. "For real, let me give you some money."

Glancing back over her shoulder, she shakes her head. "It's a soda. It's no big deal."

"But . . ."

"Really. It's okay," she replies, stopping under the awning of the sketchy gas station. Even the potent smell of gasoline and oil slicks on the ground don't make her any less pretty.

Stepping out on a limb, I close the gap by half, leaving enough distance for her to make her own decisions. "Okay, no money, but what about dinner sometime?"

The corners of her lips slope just high enough to back her entertainment, but her eyes reveal a gleam of interest in the way they shine for me. My breath gets caught somewhere between telling her she's gorgeous and reminding her to steer clear of the trouble I bring.

"You don't even know my name, and you're asking me out?" There's no offense to her tone or in her stance by how relaxed she appears.

I should probably take the opportunity she's giving me to prove I'm not a total asshole. Holding out my hand, I say, "People who know me call me Harbor. You can do the same."

She comes a little closer, the heat of her proximity reaching me. As she slips her hand against mine, her chest rises as her lips part. "Are we friends now, Harbor?"

Since not one PG image crosses my thoughts, friends aren't what I had in mind. I'm not friends with anyone these days, but she might be worth making an exception. "It depends."

I'm not sure why my directness puts her at ease, but her smile reveals only intrigue. She should probably run, get away from me as fast as she can without giving me a second thought. "Depends on what?"

"What happens next."

She laughs, rocking back on her heels. "I have to go, so I guess we'll leave it to the fates to decide."

While the distance we had just closed widens, I throw my arms out wide. "You're not going to tell me your name?" In a class of almost two-hundred students, her name is one of the few things I've not caught. I was hoping to remedy that.

The afternoon sun shines on her. "Isn't it more fun this way?"

"Fun is subjective." I watch as she turns around, her shoulders rattling with laughter. "But I'll play along." *Helps that I know I'll see her in class.*

Glancing back, she says, "I had no doubt you would."

"Do you ever have doubts?"

"All the time. See you around, Harbor." She gives me a little wave before she disappears around the corner.

I could chase her down and ask for her number, but two rejections from the same girl is enough for one day. I pull my keys from my pocket and spin the ring around my finger. Anyway, she's right. It is more fun this way. Just wait until she sees me on Monday.

I walk to my pride and joy—my Ghibli Modena—and open the car door. I don't have time to get in fully before Marina asks, "What took you so long? I thought I was going to die of thirst while waiting."

"I didn't think you'd notice since your eyes are always glued to that screen."

"Okay, Dad," she says in a deep mocking voice.

Handing over the soda, I look at her, knowing one day, if she hasn't already, she'll face assholes who will treat her like that guy in there. That's not a conversation to have now, but one we need to have soon. "Don't ever go to this station."

She looks up briefly, her eyes looking at the building behind me. "Ew. I wouldn't anyway." *Good.* "I don't even know where we are."

It's true, this isn't my usual store or gas station, but it's close to downtown, so I made the detour. I reach over to ruffle my little sister's hair, but she blocks me. "You're welcome, by the way."

"Thanks," she replies, pushing my hand away. "Long line?"

"Yeah," I lie, knowing firsthand that sixteen-year-old girls can be ruthless when it suits them.

I start the Maserati, acting as casually as I can. We don't even hit the street before she asks, "Did you at least get her number?"

The last thing my sister needs to hear about is how I hit on a woman with great legs, an even better ass, and a mouth I wouldn't mind occupying for a night. *And then got rejected.* "You saw that?"

She's at least polite enough to keep her laughter under wraps . . . *until she can't.*

"Everyone saw it."

"I didn't ask for it." *Not a lie.*

Her phone is now the least interesting thing in the car when she angles toward me. "Why not? It seems a shame to let all that flirting go to waste."

"Eh," I say, "I think I'll leave it to the fates to decide."

"If the fates have their way, you just met your soul mate."

Surprised to hear the seriousness in her tone, I glance over at my sister. "Why do you say that?"

"Because you weren't the only one flirting."

I return my gaze to the drive ahead, but there's no stopping the stupid grin on my face. I'm not sure about anything when it comes to the gorgeous girl I just encountered, but she's got me thinking about her and this main character business.

I may not believe in fate, but I believe in myself. Wonder what it takes to be the hero of her story?

2

Lark Summerlin

MY WHITE SHIRT could have used one more pass with an iron, but it's too late to worry. My skirt was in desperate need of more attention than I had to give it since I was late getting home. I can only hope Larry is too busy to notice when I get to work.

I step back from the mirror and brush my hands down the black fabric, still annoyed by the one crease down the center I couldn't iron out, but I let it slide under the good day I've had so far. The cute guy was a nice distraction, even if he made me run late.

The skirt will probably wrinkle again in the car anyway. Larry will bitch about it, but then he'll be too busy to care five minutes into the job.

Not that I'm upset about the encounter I had at the gas station. I'm not someone who flirts that often, but the minute Harbor walked in, I thought about it. I'm weak to a cute smile, and he had a great body.

It might be unfair to lump him in with the guys I've met

before, but they taught me someone that attractive loses interest easily. Giving him a hard time was a good test that he passed. Bonus: I got to enjoy his attention while I had it.

I laugh, remembering the meet cute conversation. It's ridiculous to think I'm going to meet my soul mate at a gas station. Something like that could happen in the movies that I love to watch or in the books I read, but not in real life.

Though I can admit, he got to me. The way he looked at me, his gaze penetrating me like he saw something more than what's on the outside. I smile, touching my lips as if his words were whispered against them. It wasn't the words exchanged that had me hanging onto each one of them. It was the way his eyes would settle on my mouth, the lick of his own lips, and then his tone wrapping around me like a warm blanket that had me eager for more.

Feelings that out of control, zipping through me like a live wire would have had me acting carelessly. I don't have the same luxury like they do in Hollywood.

I swipe on lipstick. Neutral, like my outfit. We're never supposed to stand out but instead to blend into the surroundings when working. I roll my eyes. Heaven forbid someone catches us doing our job.

Grabbing my keys, I yank open the door in a rush to be outside when Dane arrives. "See you later, Amanda." My roommate was in the shower moments ago, so I'm not sure if she hears me.

"Bye, Lark," echoes from the bathroom.

I grin and start to close the door, but it's pulled open. Wrapped in a towel, she peeks around with wet hair stuck to her shoulders, and asks, "Are you going out later?"

"Doubt it. I won't get home until midnight."

Her shoulders drop. "I was hoping you'd make it. Gavin's

playing tonight with the new band. I hear some of the band is single."

"Yeah," I reply, debating if I should go after work. "I'll see how I feel, but don't wait on me. Okay?"

"Text me if you decide to come, and I'll send you the address."

Amanda's been my best friend since elementary school. She was a transfer student. I was . . . *broken*. Somehow, this girl who should have had it all if looks were currency— hazel eyes and hair the color of warm sunshine—was put into my path when I needed a friend the most. We may be opposites, but our friendship stuck. We rarely fight, though we act like sisters. I have her back, and she's got mine.

Yet I know better than to tell her about the gas station encounter. She means well, but landing a boyfriend isn't at the top of my agenda. If she even gets a whiff that I've been around someone in what she has decided is "my dating range," she'll never let up. Also, judging by his friends' car and going by what the jerk cashier said, I think he might be from Beacon Pointe. That would make sense since I've never seen him around this part of town.

Everyone around here has strong opinions about the wealthy families that live north of town. Amanda's thoughts may be kinder than most, but the pressure to land a trust-fund boyfriend would be intense. So I save the good stuff for another time and keep Harbor all to myself.

Why am I even thinking about him? I'll probably never see him again.

"If I don't make it out, have fun without me." Walking through the tiny entry space, I turn back before reaching the main exterior door and point my finger back at her. "But not too much, and if you do, I've got a bail fund."

She laughs. "You're always broke."

Shrugging, I laugh. "I'm resourceful, though."

"That you are, Lark."

I hurry across the squeaking wood floor and burst through the door, landing on the sidewalk. After a quick scan down the street in both directions, I check the time. "Come on, Dane. Where are you?"

The sound of a vehicle backfiring, Dane Brody's truck to be specific, has me looking back down the street.

The beat-up white Chevy stops at the curb. Dane leans over and pops the door open for me. "Sorry. I got caught up."

I hop in and pull the seat belt across my chest. "You know Larry docks our pay if we're even a second late."

"Larry can fuck off."

"That's all well and good, but I need the money."

He's wise enough not to keep going down the path of bashing our boss because he needs the money as much as I do.

He takes off just in time to hit what feels like every red light in this town. I hate being late, and Dane has a knack for it. He's my ride, though, so I can't complain. *Out loud, at least.* Sitting at the last one before the road that leads to the estates, I grumble. "Figures."

"Tell me about it." He turns up the radio, catching a Johnny Cash song. My dad listens to Johnny, which is the only reason I know who it is. Thinking about Dad, I send him a quick text: *Still on for Sunday?*

He doesn't get off work for another hour, so I'm not surprised when I don't receive a response.

The town of Beacon disappears in the rearview mirror, the spires of the university along with it. In front of us, the street stretches into the distance like a runway to the blue sky ahead. While working for Larry, I've helped cater parties beyond the tall trees many times. The trees give the privacy, protecting the estates beyond them, but I just can't seem to get used to the grandeur beyond the gates.

What must it be like when every penny doesn't need to count?

With no A/C in Dane's truck, the window is down and whipping through my hair. Stealing a moment before the storm of work strikes, I extend my arm, waving my hand through the air.

Dane is good with silence, which is a nice reprieve from Amanda's need to always chat. I think I'm somewhere between the two. It's ironic since they briefly dated the summer before freshman year, which is how we met. Somehow, they knew they were better off as friends, and we've managed to maintain the platonic relationships over the years.

None of us can claim great luck in dating, so it helps to have others you trust who you can gripe about it to. The one girlfriend of his I avoid talking about if I have a choice, is Mia. Unfortunately, she keeps coming back into his life just when we think she's gone for good.

I hate seeing him get used, which is the type of woman he's generally attracted to, so sometimes I can't keep my mouth shut. "When you say caught up, you mean you were with Mia again?"

If the shrug didn't give me the answer, his laughter does. I punch his arm, annoyed with how weak he is when it comes to her. "I couldn't leave her hanging."

"Nope," I say, throwing my hand up. "I don't want to hear about your sex life, especially when it comes to you and Mia."

"Wish you guys got along."

The sudden serious tone to his voice has me returning my gaze. "You may have forgiven her for cheating on you, but I haven't. Not sorry to break it to you, but we aren't going to be best friends."

"Why not?" He turns onto a property, and the gates begin to open.

I lean forward and stare at the long driveway before us with the mansion at the top of the hill sitting like the cherry on top.

It's not that I'm envious of these estates, but I also can't help but wonder what it must be like living here. It's acreage of trees as far as the eyes can see, manicured lawns, swimming pools, and long winding driveways that end at the base of stunning homes so big that several families could inhabit them without running into each other.

This one is particularly pretty with white siding and forest-green shutters. I can't wait to see the inside.

"You're drooling." Dane shifts into park behind a row of event trucks.

Still staring at the structure through the windshield, I ask, "What do you think they do for a living to afford this place?"

He rests his arms over the steering wheel and follows my gaze. "Nothing." His harsh answer takes me by surprise. "This house has been handed down." Rubbing his fingers together, he adds, "The Westcotts are old money." He hops out. "Come on. Two minutes to spare."

Anchoring my shoulder against the door since it usually sticks, I wedge it open and get out. Gravel crunches under my shoes as I weave through the trucks and follow a sidewalk to the back of the house that leads to the back door. As soon as I step into the kitchen, I'm hit with Larry's judgmental gaze over the top of his red-framed reading glasses.

I raise a finger. "One minute early."

"Spare me the excuses, Summerlin. You're on refills tonight."

"What? No." I hate the whine that taints my voice. Crossing the kitchen, I lean against the fridge with the wind stolen from my sails. He knows I'd rather be serving and passing trays in the mix of the party than be stuck in the kitchen and reloading the tables all night. "That job is the worst, and you know it."

"I do know it, but you're the best at it. I need someone reliable because we're short-staffed. Johnson and Campbell both called in sick tonight. Dane's bartending, and Susan is passing the apps. I'll be setting up the grazing table in ten, and I want your help. You've got a good eye, and I intend to use it tonight."

"Are you buttering me up?"

"Is it working?"

"Maybe," I reply, hating that I smile.

He comes over and sets the clipboard on the counter in front of me. "You ready to change your major and enter the culinary program? Maybe go the hospitality route and come work for me or run Golden Lion's catering service down in Maylor?"

"I'm not working at the Golden Lion Motel. If I have any say, I'm heading to medical school next year."

Dane passes behind me with his arms filled with a box of champagne. "Heard back from any?"

"When exactly have I had time to apply? Larry keeps me working every spare minute I have," I reply, grabbing a carton of cherry tomatoes from a rolling rack and pouring them into a colander. "I'm trying to wrap up a few applications when I go to my Dad's house for the game. I might need to think of a backup plan, though, just in case I don't get in anywhere."

Pushing the door open, he anchors his foot as a stop at the base. "You don't need a backup plan. They'd be crazy not to have you."

"I appreciate the faith you have in me."

"It's easy to believe in you, Lark." The door closes behind him before I can reply. He and Amanda, along with my father, have been my biggest cheerleaders. I try to remember how much they believe in me and that it will work out exactly how it's supposed to. Some days I do better than others.

I turn on the faucet and wash my hands before running the tomatoes under the cool water. Carrying a crudité tray around the large marble-topped island, Larry whispers, "After the mess on Valentine's at the Bensimone's home, we've made it back to the estates of Beacon Pointe." He looks at me. "If we do this right, Delta Westcott will recommend us all over town."

"It will be great and run smoothly. I promise."

"I'm holding you to that." When he leaves, the event planner is right behind him with a walkie-talkie to her mouth, demanding someone leave the ice sculpture on the refrigerated truck until right before the party starts.

It's fall, but too early in the season to fight the heat. Of course, I'll be sweating now that I'll be running to replenish all the stations. *Just great.* I shake my head.

A girl appears from around the far corner of the room. Looking at her face, she can't be much older than a high schooler, but I'm sure she could get away with college if she tried. Her hair sweeps back and forth against her jaw as she crosses the room wearing a yellow sundress with nude-toned sandals as if summer was in full bloom. "Hi," she says, leaning against the island. "Sorry to get in your way, but do you mind if I grab a snack?"

"No, not at all."

"Thanks." Moving behind me, she opens the large fridge. By how at home she appears, I assume she lives here. "I'm famished, and my mom told us we couldn't come near the kitchen today. The soda I drank earlier isn't holding me over like I hoped. I should have had my brother grab snacks from the store."

I've seen the menu for the party and know Larry prepared most of the appetizers prior to arrival, so I suggest, "There are mango puddings that are really good. We always make a large batch. It's the simple appetizers that always win the crowd over. Though we'll be baking off mini beef Wellingtons later." She remains standing with the door open, clearly not interested in my suggestions. "We have skewers of deli meat and cheese that will be on the grazing table."

Her head dips into the fridge as she reaches toward the back. When she stands straight, she's scored two skewers. "Don't tell my mom, okay?"

"I won't."

I didn't expect to have an audience as I wash the tomatoes, but I'm not sure what to say to her either. I grab the figs and clean those.

She asks, "Do you go to school around here?"

Glancing up, I see her interest as she takes the last bite. "I attend the university."

"You must know one of my brothers then." She doesn't look familiar to me at all. Tossing the sticks, she then says, "You look familiar."

"Probably not. I'm here with the catering company."

Her smile is genuine as she relaxes in my company. "I'm Marina."

"I'm Lark. It's nice to meet you," I say, smiling from her kindness.

"You, too."

While she pulls a glass from the cupboard and fills it with water from a jug in the fridge, I fill in the gap, "It's a nice home."

She looks around as if she needed the reminder. I guess if you grow up here, it doesn't seem so fancy. "Thanks. My mom deserves the credit." Leaning against the island again, she looks at me as if it's not awkward at all. I like that she's comfortable around me. "Where do you live?" she asks.

"I'm from—"

"I'm sure she's too busy to be entertaining you, Marina." My gaze lands on a man entering from across the room. *Man* might be a bit of a stretch, and judging by the confidence that carries him the distance as he strides toward us, he's not just any guy either.

Marina may be smiling, but she turns back to me and sighs. "My brother's right. I'll get out of your way, Lark. Thanks for the food." Before she disappears into the back-yard where the party is set up, she starts laughing. "Loch? Are you coming?"

He passes by, but says, "Thanks for being here."

"Thanks." I'm not sure why I say that when I should be reminding him I'm paid to be here. But he's not dumb. Anyway, I appreciate the kindness. This family seems nice, especially compared to how I'm treated at some events, not being acknowledged at all.

I get back to work, focusing on food preparation. With less than an hour left before the party starts, we must get the food set up on the table outside. I finish loading the filled pans onto the rolling rack and push it toward the back door.

But the cart catches on the floor. I rattle it to free it from the obstacle, but it doesn't move.

"Here, let me help you." I hear someone say from the other side. Two hands tug the rack on the other side, and me along with it.

Stupidly, I try to help but hinder the progression instead. "It's jammed. Hold on to it."

"Ready," the male voice replies.

I try to steal a peek over a tray but all I see is his neck. It's a nice neck. Pinning my shoulder against the rack, I shove. It hits him like it ran into a brick wall and jolts back, catching my chin with the edge of the metal frame. "Ouch!"

"Are you okay?" I hear the voice ask from the other side.

Gliding the tips of my fingers across my chin, I reply, "Not sure."

"You're bleeding."

I tilt my head to spy who it is over a pan of sliced vegetables only to find the warmth of caramel-brown eyes greeting me. I recognize them instantly.

And him.

"Harbor."

3

Lark

WHETHER INSIDE THE GAS STATION, outside in the sunshine, or now in the flattering filtered light of late afternoon, his shine can't be dulled. Even the fluorescent lighting of the convenience store couldn't change my mind.

Shifting the rack to the side, he comes between the door and the metal and around, bringing him face-to-face with me. Smirking, he replies, "I didn't expect to see you again so soon, especially not bleeding in my kitchen."

The slight wave that weaves through his brown hair probably gives him hell on bad hair days, but I doubt someone so blessed in the looks department has much to worry about. He's dressed differently, swapping a black button-up for the gray T-shirt he was wearing earlier, and black pants for the jeans. Hard all over with an athletic build, his shoulders are broad, the shirt draped around his body like it's a privilege, hugging him in all the right spots—biceps, forearms where the sleeves are rolled up.

The man is gorgeous.

He looks every bit of what makes me weak in the knees in the finely tailored clothes that fit him in all the right places from his arms to his chest and backside. Dressed in black forewarns of a naughtier side while sincerity outlines the warmth of his eyes. He's a sinner and a saint battling it out inside an Adonis body.

God, I can't wait to see who wins.

Standing so much closer now than before, he towers over me, clocking in at a good six-two, six-three. Harbor's nothing less than *GQ* cover material.

I wasn't dressed up when we met, but being in my uniform isn't the way I'd choose to dress if I knew I was going to see him again. "Bleeding? Uh . . . oh right." I touch my chin again and then inspect my fingertips. "I am, and this was definitely not in the plan."

I step back and turn, searching for a paper towel or the first-aid kit Larry always brings. Neither is found.

He passes me to snatch a napkin from a drawer. Returning to me, he drops his gaze to my chin. He pauses, taking a slow breath and a slower exhale before he says, "We should clean you up."

We . . .

A thousand reasons exist to steer clear of him. He's a heartbreaker in human form if I've ever seen one. So at the top of the list, I'm just going to assume he goes through women like candy based on his attractiveness.

The thing is, I can't judge him because I don't have the best track record either. I may not have dated much, but I've made plenty of bad decisions.

With Harbor, no red flag is flying. I'm getting green all the way. I just wished that fate would have helped a girl out. Seeing him at work isn't ideal and being clumsy is even worse. It's downright embarrassing.

He dabs the napkin to my chin with the softest of touches as if it's not the first time he's taken care of a girl before. I hate that I wonder if he's always the hero to other damsels in distress. Not appearing satisfied, his expression sours just as he passes me. "Come with me."

I follow in the scent of his wake—rain mixed with a forest, ocean tides, and moonrise. *God, he smells divine.*

What am I doing? Why am I following a man I barely know without hesitation. My dad told me to trust my instincts, but I'm now questioning them. Not for the reasons I should be, but because I trust Harbor. Trust isn't something that's always come easy for me, so I can't explain why I feel such ease with him.

I take a deep breath as we cross the large room. "Where are we going?"

Without even a glance back, he says, "To treat the wound."

"You'll need more than Neosporin to heal my wounds," I say with only a hint of sarcasm.

Harbor stops and turns back. His gaze goes from my chin to my eyes. Another pause keeps me in suspense, my breath fully caught in my throat. Then he approaches, gently pinching my chin between his fingers while tilting his head down, bringing us that much closer. "Don't worry. I'll take care of this first and then work on the rest."

My thoughts blur as my heart pounds in my chest. For a moment in time, I'm captivated by the look in his eyes—one that says he could be the one to really heal me, to piece the remnants of my shattered past back together, giving me a chance to be whole again.

I'm not dumb enough to dream he can fix the past, but he makes me want to believe he can.

I look down, needing a reprieve from the intensity of his caring eyes to breathe again. "I think . . ."

"I think we should get that taken care of before the party begins."

"The party—oh shoot." I start to turn back, but he takes my hand. Warmth flows through, the feeling of calm settling my racing heart.

"I'll vouch for your absence if necessary." He nods toward the stairs. "I have a kit upstairs."

"Don't get hurt." This would be a fantastic time to heed his warning from earlier this afternoon.

Slipping my hand from his, I stay on the bottom step. "I—"

"I'll be careful with you."

Maybe it's the way he's looking at me with something more than how most guys ogle me. Or maybe it's the way he's dressed as the devil, but his voice is pure heaven when he says, "I promise."

What the hell do I have to lose? Anyway, I always was a sucker for a bad boy with a good heart. Let's hope my intuition is right when it comes to Harbor.

I follow him up the stairs. When I see the corridor at the top, disbelief drops my jaw. "This is a really big house."

He chuckles. "It really is too big."

Other than his friend's car and the cashier calling him a rich kid, I wouldn't have guessed he came from The Pointe Estates. I wouldn't say he's a perfect fit into the luxury of these surroundings, but he definitely doesn't look out of place either.

When we reach the bathroom, he says, "Hop up."

I lift myself onto the counter, facing him. I'm still not at eye level with him, but I don't mind the view from here. "Am I going to live, doctor?" I ask, teasing . . . *Fine.* I'm flirting because he's not just attractive. He's charming as well.

Especially when he cocks his eyebrow and his smile spreads slowly across his face. "I can't have you dying on my watch." And he might just be what my dad warned me about.

If we keep running into each other like this, I might not live to tell the tale. "Only time will tell."

"You don't sound very optimistic. Should I be concerned?" His touch is kind, but his skin feels like fire against mine when he taps my chin just shy of where it's pulsing.

Attempting to clear my mind of Harbor and get solid footing back in the land of reality, I shake my head, but that makes things worse, and I get dizzy. "I feel faint, but it has nothing to do with my chin."

Concern riddles his brow. "Do you need to lie down?"

"If you want me in your bedroom, all you have to do is ask." I clamp my hand over my mouth. "Oh my God," I mutter, cringing inside. *What the heck is wrong with me?* "I didn't mean . . ." I didn't know it was possible for him to be even more handsome, but he proves me wrong when he grins with pride. "Please ignore whatever comes out of my mouth."

"It's hard to ignore your mouth."

I practically collapse right here on what looks like an expensive countertop of cold stone. "I seriously can't be responsible for my words or actions—"

"I need to keep an eye on your actions as well as your mouth?" He glances at my chin again before his gaze slides to my eyes. "This is going to be fun."

I want to die inside. Did I list my dad or Amanda as my emergency contact? I know I listed them both, but I hope

Amanda is under the "In case a cute guy makes you swoon" emergency button on my phone. If she saw Harbor, she'd understand. I'm about to jump off this counter and make a run for it, probably head down that long driveway and right back to Beacon because nothing is going to save me now. There's only one problem. "I should probably get back to work."

"Let's get you fixed up first. I'm pretty sure you bleeding isn't a part of the entertainment tonight."

"I think that's a solid assumption." Treating me like a patient, he's careful as he cleans and then bandages my cut. "You're all good."

I touch the bandage and then twist to look in the mirror. If I were to go off how well he treated me, and by how long it took, I would have thought a hospital visit was in my future. But I have the smallest little skin-toned bandage on my chin. It makes me laugh. As soon as I turn back, I can still feel the heat of embarrassment from what I said, so I face it head-on. "Can we just blame the injury for my behavior?"

"Sounds reasonable."

Enjoying this little reprieve in my shift, I don't regret the wound one bit after he takes care of me. "You have amazing bedside manners. Have you considered becoming a doctor?"

Bending forward, he grins, small dimples forming on each cheek. "A time or two." Standing up, he rubs his hands together. "You're good to go, but—"

"But?"

"Are you going to finally tell me your name?"

"Oh right. That." This time, I'm the one grinning. "Ow. Smiling hurts." My fingers are quick to cover the bandage. The pain is bearable, but I sure do like his attention.

I hate to even admit it, but he makes me feel special.

"It's going to take a few days to heal," he says, covering

my fingers with his, the gesture so caring that it causes my heart to beat faster. "Do you want to take off your shirt?"

"What?" My back hits the mirror from the fast lurch of my body.

"Blood," he says, panic reaching his eyes as he takes two steps back with his hands raised in surrender. "You have blood on your shirt."

Whipping around, I see the red spotting my white shirt. "Dammit."

"I can leave, and you can try to scrub it to see if it will come out."

My eyes find his in the mirror's reflection just before I hop off the counter. Facing him, I feel panic rise like bile, making me feel sick. "I can't work around food with blood on my shirt. Larry's going to kill me or, worse, fire me."

"Can you go home and change?" He checks his watch. "The party doesn't start for thirty minutes."

"I didn't drive here, and there's no way I'd make it back in time. Larry would never let me leave either because we're short-staffed." Catching my mistake too late, I cover my mouth and stare wide-eyed at him. "I shouldn't have told you that. Please don't tell anyone." If we were found here together, in a bathroom upstairs alone, I'd be fired. Larry just got work back in the estates. I can't be the one to ruin it for him. I add, "I shouldn't be here. I need this job, Harbor." Swinging the door open, I rush down the hall toward the stairs.

"Wait. I'm sure my sister has a white shirt you can borrow."

I stop, my hand catching hold of the railing, and look back. His sister? Then it dawns on me. "Marina?"

"She's my sister."

"That would save my job." I start back but stop in the middle of the corridor. "I'll pay to have it dry-cleaned."

"That's not necessary. She probably won't even notice it's missing." He crosses the hall and goes down two doors. "Wait here. I'll grab it for you."

This could be another huge mistake, but I have no choice.

Walking back, I look around. You'd almost expect stodgy old paintings worth a fortune hanging on the fabric-coated walls. Instead, there are black and white photos that capture the family in moments of time—a cannonball into a lake, their mom standing in a canoe just as it's tipping over, a little boy with a cape soaring through a field, and a little girl holding a basket of strawberries. It's eternally summer from years back in this hallway. *And so beautiful.*

A glimpse into this family's history makes my heart ache for what I've missed.

"Will this work?" Harbor asks, holding a shirt in front of him.

"Perfect. Thank you." I take the shirt and duck back into the bathroom. As I pull the pique fabric over my head, I realize this might be the most expensive item of clothing I've ever worn, making me nervous. I'd hate to ruin it because replacing it would eat a hefty chunk out of my paycheck. But do I have a choice?

No.

I walk out, determined to find an apron to wear as soon as I return downstairs, which hopefully will protect it. "How do I look?" I spin for him. "Trick question. It's a boring uniform—white shirt, black skirt, shoes a granny would be mortified to wear, and the latest in fashion bandages." This is quite the predicament I've gotten myself into. Covering my forehead, I decide it's okay to laugh at myself. "Ignore me."

"I tried at the gas station." His words draw my eyes back to his. "It didn't work then, and it's not working now."

I turn my eyes to the floor when swallowing becomes difficult. Twisting on one of my ankles, I whisper, "Thank you for everything." Harbor's been so nice to me when he could have just been another jerk rich kid.

Packing away a bout of shame for not telling him sooner, I summon the courage to face him and finally confess, "Hi." My cheeks heat under his considerate gaze. "My name is Lark."

4

Harbor

LARK.

Her name is as beautiful as she is. "Lark," I say the name just to feel it roll around on my tongue. Her gaze slides from the floor to my face, seeming to linger just below my eyes before they finally move all the way up. "Go out with me, Lark."

"I . . ." Her chest rises with a breath she takes, making me wonder how she'll look naked. Shifting away from me with a faltered step, she says, "I could get in trouble for being here, for being with you, Harbor."

"What kind of trouble could the two of us possibly get into just from being together?" The question feels better suited for a moment bigger and more important than a stolen one in the upstairs hallway.

Her smile is so sweet that it's tempting to taste. Tilting her head, she laughs. "I think I better go before we find out." She's quick to the stairs.

"Hey, Lark?" She turns back with that smile still on her face. "What do I have to do to see you again?"

Her gaze dips between us as her smile falters. When she looks up again, a look of determination has set her features. "We don't always get what we want when we want it. Sometimes we need to follow our destinies instead."

Cocking an eyebrow, I sigh, despite enjoying the exchange. "Patience is a virtue?"

"Exactly." Her smile reappears. "Only time will tell."

"Only time will tell."

She catches my gaze for the shortest moment in time, and then she turns away.

I didn't expect to be drawn to someone, pulled toward her as if I'm hooked on the end of her fishing line. From the way she moves, so unaware of her appeal, to the mystery that resides in her eyes—pain and happiness cycling through her gaze—she's utterly captivating.

Is it wrong to long to hear the secrets she keeps from everyone else, to want to kiss her with the same determination as a thief desires the crown jewels?

Desire.

Craving . . .

I'm crude in my need to hear her call my name not just in ecstasy but in reverence when she thinks of me long after I've gone.

Fuck.

She's doing my head in. My shoulders press to the wall as I watch her descend the stairs before she disappears.

I give her enough time and distance to return to wherever she's stationed before I head down the stairs. As soon as I enter the family room, I see Lark and her boss talking in low voices to each other. He sees me and takes a step back from her as well as a deep breath as if my presence is an intrusion.

"Evening, Mr. Westcott."

"Evening," I reply, my gaze maneuvering from him to Lark. "Evening," I add for her.

"Good evening."

As I pass by, I notice the rack has been emptied and stands outside the door. I duck out, not sure how long I intend to stay. I'll greet a few guests, make the rounds to please my parents, and then hopefully make a clean escape without being noticed.

My older brother is the picture-perfect son standing beside my mom greeting guests, the first in line to helm Westcott Law Firm after my dad retires. A clap on the back and a squeeze of my shoulder signals my dad's presence before he says a word. "Your mom and I appreciate you being here." And when he does speak, his tone is lacking the judgment he has every right to feel, forgiving of the disappointments I've brought on the family.

"It's the least I can do." I shove my hands into my pockets and shift my weight to my heels. "Hopefully, this event will raise a lot of money for the university scholarship program."

"I'm sure it will." My dad may be the quieter of my parents, but he's not usually at a loss for words. We stand, both looking around for something to talk about.

I finally say, "I'm sorry I haven't been around much."

"Eh, you have your life to live." His eyes find me again, and he grins. "As parents, we're supposed to raise you to be independent." He takes a sip of his drink and savors it. "I'd say we've done a good job."

Guilt still comes in waves, reaching the shores of my conscience the more time I spend with him. I take a step away, but he notices, and says, "No one blames you, Harbor."

"I blame myself."

"Lucas made the decision—"

His *decision* almost killed me, but I keep that part to myself, always locked deep inside. He dragged me out of bed, challenged me to the edge of that cliff. I'm always so fucking competitive. *Was . . . still am, I suppose.*

As best friends, we'd push each other to do shit we shouldn't. We did with all the guys, but that afternoon it was just the two of us. I wasn't in a good mood. Cliff jumping was the last thing I wanted to do, but there wasn't a cloud in the sky and the weather had turned warm after a long and cold winter.

I gave in to shut him up, though I should have stopped him. No one saw what an asshole Lucas could be except me. He was great at getting away with murder. I used to admire his skills. *Now I resent him.*

He left me carrying the burden of the truth.

He left me to tell lies.

He left me living when so many wish that I was the one who died.

Fuck him.

I warned him not to tempt the fate at Devil's Edge. There was so much more life to live, and he chose to throw it away over a bet for a burger and fries.

Fuck him for leaving.

I close my eyes and scrub my hand over my face, then rub my temple to lessen the throb threatening to ruin my night.

"Lucas was following me," I say, the lie comes easy after two years of repeating it. I don't know if I'm lying for me or my cousin anymore, but I'll say anything to make his death easier on others. The better they feel, the less they interrogate me about how I'm doing.

I'm a quick learner. The survivor doesn't matter, leaving me caught in a purgatory between lucky for walking away and condemned to spend my life reliving it for other people's pleasure because I'm the one who survived.

If they only knew how close I came to meeting my own demise. Regret still taints the luck I had for not dying.

But I continue to tell the lies to protect him and his memory, to protect his legacy.

Straight A's.

Star athlete.

Going off to the Ivy League.

Everyone loved Lucas Westcott. Especially the girls . . . I don't do bad, but he was the golden boy.

"Harbor?"

My dad's voice brings me back to the party. I turn to him, and ask, "Yeah?"

But I'm greeted with the sadness I've put in his eyes. "How long are you staying?"

"I'm not sure. How long do I have to?"

He reaches over and squeezes my shoulder again. I've learned it's his way to hold on to me, to tell me he's here for me, to be a support when words fail him. The thing is my parents have always been here for their kids. They have a brood of four, but they love each one of us enough to make us feel like an only child.

"Your mom would like you here for a little while. If you can do that for her, I'll cover the rest of the time."

"I can stay."

He looks over at her, and says, "I should get over there and rescue your brother."

Rescue . . . the word lassos the memories I try to forget. I push them back down, the feelings growing inside, and put myself back at this moment instead like I've practiced. "Thanks, Dad."

"For what?"

I shrug, sometimes finding it difficult to locate the words as well. Like father, like son. "For being my dad."

He nods, shoving his hands in his pockets like son, like father, and walks across the lawn. My mom's eyes brighten when she sees him, her arms welcoming him into her embrace, not caring that the whole of Beacon and the estates is watching them. They've been together thirty-two years last summer. They share a love that I've come to realize is special, not often found if found at all.

Loch's eyes find me, and he nods in acknowledgment as if he's seeing me for the first time. I understand. Some days I'm a ghost among the living, going through life with one foot in the afterlife. Other days, it feels good to be alive. *Today, it's the latter.*

The accident healed some wounds with my family. Sowing wild oats was a good excuse to act out. Growing pains on my part caused some issues. There was a side of myself that needed to push boundaries to be seen. The irony is I found out my brothers, my sister, and my parents saw me all along.

I nod in return and head to the bar. No way do I plan to get trapped in conversations with my parents' friends and colleagues without loosening up first. And I can always order a car to drive me back to the apartment tonight.

My body tenses when I see the bartender. I'd never say we were friends. We're not, though we've been at some of the same parties, mutual friends bringing us together. Lucas liked to party in Beacon on a side of town that wasn't always safe to park our cars. It might have been my cousin who once introduced us. This guy acts low-key cool, but he can also be an asshole. He's big on keeping what he considers his to himself, never keen to have estate kids at his parties.

I've never cared about what side of the line—Beacon proper or The Pointe Estates—you reside. *He did, probably still does.* It would be easy for me to call it jealousy, but that chip on his shoulder seems to have a grudge backing it up, judging by the disgust on his face. When I get closer, I say, "Hey, man, I remember you." The name tag on his shirt catches my attention. "Dane, that's right."

"You're Lucas's cousin, right?" His tone is as indifferent as his expression while he runs a towel over a bottle of gin. "Another Westcott from what I remember." There's no hiding his feelings in the words. The disgust on his face is threaded in his tone as well.

I focus on the partygoers, not wanting a confrontation at my parents' home. "Yeah."

"It's too bad what happened." The change in tone—from aversion to something sounding more sincere—has me drawn to look back at him again. "We used to hang out occasionally."

"I know." Not sure if he's wanting to relate to me somehow but it's not going to happen through the death of my cousin.

"What can I get you?" he asks.

Looking over the bottles on display, I reply, "Whiskey on the rocks."

He grabs a cup and scoops ice into it. Plucking the top from the bottle, he eyes it, and then with a heavy hand, he fills the glass. "Haven't seen you at any of the parties in some time."

"Life got busy," I reply, keeping the details to myself.

"I hear ya." Rounding his shoulders, he appears to relax.

"You still partying off Dobson on Fridays?"

"Cops broke it up, and Terry doesn't like heat on his property." He sets the cup in front of me. "On the house."

He probably wouldn't have made the comment if he knew this was my family's house. "Thanks. What have you been up to?"

Chuckling, he looks around as if he doesn't want others to hear. "Busy. Like you. Heard you wrecked a Mercedes a while back." He's not asking, so I'm not sure I feel the need to answer.

"What can I say? It's been a shitty couple of years."

Shaking his head, another low chuckle punches his chest. "Must be nice to be rich." When his eyes meet mine again, he adds, "I'd be sitting in county jail if I'd pulled that stunt, but you—"

"What about me?"

His expression tells me all I need to know—the smarmy grin sitting arrogantly on his face. "It's a party. Lighten up."

I take a sip of the drink, the entertainment value of this reunion worn off, like my kindness. He's right, though, but it's not just any party. It's a fundraising event. I won't be the reason people leave or don't support the cause. One thing I've learned about this town is you either spark division or don't give a damn. I knew where he stood before, but he reinforced it. No use hanging around where I'm not welcome. I may be on my home turf, but I'll give him this bar to run in peace. "Thanks for the drink."

Stepping off to the side, I find the captivating beauty so easily in the crowd. Lark couldn't be farther away, but she still steals the attention from every other person here.

"She's off-limits." The sigh that follows warrants my interest.

I glance back at Dane behind me. "Who says?"

"I do."

Turning back, I make a concerted effort to riffle through her thoughts or read her expression at a bare minimum, as if that's possible from this distance. I only have what she's given me so far, and that impression didn't appear to include dating someone. "What would she say?"

"She'd tell you to fuck off."

I balk in laughter. She just might, but she hasn't so far. I glance back again. "You sure about that?" When he pauses too long, I start to walk away. "That's what I thought."

"Don't fuck with her. She's been through some shit," he says to my back, his tone caught in some form of big brother protectiveness like he just might give a shit about Lark.

Maybe he has the right. I have no fucking clue. I stop again, standing there, my back still to him with my eyes locked on Lark. When I look back this time, I set my stare on him. "Haven't we all." I cross the lawn to the other side of the pool.

Unfortunately, I lose the next two hours suffering through office gossip and endless questions about my plans, serving my time at the party just as I promised my dad.

I finally use my empty cup as an excuse to escape. Just when I slip out from a group of attorneys from my dad's office, Noah finds me, keeping step with me as I make my way toward the house. "If you're not going to talk to her, I will," he says with enough confidence to lead an army into a battle and then sips a beer like he's legally allowed to do so. He's not since he just turned twenty last month.

I'm not intimidated or jealous of my brothers. The threat to talk to Lark is made in jest at best. If he noticed the attention I'm giving her, he knows not to make a move on her. As for the drinking, it's a ballsy move, especially at a party of my parents' peers. "You're going to get your ass kicked if Dad sees you."

"I'm not worried." He empties the glass, gulping it down, and then turns to me. "You headed back to town shortly?"

"Probably, why?" He gives me the look, the one that says he has some girl waiting on him. I laugh. "Did you get her name this time?"

That makes him laugh. "It was one time, and the only thing that matters is that she knows mine. Very well, I might add."

We stop by the edge of the party before we reach the buffet. I turn to face him. "Look, Noah, you know I don't usually say anything, but be careful. Okay?"

"Don't worry. I will." He starts walking away backward. "You've done your duty as my big brother. Are we good here?"

Bursting out laughing, I say, "You're such a fucker."

He plucks his shirt from his chest and then throws his arms out wide. "That's why the ladies love me."

I recognize his arrogance since I still struggle with it some days as well. You would have thought almost dying would have tempered it, but alas, the Westcott brothers are in their full glory here.

With my mood lifted, I head toward the table where Lark is working. Her eyes lift, and the smile she tries to restrain breaks free. "Hungry?" she asks when I approach.

"I'm heading out, but it was good spending time with you. If you ever scrape a knee or bust a lip, I'm your guy."

"You're my guy, huh?" She comes around the table. Touching her chin, she says, "Thank you for helping me."

"You're welcome." I could linger a little longer, but I'll let her work without me interrupting. "Maybe destiny will bring us together again."

She tilts her head, looking me in the eyes, and almost knocks me on my ass from her beauty—string lights reflect in the green lagoons of her eyes, a gloss shining on her lips, and the sweetest dimple in the apple of her left cheek. "Maybe we'll be lucky that way."

After surviving on the side of that cliff, I start to think that maybe everyone is right. Maybe I am lucky to be here. If that's the case, luck is something I have in spades.

5

Lark

"DAD?" I call, letting the screen door slam behind me. *Bad habit.*

"Don't slam the door, Lark." I peer through the living room to the door that leads to the kitchen, following the sound of his voice. "In here."

I see his denim-wrapped legs sprawled across the yellow-and-white-floral linoleum. His body is revealed between open cabinets while his head is tucked under the sink. "Broken pipe again?"

His eyes find mine when he tilts to the side, a wrench in hand still attached to the pipe. "Why pay someone when you can fix it yourself?"

"Because then you wouldn't have to fix it every few weeks." I pull out a chair, the metal feet dragging through the barren spot in the flooring. The sound has been a part of my childhood, so neither of us bats an eye.

He tightens the seal and then lowers the wrench. "Turn on the water."

We've had a few mishaps over the years fixing things ourselves, but the memories only reflect good times when thinking back. I turn on the faucet. No yelping is a good start.

He untucks himself from the awkward position under the sink and sits up. "That's money in the bank."

When he stands and dusts himself off, I ask, "Did you see the new building going up at the corner of Dobson and Main?"

The wrench clangs in the rusted toolbox when it's dropped among the other tools. "I'm not an apartment kind of guy."

"They look really nice. Great views of downtown. Someone else can fix the pipes if they break, and the sale of the house would be real money in the bank." This is the only home I've known. This is the place where he and Liz . . . I still can't bring myself to call the woman who gave birth to me mom. This is the house where they once lived together, loved each other, and brought me home from the hospital. I'd be kind of sad if he sold this place. Still, it would be worth it for the gain he'd get, money he'll never have working twelve-to-fourteen-hour days in the garage.

Squatting, he packs up the toolbox and then stands with it in his hands. "She's not much, but in a few years, she'll be all mine once I pay her off. Then I never have to owe anyone for anything."

"Other than taxes."

"You know what I mean, pipsqueak." He comes over and ruffles my hair. I could complain about the nickname or the hair like I did when I was a teen, but I don't get these moments as often these days. Between work and school, I treasure our Sunday dinners. Time slows down when I'm at home, and I breathe a little easier. "There's value in not owing anybody anything."

I nod.

My dad raised me by himself since the day Liz walked out the same door I just entered. I was two when this gruff—six-one, ex-high school football player, heart of gold of a guy—took on the role of both parents, raising me with a strong work ethic, which is one of the reasons I got a full ride to college. But it's his values that never waver.

He relied on one person in life, and she let him down, so he stood on his own after that with his chin held high, even when it meant sacrificing his own needs.

I intend to make it up to him one day. It's not that I owe him that. John Summerlin would be the first to argue I don't. It's that he deserves it. He deserves to have fewer worries for all the burdens he's carried.

Opening the back door, he says, "Hope you're hungry for burgers. I've already got them on the grill. Grab a soda and seat out here and tell me about your week."

I follow him out onto the cracked concrete patio, digging through the cooler he stocks for us—beer for him, soda for me. "I'm old enough to have a beer, you know?"

"I know." He doesn't say why he only ever offers me soda, but I already know. He wants to keep me young, his little girl, for as long as he can. Not that he cares if I drink since I'm twenty-one, but I'll oblige because it makes him happy. I pop the top on a Sprite and sit in a plastic Adirondack chair I bought him for his birthday a few months ago. After almost falling through a canvas chair he'd left out in the weather for ten years, the upgrade is nice.

He returns from the garage empty-handed, grabs a can of beer, and sits in the matching chair. "Tell me about your week."

"It's boring," I reply, leaning my head back on the chair.

"Not to me."

I grin because I have the best dad. "Normal week of classes, but I was assigned a paper on Monday. It took me an hour of work every night to get it turned in on time on Friday."

"How'd you do?"

"We haven't received our grades yet, but I think I did well."

"That's good. You mentioned last week that you had two shifts this week . . ." He leaves the inquiry open-ended for me to fill in.

So I do. "Wednesday was serving the psychology department. I guess it's an annual dinner they do to talk about how their goals are being met so far after the first month of school. It was easy. Just me and Larry, but the money was good because they left a big tip."

"That's good. You socking it away?

"No, but I put it toward paying rent for next month, though."

He raises his can. "Getting ahead. That's my girl."

Hoping to distract him, I get up and open the grill. "These are looking good. I'll get the veggies ready to go."

"Already done," he says, not making a move. "Sometimes dinner with you passes too fast, so I did what you taught me and prepped ahead."

Grinning, I reply, "Who says you can't teach an old dog new tricks?"

He chuckles but gets right back on the track I was trying to detour. "And the other shift?"

I hesitate, twisting the metal top of the can around. "It was actually out at The Pointe Estates." I glance up to see his eyes stuck to his well-loved Carhartt work boots.

"Huh." Shaking his head, he says, "Larry must be doing good to get back into their graces." His tone turns just like it always does at the mention of the Estates. He looks at me as if he's seeing me in a new light, seeing me as a grown woman. "Did you make good money?"

"Yes. It was a pretty party at a big white house. Green shutters—"

"Fancy cars and buttoned-up crowd?" His grin is genuine as he takes a sip of his beer.

"Yeah," I reply, my hackles lowering when his dislike of that crowd turns into support for me. "A giant buffet, full party on the other side of the swimming pool. Grass so green . . . It was one of the most beautiful places I've ever seen."

Sitting forward, he rests his forearms on his knees. "Did they treat you with respect?"

Harbor comes to mind, standing in the hallway with that devastating smile asking to spend time with me. Feeling that weak in the knees for someone will only get me in trouble. Saying yes to him once would free the floodgates to a thousand yeses right after. It's best if I don't lose focus on a gorgeous guy and keep my attention on my school and applications. "They did. They were very kind to me."

I receive a nod in satisfaction as he gets up to check on the burgers. "Remember, don't flip until they're almost fully cooked. That way, the burgers don't dry out."

Seeing right through his own tactics of changing the topic, I ride along with him on the detour by getting up and taking the spatula from him. "Do I keep them on the flame or move them off?"

"Right on the flame, but don't walk away, or they'll burn at this stage."

When the burgers are ready, we eat in front of an old

box TV and watch the game. At halftime, he walks me outside and looks up. "It's getting darker earlier."

The cue for me to get going is his subtle concern for my safety and makes me feel loved. He'll worry about me riding home in the dark until I text him that I made it. He tries his best not to treat me like I'm his little girl, but he'll always look out for me.

I look at the sky and the golden light peeking through the trees. "I think we have another month before it gets dark earlier." Taking my bike by the handlebars, I swipe the kickstand with my foot and swing my leg over.

He gives me a hug. I bury my head against him. "I love you, Dad."

"Love you, too, Pipsqueak. Text me when you get home."

"I will."

I roll down the driveway and into the street, waving as I ride in front of the house. "Love you."

My dad is the best anyone could ever ask for. He stands there on the small steps and watches, waiting until I'm out of view. I wave one last time as I turn the corner.

Though I'm stuffed, I know it will be a late night of studying, so I ride the extra two blocks to the gas station since I know we're out of coffee at home. It was Amanda's week to buy the staples, and well, I know how that goes. She probably spent her money while out last night.

I park my bike against the side of the building near the ice and peek through the window. If that guy is behind the counter, I've already decided I'll suffer without the caffeine. I don't want to deal with him tonight.

When I spy TJ, I'm relieved. Although that's replaced with a feeling of disappointment by the absence of Harbor, which is completely ridiculous. It's not like he's a regular here. It was a one-time thing. Let it go.

I tug the door open, setting off the bell to chime above. TJ, the owner and the convenience store's namesake, spots me when I pass the lottery ticket machine. "Lark, what brings you in tonight?"

"Coffee." I trek straight for the aisle, hoping he has stocked a variety to choose from. "How are you?"

"Hanging in there. Debbie, that beagle down the road had a run-in with a porcupine a few days ago. Patsy asked me to deal with that disaster."

I stop and turn back to ask, "How's she doing now?"

"Patsy's always been a hot mess."

I laugh. "I meant Debbie, the dog."

"The vet says she'll heal right up and be fine."

Scanning the aisle, I find the tiny coffee selection. "That's good. She's a cute dog."

"She's about to have another litter. Want one?"

I start to laugh. "I can barely pay my bills, TJ. I definitely can't take care of a pet."

"I hear you. Did you see I got pumpkin spice coffee?" The door chimes just as I bend down to see the bottom shelf with the new coffee. It's a few dollars out of my league this trip. He adds, "Figured you'd like that."

I grab the smallest and cheapest bag of coffee before heading to the counter. He rings me up, but when I reach into my pockets, I can cover the three dollars, but I'm short twenty-three cents. "I'll try it after payday." Glancing at the spare change tray, which I've probably donated enough change over the years to pay for a lot more than cheap coffee, I discover it empty this time. "I'm a little short, so I'll find something else inst—"

"I'll cover it."

When I look behind me, I'm greeted with that smile that weakens my knees and the warmth of the fire lit in his brown eyes. I'd like to act like I'm not over the moon thrilled to see Harbor again, but I'm not that talented of an actress. But then I realize he's bailing me out. So embarrassing. "It's okay. I don't need a handout."

Harbor sets a bottle of fancy water on the counter and a pack of gum. Peppermint, my favorite flavor. "I owe you, and I always pay my debts."

"I'd hardly call a soda a debt," I start but then see the coffee and think of tonight when I'll need it most, and then the morning trying to function without it. "Okay. It's only twenty-three cents." I roll my eyes at myself. It's like one embarrassing moment after another.

He probably didn't have to think twice about it, put it on his card, and not worry how the bill gets paid when I'm standing here worried about twenty-three cents.

I say, "Thank you," and take the coffee.

"Need anything else? I only have a credit card, and it's a ten-dollar minimum charge."

TJ says, "There's a pumpkin spice coffee Lark said she'd like to try."

Harbor grins, knowing TJ just sold me out for a delicious-flavored coffee drink. "Perfect. Add it to the tab."

I whisper, "Traitor," under my breath.

Under the sounds of the keys of the register, TJ laughs. "He offered."

I roll my eyes and take my cheap coffee. When I head to the door, Harbor says, "Don't forget your pumpkin spice."

Pausing, I glance back at him, and as if I'm spiting him, I turn abruptly and head down the aisle to grab the bag of beans. Like my dad, I hold my head high and march myself outside.

It's gotten dark since I was inside the store. I walk to my bike and mount it while waiting for Harbor to come out. He sees me as soon as he does, his smile growing like I just made his day.

With the coffee tucked in the small basket on the front of my bike, I say, "Now I owe you eight dollars."

"You don't owe me anything, Lark. Just a friend helping a friend." He walks toward a car.

Oh.

My.

God.

Is that his car?

How'd I miss this amazing sports car the first time we met? Sleek and silver, it's a dream, and the prettiest car I've ever seen. And by far the most expensive I've been near other than maybe the car shows my dad used to take me to when I was younger. But this one might still win that award.

How does he afford this car? Oh wait, that's right. He's a Westcott.

I'd almost forgotten.

Popping open the driver's door, he stops with his hand on top and eyes my bicycle. "It's pretty dark out. Is it safe to ride home at this hour?"

His words remind me of my dad's, causing warmth to spread across my chest.

I swing my leg over and stand on my tiptoes to balance. "It's all I got." Not a dig at his car, but I make do with what I have.

"Since destiny brought us here together tonight—"

"Or you're stalking me?" I laugh, loving to tease this man.

"Ironically, I had the same thought about you being the one stalking me," he volleys right back while also laughing.

"*Me?*" I ask, stabbing my finger into my chest. "You're the one who doesn't live anywhere near here."

"Only a stalker would know where I live." Raising an eyebrow in challenge, he nods as if he's won.

"Or someone who just worked at your house last night." Maybe he is winning . . . winning me over. The more time I spend with Harbor, the more time I want to spend with him. I don't always trust guys when we first meet, but there's something about Harbor that makes me believe he's being genuine with me.

Chuckling again, he rests his arms on the roof and says, "Touché." His shoulders drop as he eases against the car. "But it is really dark out. I'm happy to give you a lift if you'd like a ride home."

His argument holds water. It's just a friend helping a friend. And maybe it's a little, or a lot, of me wanting to ride inside something so luxurious. I may never get this chance again. "I've almost been hit a few times riding at night, so I guess it would be safer if I ride with you, but how will we fit my bike? There's no room for it."

He's grinning, nothing less than gorgeously, as if it were even possible for him to sport anything less. His gaze runs the length of the car and then lands back on me. Waggling his eyebrows, he replies, "Don't worry, we'll make it work."

6

Lark

I'M NOT sure how everything Harbor says feels like it has
layers of other meanings built in, but he did make it work.

Kneeling on the sidewalk that leads to the door, he puts
the last bolt back in place and then spins the wheel. "Good
as new."

"Thanks." I spin the tire, not because I don't believe him,
but I'm not sure what to do and need the time to decide.
Should I invite him in, take the free ride in the fancy car and
then make a break for it inside, or hang out here in the dark
with him a little longer? One and three are tempting, but my
sensible side says two should win out. "Would you like to
come in?" And there goes all reasoning . . .

"Sure." He rights the bike.

"Let me put this up." I take it by the handles and start for
the side of the house where I store it behind the bushes.

Shoving his hands in his pockets, he follows me through
the grass. As I hide it from sight behind the shrubbery, he

looks down the street and then back at me. "Should you lock it up?"

"I don't have anywhere to lock it, and my neighbors inside the house complained when I used to keep it in the entryway." I walk back around the house to the sidewalk. Harbor keeps up, his strides double mine. "They had a point since it's a small entry, but now I take my chances." I'm about to take the coffee from him when my phone buzzes in my back pocket. "Oh no, my dad."

Panic widens his eyes as Harbor looks around. I would laugh, but my dad is actually here in his truck, parked at the curb with the passenger side window rolled down. "You didn't text me back," he says, but his eyes are glued to the guy beside me.

With the phone in my hand, I see the three missed texts and one call that went to voicemail. *Yikes.* "Hey, Dad," I say, sounding as chipper as I can despite being not only busted with a man he doesn't know but said man also making me forget to text my dad. I move to the truck quickly before he gets out and this becomes a whole thing that it's not. "I'm sorry. I stopped at TJ's to grab coffee and ran into a friend."

My dad glares over my shoulder, and mumbles, "A friend, huh?"

"Hello, Mr. . . . ." Harbor goes quiet after approaching.

Under my breath, I whisper, "Summerlin."

"Mr. Summerlin. It's nice to meet you."

My dad was never a cop, but he gives off the vibes when he wants to intimidate. Resting his arms on the thin steering wheel, he eyes Harbor. "And you are?"

Harbor moves to my side and holds out his hand. My dad doesn't bother, standing his ground. The left side of his face pinches as he looks him over, and from experience, that's never a good thing.

Lowering his hand, Harbor replies, "Harbor Westcott, sir."

"Let me guess," my dad starts and then leans back. "From Beacon Pointe?" His tone isn't rude, but he calls things how he sees them.

"Yes, sir." Harbor's tone stays as solid as his demeanor, which I think matches his character. My dad will appreciate that. "How did you know?"

"The car might have been a giveaway."

"Right. Well, speaking of cars, I should probably go."

Jumping into the exchange, I say, "Harbor gave me a ride home since it was dark."

My dad looks into the rearview mirror and then back at us again. "How'd you fit her bike in a Ghibli Modena?"

Harbor's surprise matches mine. He asks, "You know cars?"

I start to laugh when my dad shakes his head. "Yeah, I know cars." He finally directs his gaze on me. Since the engine is rumbling, he shifts the old Ford truck into gear. "Next time, text me, Pip. I'll come get you."

"I will. Sorry for worrying you."

My dad looks at Harbor one more time. "Thanks for making sure she got home safely."

"My pleasure." He receives a glare for that. Harbor is quick to add, "It was nice to meet you, Mr. Summerlin."

"Yeah. Yeah." Pushing the gas, he pulls away from the curb, leaving the two of us alone again and standing in awkward silence.

When the taillights disappear down the street, Harbor turns to me, and says, "That was fun."

I burst out laughing, but I feel my cheeks heat. "That was mortifying."

Gently knocking his elbow into me, he grins. "Nothing

to be mortified about. You met my mom. Now I've met your dad. All seems right to me."

Crossing my arms over my chest, I quirk an eyebrow at him this time. "How'd you land on that?"

"I'm just saying that things are happening. Maybe faster than usual, but I don't think you can deny destiny or the chemistry."

Now both eyebrows shoot straight up to the sky. "Chemistry?"

Leaning closer, he whispers, "Don't you feel it?"

I definitely feel it.

"I'm . . ." It's not just my cheeks heating anymore. His words warm my chest like a hug. A little flustered, I take a step back in a bad attempt to clear the thoughts that have me wondering what it would be like to kiss him that are presently running rampant. When he pushes the strands of hair that had fallen in my eyes away from my face, a shiver runs up my spine. "I'm cold and should probably go in."

I start walking up the sidewalk but stop and turn back when I realize he's not next to me. "Hey, Westcott?"

"What's up, Summerlin?"

"You coming?" I smile with a nod toward the house and then head for the door.

I hear the hurried steps behind me. "Wouldn't miss it."

Using the house key, I unlock the main door and then have him follow me to the door leading to Amanda's and my apartment. "We're over here."

Leaning against the wall while I unlock our door, he asks, "We?"

"My roommate and I live here. My best friend, Amanda."

"Ah." I unlock the door and open it wide, silently inviting him in. "It's nice in here. Which apartment is yours?"

"Over here. This apartment was a good find, affordable and close enough to campus." I laugh to myself about the surprise visit from my dad. "It's also only about five blocks from my dad."

Harbor walks in and stops in the living room. "Nice guy."

I shut the door and lean against it. "Tell me the truth."

He chuckles. "I'm not easily intimidated." Rubbing over a shadow of scruff on his jaw, he adds, "But he does a good job."

Pushing off the wood door, I take the coffee from him and then drop my keys in the bowl on the small kitchen bar. "He tries."

"Does he come by often?" Harbor's presence fills the space. This place would be too small to ever adequately house a guy of his stature, his shoulders that appear broader in this small apartment, and standing at a height that has him caged in by the ceiling.

"Not that often." Moving around into the kitchen, I set the small bag of coffee and the box of pumpkin spice next to the coffee maker on the counter. "Thank you again for the coffee. You really didn't have to do that."

"Coffee is the nectar of the gods. I have an addiction, so I can appreciate the need to be prepared when you wake up."

Opening the cabinet, I reach for two mugs. None are matching, which never bothered me until Harbor Westcott was standing in my apartment. His house is so beautiful that I'm sure their dishes match. They probably have formal sets for special occasions and daily plates for everyday use as well.

I grab my favorite ones since that's all I have to fall back on. "I'll actually be up studying tonight, so I needed caffeine. Would you like a cup?"

"Sure. Thanks."

Staring at the options, I splurge and go for the good stuff —pumpkin spice—and hold the box up. "Are you good with this?"

"I've never had it, so it will be a first."

I put the beans in the grinder and then into the machine. "I don't have the fancy syrups or anything, but I do have sugar and creamer."

"I'll take mine however you take yours."

"Are you always so agreeable?"

He chuckles. "Guess it depends on who you ask."

While the coffee percolates, I lean against the counter facing him. "Name a person who would disagree with my assertion."

"Bailey Bensimone." Not one hesitation. No waffling about who to choose. Not even shy about throwing a name out there. He just did it when most wouldn't.

The thing is, I've heard of her. I suddenly feel uneasy. "She goes to the university."

His eyes latch onto mine. "Do you know her?"

"No. Just her name."

"I probably shouldn't have said anything."

"You were just being honest." I come closer, standing with only a sink and a small bar between us. "But you have me curious. Why would Bailey Bensimone call you disagreeable?"

I hate that he clams up, but he does, turning his back to me and walking to look out the front window. "It's a nice street. Quiet." When he turns back, he asks, "Where's your roommate?"

"Working. She's a server and closes on Sundays."

The water stops filling the full coffee pot, drawing my attention to it. Pouring powdered creamer and a dash of sugar into each mug, I stir, and then present the blue mug to him. He takes one look and smiles. "You're a Yankees fan?"

"It's my dad's favorite team, so I grew up watching the games with him. I asked for tickets for my fourteenth birthday." I sip, letting the warm liquid meld with the good memories. "My dad said I could pick out anything I wanted from the gift store."

Both his hands wrap around the mug like it's the most precious thing he's ever held on to. "You chose this mug?"

"I remember flipping over price tags on the jerseys and T-shirts. They cost way too much. I couldn't let my dad spend that. He'd worked late for months to pay for the game tickets and the night at the motel. I really didn't want a pennant or a foam finger, so I chose the mug."

"If you could have had anything without worries over money, what would you have picked?"

"A jersey." Approval reflects in his eyes. I add, "But I love that mug."

He takes a sip of coffee, staring at the mug even once lowered. "Not sure I can agree on the team, but it's a good mug. A New York classic."

I move into the living room and set my mug down, one I got when my dad forgot it. He got it from Dell's Creamery when Dell was trying to butter my dad up to cut the bill for fixing his delivery truck.

"So," I say, sitting on the couch. "Did you just happen to go to the gas station tonight or—?"

"Or did I show up hoping to see you?" He comes to sit next to me. Setting his mug on the table next to mine, Harbor then rests back and spreads his arms wide across the back of the couch. He looks me in the eyes and replies, "The truth?"

"Always."

"I went there hoping to see you, but when I didn't, I grabbed a bottle of water since I was there."

"You really didn't know I was there?" I laugh, remembering how I was bent down on the food aisle. *Did destiny play a hand in our meeting?*

"Not until I saw you at the register." Not a lie is detected in his eyes. That leads me to believe that maybe it was meant to be.

Just like in the movies.

7

Harbor

LARK STILL EMBODIES the bravado she had the first time we met, even if we've moved past the cat-and-mouse game we were playing. She owns every sway of her hips and the way she moves in her body.

For all her certainty in who she is, she doesn't fully trust me. She's not unwise. Quite the opposite. I like that she's guarded. It makes the reward of being on the inside of her walls all the sweeter.

"I was going to study," she says next to me on the couch.

Her hair tousled from being outside, her green eyes still bright as if it were still daylight outside. I search for makeup but can only find maybe darker lashes than her natural ones and a hint of pale pink on her lips that could be mistaken for when they're nude. She doesn't need any.

She's just as beautiful without makeup, if not more, than when I saw her working last night and wearing it. I pivot my gaze away from her and to the mug on the table so she doesn't find me creepy for staring at her too long. Though I could stare at her all day and still find something new that fascinates me.

I reply, "I can go if you want."

There's no rush to respond. She sips her coffee with delicate lips pressed to a mug that I'm sure she got from that junkyard of a car dealership just outside Beacon lines. The juxtaposition is interesting. That she doesn't have a car gives me the feeling there might be a story behind the acquisition of the mug.

"I'm okay." Leaning forward, she adds, "If you are."

"I'm good. What's your favorite color?"

"Blue."

I chuckle. "Yankee blue or sky?"

"Somewhere in between." She grins, and then asks, "What's your favorite color?"

"I don't have one."

She sits back again, propping her elbow against the couch and her head to her hand, and then furrows her brow. "How can you not have a favorite color? Everyone has a favorite color."

"I'm not everyone."

"No." She tilts her head down, but her eyes stay on mine. "You're definitely not, but you're telling me there's not one color that makes your day brighter? The yellow of a daisy or sunshine, the green of freshly mowed grass in spring, a patch of clovers, or delicious pesto pasta?" She sits up, determination anchoring her spine straight, and continues, "The red bird of the year you see or a peppermint stick? The leaves when they turn orange or a patch of pumpkins in fall? Even brown like the smoothest Belgian chocolate or the trunk of the tallest pine trees?"

"You're very good at this. How about purple or gray, or even black."

"We may love to wear black, but it's no one's favorite color."

"It could be."

"I think if someone said their favorite color is black, they're caught in the idea of it more than the hue because it's the absence of color. The gray of a cloudy day or the stunning cliffs overlooking the emerald lake out at Devil's Edge." She doesn't notice me bristle or my hand fisting, my breath growing deeper as I try to calm myself. "They say those cliffs sparkle from the water, but I've never been on a boat out there to see for myself."

"They do." My tone is clipped, which makes me angry. She doesn't deserve to be on the receiving end of my reaction to mistakes I've made.

"Harbor?" Her hand rests on my forearm when my gaze slides from my lap to the woman beside me. Her smile is small and makes me feel worse for making her feel that way. "Are you okay?" Licking her lips, she then drags the bottom one under her top teeth.

"I'm fine. My apologies. What were you saying?"

She doesn't rush to answer. Instead, her hand gives me a little squeeze before she pulls it back to her lap. "I was rambling."

"No, you weren't. I'm sorry. I just . . ." I push up as anger at myself gets the better of me. "I'll let you study."

Grabbing my wrist, she stands. "Stay." Still latched onto me, there's no room to make excuses, so I stay, unsure of what she wants from me. Her breath has quickened, her chest rising and falling as fast. "What happened? What did I do?"

"No, you did nothing wrong, Lark. I . . ." I look away from her before I'm tempted to caress her cheek, to lean in and kiss the shine from her freshly licked lips. "I got caught up in a past I've tried to forget."

"It was something I said?"

The truth isn't something that needs to shroud our conversation. She didn't mean to push my triggers. They're mine and a fucking annoyance for ruining our time. Despite me escaping the question, I focus on her, the pretty girl, who looks at me like I might have a chance at being someone good, someone she can trust. "I haven't eaten in hours. Want to go out and get something?"

Her hand falls back to her side as she looks away from me. "I don't think I can." I wouldn't say she's lying, but she is looking for excuses. I follow her gaze to the mug on the table and remember she couldn't cover the coffee at the gas station. I'm a dick for putting her on the spot.

I reach over and take hold of her wrist this time and then slide my hand until her palm rests against mine. This connection is different than the ones we've shared before. Not less important, but more potent as if I'm being given a second chance. With her, my cousin's death doesn't over-shadow who I am.

God, I could drink this in, savor her for hours if given the chance.

I wish I could.

I wrap my fingers around her just enough to hold her before she's gone.

Her breath catches, and the tips of her nails send my pulse racing through my veins. Only seconds have passed, but I've lived a lifetime of bliss inside them with her. I don't want this to end. "Hey," I start with a whisper, lifting her chin so her eyes meet mine again. "I know paying your way is important but let me take you to dinner. I promise to let you take me another time."

She giggles softly. "You'll let me take you out on a date? You're good, Harbor." Waggling her finger, she adds, "Very good." She takes a deep breath as her eyes search my face and then nods. "But I also can eat, so okay."

I've had more enthusiastic reactions when asking girls out before, but that okay was worth the wait.

"Give me five? I need to change clothes." Her hand starts to slip from mine as she walks away, so I tighten my grip on her just enough to bring her eyes back to mine. Questions fill her greens as we stand there in the briefest moment of silence.

"You don't need to change one thing, Lark. You're perfect as you are." Dressed in shorts and sneakers with a cropped pale-pink T-shirt, she looks great. But even she knows I wasn't talking about her clothes. "Don't change."

Angling on her ankle, she tilts—her body and head, "Ever?" Her voice is low, quiet . . . seductive. My body vibrates, reacting to the sound. I don't think she even realizes what she does to me, and probably to every other guy on this planet.

Her naïveté makes her more enticing.

I step back, needing a breather before this night goes sideways. We're not fucking, after all. At least not before I have the chance to buy her dinner. I run my hand over my head and clear my throat. "So dinner, then?"

Crossing the room, she replies, "Dinner, then." She pulls out a little yellow-and-red wallet, she takes her keys with a smile that feels personally tailored for me. She sweeps her hair off her shoulders and into a knot on her head. "I guess I'm ready."

We walk to the car, and I open the door. Lark slips inside, her eyes roaming the interior, and her hand rubbing the leather beneath her. I close the door and walk around the front to the driver's side. My chest tightens from the sight of her tucked inside my car. It's not a feeling I'm familiar with or one I can pinpoint. Just feels good to be around her, and I'll take that good and try to hold on to it because it's not as common after the accident.

As soon as I start the engine, she rests her head back, and smiles at me. "What are you craving, Harbor?"

"What am I craving?" *Fuck.* She's going to do me in. "Pizza, burgers, tacos, or there's a little Italian place in the far corner of the square? I think they close just over an hour from now, so we need to get going."

"I love Moretti's. It's always a treat."

"Moretti's it is, then."

She lives close enough to downtown to get to the restaurant within five minutes, even with the two stoplights. Even though it's not that late, Moretti's closes earlier on Sunday nights. When we walk in, Lark asked the hostess, "Is it too late for dinner? We don't want to keep you."

Most people I know don't give a damn about other people's schedules or lives that might be affected. I think that's why Lark stands out so much . . . Or should I say even more at this moment?

I may have only just met her yesterday, but I can tell she doesn't have a pretentious bone in her body. I add that to the list of things I find so attractive about her. It's a list that's getting longer with every hour we spend together.

The hostess smiles, tapping Lark on the arm, and says, "You know you're always welcome here, Lark." Her eyes shift to me and then back to her, giving her a little wink. "I have the perfect booth for you right back here. Follow me."

They chat as if they've known each other forever, asking about each other's families and how their classes are going this semester.

The restaurant isn't big, but it's quaint, and the food is good. As we pass through the dining room, I can't help but notice it's quieter with only a few tables occupied. The Italian music can barely be heard, low enough to allow for private conversations.

We slip into the booth near the window and open our menus. I'm scanning the specials that are clipped inside when I feel Lark's gaze on me. I look up to see her attention shift down, but I know I just busted her. "What sounds good tonight?" I ask.

"I'm thinking about the carbonara. It's my favorite." She sets the menu as if she's more than thinking about it. She's decided. "You?"

"Lasagna. It's been a while since I've had it, and it's not something I'll ever make."

"Do you cook?"

I lean forward as if I'm revealing some great secret. She does the same. I reply, "Not at all."

Surprise doesn't contort her expression, but it does bend her brow. "You don't cook, not eggs or anything? Ever?" Her voice starts pitching even through the whispering exchange.

"No. Never. I should, though."

"I don't under—"

"Ready to order?" the server asks, a kid I might recognize from campus, but I'm not sure. Though his blond spikes tend to stand out in this small town. He sets down two glasses of water, and then pulls a pen and pad from his apron. "We can start with drinks. Wine, soda, tea?"

I look at Lark. "We can get a bottle of wine if you'd like."

She glances up at him. "I think water will be fine for me."

"I'll stick with the water as well."

He takes our food order and quicksteps it back to the

kitchen. While we unwrap our napkins, she asks, "Do you have a chef? Or you order food every night? Or . . ." She leaves it open for me to reply. Curiosity shapes her face, but her features remain soft.

"I order a lot of food, I'm a whiz at heating up food—frozen meals or dishes that my family sends me. I eat out a lot or grab something quick from a fast-food joint."

"I don't understand. Do you live at home, the home from yesterday?" She adds, "You had a room upstairs?"

"That's still my room. Whenever I stay over, that's where I sleep. My childhood, my life before moving out, remains there for me. I suppose one day I'll have to pack it up, but it's there now, maybe always will be. Who knows?"

She relaxes across from me, her shoulders rounding as she takes a deep breath. "I still have a room at home. My dad keeps it just as I left it. Sometimes I wonder if he hopes I'll move home, and other times I think about it because I feel guilty for leaving him."

"You didn't leave him. You're just living somewhere else right now."

Hope returns to her eyes and raises a smile. "That's a nice way of looking at it." She toys with the red pepper shaker, spinning it mindlessly as if her thoughts are else-where. "I'm not sure if I'll ever live there again. Growing up is weird." She looks at me. "I'm twenty-one, living on my own, paying my own bills, but I feel caught in this age, like I'm not an adult but I'm no longer a kid anymore." Shaking her head, she says, "Weird. And every time I see my dad, I still feel like a little girl?" She whispers, "I think he'd keep me young forever if he had a choice."

There's such a sweetness to her that I can see what she means about being trapped in the age in between. It's almost like the darkness of life hasn't touched her yet. She's lucky that way.

Lucky.

Fuck luck.

Luck doesn't exist.

Only this.

She and I right here.

Right now.

This is the luck *I* created.

8

Harbor

I THOUGHT we were getting heavy and heading for a conversation about the meaning of life. Nope. Her mood goes from introspective to animated with a wave of her hands. "Where do you live?" she asks.

Taking her in is a treat I didn't expect to get tonight. I gulp some water and return the glass to the ring formed on the table from condensation. "I'm in an apartment a few blocks from here. The house out in The Pointe wasn't 'conducive' to my behavior a few years ago. My dad's words."

Not missing a beat of what I mean, she says, "That's a nice way of phrasing it."

"I don't blame him. I was a freshman at the university and wanted to party." Shame rattles through me as if I'm saying something I shouldn't. I would never want to make my family look bad. At least, not more than I already have. But, if my honesty ends what Lark and I have started, then it's best she knows to get out now because I can't change my past. I am who I am. "I partied hard."

"A lot of people do," she says, not a word of mine fazing her. "I have good friends who still do, but I guess if there were ever a time, it's this time in our lives."

"You sound like you didn't."

She ponders the question, a family walking by drawing her attention to the window. "I drink occasionally, but otherwise, I never had the time to party. Even most weekends now, I work a catering shift."

"Is it hard to see others go out when you're working so hard?"

"I need the money, so I have to work. But it's hard to hear about the fun after the fact. My roommate goes out all the time. She'd love for me to go out after my shift."

"But you don't?"

"It sounds so bad because I'm young, but I'm exhausted most of the time." Her eyes return to me, and she smiles, but some of the joy is lost. "Getting home at midnight, pulling on a dress and heels, full face of makeup, and doing my hair," she says, her arms making circles in front of her, "and then going to party after all that? I don't have the energy."

"Sounds like a lot, but you know, you don't need all that. You always look great."

Her chin dips to her chest as she hides her smile. "Thank you." Taking her water, she sips again, and then says, "You didn't finish the story about when you moved out."

"Right," I start where I left off. "My dad had a point. He didn't say that, but I knew I wasn't setting the best example for my younger siblings. So instead of living by the rules, I decided to move in with my older brother who was already in the apartment. It's two bedrooms, so that made the transition easy."

"And that's Loch?" Even though she sometimes appears

shy around me, she's not shy about asking exactly what's on her mind. *Adding that to the list.*

"Yeah, Loch is my older brother."

"I met him yesterday. He was nice."

Not sure why, but she's easy to talk to. I think it's because she appears genuinely interested. Most girls I know don't have that skill or natural inclination. "He's a good guy. I also have a younger brother. Noah. Don't know if you met him." I'll kick his ass if he hit on her.

"No, I didn't."

Thank fuck. I can give that kid some credit where it's due. We're all talented in the charisma category, but Noah's turning into the biggest charmer of us all. "My little sister is Marina, and now you know my family tree."

She laughs. "I have a feeling there's more to the Westcott family tree, but since you're giving me the short version, how about we talk about that some other time?"

"I like the sound of 'some other time' when it comes to you."

She shrugs. "Well, I do owe you a dinner now, so I figure we don't have to learn our whole life stories tonight."

"True."

Clasping her hands together on the table in front of her, she says, "But I need to know because I'm sensing a pattern. What's up with the water names? Harbor, Marina, Loch—"

I chuckle. "There's more, but I'll leave it for some other time."

"You've got yourself a deal." Lark smiles, leaving the topic where I left it. "How about you and Loch. You live together, but do you get along?"

Nodding, I reply. "Yes, ever since he moved out."

"Ah," she says, not surprised at all. "I hear siblings can

be a pain in the ass." Touching her chest, she adds, "Not that I would know since I'm an only child."

"He graduated from Beacon U. two years ago. Now he spends most of his time in New York City, my dad's right-hand man in the Manhattan office. He stays at the house when he's in town."

"That's exciting."

I shrug. "Loch is working on his career, networking, doing everything a good son does for his family." Her smile falls. "What is it?"

She sits back and adjusts the napkin on her lap. "That sounds like a good employee more than a son."

As an outsider, she doesn't understand the full scope of Loch's role in our family. But she just nailed me, under-mining all my brother does for us. She sees me so clearly. I have a feeling I can't pull anything over on her, so I straighten my shoulders and try to ignore the unsettling feeling creeping up the sides of my spine.

She asks, "What are your plans after graduation? Following in the family footsteps?" There's no judgment in her tone or the way she looks at me, like what I say next will give insight into who I am.

Despite being called on my BS, she gives me the floor to say what I'm comfortable with sharing. "No. I've chosen the noble profession of medicine to pursue."

Her mouth falls open, her lips parting in such a deli-ciously subtle way. "You're going to medical school?"

I shift across the vinyl, still trying to come to peace with the decision I've made regarding my future. "That's the plan."

As if I've made her day, she says, "Incredible. I'm also going to medical school. Well, trying to. I'm working on applications and took the MCAT over the summer." Resting her arms on the table, she sits on the edge of the seat and closes some of the space between us on the table. "I can't believe we have that in common. You're a senior and pre-med, right? How have we never met?"

The heat of my stalkerish ways begins to catch up with me. Do I confess now or do I surprise her in the morning? There's just something about her that makes telling the truth easier. "Guess it just wasn't our time, but you know what's even more mind-blowing?"

"What?" she asks with anticipation filling her eyes. "We actually have a class together."

"We do?"

Taking my glass, I pull it across the wooden table. "First class. Mondays, Wednesdays, and Fridays."

Disappointment wedges into the greens of her eyes, darkening them just enough to wish I hadn't said anything. I prefer the happiness found in the brighter version.

Row 14.

Seat 20.

I keep that to myself and instead offer her an out. "I sit in the back, and you sit closer to the front."

The dim restaurant has only flickering candles on the tables and soft lighting above our heads. When she smiles, her beauty can't be hidden in the shadows or by low lighting. "So you were stalking me?" She's clever, entrapping me from our earlier conversation when I denied everything.

"If you want to get into the weeds, I *noticed* you versus the alternative."

A rosy color fills her cheeks, and although she's usually been bold in our interactions and quick with comebacks, she seems to be without any for the time being. But there's no fear or concern written on her face either. She takes a sip of water and then rests forward again, keeping our conversation quieter between us. "I—"

"Here you go." The server sets down the plates in front of each of us. Lark's eyes are on him but move to the food, completely stolen from me. Resentment fills me but dissipates just as quickly, knowing I'll have her full attention again in a minute.

As soon as he's gone, she picks up her knife and fork. Her lips twist to the side as if she's fighting a smile, but she says, "I have a secret I've been keeping from you, Harbor."

I hate secrets. Secrets cause more problems than they solve. Like now. A thousand possibilities cross my mind of what she might tell me, but I land on only one, hoping I'm right. *Did she notice me like I did her?* Please say yes. "Tell me."

She looks around, and then a devious smile crosses her lips. "I had dinner two hours ago."

Fucking hell, she's cute. I pretend to take this matter very seriously, though. "You misled me, Ms. Summerlin."

Already spinning pasta around her fork, her shoulders pop up and down twice. "My apologies, Mr. Westcott, but how could I say no to this?" She takes a bite, her eyes practically rolling back in her head as she moans in ecstasy.

Fuck. I shift in a poor attempt to create more room in my pants. "You couldn't."

She chews, and then when she's ready for another bite, replies, "Exactly. I couldn't."

I cut through my lasagna as if I don't have an erection hiding under the table. Before I take a bite, I ask, "And why exactly couldn't you say no?"

"Because of the company, and . . ." With another fork full of creamy pasta, she adds, "and did I tell you how much I love carbonara?"

"You did mention your love of carbonara. Since that

ground has been covered, let's talk about the company you couldn't resist."

She giggles. "That escalated quickly. That's a big leap from not being able to say no to the company I keep to said company being irresistible."

"Not much of a leap, but to be honest," I say, and then smirk. "It wouldn't be the first time I've been called irresistible."

This time a bellyaching laugh escapes her. So much so that she sets her utensils down and covers her mouth as she falls back. When she calms, she waves her hand erratically in front of her, still giggling, but says, "Thank you. I needed a good laugh."

"Glad to oblige, but care to share what's so funny?"

Catching her breath, she settles back at the table and picks up her fork again. "I have no doubt you've been called that many times over, but that aside, I'm so glad I came out tonight. This is the good time I didn't know I needed."

She's refreshing in her honesty.

A natural beauty.

And not afraid to say whatever is on her mind.

"I'm glad you're having a good time, but let me include you in on a little secret, Lark."

Her brow rises, and she whispers, "Go on."

"I'm having a good time with you."

This night feels different.

And I have a strong suspicion that Lark Summerlin is proving to be just the distraction I need.

Harbor

HER CAR WINDOW is down despite the chill in the air as I take the long way back to her place. The wind blowing through the loose strands of Lark's hair twist like tiny tornadoes, making it hard to look away. Something is comforting about not seeing one worry wrinkle her face when she's with me.

Beacon is small town in all ways except for the university. The school hosts the largest population in the area at thirty-three thousand students. Pre-med is much smaller, but the school has a great reputation, so it's one of the more popular majors.

I'm still perplexed by how I'd never seen her before we shared a class this semester. Was I not paying attention? It's a large school, so maybe our paths never crossed before.

If I follow Lark's reasoning, our "meet cute" was in the hands of fate. If I gave that much credence to superstitions, then we met when we were supposed to. Doesn't matter when we met, though, only that we did meet.

I find myself forcing my eyes to the road ahead instead

of staring at her like the stalker I am. But there's nothing typical about her. The girls in my world have hair with every strand in place and lip injections to have the perfect pout for social media posts. By the small rise in the middle of Lark's nose, I'm sure she hasn't had anything about her "correct-ed," as others call it.

Her body's an aphrodisiac, whetting my palate. With a face perfect exactly as it is—natural and confident—an inner beauty shines through in the simplest of glances we're sharing.

"Why are you staring at me?" she asks, no accusation woven in her tone, just curiosity.

I tighten my grip on the steering wheel and exhale a puff of air. "Sorry. It's a bad habit."

She angles her knees toward me. "You make it a habit of staring at people?"

"No." I glance at her with a smirk fully in place. "Just you. You're very distracting."

"Good or bad?"

"Good distracting. Bad for our safety."

She reaches over and presses her fingers to my cheek until I'm facing forward again. I chuckle because she doesn't manage to wipe the smile away. In fact, it grew wider. "Eyes on the road, mister."

"I thought you liked to take risks. Something about pain being worth it."

The question leaves her in silence but not long enough to be concerned. "I was speaking of the heart, not life-or-death situations."

"Ah. That makes sense." I give her a wink. "Don't worry. I'll get you home safely."

She looks at me with the moonlight pouring in and shining in her eyes. "Harbor?"

I like the way my name rolls off her tongue and kisses her lips.

"Yeah?"

"Can I tell you a secret?"

"Another one? I feel honored," I tease her after the last one she shared with me, which wasn't much of a secret.

"Maybe they're not so much secrets as confessions."

"Okay, confession or secret, I won't share with anyone else."

Her smile warms me more than the car's heater ever could. "I rarely go out, but I'm glad I went out with you tonight."

"Me too. It was good spending time with you."

I slow down to turn left, which goes against every urge inside telling me to keep driving just to steal a few extra minutes of her time. "Can I ask you something, Lark?"

"I don't have anything to hide."

Everyone has something to hide. But I believe her. "Why'd you decide to come?"

Her eyes return to me as she snuggles up on the passenger's seat. "You made me an offer I couldn't refuse."

"Dinner?"

"Moretti's."

I click my tongue in amusement. "Noted." I turn onto her street, dreading the night coming to an end.

She says, "You know . . ." I glance her way. "It wasn't just the restaurant."

"Oh yeah? What was it?"

"It was also the company. You are definitely better than a can of frank and beans any day." She gives me a flirty wink, holding her sexy own with me.

I burst out laughing. "So what you're saying is I was right."

"You weren't wrong."

I catch her smile fading just as I pull up to the curb in front of her house. She looks at the house for a long beat or two, and then says, "You can come in if you want to."

I've wanted this offer since the minute I laid eyes on her at the beginning of the semester. Standing so close to her, touching her chin, and being alone with her, there's nothing else I've been able to think about other than what it would be like to sleep with her. Even tonight, in her apartment earlier, it felt right being alone with Lark, but not taking advantage of the situation.

Now, she's rolling out the red carpet for me and offering me a golden ticket inside her world, and maybe even her bed. My fingers tighten around the steering wheel as I mentally kick my own ass for what I'm about to do. "It's been a nice night, and although I'd like to go in . . ." Her gaze is locked on mine, but rejection doesn't taint it. "I should probably get going and let you study."

A gentle nod rocks her head as she reaches for the handle. "You're right. Anyway, we always have class tomorrow. Thank you for dinner."

"You're welcome, but you still owe me."

She grins. "Don't worry, I'll pay up." Opening the door, she steps out before I have time to get out and run around the car to do it for her. I stop on the sidewalk, though, after making my best effort. She says, "I'll see you tomorrow, Harbor."

I raise my hand. "Yeah, tomorrow." I wait as she lets herself in, only looking back to give a quick wave of her hand before she's inside.

There's nothing but a quiet apartment to rush back to but I decide to follow her lead and study. It would make my parents proud to hear about this. Not that I'll send them an alert or anything, but it's always a good hand to hold in my back pocket for the next time I get into trouble.

Not fifteen minutes later, I'm tossing my keys onto the kitchen counter, listening to them slide across the slick surface as I walk straight to the bedroom. Yanking off my sweater, I toss it in the closet. It lands on a shelf before it falls to the floor. I unbutton the shirt and then tug the undershirt off, tossing both in a hamper.

After I've stripped down to my boxers, I head back into the living room and tap my keyboard, bringing my computer to life. I need my thoughts to detour to anything other than the woman I just drove away from. I'm a fucking idiot for turning down her offer. If I don't get engrossed in something else, I'll end up getting dressed and heading right back over there.

My dick is hard and in need of some relief. I return to the bedroom and cross through to the bathroom to start the shower. I should turn the cold water on so I can get on with my night, but every time I think of Lark, I can't concentrate on anything other than the way the candle flickering reflected in her eyes when she looked at me with a smile, the little bow at the top of her lips, and the tiny mark on her chin that she didn't bother covering. I'm starting to believe it's the culprit that brought us together.

I tug down my boxer briefs and step under the warm water. Yeah, I'm weak to that body of hers. I tilt my head under, getting my hair wet. It feels good as the heat penetrates beneath my skin, easing my muscles and relaxing my mind.

The swell of her hips.

The rising and falling of her chest.

The sound of her lips parting just before she licks them.

Taking hold of my erection, I let the images of her fill my

head as my senses kick in from when I stood so close to her when she was seated on the cabinet in front of me as I bandaged her chin. I remember her smelling of springtime and freshly picked flowers, and her skin being as soft as a rose petal. I breathed her in just to taste a part of her.

Stroking slowly, the urge to release builds inside me as memories come flooding back—the sound of her whispers as if we were Bonnie and Clyde, just the two of us escaping together.

I pick up my pace.

Pinning my palm to the shower wall, I can see her as clearly as if she were here now. Her eyes were closed, and her trust on full display. I could have leaned in to kiss her vulnerabilities, but I savored the sight of her instead. Her body so close to mine in the doorway . . .

My hold grows tighter as an orgasm rushes forward.

That look in her eye . . .

The sway of her ass . . .

The way she looked back as if she wished she could stay . . .

"Lark. Fuck. Fuck. *Fuck*." My voice trails off, the last words faint under the sound of the shower as I lean against the cold tiles to recuperate.

The release? *Worth it.*

A POKE to the ribs startles me, and I turn around. "Busted," Lark says, beaming in victory.

Turning around, I lean against the brick building to face her. I take the high road . . . Okay, I don't, but I do feign innocence. "Busted me doing what? Hanging out before class?"

She smirks, crossing her arms over her chest with a large tumbler in her hand. Shrugging it off, she says, "Aw, come on, Harbor. Don't be a poor sport. Admit it, you were waiting for me."

"Hi, Harbor," some girl I met at a party last year purrs as she passes behind Lark.

Lark rolls her eyes, but then something dawns in her eyes, and she sucks in a breath. "Oh my God, you weren't waiting for me, were you? I'm so sorry. Ugh." She tries to escape through the double doors, but I catch the tail of her sweatshirt and tug her back to me.

"No. I wasn't waiting for anyone else." I get her to turn around. She leans against the wall where I was just a moment earlier. Pink-cheeked and giggling, she looks up at me with bright-green eyes catching the sunlight inside.

The golden morning highlights the beauty that some might miss when passing by, rushing in their lives instead of soaking her in. Lighter strands that have forgotten to fade after last summer hang freely around her face and her lips, just moistened, glisten like an invitation.

And here the best I did was narrow her eye color down to green, but they're so much more than I had previously seen. Gold flecks shine in the sunlight as if I've discovered treasure.

Fumbling for words that could do her justice, I lean in, so close to kissing her and easing my misery from the anticipation.

"Harbor?" she whispers, her lips barely parted as her hand fists my shirt.

"I was stalking you."

Her head jerks back and a restrained smile tilts the corners of her mouth upward.

What the fuck am I saying?

I turn to make a quick getaway, but she holds tighter to

my shirt, and with both hands, she brings me back to her. "I knew it," she says, giggling.

"And I'm humiliated." I run my hand through my hair. "You're fucking with my cool."

She doesn't give me any sympathy, though. Not surprised by how she's eating this up. "I'm not fucking with anything. You don't need cool with me. You just need to be you and *the you* you're being is pretty darn smooth." Closing the space between us, she adds, "Do you know how hard it was to walk inside that house last night with you standing by your car looking like Jake Ryan?"

"Who?"

"It's a movie."

"Ah. Are you saying I give main character energy?"

"You could most definitely be the hero of a story."

I plant my right hand on the brick wall above her head. "What about your story?"

The smile has softened like her gaze. Still holding me close, she says, "Yes."

Nothing more is needed. I cup her cheek with my left hand and tilt down. "I'm going to kiss you, Lark Summerlin."

"I wouldn't have it any other way, Harbor Westcott."

Our lips come together, meeting in the middle as if she couldn't wait any longer than me. Pillow-soft pressure turns heated when our lips part and our tongues meet, tangling together for the first time.

The taste of her is just the appetizer. My body presses to hers, sending her against the brick wall and giving us purchase against each other. Her hands run over my chest as I caress her cheek and slide my hand to the slope of her shoulder.

When I hear some guy say, "Get a room," I pull myself

off her because not only is that guy right, but I don't want to sit through class as hard as a rock.

Fuck.

Too late.

Lark tucks strands that have escaped the elastic on her head behind her ear and then runs her fingers on my chest. "So we kissed."

Grinning, I say, "We did kiss." I give her enough space to decide what she wants to do next.

Taking my hand, she leads me to the door. "What does it mean?"

I shift to her side. "Guess it means we're main characters in each other's stories."

Stealing a glance in her direction, she grins. "Too soon to root for a happily ever after?"

As soon as we enter the building, I wrap my arm over her shoulder and hold her close. "Guess it depends on the risk."

She laughs, the sound a melody to my ears. "I'll take my chances."

10

Lark

HARBOR WESTCOTT IS bad for me.

My grades.

My schoolwork.

My attention.

"Ms. Summerlin." My professor calls me out in front of everyone. "Why don't you share with the class what you find so funny about the preservation of cadavers?"

I look up from my phone and the text from Harbor asking me out for Saturday night. "*Um* . . . there's nothing funny about cadavers—"

"Correct!" Professor Brown says, pointing the marker in his hand at me and causing me to jump in my seat. "There is nothing funny about cadavers. The donors deserve respect for the sacrifice they've made to science."

"My apologies," I say about ready to kill Harbor for texting me in class. *He's bad for me.* That's all there is to it. Yet he's so darn irresistible. My lips still tingle from kissing him.

Glancing back down at the screen again, I smile.

"Ms. Summerlin, bring me your phone. Apparently, it's too much of a distraction today. I have you for ninety minutes, and your shenanigans have cost the class five of them. We won't lose any more to your screen addiction."

My hands begin to tremble. I've never been in trouble in my life.

"I think we should keep going with the lesson," Harbor says from where he's seated. I glance back along with the entire class.

The professor replies, "That's what I want to hear, Mr. Westcott. Eager minds create great doctors, but thorough research should always be your guide."

Harbor is gifted. Trying to save me just earned him brownie points with our hard-ass professor. *Impressive.*

Then Professor Brown says, "I'm going to give you two options, Ms. Summerlin. Bring me the phone or leave my class."

I hoped this would go differently, but no luck. Still debating if I should swing my backpack over my shoulder and leave in shame, I choose option one and start down the row toward the center aisle of the auditorium. My throat is dry as I tell people to excuse me, not daring to glance back at where Harbor is sitting.

When I reach the front of the room, Professor Brown says, "Show me what you were looking at."

Wait, what? Oh no. "I thought you were just going to confiscate it until the end of class?"

"No. I could use a good laugh, though." I knew I should have chosen option two.

He's waiting for me to show him the screen. I take a shaky and just do it to get it over with. His eyes roll across the screen and then looks up in the auditorium and finds where Harbor is sitting.

Slumped in his seat.

Cocky smirk on his lips.

Eyes glaring back at the professor.

Lowering his glasses, the professor says, "A lot more makes sense now." Looking at me, he keeps his voice low. "Return to your seat, and like the cadavers, please give me the respect I've earned during our ninety minutes together."

"Yes, sir."

My body feels like fire as heated embarrassment consumes me whole. I return to my seat, sinking into it while wishing it had a hole I could disappear into forever. The girl beside me whispers, "Don't worry about him. He'll forget all about it soon enough when someone else pisses him off. Just lay low until then." She leans back in her seat.

"I will." *Oh trust me, I will.* "Thanks."

Suddenly, she leans over again, and whispers, "And quite the coup scoring a date with a Westcott." She wags her brow once. I'm about to ask her how she knew, but she points at my phone. "Couldn't help but see the text."

"Ah. Gotcha." Note to self: everyone can see everything in this auditorium.

A text comes in . . . from Harbor again: *You okay?*

I debate if I should reply just in case I get caught again. The professor is caught up in writing a timeline across the whiteboard that I remember reading about online. So I text: *Sorry, I can't reply. I've died from a peculiar strain of mortifica-tionitis.*

He texts a reply: *I know just the cure for that.*

My fingers slide against the screen: *Oh yeah?*

The next text reads: *It's a cure-all. Trust me.*

It is too.

The moment he kisses me after class, I forget all about what happened inside. With his lips pressed to mine, I realize that he may be bad for my school career, but he's *oh-so-good* in every other way.

"WHY ARE WE DRIVING SO SLOW?" I ask Dane impatiently.

I'm anxious to get back to Beacon after our shift at the DeRoy's anniversary party. A lot of the same faces were there that attended the last week's party, including the West-cotts. Mrs. Westcott even came by the buffet specifically to say hello to me. She's very sweet.

Still, there was no way I would dare mention my late-night date with Harbor to her. For one, meeting at midnight makes me feel more like a booty call than a proper date. And two, being nice to me as part of the catering crew is one thing. Dating the part of the catering crew is quite another. I'm not sure where she would stand on that part of the equation.

Dane's been lost in his thoughts most of the way back, the truck absent of our usual small talk. "Dane?"

He glances away from the road like I woke him from a slumber. "Huh?"

"The speed limit is sixty. You're going what, like forty-five tops?"

His eyes glance down at the dash, and then he says, "Oh."

When he sits up to adjust in the seat, his knuckles whiten from his firm grip on the steering wheel as he gives the old truck some gas. The radio can only shed so much light in the cab, but there's enough to see he's tense. "Want to talk about it?"

"Talk about what?"

"Whatever is on your mind," I reply, angling his direction. "Is it Mia?"

"No." He shakes his head. "We're good, better than it's ever been."

Mia may not be my favorite person, but that's based on their past. If they're good, *better than ever*, then I'll support my friend. "That's good to hear."

I leave room between us for conversation, which he eventually fills. "Do you ever think about the class divide between Beacon and Beacon's Pointe? There's what? Ten, fifteen miles max dividing the two towns, but they're worlds away in more ways than financially."

"I've thought about it, but does it matter?"

"Of course, it matters." He looks at me like I'm not speaking the same language. "We drive out there to serve them at their pool parties and children's pony shows or whatever shit they decide to throw a random celebration for. That doesn't ever get to you?"

Dane's never been a friend who requires accolades, pats on the back, or anything more than knowing you're loyal. We're alike that way. So his insistence that I understand or agree with him is not typical behavior. "I don't think I can give you an answer that will suffice." I hate arguments in the car, not that we're arguing, but the growing intensity of the conversation is unsettling.

"It's like they live on another planet. They have fancy-ass parties while we struggle to pay our bills."

"I hear what you're saying, and sure, I've wondered what it would be like to be rich, but it does us no good to wish for what they have, and we never will."

"You might." He grins, and though I never had a brother, Dane's always tried to fill the role.

"Maybe." I watch the road. "Hopefully." I can't shake the feeling that he's acting strange. *What rattled him?* "We've worked many parties in The Pointe. What brought this on tonight?"

I'm answered with a shrug as he resettles with one hand on the steering wheel and the other tuning the music station. "I'm glad you're getting out of this place."

Life is usually less complicated on these drives, but not tonight for some reason. He's never been high-strung, but he'll defend himself or those he cares about without a second thought, which makes me think there's more to this conversation. *What is he protecting me from?*

He turns into town and takes the first right, traveling slower like the speed limit requires and passing busy bars and restaurants on the way. Doesn't matter that it's almost midnight. This college town is bustling with people ready to blow off steam after a long week.

Traveling to the far end, past the entertainment district, the street we turn onto is quieter. The lights and sounds from town are just out of reach when he turns down my street.

Dane parks in front of the house. I don't jump out since I'm kind of worried about him. "Working the late shift tonight?"

"I'll be at the tattoo shop until two if you get bored and don't want to go to bed."

I still stay but open the door. Although I know he takes these after-hours shifts because he needs the money, I say, "Be careful. It's still illegal to serve alcohol at a tattoo shop."

"Getting paid under the table means twice the pay when not having to dole out for taxes."

I nod in response, knowing he won't give it up because of my warning. "I still don't know how you manage the lack of sleep."

"I sleep all day."

"Good point. I have classes I can't miss." Hopping down onto the curb, I say, "I won't be able to make it, but I'm sure Mia will be more than enough to handle tonight."

He cracks a smile. "That's what you never understood. You're the only chick I know who I don't have to handle. It's just easy being friends with you."

"Should I take offense to being called easy?" I grin, but he doesn't. I snap my fingers. "Hey, that was supposed to be funny."

"Sorry," he says, forcing a smile. Leaning on the steering wheel, he looks ahead through the windshield, seemingly lost in thought again. When he turns back, he says, "Don't settle for less than you deserve, Lark."

This is unlike our typical conversations, so I can't help but laugh awkwardly. "I'll try not to."

"No, I mean it. There are a lot of . . . There are a lot of shiny fucking objects that will draw your attention away and steal your heart. Underneath the gleam, they're not like us."

"Who's they?" The words remind me of when Harbor asked the same question.

"You know who. The Pointe kids."

An ache threatens my stomach as an image of Harbor fills my head. It's as if Dane can read my mind. *Am I that obvious?*

He continues, "Their motives will always outwit your good intentions." He shifts the truck into drive. "Don't settle, okay?"

"I won't," I reply, not entirely sure what he expects from me. I step back from the truck and shut the door, though, as some form of guilt inches its way into my subconscious.

"See ya, Lark."

"See ya." His words slow my steps as I walk to the front door. *Did he see Harbor and me talking last week at the party?*

Catch us alone upstairs? Or is Dane just looking out for me in general?

He may be sharing what he thinks is best, but he also tried to plant a seed of doubt.

He seems to have forgotten that I'm usually a good judge of character. I might have been blinded by Harbor's good looks, and he certainly has a way with words, but our interactions have been sincere and not fake in any way.

Although Dane's looking out for me, he's also being overprotective when he has no need to be. Irritation covers me like an itchy wool sweater. I scratch my chest before the seed embeds itself and go inside the apartment.

I work hard.

I study all the freaking time.

No one needs to worry about me.

I'm the same girl I've always been.

I'm not like the typical Pointe crowd, and that's why Harbor likes me.

He likes me for me.

Genuine.

But just in case, I should take a shower and wash away the smell of work. I set the tip Larry gave me aside for tonight and then hurry to take a quick shower.

As soon as I'm dry, I pull on a dress that I never thought I could pull off, but Harbor inspires me to want to try. The T-shirt material of the dress clings when I roll it down my body. The dusty-rose color makes it lean toward sweet instead of being too showy, which I prefer.

The lace line of my undergarments wraps around my hips, but it doesn't bother me. Trying to be as fast as possible and still look my best, I run a towel over my hair once more and decide to let it hang naturally.

I struggle to apply my makeup while taming the butterflies that have been fluttering inside my belly since I got home. I left Dane's words at the door. Harbor's given me no reason to second-guess his intentions and given me plenty of reasons to trust him and continue to do so until he proves me otherwise.

Like I told him, he's a risk I'm willing to take.

I grab my phone from the dresser, finally almost ready. I text him: *Hi, I'm ready when you are.*

A return text pops up: *Is it bad that I've been here for twenty minutes?*

I can't stop the giddiness from swelling inside and let the butterflies fly freely as I slip on a pair of white Converse sneakers. I know myself too well, and unlike Amanda, I'm not great in heels.

I text him: *Not bad at all. I'll be right out.*

Looping my purse over my body, I realize it's midnight. I don't stay up this late unless I'm studying. I definitely don't go out this late to start partying. *Who am I?*

I laugh as I hurry out of the apartment and through the house's entry. Leaning against his sleek car, he waves, his lopsided grin endearing.

My heart just about beats right out of my chest when I realize what he's doing.

"Me?" I mouth.

"Yeah, you."

Standing so assuredly in front of me with his hands in the pockets of his jeans and pushed-up sleeves of a gray Henley, he gives me a good look at his biceps. Every dip and peak of his muscles pushes against the fabric. He finally pushes off the car, starts up the path to greet me, and says, "That movie doesn't age well."

"The romance of it clouds my mind, and I saw it when I was seven, so I probably didn't understand it, either." We stop in front of each other, and he takes my hands in his, holding them between us. "He cheats on his longtime girl-friend." I didn't understand that at seven, either.

"It was justified. His girlfriend wasn't his soul mate."

My cheeks flame but with the broken streetlamp and the burnt-out bulb behind me, I'm pretty sure he can't tell. I smile. *I mean, how can I not when he's speaking about destiny?* Lifting on my toes, I close my eyes and kiss him under the stars.

When our lips part, and my heels hit the pavement again, I will my knees not to go weak from the presence of this man. I ask, "What's the plan?"

"You kiss me like that again, and we'll stay in for the night."

"You say that like it's a bad thing."

He shrugs. "Good or bad, life is what we make it."

We walk to the car, and I ask, "Did you watch the movie for me?"

Opening the door, he says, "Yes. I'm taking a crash course in the study of main characters." After I get in the car, he shuts the door, but when he slides into the driver's seat, he adds. "I want to perform my role to the fullest."

"I'll let you in on a little secret."

He leans over the console. I run the tips of my fingers over the day's scruff shadowing his cheek, and whisper, "To me, you're already an Academy Award winner for making me feel so special."

"You are special. I've never met anyone like you, Lark." He puts a finger on my lips. "And because I know you were about to ask, that's a good thing."

His lips replace the finger, and we kiss until the wind-shield starts to fog up.

I've never had the luxury of being someone special.

Believe me, I'm not the girl to think poorly of myself. I was raised to know my worth, and I know I'm attractive, but I've also never been the girl who outshines all the others.

"Where do you want to go?"

"Anywhere as long as it's with you."

God, he makes it so tempting to stay home and invite him in, which is so unlike me. Amanda calls me sweet and innocent, but I can be wild and spontaneous. And tonight, Harbor is making me second-guess my inhibitions. The jaw that ticks when he's in thought, the brown eyes that anchor trust in the centers like a haven, and that muscular build of his have me feeling the opposite of sweet or innocent.

And I haven't even had a drink yet.

What about him has me ready to trade my V card for more experience?

It might be these soft seats and the fancy car. Although I'm not usually superficial like that, I'm impressed. But it will take a lot more than a Maserati to get me into bed. I glance over at him, and that smirk, the perfection of his face, and those eyes looking at me like I'm something he wants to devour have me feeling this way.

He's no boy and not a guy.

Harbor Westcott is all man.

Oh my, oh my, I don't stand a chance. "You'll do anything I want to do? That's very amenable of you."

Harbor starts the car and then sits back, buckled in, looking every bit the playboy I was warned about. Something about bad boys is just so irresistible.

With a wink, he replies, "What can I say? I like to hedge my bets."

11

————

Harbor

I HATE NIGHTCLUBS.

Especially small-town clubs that think they're edgy by playing pop music from the previous decade.

I don't hate it so much tonight, though. Lark's body glides from side to side while her shoulders sway under the lights of the dance floor. She claimed in the car that she had no moves, but I could argue otherwise after watching her for the past few songs.

She's magnificent in her blend of virtue and vixen, a body caught in the middle of two identities, her sneakers lying in distinct contrast to her dress.

Eyes closing.

Tugging her bottom lip between her teeth.

The skirt of her dress rising when she raises her arms in the air.

A fascinating and so fucking sexy creature in a small package.

Plenty of women are showing more skin. Even her

cutoffs at the gas station were shorter. But in this environment, with other guys staring at her as if she's their next meal, she dances for me.

Every time her eyes find mine, her smile grows.

Such a fucking turn-on.

I could watch her for hours, and it still wouldn't be enough time to riddle through how this woman has become my sole fascination in such a short time. I've started to miss her when we're not together. We sit together now in class, but between her other classes and work, her studies, and mine, we've not had much time together since we went to dinner at Moretti's. So I've been looking forward to seeing her free of obligations all week. Even if it had to be a late-night date.

Lark Summerlin is worth the wait.

The lights flicker, warning that it's almost two o'clock, and the music is turned down. Disappointment fills the air as the sea of dancing bodies begins to dissipate.

I wave and then finish drinking my bottle of water, ready to have Lark to myself again. I push off the wall, toss my bottle in the trash, and work my way toward the dance floor.

Cutting through the crowd is easy but keeping an eye on Lark is a little harder. She's not short, but it's easy for her to disappear in the crowd. Like Moses, the sea of heated bodies part for me as I cross the dance floor.

She runs into my arms, our bodies slamming together. I catch her just as she says, "Hey there, stranger," while gripping the front of my shirt.

Having a conversation in here is impossible, though, so I tilt my head and signal toward the door. "Let's get out of here."

Those teasing pink lips are licked, and she nods. I wouldn't say she's drunk, but she's tipsy. I wrap my arm around her lower back to guide her to the door. If I didn't, we'd end up in a corner by the way her hands are rubbing all over me. Like a bodyguard, I use my other arm to keep others out of her personal space.

We make it out of the exit and take a sharp right to head toward the car. She bumps into me and then snuggles under my arm. "Did you have a good time?" she asks when we're clear of the crowds.

"I did." A half-truth is better than a lie.

"I'm not ready for the night to end."

The unsubtle batting of the eyelashes, the way the back of her hand is practically glued to mine, and the shared glances, I think it's safe to say, "I was hoping you'd say that."

With the crowd flooding down the street around us, we stay with the flow. I keep her tucked under my arm when a group passing is oblivious to her presence.

She looks up at me, and asks, "Why?"

"Why what?"

"Why were you hoping I'd say that?"

Oh. Um. I scratch the back of my neck. "I'm not ready to say good night to you either."

"You say such sweet things to me, Harbor." She double steps, walking backward in front of me. "Why do you have to be so good?"

"Good to you? Because I like you, and you deserve it. You have a good heart, Lark."

Though others are rowdy in the vicinity, I'm more in tune with her. She's the kind of good that needs to be protected at all costs, the light that makes a day shine brighter, and my night worth staying awake longer. I scratch the back of my neck as my head fills with nonsense. What am I doing?

Lark's great, but I haven't been in a relationship in a long time. For good reason. I'm a fucking mess. She doesn't need me to dump that on her. But fuck, she's gorgeous, and that mouth—whether speaking or kissing—tells me to fuck it all and go for it. She's worth the mess and pain, the lost early morning hours.

She takes my wrist, holding it between her hands, and double steps. "This was fun."

"It was." I give my trust to the hands of fate and swear I'll never complain about the direction our lives take if it means more of Lark in my life. I ask, "Are you hungry?"

"I wish we had somewhere else we could go, grab a meal, and spend time together."

"Everything's shutting down at this hour."

She sighs. "That's too bad." Suddenly, she pulls me to the side of a building, out of the main foot traffic of the side-walk. Stopping abruptly in the middle of the sidewalk, she digs into her bag and pulls out her phone. With her eyes on the screen, she says, "My friend invited us to a party over on Delaware Avenue." She looks up at me. "Do you know where that is?"

Too well. It's not an area of town I visit anymore. I run my hand through my hair and look to the side. It's quieter, most clubbers already gone from the area. I reply, "I know."

She drops her phone back in the small bag looped around her body and takes my hand. The connection is felt strong in my chest, causing me to stand straighter as energy vibrates between us. Anticipation. Exhilaration. The feeling of something new, something beautiful blooming between us. She asks, "Do you want to go?"

Despite this growing bond I feel with her, I hesitate, not wanting to unpack my baggage in the middle of our first date. "What do you want to do?" *Please don't say the party.*

She holds my hand like a lifeline, the streetlights

bouncing in her eyes as if dancing just for me, and her smile exudes happiness. I'll give her the world if it means she'll always be this happy. Taking a quick breath as her body still wriggles with adrenaline from the club, she says, "I'd rather be alone."

Not what I expected, but exactly what I want as well. I'm hoping she means alone with me since I'm not ready for the night to end. "Would you like me to take you home?" I ask to make sure we're on the same wavelength.

She grabs the front of my shirt, tugging me closer. Lifting, she kisses my chin until I dip so she can reach my lips. There's no way I'm going to be able to resist her once we're alone. "Yes, with you."

I take in the sight of her before me. Her hair is up, but strands have escaped the elastic and hang wildly around her head. With her eyes locked on mine, her tongue runs along the corner of her lips completely unaware of the reaction it causes. *So fucking innocent.* "Is that an invitation?"

"Yes." She kisses me, her arms wrapping around my neck and holding me close. "And sealed with a kiss."

I smirk. *How can I not?* Judging by how she's looking at me, like I might make a tasty snack, I'm starting to realize that alcohol might be involved in the action. I caress her cheek and then kiss it. "Let's go home then." *Home?*

I'm not sure why that came out so effortlessly, but with this incredible creature clinging to me, I'm not going to stand here to work it out. Not when I can be working other things out, like pent-up sexual frustrations, in the privacy of her bedroom.

I take one of her hands and hold it because I like having the connection. And by how she moves closer to me as we walk to the car, I'm certain she feels the same. Guess even the feisty aren't immune to the Westcott charms. *Go figure.*

Holding her close feels natural and not like this is the first time. She feels good and fits nicely in the nook of my arm.

Plenty of girls are clingy with me.

Lark feels different.

Lark *is* different.

It's how she makes me feel, lighter, like she doesn't see the mistakes I've made in the past but only sees the me that exists now. *She's utterly addicting.*

It's been quite a whirlwind week. I went from just fucking around to having a full-on girlfriend. *Am I insane?* Maybe I am, but I don't care. Lark Summerlin has become an addiction that I have no intention of quitting anytime soon.

"I think we jumped a few steps ahead in this relationship." I realize how that might be taken if she takes it wrong.

She asks, "Is that what this is?" When I look down at her by my side, she's already got her eyes on me. "Are we in a relationship, Harbor?"

I stop because what the fuck? Nothing I've done in years has made sense, except one. *Lark.* Taking both of her hands in mine, I search her eyes, praying to God that she's as deep into us as I am. "I want it to be."

There's no humor or jokes, no lightness that usually comes from being around her. My heart thumps in my chest as I stare at her, silently pleading to end my misery. This woman can't fix my past, but I'm hoping that my future plays out differently. If anyone has a shot of doing that, it's her.

Reaching up, she cups my face. "You want to be in a relationship with me?" she asks wistfully.

"I do," I reply, sounding a fucking lot like I'm ready to commit to more. "I want us to be together and date exclusively."

A smile wiggles into place where it always should be on her face. "You want me to be your girlfriend?"

I hold her by the waist, the thin material not able to hide the shape of her body. I run my hands up and down her middle and then pull her even closer. "I'd really like that."

"What's the criteria?"

"Huh?" I should have known this wouldn't be easy. This girl has a wildly independent streak. I don't want to tame it, but I would like to be a part of her journey.

She takes my hand, and we start walking again. "Expectations."

"Uh . . . huh. Well, we'll spend some of our free time together . . ." I glance at her. "We can even study together. As the relationship progresses and our feelings evolve, we can review the agreement."

She stops again, laughter shaking her body. Tapping my chest, she says, "I don't want agreements. I want investments —my heart for yours."

I tuck some of her hair behind her ear and grin down at this stunning woman. How did I get so lucky? Guess I've been given a second chance. "You've got yourself a deal." I kiss her, good and hard, firm and with passion. "Sealed with a kiss."

12

Lark

WHAT AM I DOING?

It's three in the morning, and I'm currently brushing my teeth next to the sexiest man alive. *And yes, he was nominated, voted on, and presented the award by me.*

Although he's been staring at me in the reflection of the mirror as if he's about to seduce me while brushing his teeth with a spare toothbrush, I have a feeling that he's just built like that, put on this planet to make women weak in the knees and melt in his arms. I was close when we were down-town, but now in my apartment . . . *I'm even closer.*

Especially after becoming his girlfriend. I giggle internally. Okay, it sneaks out.

Harbor isn't like other guys. I mean, he probably wants to get me in bed, but not more than I'm willing to jump right onto that mattress with him.

Sure, he's drop-dead gorgeous, but he's also intelligent and thoughtful. We talk all the time, but there's comfort in the silent moments with him.

Oh Lordy, I'm already in way over my head, and I've only known him a week. Everything with us is moving so fast, but it doesn't bother me. It actually feels right.

Just like that body of his. So right. My *boyfriend* is built like a Greek god. And I'm feeling enough confidence in this dress to be his Aphrodite for the night. Yep. I feel great. He could have any woman, but he chose me not just for the night but to be his girlfriend.

I'm someone's *girlfriend.* The shock of that causes my jaw to slack and toothpaste to dribble down my chin. I bounce around, trying to scavenge toilet paper to wipe my face. "Holy wow! That burns like a mother."

He laughs. "Isn't it usually motherfucker?"

Tapping the paste away with a square of toilet paper, I reply, "Usually, but it wasn't my father who left. It was the woman who gave me life." I clamp my hand over my mouth, realizing a second too late that I've said too much.

Harbor's staring at me again but with concern this time. "Your mom left you?"

I sigh and rest back on the counter with the paper stuck to the little bastard of a wound. "I have a suspicion that talk of a parent leaving their kid when they were not even two years old isn't the aphrodisiac we were hoping for."

Gently pinching my chin, he runs the pad of his thumb over the almost-healed cut. "It's not, but that doesn't make it less important." He leans down and kisses my chin. "Is it painful like a paper cut?"

"Worse," I reply with a slight pout to my tone, basically hoping he puts his healing lips on me again.

Harbor's expression is as steady as he is while he studies the wound. He kisses it again and then smiles. "Yep. You're still going to live."

"Barely," I bemoan, tossing the paper in the trash.

Cupping my face, he presses his lips to mine, and whispers, "You think you'll survive the night?"

My heart kicks in my chest, and my breath staggers. I close my eyes and breathe him in. Desperately trying to hold on to my better senses while wanting to toss reasoning in the wind, I slink my body against his. I kiss under his jaw and place two on his neck before leaning my head on his chest. "Depends on what happens next."

Everything is hard under my hands . . . and parts they're not touching. I smile, doing a mental victory lap.

He wraps his arms around me and kisses the top of my head. "What if—"

"What-ifs make me nervous."

"I know, so please hear me out. What if we didn't detail out the night and just do what feels right . . . or what comes naturally?"

My eyelids bolt open. There's no denying I'm horny for the man, but letting things come naturally means giving up all control. "I struggle with the unknown."

Leaning back, he brings my chin up, and says, "No, you don't." His tone is soft as if he knows exactly what I need to hear right now.

"I don't?"

"No, you believe in destiny and romance, like in the movies. That all falls under living in the moment, aka the unknown." My eyes water, and I hate feeling weak when his eyes are on me.

His brow furrows. With the back of his finger, he swoops in to catch a tear. "Why are you crying, Lark?"

"I think you know me better than I know myself."

"Well that's nothing to cry about. That's a good thing."

"It's happy tears."

He reaches over and pulls more from the toilet roll and

dabs under my eyes. "You're making it hard to seduce you when you're crying. You have me torn between throwing you on the mattress or asking if you need to talk."

Pushing off him, I stretch out my arm and point my finger at him. "I knew it! I knew you were trying to seduce me." Circling my finger in front of his face, I say, "With those eyes—"

"Those are my eyes."

I shake my head. "But they were extra seductive tonight."

"So were you, if we're being so honest."

My head jerks back, and I plant my hands on my hips. "Me?" Feeling the fabric under my fingers, I realize I'm wearing the dress—the one that reveals everything I absolutely wanted him to see in hopes of seducing him. "Scratch that." Raising my hands in surrender, I claim, "You busted me all right."

I walk out of the bathroom with my chin held high and a sexy thrill running through my . . . attitude. I add, "And you're right." With my back to my bedroom door, I turn around to face him. "All great—" I stop myself before I throw the word love into the mix. That's probably jumping ahead too many spaces at this juncture—the juncture between me crying over him, understanding what makes me swoon, and my bedroom, that is. "All great movies start with the main character being spontaneous. *When Harry Met Sally*, *Serendipity*, *Pride and Prejudice*. The list goes on, but you get the idea."

Harbor's leaning against said juncture with his arms crossed over his chest and a smirk on his face when he replies, "I do."

"We should be spontaneous and do what feels right," I say more for myself than him and shrug as if this is what acting casual looks like.

"Sounds like a plan."

Wrinkling my forehead, I hold up a finger. "But it's not a plan. It's living in the moment."

"Right." He shakes his head. "It's not a plan." He stands, his arms falling back to his sides as he eyes the door behind me. "Are you going to show me your bedroom, Lark, or would you prefer to do what comes naturally out here?"

I laugh awkwardly, unsure how to go about this bedroom situation.

Do I present it like a game show host?

Do I open it and let him meander around, snooping through my stuff and just stand here while my whole world is exposed through old videos and books I love, to the color that seems to touch everything from wall to wall?

Did I make my bed? Put away my clothes that I was trying on earlier and got vetoed? Are my birth control pills displayed like candy on my nightstand?

He finally cups my face and looks deep into my eyes. "What's going on in that pretty head of yours?"

"I . . . I don't do this." Another nervous laugh escapes.

"What are we doing?"

"I don't have guys over like this." My arms go out, and I press my palms to the wood door behind me. "There's stuff in there that you might judge me for or think differently about me."

Tapping the door above my head, he says, "There's stuff in there that gives me better insight into who you are and what you like."

"Okay, but—"

"No buts. Don't worry. I'm not judging you, Lark. I mean, what's the worst that could be in there? Stuffed unicorns covering the bed or blue covering every surface."

"You don't like blue?"

"Is it blue?" A smug grin appears, backing the accusation. When I don't answer, he dips his head and whispers in my ear, "I fucking love blue, just like you."

Oh my God. Did he just tell me he loves me? Or was he saying he *fucking loves* blue like I love the color? Or does he *love* me like he *fucking loves* blue?

What do I say?

I feel very strongly for him, but it's too soon—

"Hey, Lark?" My eyes find his and that sexy smirk of his. "I love the color. It's too soon for other types of confessions."

Falling back against the door, I wipe my brow with the back of my hand. "Phew because it's way too soon for exchanging I love yous."

And with that matter cleared up, I present my bedroom like a game show host and open the door.

His gaze slides over my shoulder as he straightens his back, peering in over my head.

What am I doing with him in my bedroom? Does inviting him in give the nonverbal go-ahead for sex? I wonder how he feels about making out?

He kisses me, reminding me exactly what I might want to be doing with him. Stepping aside, I take a breath and let him enter the room.

Wandering in, he looks around, keeping that grin firmly in place. He takes a stroll to the bookcase, bending down and eyeing up the titles I've displayed. "Darcy. Rochester. Heathcliff and Cullen." He raises an eyebrow as he looks over at me through the corner of his eyes. "Questionable in their motives, but I can appreciate your love of a broody male."

"In this room, those are the classics," I reply with a shrug as if he asked me something. I move to the wall and lean against it, crossing my wrists and entwining my fingers.

His finger runs along the front of old DVDs on the next shelf, titles I keep for the memories. "*Pretty in Pink. Casablanca.*" He shoots a glance my way. "*Pretty Woman.* If this doesn't reveal the heart of a romantic, I don't know what does."

"I have *Fight Club* and *Gladiator* as well." I don't know why I feel the need to defend myself.

"A lover with a fighter's heart. I can respect that." Sitting on the end of the bed, he rests back on his hands and turns his attention on me like I'm the entertainment.

"So . . ." I let it linger, hoping to gauge the temperature of his mood.

Should I let him lead? Should I take control? Or do we spend the rest of the night looking at each other like we were forced to attend the ninth-grade dance by our parents?

Oh, that's right. I'm supposed to be going with the flow.

I can do that . . . *I think.*

"You know," he starts. Standing, he crosses the small room and returns to me, caressing the side of my neck and then running his fingers into the hair at the back of my head. "If you're uncomfortable or have changed your mind, I can go. I know how things can spiral in unexpected directions at this hour." His voice is deep, the tone befitting the night.

I'd like to think I'd choose self-preservation, but with his lips against that spot just under my ear and his breath heating my skin, I wrap my arms around his neck and give him more access. His sharp inhale causes goose bumps to ripple against my skin, and then the lightest of kisses are sprinkled along my jaw until he finds my lips.

"I want you to stay."

He tilts my head back, my chin nearly touching the bottom of his, and then presses his mouth to mine, and whispers, "I was hoping you'd say that." Holding my face between his hands, he kisses me so hard that my back hits the wall.

My breathing is as wild as my hands, which travel across the broad width of his shoulders to find purchase. Then he stops, his eyes searching mine between panting breaths. Goose bumps ripple across my skin and as good as he feels now, greedily, I want more.

Taking my hand, he leads me to the edge of the bed, and whispers, "Are you sure?"

"You warned me the first time we met."

He nods, his gaze dipping down momentarily. "And you foolishly let me in."

This time, I lift his chin with my hand. "I don't know what happened in your past, but believe me when I tell you, I love a redemption story."

"Where have you been all my life?" His deep and smooth voice is sexy as he speaks so close that his breath coats my lips in a gentle sweeping kiss.

"I've been right here all along."

Without a word, his eyes skim over my body and then he reaches down to the hem of my dress. Pulling it slowly up my body and then over my head, Harbor looks at me with lust coloring his eyes a deeper shade of brown. So I stand there, basking in his gaze.

His jeans and shirt come off, and we're left standing practically naked together. The room suddenly feels hotter, but a deliciously forbidden sensation sparks in the air like two live wires coming together.

He sits down on the mattress and takes my hands, holding them between us. I've never felt more beautiful than I do when he's staring at me like he's the luckiest guy in the world.

Bringing me to his lap, he kisses my shoulder, and then looks into my eyes. "Does this feel right?"

"No." I turn in his arms, straddling him and kissing him on the mouth. Pushing him back, he falls on the bed lying flat. I drop my hands to either side of his head and kiss his shoulder.

He asks, "No?"

Feeling sexy.

Feeling powerful.

Feeling more myself than I ever have before.

I kiss his mouth, and then whisper, "But this does."

13

Harbor

Fucking comes naturally.

Fucking Lark though . . . there's no way I'm going to be able to make this last by how she's moving on top of me— kissing me like she'll lose the chance and grinding her hips against mine, her heat against my erection.

Little coos become mewls with each gyrate. I swear she's going to get off on me before I even have a chance to slip on a condom. I run my hands from her shoulders over her blades down to the small of her back and then lower over the mounds of that great ass. Keeping it right there feels so good that I might just get off as well.

But patience has always been a struggle of mine. I flip around to the mattress and roll over on top of her, my knee holding her legs apart so I can settle between them. And the scrap of material covering her pussy is not going to do anything to keep me from making her feel incredible, except this underwear which is strangling the fuck out of me right now. I need to get some relief so I can focus on her instead.

I push up above her, and ask, "You want to take them off, or do you want me to do it?"

There's enough light from the open blinds drifting in to see her eyes locked on mine when she reaches for the waistband. She starts rolling my boxer briefs lower and when she reaches the tip of my dick, she licks her lips and looks down between us. My body throbs from the sight of her watching me, anticipation teeming in her eyes.

The fabric is lowered, and her chest fills with a sucked-in breath and the feel of her fingers run along my length. That's not going to help me last, not in the least bit. The weight of my dick drops against her leg as I help her finish the job, kicking them off my feet to the floor.

I'm not shy.

I know how to please women. But something tells me I need to go slow with Lark. I need to claim her in a way where she feels in control, even when all I want to do is mark her with my fingerprints and ruin every memory she has with any other man.

Repositioning myself over her, I run my hands over my abs and then dip down to stroke myself before sliding my fingers between her thighs. I'm gifted with a moan and her lips parting. I glance down as her body moves against my hand. Reading her reactions, I find no doubt in her eyes, only the desire for more as her hands glide across my shoulders.

I go slow, appreciating her response to even the smallest of movements. Sliding down her body, I kiss the valley between her breasts, selfishly lingering as I take in the scent of her skin—a hint of orange and whiskey mixed with sweat from dancing. I lick the curvature of her tit and then cover one with my hand.

Trailing the fabric down like she did for me moments before, I like that her tits aren't big but a good handful. The pert nipple, a tawny tease, puckers for me. I dip down and run my tongue over it before blowing the slightest of breezes and then wrapping my lips around her.

Lark's back arches ever so gently as her fingers run through my hair.

I treat the other nipple the same, squeezing both at the same time while trailing wet kisses down her stomach. Peeking up every so often, I meet her gaze, and she whispers, "I'm ready, Harbor."

By how she moves and sounds, I'd already picked up on her desire. But I'm not finished with her yet. "I want you to come on my tongue."

She doesn't say anything, but her eyes widen when I slip between her legs. I toy with the panties, knowing I could easily rip them, but I'm not sure how she'll react.

I'm usually a hit-it-and-get-out guy, but I won't do that with her. I'll take the time and make the effort because Lark matters to me. I want to know what she likes and learning what she enjoys sexually isn't just about wants or desire. It's about knowing what she needs and making sure she's mentally *and* physically satisfied.

Sliding down one side of the lace, I kiss where it laid against her skin. I do the same to the other side and then pull them down her thighs, discovering the sweetest meal before me. I'm ready to devour it. I look up at her once more, taking my time to appreciate her. "You're stunning," I say. "You know that?"

She bites her lip because no response is needed. I already know the answer, feeling the connection with her body and mind.

Grappling to touch me in any way, she barely reaches my scalp with the tips of her nails. Her beauty had caught my eyes, but it's knowing her, tasting her sweet side that has me wanting more. I lower, running my nose across her softness before a deep inhale.

Goose bumps rise over her skin as she starts to writhe underneath me. I don't wait. I dip my tongue between her lips and drag my tongue from bottom to top. Her hips buck into me and then squeeze against my head, so I pin her thighs down and make love to her with my tongue.

My hair is pulled with each thrust of my tongue. My dick seeks relief I know I won't find against the mattress. Nothing will satisfy me until I'm inside her.

Letting go of her legs, I push against the bed to leverage myself to make the most of the orgasm that's twisting through her body and about to release. I keep licking, flattening my tongue against the apex of her thighs. I lick the crease and then between her lower lips again, sucking on her clit until her back arches off the bed, and she yanks my hair.

Ecstasy rips my name from her lips as she peaks in her release and coats my tongue. Her body trembling against my lips, my hands, and my chest. I don't stop until the last wave has rumbled through her. But then I'm quick to move higher, stealing her breath with a kiss. Her arms wrap around my neck and when our lips part, she sighs in contentment. "That was better than I ever imagined."

I pause—my mind and body—her upper lip still between mine, frozen in a kiss. Did she just say . . .? My thoughts were muddled under her bliss; maybe they still are and I heard her wrong. I lift so I can see her eyes, and say, "Call me dumb, but that sounded like you just said this was the first time you had an orgasm."

Tucking an arm under head, she's tilted with a smile on her face. Her nails rub gently around my ear, and she replies, "It was . . . well, with someone else. I have a few times alone, but it's never been like that." I don't know what I look like to her, but her brows pinch together, and her smile disappears. "Harbor?"

This night just took an unexpected turn. "Are you a virgin?" I can't take my eyes off her. I won't. What she says next will determine the rest of the night. Not that I haven't gotten a few V cards over the years—some girls told me before and others didn't—but this is Lark.

Lark is the "different" I didn't know I needed in my life, the change I never saw coming, the breath of fresh air and my girlfriend. She's my fucking girlfriend, and I almost had sex with her like it meant nothing. Not that it wouldn't mean anything, but yeah, I'll do things differently if it's her first time. "Are you?" I ask when she seems to consider the question.

Her hands slide onto my shoulders, and she smiles again, gentler this time with a hint of apprehension in her eyes. "It might be my first time."

"Might be? Or will be?"

The smile is wiped with shame. "Will be," she whispers. *And here I almost fucked it up.*

I push the hair away from her face and lean down to kiss her. "It's sweet that you held on to your virginity."

"I don't want to be sweet anymore, Harbor. I want to feel sexy and in control for once in my life. I'm tired of making it a bigger deal than it is and worrying about who's going to be bothered by it."

"That's a lot to process."

"Tell me about it." She sighs. Her gaze reaches the window and beyond, but I don't want to lose her or have her perceive this as a rejection. It's not. Before I say anything, she adds, "But I don't want us processing it. I just want to do it and get it over with."

"Lark?" When she looks back, I say, "You're my girl-friend, and I hope you believe me when I tell you that I care about you. More than I expected so soon, to be honest. I don't want to fuck this relationship up before it really begins. Getting it over with when it comes to you is the last thing I want to do." Cupping her face, I kiss her cheek and then lie back down. "Don't ask me to take something you're not ready to give."

She huffs, flopping flat on the bed beside me and tossing her arm across her forehead. "I can't even give it away these days." Facing me, she adds, "And for the record, I don't think you're taking advantage of me or my situation. *I choose you, babe.* I just want you to choose me as well."

I can hear the plea in her tone as if having sex will fix everything that's wrong in her life. I know firsthand that sex doesn't have that power. "Believe me when I say this, baby, I am choosing you but please let me make this special for you?"

"Do I have a choice?" Her eyebrow quirks higher.

"Sure, you have two options. I can fuck you right now, or I can make it worth the wait. What do you choose?" Please choose two. She's already gotten under my skin, so fucking her like she's any other girl isn't going to be something I'm capable of.

I can see the debate in her eyes. I don't know whether to laugh or take the compliment. I take her hand instead, and say, "Your first time should be special."

"It would have been," she fake grumbles, but then laughter bounces through her. "Geez, what happened to being spontaneous?"

"That was before I had all the facts."

She rolls over, the cups of her bra hiding her breasts. Disappointment runs through a vein of my greedy side. Not only have I lost visual access to those perfect tits, but I can't seem to find the silver lining to the reality that I'm not getting laid tonight. *Fuck.*

Whipping herself on top of me, she straddles me, and my dick is instantly hard again. But knowing I'm not getting any gratification tonight, I take her by the hips and lift her to the side, putting her back on the mattress again.

"Hey," she says. "I made my choice."

I get out of bed to find my underwear on the floor but stop and look back at her propped up on her elbows. "Well, I'm choosing the other for you. I'm not going to fuck you tonight."

Crossing her arms over her chest, she asks, "What if that's exactly what I want for my first time? I don't want hearts and roses or picnics by the lake. I want to feel normal like every other twenty-one-year-old."

I don't bother with my boxer briefs. I climb back on the bed and then push the covers down so we both can slip our legs under. For someone so sure of herself, she falls in bed and curls up right beside me. Lying with our heads on the pillows, we face each other. "You are normal, Lark," I say, lying. I don't know any twenty-one-year-old virgins, but I chalk it up to the fact that I just didn't care enough about my first time to think twice. "I respect that you value that part of yourself enough to wait for the right time—"

"The right guy works, too." She drapes her arm over my chest. "I'm ready, Harbor."

Her whole body vibrates, and she's still grinning. *I remember the delicious feeling.* She's still reeling from the high of her first real orgasm—one that I gave her. *Shit, I'm getting hard again.* "For someone who is basically begging me for sex, you sure do look cozy and content."

She laughs. "I can't help it. Look at us all naked and cuddling. I would have never guessed that I'd end up with the guy from the gas station." She yawns, and I'm reminded of the late hour.

"I've been thinking about that. I'm not thrilled with being the 'guy from the gas station.' We need a redo." I lean over and kiss her quickly. "I also think we need some sleep."

"I agree on the sleep, but as for the redo, I'd just like the first 'do.'" She giggles and then lifts the covers, and asks, "What about the situation down there?"

I cover up again and shake my head slightly. "I don't have a 'situation down there.' It's a hard-on. It will go down."

"Won't that hurt? I always heard it hurts."

Is she fucking with me right now? She might be, but I have a feeling she's not. "I wouldn't call it pain, but if you want to kiss it and make it feel better, I won't stop you."

Eager, she moves under the covers. "I've always wanted to try this."

"What?" My head bolts up from the pillow, and I lift the cover to see her eyes. She's got to be fucking with me. "You've never given a blow job?"

"No, but it seems like a good skill to have."

My eyes practically bulge out of my head. *Skill?* Her having great blowie skills is not the reputation I want her to have. "No. No. Absolutely not. You don't need that skill."

"What about you?"

What the fuck? "I don't need that skill either."

She bursts out laughing again. "I meant me using that skill on you."

"Oh right. It's late, and I'm—*oh fuck*." I lay my head back on the pillow as her tongue travels over my erection.

Reaching under the covers, I rub the top of her head, the only part of her I can reach.

For someone who's never done this before, she's doing a fucking fantastic job of it. Taking me into her mouth, she sucks, causing the inside of her cheeks to hollow around my dick, and I'm about done here. A few more rounds of her mouth and my release hits fast, and I come hard.

Her hair tangles between my fingers as I give in to every sensation.

When I finally catch my breath, I find her kissing my chest and moving higher up my body. When she reaches my mouth, she kisses me, and then says, "How'd I do?"

"Yeah, you don't need any guidance from me."

"If that didn't feel so fucking amazing, I might be embarrassed that I didn't last longer." I stroke her cheek with the back of my hand. "Where'd you learn to do that?"

"Guess it just comes naturally." She laughs, kissing me again, and then slides off to snuggle against me.

This woman, what am I going to do with her?

Rubbing her back, I hear the sound of her sighing in satisfaction, which relaxes me in a way I haven't felt in quite some time. Every bone feels pliable to the bed as I hold her close. I ease into sleep so quickly, but before I do, I kiss the top of her head, and say, "I'm glad I stayed."

Her smile growing is felt on the side of my chest. Her arm tightens over me, and she whispers, "Me too. Good night, babe."

"Babe?"

"All's fair in love."

"And war." I've never bothered with terms of endearment before, never feeling that invested. But with Lark, I'm all in. "Sweet dreams, baby."

She squirms under my arm and looks up at me. "Baby?" she asks through a smile.

"It feels right."

She feels right.

14

Lark

JELL-O.

My body feels loose, limber, and pliable on the mattress and more at peace than I've ever been.

The clouds of my mind have cleared, though there's a slight thunder in the temple of my brain, but then I remember him calling me baby last night. Me, Lark Summerlin from small-town Beacon is Harbor Westcott's baby, and all is wonderful in the world. I giggle in delight but am quick to silence myself so I don't wake the sleeping giant.

I roll over ready to kiss him awake, but I roll right onto my face instead of finding Harbor. I open my eyes, hoping I'm wrong, but also to verify the bed is empty beside me. My heart starts racing as a wave of emotions overwhelm my head. My stomach turns from the sight of the spot where he lay when we fell asleep last night. Wrapping my arm around it, I realize I need to cover more than my stomach.

Instead of lying there in my growing anxiety, I slip out

from the covers, still wanting to prove my suspicions wrong. I grab my robe and punch my arms through as I swing my door open only to find the bathroom unoccupied.

Glancing left, I find Amanda's door closed as usual, so I walk down the short hall. My hands begin to shake as I have the view of the entire apartment in my grasp.

And there's no Harbor.

He left . . .

After what we did, what I was willing to give him, he still left me like I didn't matter at all.

A deep hole I thought was long buried is exposed like it didn't take me years to come to terms with someone abandoning me. Tears fill my eyes as my heart is squeezed a lot like I remember having the good memories ripped away from me back when I was little.

"Harbor?" I call for him like an idiot. He's not here. I can see that with my own eyes. I feel weak and not the good kind like Harbor usually makes my knees. I grip the kitchen counter to support me, unsure why I'm feeling so off and more than only disappointed.

We'd agreed to date, to be exclusive, to use the cheesy terms of girlfriend and boyfriend, so why would he leave me without so much as a note?

I return to my room and grab my phone. No texts or missed calls. Tossing my robe off, I drape it on the bottom of the bed and climb back under the covers. It's not even nine o'clock, which makes me wonder what time he left.

Sleep would be awesome, but I'm left lying here alone when I thought I'd be waking up with him. Such a disappointment.

The door creaks open. I roll away from it. "I'm sleeping, Amanda."

"That's too bad." His voice is deep, the dulcet tones drawing me to sit up and turn back.

"Harbor?"

Carrying a tray with coffee and a bag on top, he shuts the door behind him. "Did you miss me?" That smile would usually work wonders on me, but the joy in seeing him still competes with the fact I thought he had abandoned me.

"I thought you left."

"I did." He sets the tray down on the dresser and pulls a cup from it. "I got us coffee from the shop downtown."

"No, that's not what I meant."

He sits next to me, sets the bag down on the comforter, and hands me the cup. "What did you mean?" But the answer seems to come to him before I can reply. "You thought I left you, like not going for coffee but went home?"

"I—"

"You thought I'd do that to you even after last night?" He stands, the bag forgotten. Running his hand through his hair, he turns away from me.

I felt sick before, but now it's worse, my guts twisting in knots. I get to my knees and touch his back. "Harbor, I don't know what to say. I thought you had left."

He turns back, looking down at me. "You thought the worst of me when I was thinking I would do something nice."

"I feel terrible."

"Because of me. You feel terrible because you thought I would sneak out in the night to get away from you." Taking the bag, he drops it next to me. "No good deed goes unpunished. Enjoy the muffin."

He's about to leave, but I say, "Stay, Harbor, and let's talk about it."

When he turns back, the disappointment I felt minutes

ago is personified in his eyes. I did that to him. The knot in my stomach pulls tighter. I slide down on the mattress again, and say, "Please." It may only be a whisper of a request, but it reaches him by the way he drops his head.

As if his willpower is lost in the moment, he moves closer and holds me under my chin. He angles my face upward, and our eyes connect in the morning light. "Don't grovel or make apologies. Not for me or anyone." His eyes meet mine in a moment of intention. "You're not a damsel in distress. You never were. So if someone wants to go, don't beg them to stay."

"But I misunderstood—"

"I know, but no one is worth sacrificing your pride."

"Not even you?"

He sits on the bed beside me. "Especially not me." With his hand on my knee, he sighs. "I've disappointed so many people in my life, but I can't handle disappointing you, Lark. So if I need to walk away to figure some shit out, you need to let me because I won't be any good for you otherwise." His arm comes around my shoulders, and he pulls me close. Kissing my head, he then tilts down until he can see my eyes again. "I will always come back to you."

Statements like those that he makes, ones that are definitive when spoken make me believe him. Through his honesty, I find my own power again. I'll know what to do and what to expect next time.

But a flicker of pain shelters in the depth of his irises, one that doesn't belong there. I'm not sure if it's his trust I broke or the thought that I might have lumped him with his past that hurt him more.

Wrapping my arm around his, I lean my head on his shoulder. "Sometimes sorry isn't a weakness but a strength.

It all depends on the intention behind it. I'm sorry for thinking the worst, Harbor."

He rubs my leg several times and then looks at me. "Don't worry about it. As I said, I'm used to it."

"I don't want you used to it with me, though." I sit up straighter, feeling the importance of the moment. "I was thrown, but it wasn't you who caused me to get upset. It's stuff that I need to work through." I cover his hand with mine. "I trust you, Harbor."

"Thank you." Flipping his hand, I press our palms together on his leg. "Why did you leap to the worst conclusion first?"

Taking stock of my emotions, I don't feel so empty with him. "So much has already been said. I think I just want to continue this some other time. Is that okay?"

"Of course." Getting up, he takes his coffee from the tray, and then returns to sit back down. "You should drink your coffee before it's cold."

I take a sip, savoring the foam on top. "That was really sweet of you to go out to get these for us. I'm just surprised you were up so early."

"I run in the morning before class. Waking up early is a habit now, even on the weekends."

I get back in bed, sipping my hot drink while he starts to undress. Wow. That body is impressive. As soon as he climbs in next to me, he says, "I'm usually tired from a shift, so it's easier to sleep in on the weekends."

He hands me the bag. "You didn't get a muffin?"

Sliding down until he's lying flat next to me, he says, "I was starving for more of last night." He winks with a click of his tongue. "But I decided to let you rest and settled for a muffin from the coffee shop instead."

I nibble on the muffin, but seeing him lying there—tan,

muscular, and so attractive—I set the rest on the nightstand and cuddle with him. A kiss here leads to placing one there, and soon enough, we're kissing for the next hour.

Exhaustion catches up with us eventually, and we close our eyes, falling asleep together again.

"OH MY GOD!"

The door slams shut, causing both Harbor and me to bolt upright. My hand flies up to contain my heart before it beats right out of my chest.

We look at each other.

Shirtless.

A muss of hair that's looking more like bedhead at this point in the day.

A jaw so cut that it shadows his neck.

Harbor Westcott is quite the delightful sight, every bit *GQ* model material, and he's in my bed.

With his eyes set on mine, they both comfort and call me to him without exchanging a word. He asks, "Roommate?"

I shift closer to him, gliding my hand over his chest. "I think so. Sorry about that."

"No worries. Do you need to let her know that you're not being held hostage by a strange man in your bed?"

"Probably." I slip out of bed and into my robe as I pad to the door. "I won't be long."

He tucks his hands under his head, watching me go. "I'll be here."

Glancing back, a surge of giddiness rolls through me at this sight of him. "You'll have my undivided attention when I return."

"I appreciate the declaration, but you should probably talk to your roommate to make sure she's okay."

"Yes, right . . ." He's very distracting. I turn around and open the door. "Going to talk to my roommate." I peek back. "Be right back."

"I'll be here."

I close the door and instantly sink against it, feeling pliant all over again. I'm shocked I'm even standing after the past twenty-four hours.

The sound of the water running has me moving into the kitchen and rounding the corner. "Aman—" I'm pinned to the fridge before I can scream. A hand is clamped over my mouth and my best friend leans in so close our noses are practically touching. Whispering, she asks, "Why do you have Harbor Westcott in your bed?"

My words are muffled because yeah, her hand is still blocking everything I say. She gets the hint and removes it, and I slide free. "How do you know Harbor?"

She looks at me like I've suddenly grown a third eye. "Everyone knows Harbor, Lark."

"Guess I'm out of the loop because I didn't know him until recently."

She punctuates her dramatic eye roll with an exasperated sigh. "See? If you went out more, you'd know these things."

"Apparently, going out doesn't matter because I met him anyway."

"And how exactly did you meet him?"

We've been whisper-yelling out of panic. I just wish I knew why we're freaking out. I grab a paper towel to wipe my brow during the interrogation. "At TJ's, but how do you know him?" I ask, dabbing my forehead.

"Parties."

My stomach drops. "Have you hooked up with him?"

"No." She flips her hair over her shoulder and then crosses her arms over her chest. "But thanks for assuming I have sex with every guy I meet."

"I didn't mean it like that. It just sounded like you knew him better than someone at a party."

She laughs and reaches over my shoulder to get a glass from the cupboard. "I'm just giving you a hard time. *Anywho*—"

"Sorry to interrupt." Harbor's deep voice flows between us, and we turn toward the hall with a gasp to our breath. He's leaning from around the corner, looking at me. "It's coming up on noon. Do you think we'll be staying in bed, Lark, or should I get dressed?"

"Don't get dressed." I throw my hand over my mouth and clench my eyes closed. *Oh my God!* I did not just say that. Unfortunately, I did. When I peek one eye open and then the other, I'm met with a stupidly handsome lopsided smirk. He's trying to do me in one grin at a time.

I glance at Amanda, whose mouth is currently hanging open as she stares at him. "Oh, by the way, this is my room-mate, Amanda."

"And best friend," she adds, raising her hand and then sticks it toward him. "Hi, I'm Amanda."

"Hi, Amanda," he says, his voice smooth like chocolate syrup. Delicious. Coming from around the corner, he's in jeans that didn't manage to get snapped at the top and still shirtless. I bite my bottom lip. *Good lord, he's amazing.* "I'm Harbor Westcott," he adds as they shake hands. A stolen glance at me has him smiling as if we have a shared secret.

I think we've shared a few in the short time we've known each other.

"You two grew up together?" he asks.

"Yeah, just east of Calhoun Road. You're familiar with that area. I've seen you at parties over there." Her eyes narrow in his direction. "I'm just not sure who our mutual friends are." She raises an eyebrow, leaving the question she didn't ask directly hanging in the air.

His hand finds the back of his neck, and he scratches. The lighthearted grin now gone as he looks at her, trying to place where he's seen her before. "It's been a while since I've been to that part of town."

"Lucas Westcott," she starts. "That's how I recognize you."

"Probably." He shoves his hands in his pockets, but I notice him glancing at the door a few times. Discomfort? Wanting to run out the door? Hungry? I can't read his needs right now and that bugs me.

Amanda says, "Seems like quite the drive from The Pointe Estates."

His smirk is gone. "Lucas tended to look for trouble, always managing to find it in Beacon."

She nods, but then says, "I knew him. Met him a couple of times. He was always nice to me. I was bummed to hear about his accident."

"Accident?" I ask, stepping closer to Harbor, but when I search his eyes, I don't feel the timing is right to lift the lid on that topic of conversation. Not sure if it's how he keeps looking for an escape though that's a solid tip-off. It's more that the pain I saw a few hours ago has returned in the current circumstances.

"Another time," he replies quietly.

I understand the need to push certain things away. I wrap my arm around Harbor's and lean my head on his bicep. "I'm still tired, Amanda. We're going to head back to bed."

"Yeah, no problem. We'll catch up later, Lark." Just as we round the corner, she singsongs, "Have fun."

"We will," I reply innocently, and then I catch her drift and giggle.

Sunshine floods the room, leaving shadows of stripes across Harbor's body as he sits on the bed. I ask, "How was meeting the roommate?"

"I think it went well, as well as it could since she was surprised to see me."

I sit next to him, leaning my back against the wooden headboard. "I think you made quite the impression."

He starts to laugh. "I bet."

Reaching over, he takes my hand and brings it to his mouth. One kiss and then two more are placed on the top of it. It's not sexy like the idea of sitting on a bed together might summon, but it's sweet like first kisses and the excitement of newly dating should be.

He slides down lower, settling in again. Looking up at me, he slips a wry grin into place. "So what do you want to do today?"

15

Harbor

I DON'T RECOGNIZE who I am when I'm with Lark, but for some fucking reason, I don't mind the difference.

She's as innocent as can be, but she smarts back, like at the gas station when we first met and last night when she tried to convince me to fuck her.

It's good that she has bite and speaks her mind. She'll have no problem handling when my inner asshole shines through after walking a straight fucking line all day in order to appease everyone around me.

My current mood is courtesy of her having prior plans with her dad and me getting a text from Marina guilting me into coming to the house for dinner.

I shift the car into park and cut the engine, sitting, and staring at the house through the windshield. I unlatch my seat belt and pop the door open. With one foot planted on the ground, the other stays firmly inside the vehicle. My hesitation to attend this dinner comes from months of building my tolerance for avoidance. It was better not to see too much of my family than for them to see the pain I was going through. I wasn't going to add to the devastation of what happened.

I've mastered the character flaw of avoidance, but I always was a fast learner.

The door opens and Marina steps out, looking right at me. Standing there on the brick landing, she leans against the railing. She shakes her head but then smiles and waves me in.

After a great night with Lark, I'm not in the mood to disappoint anyone today, especially not my sister. The way she viewed me never changed. That's the bliss of youth. The dirty details are left out of the conversation when a story is explained.

"Come on, Har. I want to show you something."

I get out and make my way up the steps. "I'm coming. I'm coming," I reply, sounding a lot like an old man. Closing the door behind me, I follow her into the kitchen.

"Hey, Mom." I come around the island just as she turns around.

"Harbor." Her arms go out to bring me into a hug. "I'm so happy to see you."

She holds me tight, and for a minute, I'm reminded how she always made me feel loved. If I wouldn't have lied to protect Lucas's memory, I know I wouldn't have left home. But I had to because Mom would have seen right through me. Now I only grant her glimpses. "Happy to see you, too."

She leans back and takes a good look at me. "You look tired but happy." My mom notices every little detail about her family. If I let her look closer, she might even see Lark hanging around my thoughts tonight. "Oh, to be young. I just look tired these days." She laughs as she stirs what looks like a soup on the stove.

"You look beautiful, as always," I say, knowing she'll never believe me as if it's my job to tell her what she wants to hear since I'm her kid. But it's the truth—my mother is the embodiment of grace and class. Plus, she's basically a saint for dealing with us four kids. I'm quickly waved off, exactly as expected.

"Something to drink?"

"I can get it when I'm thirsty." I know she tries to make me feel at home when I'm here, but it feels strange to fall back into the kid role after living on my own for the past couple of years. I don't have anyone offering me anything in my apartment, so I'm not used to being catered to anymore.

I take a seat on the other side of the island next to Marina. Her laptop is open, and a page from Beacon University is loaded. I ask, "What is it that you wanted to show me, kiddo?" I like to remind her she'll always be my baby sister.

She rolls her eyes from the moniker. "I'm not a kiddo anymore, Harbor."

I chuckle from the staunch stand she takes. "Noted."

Tugging me by the shirtsleeve, she says, "Pay attention. Remember the girl from the gas station that you tried to pick up?"

"What girl from the gas station?" my mom asks, angling to look back at us.

"What gas station has chicks hot enough to pick up?" Noah asks, joining in the conversation. I look behind me as he crosses the family room and comes to stand behind Marina to look over her shoulder.

Fuck me.

I knew Marina being in the car that day would bite me in the ass.

The back door opens, and Loch steps inside to our

silence. He stops, his eyes darting to each of us before then closes the door. "What's going on?"

Noah replies, "Harbor picked up some chick at a gas station but won't do us a solid by telling us where the hot girls pump their gas."

Opening the fridge, my mom says, "Don't call women chicks. It's disrespectful."

Loch's eyes are still pivoting between us as if that will give him a clue as to what the hell we're talking about.

I lower my head while shaking it. "This conversation is bordering on ridiculous."

"I think we crossed that border," Noah starts, drawing our attention to him. "When my brother decided to refuse his own blood the opportunity to meet hot chicks." He glances at Mom. "I mean girls."

Keeping her eyes on the large pot on the stovetop, she replies, "Better." Loch or I would have gotten the "Mom glare." Noah, the baby of the brothers, gets a gentle correction. *Little fucker.* Well, not so little anymore, but he's still a fucker.

Loch keeps walking. "I don't even want to be a part of this. I'm heading to Dad's office."

My mom looks up, and says, "Tell him dinner is in ten minutes."

"Will do," Loch replies, the words trailing around the corner with him.

Marina pounds the counter with a balled fist. Just one time, but it gets everyone's attention. I chuckle because she's feisty. It's a good quality for her to have, especially considering all the assholes she'll have to deal with in life. She says, "Can we get back to this, please?" Sitting up straighter, proud of her project, she looks at me. "I found her."

The grin is wiped clean from my face as I whip my gaze to the laptop. "What?"

Proud is an understatement for how Marina beams at me. She repeats, "I found the girl from the gas station." This time, it sounds a lot more like a question than a statement. Tapping the screen, she leans in closer to see the picture. "Right here. Lark Summerlin. Senior. I found her for you."

"What do you mean for me?" I ask, feeling the heat of not only Marina but also my mother's and Noah's eyes on me.

"You seemed to be really into her from what I witnessed, so I thought I would do some matchmaking."

"What do you mean by matchmaking?"

The soup is forgotten when my mom comes around the island to see the photo on the screen. Since the laptop is smaller, they all lean in closer while I plan my escape route.

Mom smiles at me and then turns her attention back to the webpage. "She's one of our scholarship recipients." Her hands clasp together against her chest. "This is exciting, Harbor. She must be a stellar student to receive a full ride like she did."

Not that I believe they've done anything intentionally malicious, but I stand, uncomfortable about this topic of conversation without Lark being here. I don't think it's right to be discussing her finances behind her back.

She grew up on the skirts of downtown and works her ass off at her job. It's not difficult to piece together that she doesn't come from money.

Leaning in again, my mom squints her eyes at the screen. "Lark . . ." She stands up and returns to the stove to turn it off. "She was the lovely girl from Larry's catering company." Humming cheerfully as she stirs the pot, she stops, and adds, "That's why I love supporting the scholarship organization. It's good to know the fundraising is helping. You met her at a gas station, Harbor?"

"I did." I hate this attention, not sure if Lark and I are ready to share our new relationship with the world. Or even family. Glancing at her poised photo on the screen, I can't help but admire her again, but now I know that her beauty is inside and out. "You know, we can talk about other stuff like the game that was on or how nice the weather is this fall."

Noah hits my arm and laughs. "Nah, we're good. Tell us more, Harb." I hate when he calls me that. He does it purposely to annoy me, and it's working. But it also has me wondering if she's telling her dad about us.

After spending the morning together, Lark went to the library to study. I went home, but I probably should have studied like she did. I watched football and ordered a pizza instead. It was the third quarter when Mom texted me asking to come for dinner. The text I usually say no to most of the time came as an opening, an invitation, but I was ready to accept.

From what it sounds like, Lark is close to her dad. If she had been free tonight, would I have said yes to my own family?

They've given me everything I could ever need—love, emotional support, independence when I needed it, financial backing, and most importantly, forgiveness. So why do I still keep them at a distance?

Even when I wrecked an $87,000 car, they forgave me. No lecture. In fact, they gave me a Maserati as a replacement. I make the payments, but they signed the loan papers. If I wasn't so fucked up about the accident, maybe I wouldn't be so fucking ungrateful. I just don't know how to find my way out of this misery.

Whether thinking of her or seeing Lark on the screen, it feels good like there's light at the end of the tunnel. I'm starting to believe she's the one who can turn things around for me.

I don't want to just take from her, though. *What value can I bring to her?*

Getting caught in a spiral never ends well. I need to stop holding everything in. Focus on the day, the hour. The time with my family.

The here.

The now.

"I'm dating Lark Summerlin."

Everyone stops.

What the fuck am I doing?

I just stand there like Romeo, who just confessed their love for Juliet and not one person is going to rescue me from this tragedy. I grin, thinking about how amusing this would be to my girlfriend. What would Lark do? She'd lean right into this romance, just like in the movies. "She's my girlfriend."

I don't know what's happening. I guess I expected a different reaction. Their silence is starting to unnerve me.

"You should invite her over sometime. We'd love to meet her."

I turn around to the sound of my dad. He and Loch come toward the kitchen.

Mom's quick. "I don't think your dad met Lark at the fundraiser." I glance over my shoulder as she says, "We could meet at a restaurant if you don't want to intimidate her with a crowd."

"Mom." Marina hops off the barstool. "I should be there since I was there when they met."

"You weren't there, Marina," I correct. "You were *in* the car."

"But it's only because of me that you met her. If I hadn't wanted something to drink—"

"We have a class together, so the odds were already in our favor."

"You do?" my mom asks, dinner entirely forgotten due to my love life announcement. Luckily, I had pizza earlier. "Is she pre-med?"

Dad moves around us and looks in the pot on the stove. "We're having more than soup, I hope. I'm hungry."

"If you're that hungry," Mom says with a laugh, but the humor isn't quite reaching her eyes. "You should have come in here and helped to make dinner. You get caught up in work and forget you have a life. That needs to change, Port."

"You're right." Coming behind her, he dips to kiss her cheek. "But I'm really good at ordering." He pulls her hair behind her shoulder and kisses her neck.

"Ew." Marina is the most vocal as we all fake vomit at the sight of my dad making the moves on Mom. Doesn't matter how old we get, that's just not something we should be subjected to. Though, as I've gotten older, I appreciate the playful side to their love story.

Laughing, they put space, and then an island, between them. My mom says, "I'm grilling steaks. Soup is just the appetizer because I love soup."

The family disbands—everyone falling into their old jobs from when we were little. Marina oversees the distribution of napkins, Noah grabs plates, Loch walks out to help Dad with the grill, and I pull the silverware from the drawer. Mom pours a glass of wine.

I don't know why it took me so long to find my way back

"into the fold" as Mom calls it. Being here and being with them is good for the soul.

The teasing about my dating life ended after the first course. Although I'm ready to see my girl by the time dessert rolls around, the goodbyes are a little harder tonight with my family.

I carry that feeling with me, the one that adds to a great weekend that started with a girl I met at a gas station. Chuckling, I turn on music to pass the time until I'm back in her neighborhood.

Amanda tells me she's at her dad's place and gives me the address with some valuable insight. "Her dad lives for three things in life, in this order. His daughter. Pro sports. And cars."

That's some irony right there.

Seems to me that John Summerlin and I have quite a lot in common.

I drive over and park out front. It's tempting to try the Jake Ryan move on her again, but I have a feeling her dad won't be as entertained. I knock on the door and then step back, letting the screen door close again.

The door swings open, and her dad answers.

No smile.

No greeting.

Nothing but a question. "So you're the boyfriend?"

16

Lark

"Yes, sir."

Harbor tugs at the collar of his crew neck T-shirt and then loosens the jacket he's wearing, his nerves getting the better of him.

It's funny seeing him sweat being face-to-face with my dad. If asked a week ago, I would have said Harbor Westcott doesn't sweat over anything. I grin, knowing that he's nervous because he wants to make a good impression. He cares about me, or he wouldn't give a dang about seeing my dad again. *And he calls me the sweet one.*

I give him a wave from behind my dad. When he sees me, relief eases his shoulders. I nudge the back of Dad's boot and clear my throat. *Hint. Hint.*

"Are you coming in?" my dad asks, his tone as unwelcoming as the invitation.

Stepping around him, I push the screen door open and fill the doorway. I hold out a hand, and say, "Come inside, Harbor."

His grin says it all. I'm happy to see him as well. "The steps are cracked," I warn since night is falling, and he might not see how crooked they are. He comes up and takes my hand. I pull him inside, where my dad has moved into the kitchen. "Something to drink? Water? Tea? Beer?"

"I'm driving, so I'll stick with water."

The sound of the tap running gives me a quick second to lift on my toes to kiss him. "What are you doing here?"

"I stopped by your place, but Amanda said you were still here. Since it's getting dark, I thought you might want a ride home."

"That's nice of you."

My dad returns, and we take a step back from each other. I saw Dad wasting time in the kitchen to give us some time alone. He's good like that. He hands a cup to Harbor and says, "Have you been watching this game?"

"No. I was out at my parents' house visiting with them."

"You're lucky."

"So I've been told."

My dad doesn't catch his response, but I do. Dad just carries on, bothered by the loss, even though he doesn't care about either team. "It's a shit show on that field."

Harbor widens his stance and crosses his arms over his chest as he stares at the TV . . . well, I assume the game on TV, but I'm now remembering how beautiful his family's home is, where he just returned, compared to this home where I grew up. Nothing's newer than ten years, if not double that in age. Even the cup he set on the coffee table was free from the school carnival when I was in fourth grade. It's a good cup that's held up, but not the same as what he was most likely drinking out of an hour ago.

He asks, "Who are you rooting for?"

My dad laughs, kicking back in his chair. "For baseball

to return. I just pass the time with this nonsense."

I say, "We've always watched sports together on Sunday night. Whatever season it is, that's the sport we watch. Unless it's the Yankees, most of the games are just background noise while we hang out and eat." I signal toward the back. "Want to see my room?"

"Only if you're going to show me embarrassing photos of when you were younger."

I'm already walking toward the hallway. Shrugging, I call over my shoulder, "I would, except I don't have those. I was always an adorable kid."

Strong arms grab me from behind, wrapping around my waist and lifting me. I burst into laughter but quickly remember my dad is less than twenty feet away, and I don't know how kindly he'll take to Harbor carrying me into my bedroom.

Wriggling free just outside my door, I turn abruptly and put a finger to my lips. "Shh," I mouth. I know my dad too well. He's probably in the living room pretending to watch the game while secretly plotting how to get Harbor back in the living room and out of my bedroom.

Boys are never something he had to deal with when I was growing up since I was too shy. This is all new to him. And I'm guessing if he hears a door shut, he may jump out of his skin, so I opt to leave it open. That way, he's not forced to come investigate.

As Harbor stands in the middle of my room, I start to feel a lot like I did last night, introducing him to another part of my life. This room is more of a flashback and a homage to my childhood than who I am these days.

He circles the room, giving it a once-over before homing in on a corkboard above my desk. "You won so many awards." *Too many to display.*

"I knew I had to be the best at everything if I wanted to get out of this town one day."

Glancing back at me, he asks, "Is that the plan? To get out of Beacon as fast as you can?"

"Nothing about my journey has been fast. I even went to the university here because it gave me the best shot of having my school paid for." I sit on the edge of the bed, my hands resting back on the mattress, and let him explore. "I would have gone wherever I got the best offer. It just so happens I got a four-year scholarship, including supplements for books and cost of living. That part of it doesn't cover anything but my supplies, but I wouldn't be going if I hadn't gotten it for academics."

Taking a seat at my desk, he spins in the chair to face me. "I knew you were on scholarship, Lark."

My hands go out. "That obvious?"

He shakes his head, though. "My sister actually found you on the university's website. You're featured on the scholarship page."

"That's odd. Why was she looking for that page? I'm not trying to make judgments, but it seems like your family probably doesn't need scholarship money."

"She wasn't looking up scholarship information. We'd never qualify for needs-based assistance anyway."

I'm trying to connect the dots, but they aren't coming together for me until I read between the lines. I'm not sure how to feel about being a research project. I sit up. "She wasn't looking up scholarships. She was looking for me?" My arm flies out. "Did I pass your background check?"

"No. You're misunderstanding," he says in a calming voice. *Maybe that's his serial killer voice . . .* I really need to lay off the podcasts.

"Am I? Because it sounds a lot like you were digging up information on me online."

Sliding the chair across the floor, he stops in front of me and leans forward to rub my legs. "It was innocent on her part. I promise. After seeing us together at the gas station, she knew I was attracted to you and wanted to help me find you again."

My hackles lower. "I didn't even know she was there."

"She's the reason I stopped. She wanted a soda."

"The soda I bought for you?"

He nods. "It was for her."

I get up and sit on his lap. Wrapping my arms loosely around his neck, I ask, "Why were you worried I'd be upset?"

He shrugs, resting his head to the right. "I don't know. I didn't know how you'd react to hearing that my family looked you up online."

"It doesn't sound like you were in on the plan, and what she found is there for everyone to see. It doesn't bother me. I'm grateful for the scholarship."

Money doesn't set me apart simply because my dad and I have never had any.

I could serve at the Dime Diner at thirteen and get enough tips to pay for a bill or two, and then have some left over to save for college. Debt isn't something my dad or myself want to be buried under. We've been close to losing everything a few times, and I hope to never experience that again. Tightening my hold on him, I ask, "Was anything else said about me?"

"I may have told them you're my girlfriend."

Whoa. "You did? You told your family about me?"

"It just came out."

Okay, I can handle this confession one of two ways. I can

swoon or tease him mercilessly. "Right out of your heart?" I never claimed to always take the high road. Since I'm already swooning over this man, I choose to joke with him instead. I love the way he laughs, instantly knowing I'm giving him a hard time.

With his arm wrapped around me, he brings me closer and gives me a kiss. "It sure did."

"Save room for Jesus." My dad's voice reaches the bedroom.

Harbor's eyes widen, and he stands, lifting me with him and setting me on my feet. He whispers, "Is your dad religious?"

"Not at all," I reply, laughing. "But that line always worked."

Resting back, he stretches out his legs and smirks. "Are you telling me that you had a lot of guys in your room?"

I get up, laughing. "I think you already know the answer to that based on what I told you last night. And I have a feeling you can't tell me the same about your room."

"You're right, but we don't need to get into the weeds of my sex life." He pushes off the floor, laughing, and slides back over to the desk. "Trust me, nothing is interesting about that until last night."

I walk to my closet to peek in. It's been a while since I've gone through my things, and I can't remember what I left here. "And what was so interesting about last night?"

"You."

"You know how to make a girl feel good about herself."

Our eyes connect across the room. "I only speak the truth."

I flip through old clothes on hangers, trying to settle the anxiety of Harbor seeing a part of my life that few have or ever will. From the house to my room, he'll have a fuller picture of who I am and where I came from. *Will he still like me the same?*

For someone who comes from so much money, he hasn't shown me an ounce of elitism, staying true to who I believe he is. But when he pulls a yearbook from the shelf above the desk and starts flipping through the pages, I second-guess giving him free rein of the place. Especially since I don't know which grade is in his hands. I say, "When I said I have no embarrassing pictures, I was kidding. I don't think I've taken a photo that's not awkward in some way."

"I beg to differ." He holds up the book, and it's flipped open to the page with me at the graduation podium.

I shrug. "One pic doesn't make a nerd more popular. *You* can trust *me* on that." It's all so easy being with him that I almost forget that we've only been relationship official since last night.

Not finding anything worth taking to my apartment, I close the closet door and sit on the bed, but this time with my back to the wall at the head. I grab a worn paperback, *The Great Gatsby,* sitting on my nightstand when Harbor says, "Is this your mom?"

My gaze races to the dresser where the photo of Liz holding me as a newborn has taken up space my entire life. It's one of the few items I have of her, especially after the house was burglarized a few years ago and her brooch was stolen. It was the only thing of value that I had, but more importantly, it was the only thing she left before leaving for good.

Seeing Harbor bending to get a closer look has my heart racing. I toss the book and jump from the bed to hurry over to him. "That's her. That's . . . Liz and the stolen brooch. Sounds like a book title, but it makes me sad to think about."

"I bet. I'm sorry it was stolen."

"Me too. It's one of the only things I had of her. That and the photo."

"Liz is your mom?" he asks, looking back at me, but he returns his narrowed gaze to the photograph and leans in even closer.

"The lady who gave birth to me," I reply curtly. "I call her Liz because calling her Mom feels like a stab to my heart. And the truth is that I don't have a mom."

Taken back by my tone, he steps away from the dresser. "Did I do something wrong? You seem upset with me."

Guilt washes through me for overreacting. Harbor doesn't know the story. He just asked a question. "No. I'm sorry. I just . . ." I move closer to the picture frame and stare at the faded photo. "My heart shouldn't ache from the pain she caused nineteen years ago, but it does, and I hate it. I hate how weak, how empty she makes me feel, even after all this time."

His hands cover my shoulders, and I feel his warmth through my sweatshirt. He rubs gently and then kisses the top of my head. "The pain sticks around long after years have passed. Even when you think you're healing, something always lurks to make you feel it all again." He wraps his arms around me, his front to my back, and I feel safe in the strength of this man—not just physically, but emotionally. *He understands.*

Looping my arms over the front of his, I rest my head back, still staring at the photo. He asks, "Can I ask you something, or would you rather drop it?"

"You can ask."

Holding me even closer, he whispers, "Why do you keep the photo on display?"

"It's a reminder that she once existed in my life."

17

Harbor

LARK HAS BEEN quiet since we got to her place.

Amanda even pulled me aside to ask what was going on. All I could say was Liz is on her mind. That's all Amanda needed to hear. She made a cup of tea, set it in front of Lark, and then turned on *When Harry Met Sally*.

The three of us watched half the movie before Amanda told us good night and went to bed, leaving Lark and me to deal with the silence. Leaning back on the couch, I look over at her, and ask, "You know how sometimes we say we'll talk about things another time? Are we waiting for a better time, or will we never talk about them?"

Lark pulls the elastic from her hair and runs her fingers through the wild curly strands. "I took it as we were waiting for the right time to bring it up and discuss it."

"Funny thing about time is that it never changes. It's consistently the same. We're the ones who change."

She looks at me, the happiness she usually can't hide from me void in her expression tonight. Her eyes, though, those greens aren't taking time off. She's listening, seemingly taking in what I was saying. She says, "I'm not afraid to open up to you, Harbor. It's just not a great story. There's no happy ending."

"I don't need happy endings, and I don't need your life to be entertainment for me. I want to get to know you, but I can see how painful this is for you, so there's no pressure from me to talk it through."

Curling her legs under her, she gets more comfortable on the other side of the couch. "I don't know every detail of what happened to her, and I'm certain some things my dad will take to the grave with him. But what I do know is that she grew up in The Pointe and graduated from Beacon Pointe High School. Somewhere in that period, she met my dad, and along came me." She frames her face and puts on a fake smile. She doesn't have to put on pretenses for me, but maybe it helps in some way.

I've done it plenty of times when it came to Lucas, and plastering on a fake smile has helped me out of plenty of situations.

I'm surprised by how few details she knows, or is she not ready to share? I'll wait for when it feels right for her. Reaching over, I rub the top of her thigh. "Come here."

She unfurls herself from the cushion and slips into my arms, her back to my chest. Her body is calm against mine, but I know her mind is spinning. She says, "I don't know anything about their relationship, but something wasn't working. That aside, how does someone leave a two-year-old?"

I promised not to pressure her. And I want her to know she's in control of this. As much as I want to give her answers, I don't have them, and I'm not sure I can find them. So right now, I just want to make sure she doesn't feel alone.

I hold her a little tighter. She didn't open up to me for answers. She knows I don't have them. She just needs me to be there for her. I can do that. *I will do it.* Seeing her in pain in a way that hurts the core of who she is is all wrong. *Lark deserves better.*

She says, "No one's perfect, but the little I've gotten from my dad is that she never asked for this life. She was from a whole other world and got stuck here in a run-down shack with a kid and a mechanic."

"Your dad's a mechanic?" This is new information. Amanda sharing with me that he likes cars is an understatement. He's a trained professional. No wonder he knew what my car was just from a quick glance. This is something I can work with.

She nods against my chest. Angling to look at me, she fidgets with the hem of my shirt. "She was young, about the same age we are now, so I try to give her the benefit of the doubt. She was overwhelmed and cut off from her family. That's all I know. It must be why she abandoned me." Suddenly looking at me, she asks, "What do you think?"

What do I think?

"Um," I start, not sure what to say. "I don't know. It sounds like there's a lot of information missing. That must make it hard to move forward."

"Yeah. It does. It's like, if I could just get a fuller picture of the situation, I'd be able to close that chapter. Instead, I've been left in limbo my whole life."

"Is there anyone else you can ask? Grandparents? Siblings of your parents?"

"No, my dad's parents split up when he was young. My grandfather took off, and my grandmother died before I was born. As for Liz, something in my gut tells me she's still alive. I don't know anything about her family, though. My dad was really kept out of their lives. They never approved of them or their marriage."

Lark pushes off the couch and from my lap. She pads across the room into the kitchen, and without needing to ask, she pours us both a glass of water. I follow her in there, holding her by the hips and kissing the side of her head. That's when it dawns on me that I'm holding her the same way Dad held Mom.

My instinct is to push away and change positions, but my head tells me to stay. Because they're my parents, I've always given them a hard time about their PDA. But the way they publicly showed each other love was modeling the behavior.

Before I have more time to second-guess myself, Lark's arms cover mine, taking my hands and holding them to her chest. Giving her the security of my arms is an extension of how I feel about her. It's us, baring our souls for each other. Though the words don't come, the feeling is still between us.

I kiss her once more before she turns in my arms, leaning against the counter. Caging her in, I lean down and get the pleasure of her lips again. But gentle pressure has our mouths separating. Lark wraps her arms around my neck, and asks, "Who is Lucas Westcott?"

Hearing his name come from her mouth hits like a ton of bricks. Unable to answer what to her is a simple question, I move away, my back hitting the fridge. I run my hand through my hair, wondering if it's time for me to go home.

"Harbor?" My eyes are on her as she approaches like she's sneaking up on a wild cat. Caressing my face, she rubs the space between my brows and then my temples, the skin at the corners of my eyes, and then my frown. "I'm sorry. I didn't mean to upset you."

Taking her hands in mine, I lower them between us. "It just didn't . . . I need—"

"What do you need?"

"A warning next time. I understand the interest, but you can't trade my pain for yours. They're two different things."

"I don't know what you mean," she says, freeing herself and moving back against the opposite counter. "I could have asked Amanda who he was. She knew him."

"Then ask her." I leave the small kitchen, the space too confining for a confrontation.

"I'm asking you."

I stop a few feet away and look over my shoulder, our eyes meeting. "I heard you, but there's no fucking way I'm having this conversation, not tonight, and if I have my way, not ever." I turn the bolt to unlock the door.

"Why are you leaving?" Lark runs to block me by pressing her back to the door.

My hand is on the doorknob, ready to help me escape. She only asked about him, nothing more, but I stand there, looking at her as if she's changed. She hasn't. I have, which isn't fair to her. "You were sharing your hurt with me." I touch her cheek, rubbing the pad of my thumb over her soft skin. "And it means a lot that you trusted me with that part of yourself. But it doesn't mean I'm ready to do the same."

"Harbor," she says, her tone dripping in sympathy. My hands have lowered, but I don't move away from her because I've done her dirty by making her grovel for me. "I'm—"

"It's okay. I'm just telling you how it is with me. Lucas Westcott isn't a story I'll be sharing."

"You don't have to talk about him if you don't want. I won't ask again. Just please stay."

My throat feels thick with remorse—not for standing my

ground about my cousin but for making her feel bad for even asking. "I'm sorry, Lark. Maybe I overreacted. It's just—"

"You don't have to explain. You're allowed to keep parts of yourself private." She's too understanding.

"That's just it. It's not private. It's all out there. You can google it."

"I don't want to google it. I don't want to learn about you from the internet. I want to know the person you want to share with me."

Fuck. I feel like shit now. I move in, bringing her into a hug. She lets me without resistance, which makes me feel worse instead of better.

Generally, I'm as honest as I can be, but Lark speaks her heart, which can be a dangerous proposition. But I speak from mine as well when it comes to her, so I guess we're both taking a risk.

Getting to know someone—about their family, their upbringing, and their life—isn't always easy. Her arms finally come around me, and she rests her cheek on my chest. "This is going fast . . ."

This.

Us.

I step back—emotionally and physically—to deal with the tightening in my chest by rubbing the forming knot before it settles in. "What are you saying?"

"I shouldn't have pushed." She walks to the bedroom, still talking. "That's all." Turning in the doorway, she leans against it. Nothing about her stance is open to me.

Crossed arms.

Pursed lips.

Eyes with no shine for me to find.

What have I done?

I've fucked up. *That's what.*

But it's easier to think she's the fool for opening the door and letting me into her life. Although I hope I won't be a regret she has one day, I have a feeling I don't have a say in the matter. She's already made the sacrifice—herself.

This time, I won't play games. I won't toy with her or her feelings. She deserves to have honesty, something that I'm used to burying to protect a ghost.

"I wasn't believed when I told the truth, but the lies were as if everyone was waiting for this day, anticipating my downfall. I had no choice but to embrace what benefitted my cousin more. I gave them what they wanted and told them I caused the accident."

Her guard is down, and worry wrinkles her face as she comes back to me. Taking my hands, she kisses one and then the other. "I'm so sorry." She reaches up and wraps her arms around my neck, hugging me with all her strength. "I'm so sorry you had to go through that alone."

Her response takes me by surprise. I've never had anyone take my side before. I lean back to see her face. "What?"

"Harbor," she says, caressing my face. "I can't imagine feeling so alone that you have to lie to please everyone."

I've unlocked the gates, and memories begin to flood back. "You don't understand. I didn't deserve a shot to set things right or to make amends. I'd fucked up so many times."

"Not enough. Not ever enough to be dismissed." She takes my hand and leads me to her bedroom. "We should be in bed."

"Why?"

She starts on her shirt, pulling it over her head and dropping it to the floor. She nods in encouragement. Not that I need it to get naked with her, but what the hell, I'll go along with her plan.

"We're not rushing into this just because we're addressing real feelings."

"I don't have some elaborate plan to lure you into my bed, Harbor. I just want to be with you. Now take off your clothes and take me to bed."

I reach over my shoulder and tug my shirt off from over my head, dropping it to the floor like she did. When she starts on her jeans, I start on mine. "You don't have to ask me twice."

She grins and then laughs, bringing my own laughter to the surface. Her light is giving me the reprieve I didn't know I needed until we arrived here.

Like every other time we've spent together, this is right. This is us. The levity feels good, even if it comes in the darker hours of our lives.

I take a deep breath when only our underwear is left hiding our secrets. But soon, even that barrier is removed. First her bra and then her panties. Both left in a pile at the foot of her bed. She stands there, baring herself to me. It doesn't feel erotic, though she's incredibly sexy.

There's more weight to this moment we're sharing. I remove my boxer briefs and stand across from her. She doesn't rush to me to hide herself, and I don't close the gap to cover us in an embrace.

As the laughter fades, we just are right then, just us, and the light from the small lamp on the nightstand. Lark moves to the side of the bed and then climbs in. I climb in on the other side and move to the middle to be close to her again.

She rolls to her side and snuggles against me. Her breath drifts across my chest, warming me, and her heart beats against my ribs.

I wrap my arm around her, not knowing what I did to deserve this woman in my life, but I vow to always protect her. I've never felt this strongly for someone. I won't lose her, and if that means putting my heart on the line, I'll do it. "I love you."

Those three words come so easily that I realize that a timeframe can't dictate what the heart already knows.

"I love you, too," she whispers.

Kissing the top of her head, I'm aware that it's too soon to share those words. But if we're doing what comes naturally, I couldn't hold them in any longer.

She mindlessly doodles with her nails lightly across my skin. Tilting her head, she kisses the underside of my chin, and then asks, "Do you want to start at the beginning?"

18

___

Lark

I BARED my soul to him.

Lying beside me, now he bares his to me. "My aunt called Lucas the golden child of the family." He glances at me as I lie beside him. "My mom isn't the type to argue about such things, as she puts it, but it always stuck in her side." He grins as if the memory invokes it. "She would tell us that she was gifted with four beautiful children, so she wasn't looking to get into a fight over her sister-in-law's only child." He looks back at me again, the smile still on his face. "She loved Lucas like one of her own, so I think she just let it go."

"Your mom is nicer than I would have been."

He gives me a wink and then rolls to his side to face me. "Lucas was my age, so we were always directly compared to each other. It's like what they do to twins. There's always one deemed an angel and the other a devil. That was true for Lucas and me, too. But with his mom always campaigning for the top slot, she pegged me early on as the troublemaker."

The lighthearted tone weaving through the story has disappeared, and I have a feeling this is where truth and lies get confused.

"The thing is," he continues, "I wasn't trying to be an angel. There's not a bone in my body that struggles with confrontation. But sometimes, trouble knew how to find me. Nothing big. It was petty shit, like a pack of gum that was too tempting not to nick behind my dad's back. Or trekking muddy shoes in the house and blaming my younger brother." He shakes his head. "I always got busted. They matched the soles of our shoes to the footprints." A light chuckle rocks his shoulders but then stops. "But Lucas, despite the angelic reputation his mother had built, he looked for trouble."

"Maybe she knew, and that's why she petitioned so hard for that perception."

Reaching over, he finds my hand between us, and our fingers fold together. "I always had a similar thought, but it's nothing I could prove."

"What kind of trouble did he get into?"

"He was stealing liquor from his house at fourteen, smoking weed at fifteen. When he got a car on his sixteenth birthday, he drove us straight to Beacon . . ." Harbor stops, seeming to shuffle through notecards in his mind that will detail the memory.

"What did you do in Beacon on his birthday?"

He exhales and looks down. I'm naked next to him, but he doesn't ogle me or do anything that makes me feel vulnerable or exposed in an uncomfortable way. I'm treated as an extension of him, our hands exchanging energy between us.

His hands slide over my shoulders and then up my neck until I look him in the eyes. "He found the trouble he was looking for, but I made the mistake of being there. We were best friends. Wherever he went, I went. When he drank, I drank. The first time I ever smoked weed was from a blunt he handed me. That's just how it was with us. We were like brothers but almost closer." He suddenly sits up and puts his back against the wall. When he scrubs his hands over his face, I can already see the toll this is taking on him.

I sit up next to him, bringing the sheets over my chest. "If this is too much—"

"I'm okay. I just haven't thought about some of this stuff in years. It's weird now, like it was a different lifetime and not my own. We had some good times, but my eldest brother, Loch, was onto us. He'd threaten to tell our parents if we didn't stop. We always told him what he wanted to hear. Then the next day, without a second thought, we would be up to the same old shit." He yawns, but I don't think he's tired from the day, but from the exhaustion of reliving a life he dug up today.

"Harbor?" He looks at me, and that's when I see the torment in his eyes. I rest my hand on his arm. I kiss his shoulder and then mold myself to him, holding him the best I can. "I love you." I do, too, more than seems possible in such a short time. But like his life with his cousin, our connection runs deeper than the time we've had together.

Our bond is stronger with every day that passes, and in each hour, I feel more myself when I'm with him than I ever have alone.

His arm comes around my front, and he rubs my back. "I love you." A kiss is placed on my forehead, and he whispers, "I love you so much."

We sit in silence, letting the moonlight stream in

through the blinds and mingle with the light stretching from the lamp in the corner.

He says, "My shoulders don't feel so heavy when I'm in this room with you. It feels good to feel like myself for the first time in years." We're so alike, but I don't want to distract from his story, so I stay quiet, though I'm impatient on the inside. "Lucas died on my birthday."

The punch to my gut elicits a gasp. I can't hold him any tighter than I already am, but I wish I could ease the pain. "I'm so sorry. I know it's just words, but please know I mean them."

"I know, and it's all right. There's not a lot to say about it. We spent years fucking around, but when I turned eighteen . . . I don't know. I was over it. I was over taking the blame for him. Watching him be rewarded for coming out of the mess he made unscathed finally got to me. He kept going to parties in Beacon, mixing with people who didn't give a damn about him while I started focusing on what I wanted to do with the rest of my life." When he exhales a deep breath, we readjust and lie down on our backs again. "Did I mention his mom wanted him to be a doctor?"

"That was the plan?"

"He was going to Princeton, and I was going to Beacon. He told me better luck next time, gave me a pat on the back, and told me to work harder so we could go to medical school together. He even suggested I get my parents to make a large donation like his had done."

I have so many thoughts about how this picture has been painted but only one conclusion. "You got into Princeton." I don't bother asking because I already know the truth. Harbor lied to get away from his cousin. "Do you want to be a doctor?"

He keeps his eyes forward on the blanket. "I have to be a doctor. For Lucas, to make his dream come true."

"Why?" I sit forward, angling to face him. I need a better view of this man. I need to see his eyes, and the truth inside he won't be able to hide. "What about your dreams? Don't they matter anymore?"

Closing his eyes, hiding them from me, he shakes his head. He finally turns to me, and says, "My dreams died the day my cousin passed away."

"No." I cover his hands with mine. "That's not how life works."

"You're right, but we're not talking about life. We're talking about his death." His tone is firm, his eyes determined despite knowing he doesn't believe the words coming from his mouth. "My aunt told me he would want me to still become a doctor. She told me over his grave and made me promise."

"Who does that to someone?" He can't answer that. No one can. It's not her right to saddle him with the burden of her son's life. "Harbor? If you're living your cousin's life instead of your own, you're not living."

"It's all I know anymore." His tone is resolved, the fight for his own life left his eyes long before I met him.

"I've met your mom, Harbor. You cannot convince me that this is what she wants for you."

He levels a glare at me. "My mom is thrilled she'll have a doctor in a family of lawyers."

"Not at the expense of your happiness."

The tips of his finger graze my neck as he slides his hand into the hair at the back of my head. "I'm happy, Lark. I'm happy with you." Bringing me in for a kiss, he does it twice before saying, "Medicine is a noble practice."

"Who are you trying to convince? Me or yourself?"

"No one. I don't have to convince anyone. It's a done deal."

"What if you don't get into medical school?"

He scoffs, the sound more likened to an arrogant prince than Harbor. "Of course, I'll get into medical school. I'm a Westcott." It's then that I realize. Right now, he's not the guy who bandaged my chin with loving care. He's the creation of what he thinks he's supposed to be. He's what happens when your life is formed from tragedy.

I move away, an inch at first, and then climb out of bed. He watches but doesn't try to stop me. Grabbing my shirt from the floor, I put it back on and stand at the end of the bed. "You should go home and get some rest."

"I'm not tired."

"I am."

The covers are flying so fast from his body that I flinch. Stopping, his shoulders are straight and muscles are tense. "Don't do that, Lark."

"Don't do what?" I ask, raising my chin as I cross my arms over my chest.

"I would never hurt you, so please don't flinch."

"Like I can help it," I gripe. "It's an involuntary reaction."

"It's distrust."

Kicking out my hip, I plant my hand on it and push every one of his buttons. "It is what it is. Isn't that what you say?"

He grabs his clothes, and says, "Fuck this." He dresses as he moves to the door, and his pants are up by the time he leaves my room.

I hear Amanda say, "Hot damn," and the sound of her door shutting. I'll apologize to her later, but for now, I follow him. His pants are up, though the fly hangs open. Still shirtless, he pulls on his shoes and hops on one foot. Then he grumbles again, "Fuck this." Pulling open the door, he doesn't look back before walking out.

Wow. I stand there in shock, dumbfounded by the turn tonight took.

And I'm pissed.

How dare he treat me like I'm one of them, like I'm supposed to just let him follow someone else's dream and not say something? Fisting my hands, I lock the bolt, then go back to my room and shut the door. I lean against the back of it, and my blood is boiling. I go to open a window, needing the fall air to help me cool down, but stumble over something sharp. Looking back, I see what stabbed my foot —keys.

Harbor's keys, to be precise. I recognize the Maserati fob on the keychain.

Who's laughing now?

Not me because I'm still too mad to find the humor in him being stuck outside without his keys to help him avoid having a real conversation with me.

My phone buzzes on the desk and his name flashes on the screen before it goes dark again. It seems his arrogance still gets the better of him. But I'm not going to stoop to his level.

With the keys digging into the palm of my hand, I walk out of my room again, unlatch the bolt, and cut through the entry, landing outside on the sidewalk and looking around for him.

I'm left shocked again when I see him riding *my* bike down the street. *How dare he!*

Unbelievable. He'll let his pride win before resolving things with me? Good to know now before I sink even deeper into this relationship.

My anger morphs as my stubbornness kicks in. I stomp

in my bare feet and the cold air straight down the path to his vehicle. I've seen him unlock it several times and don't struggle with that part. It's the starting of the engine that I can't figure out. I sit in the driver's seat, the leather chilly against the back of my thighs and ass, searching for where I stick the key.

A button labeled "engine" stares back at me, so I put my foot on the brake and press it. The car purrs to life and music streams from the speakers. I didn't take him for a rock guy, but I guess we haven't dated long enough to find some of these things out.

Thank God it's an automatic. I never did master my dad's truck. It was just easier to ride my bike everywhere.

I put my seat belt on and then shift into drive. This car has power, and if I'm not careful, she'll take over and I'll lose control. Looking ahead, I don't even see Harbor anymore. I drive slowly at first as I get accustomed to handling it. I stop at the stop sign at the corner and then keep rolling forward. I know the general direction he lives in, although I've never been there.

Scanning every street I pass, there's no sign of him until I get a block shy of downtown. He's sitting at a red light, waiting for it to turn green. How does that even make sense when he just stole my bike?

I don't know why I find it funny but seeing that big guy sitting on my pale-blue bike with that white seat, a few streamers still attached to the handlebars fluttering in the breeze, puts a smile on my face. I roll up behind him, keeping enough distance to keep him free from my head-lights, and then lay on the horn, which startles him so much that he almost falls off.

Upset and flailing his arms, he swings the bike around and moves into the breadth of light from the car, saying all kinds of things that I can't hear over the music filling the interior.

The light turns green, but he stays exactly where he is. With no other cars in the area, I pull up next to him and roll down my window. "You stole my bike."

"You stole my car."

With the accusations thrown out, our eyes narrow as if we're determined to win a staring contest. Neither one of us blinks. But we can only do this for so long, so I blink and let him win this round. "You left me because I called you out on that bullshit."

"I didn't leave *you*, Lark. I left the situation."

He's still sitting on my bike like he intends to ride it. It's not exactly an even exchange, but he doesn't budge or make a move to get me out of his car. I rest my arm on the door, my elbow hanging out, like I'm settling in for the night knowing I have the sweeter deal right now. "Same thing, Harbor."

"I didn't leave you. I swear." His tone is as genuine as his expression. Giving up the fight, he gets off the bike and comes to the open window. Kneeling beside the car, he rests his hands on my arm. "I made the decision to honor my cousin and my family a long time ago. You may not understand why, but it was something I've come to terms with before ever meeting you."

The stubborn wind leaves my sails because secretly, I like the way he feels with his hands on me like I'll slip away if he doesn't hang on. And because his eyes never lie to me, I believe him.

I let out a deep breath, my body eased against the seat, and say, "Okay."

He stands with his hands still on me and says, "I'm sorry. Relationships are new for me. I'm not making excuses. I've really just never had to consider someone else's feelings. I want to change. *For you.*"

"I don't want you to change for me." I'm freezing, but I try to keep my teeth from chattering. "I want us to learn how to handle these situations together." I fail, and my chin trembles.

He notices the goose bumps popped on my arms and cups my jaw. "Let's get you back home." He says, "Pull over there and roll up the window. Crank on the heat. I'll take the wheel off and get the bike in the back."

I do as he says ready to be warm again. A few cars stop to offer him help, but he's become a master at deconstructing my bike and fitting it in the car. When he comes around to the driver's side, he opens the door for me to get out.

I say, "I'm good to drive home."

I don't think he hears me because he's staring at my legs. Looking down at my lap, I realize the shirt isn't as long as I thought, just covering my butt and barely reaching the top of my thighs. His eyes lock on mine, and then I see him take a long, slow breath. On the exhale, he says, "We need to go."

He runs around the vehicle and gets in on the other side. "Hit the gas."

I don't.

The last thing I'm going to do is wreck this very expensive car. Harbor accuses me of purposely torturing him. "Going the speed limit isn't a slight against you, babe."

As soon as I park at the curb, he grabs the bike and wheel hanging out of the trunk and runs it to the side of the house before I've even locked the car and set the alarm. Standing at the front door, he says, "Shake a leg, baby."

I do.

I shake my ass, too, realizing that I might just get my wish, after all.

19

Harbor

LARK JUMPS INTO MY ARMS, wrapping them around my neck and kissing me like she wants to medal in the Olympics for it.

I kiss her right back, holding her bare ass in my hands, and carry her inside not only to get her out of the cold but to fucking apologize.

When I kick her bedroom door closed, our lips remain attached until the very last second when I lay her down . . . a few inches above the mattress. Laughter erupts from her as she lands with a bounce.

She has a way of getting me to confess my darkest secrets, the desire to have someone else sharing the burden in carrying them runs deeper than I could have imagined. I've never had the inclination to share at this level with anyone else. She bared her body, but I know she was also baring her soul to me. Me doing the same wasn't as hard as I would have thought.

It was our way of communicating, to get to the core of the issues, reminding me of something I once overheard my mom telling Loch. Every couple has their own way of working through a problem. As a team, they have to find their method and always respect each other.

"When I said I love you, I meant it, Lark."

She catches her breath and lies on her back, studying my face when I sit down. "I know you love me, babe. I wouldn't have let you come back here if I didn't love you just as much." Sitting up, she anchors her hand to the bed, and says, "You said you'd always come back to me."

"I will. I promise you, I will."

Grabbing hold of my arm, she pulls me down until we're both lying flat on the mattress, our heads barely touching and staring up at the ceiling. *It's been a night already.*

Talking about her, Liz, and then when I shared some of my history with Lucas. We talked more than I have in years. I'm usually one more for listening, but for Lark, I'll stay up all night and talk if that's what she prefers.

There's just the matter of this not-so-small issue of my erection. It's not going away. As if knowing that she's naked under that T-shirt isn't enough to keep me hard, I will never in my life forget the sight of her in my car, dressed the same. She's a fantasy come to life.

I'm not usually one for sex in cars. They're cramped and uncomfortable, but an exception will eventually be made for Lark Summerlin. I'm an asshole for thinking about her body, but she's very distracting, and currently oblivious to how sexy she is.

Our hands bond together in the space between us. She says, "I know you will. I really do, but for me, it cuts deep that you'd walk out during an argument. You're asking me to stand by while you process your emotions. It doesn't work like in an argument. I need to know you're going to stay, that you'll fight through whatever's upset us, and that you'll fight for us in the end." She turns to look at me, seeking an answer by the questions in her eyes.

The heat of her hand against my skin has me pulling her in closer, and the vulnerability in her eyes makes me want to be a better man. "We're new at this, not just being together but being in a relationship. Relationships take time and effort. I'll give you both."

Although she's silent, her expression remains thoughtful. I feel like I'm holding my breath. Not that I think she'll break up with me, but more her believing in me enough to give us a real chance, a third chance to get this right.

She sits up and faces me. "For all the times we lay here and talk, which I love to do with you, I've come to learn that you're not a wordy man. You hit straight to the heart of the matter, so I'm going to as well. I'll give you room to process if I can rely on you to stay."

I don't think I've ever been held accountable for anything before. So I give her a lot of respect for doing it now. She knows what she wants and won't settle for less. I don't want to be the "less" in her life either. I want to be more than she could ever dream of. "I can't argue with that."

Her smile blooms for me like a night flower that opens for the moon. "Good because I don't want to argue with you anymore." Leaning over, she kisses my cheek, her hand leveraging my leg to get her closer. With our mouths pressed together, she whispers, "Unless it's under the covers."

I close my eyes to kiss her, but she's off the bed and standing before me with her hands on her hips. "I think we need ground rules, Mr. Westcott." *And my dick is hard again.*

Gulping obnoxiously, I then say, "Rules? I never did well with rules. I'm more of a rebel type."

"You wear button-ups and drive a Maserati, babe. So let's correct that statement to you were a rulebreaker. Now, you're my boyfriend." She has a point. I'm not so rogue these days. Standing in front of me, she toys with the hem of her T-*shirt. .. or what I call*, teasing. "And as my boyfriend, I promise you two things."

I lean back with a cocked eyebrow. "Go on."

"Loyalty. It's one of the traits that I value most in myself and in others."

That's an easy one. "I'm ride or die, baby."

Running her hand up her hip, the fabric is dragged with it, giving me a peek at her sweet little pussy. She's determined to torment me. I run the tip of my tongue over my bottom lip as a little reminder of what she's missing.

Losing some of what I call the upper hand, my peekaboo view is covered, and she crosses her ankles. I'm getting to her, wearing her down, and ready to blissfully deplete her of all releases. "And the second promise?" I ask, feeling quite cocky about now.

"Honesty." *That stings a bit.* She adds, "You've mentioned being someone else for your family. I don't want someone else. I want you—the good and the bad, the dark and the light. The truth. Promise me you'll be honest with me, Harbor."

I stopped tracking the lies I was living years ago, but there's something I can say without a doubt. "I've always been honest with you; I promise never to lie."

This time, I'm rewarded when she straddles my lap and pushes me back. Leaning down, she says, "I won't lie to you, not ever." I'm quick to wrap my arms around her and hold her there. It's not a frenzy to get off or anything like that.

It's a slow seduction of our mouths coming together and then our bodies. Her thighs are tight around my middle as she seeks relief I'm more than happy to give her. Maneuvering my hand between us, I reach lower until the tips of my fingers find her clit. Like a shock of electricity running through her, her head falls back as I rub circles to get her off.

Her body dances against my hand, erotic, craving, her chest pushing against mine as I hold on to her hips with my other hand and listen to soft moans in my ear. "Talk to me, babe," she whispers.

Pumping in and out of her with two fingers, I slide my free hand around to her backside, dip under the shirt, and take a firm hold of that great ass of hers, squeezing. Hard. I whisper in her ear, "I want you to take off my jeans."

She stops like a good girl and moves to the side to give me access to pop the button and drag my zipper down. I shift to get them to my ankles.

Lark moves to the floor to take my shoes off before helping me remove my jeans altogether. When she starts on the waistband of my underwear, I stop her by the wrist. "What are you doing?"

"We don't have to have sex, but I want to feel you."

And she just graduated to vixen.

In all fairness, I want the same. I want to feel all of her, but I'm not sure if I'll be able to handle her riding me bare and not push in. I've never had the challenge before. "I want that with you."

She takes my boxer briefs off and then slowly settles back onto my lap. Her arms hang loose over my shoulders, and her gaze is soft when she starts to move on top of me again. Running my hands over the curve of her waist and lower, I move my hand back to the apex of her thighs.

Though she has a steady rhythm going, she pauses to spread her legs wide enough for my hand.

I could tease her and only fuck her with a finger, but I'd rather see her come undone. I push two fingers inside her, anchoring my hand next to my dick. Each rub of her pussy against my erection is another strike of a match. With every thrust and push-pull of her body, a fire is lit deep in my belly

When her head falls back and her mouth falls open, her body starts bouncing on top of me, chasing her release, and then mine hits. The stars burst behind my closed eyelids as she continues to roll of her hips, insisting on every ounce of my pleasure releasing. She cries out my name just as she drops her head onto my shoulder and comes on my hand.

Her body rocks from the inside out and when she finally takes a breath, her head resting on my shoulder, she says, "I could get used to this."

I push her hair out of the way to kiss her neck. "I hope you do."

We only give ourselves a minute to unwind before we take turns leaving to clean up in the bathroom. Feeling more relaxed than I have in long time, I lie in bed beside her with the lamp turned off. I say, "It's going to be a rough day ahead if we stay up much longer." I don't put this pressure on her, but I'd fight sleep just to spend more time with her.

Her smile blooms in the middle of the night, just for me. Touching my cheek, she says, "Let's get some sleep then." She kisses me, and then I lean over her and steal another.

She must have been more tired than she realized. It takes her no time at all to find her slumber, but I stay awake, fighting against it just to have a few minutes to think.

I've fucked up in the past and almost got kicked out of

my house and school *a couple of times*. I don't blame anyone else involved but myself.

I didn't have to drink like I'd never get another.

I didn't have to smoke weed.

I didn't have to let my ego get the better of me.

But I did.

Holding her now while she sleeps, I don't know what good I did to deserve this peace, even if temporary, but I recognize when there's an angel in my midst. I kiss her head as the past is forgotten, and an opportunity for a new beginning fills this room.

Lark.

I stare at her, almost willing her awake just to selfishly see her eyes again. She stirs, so I lie as still as I can, hoping she can fall asleep again. We stayed up late, too late to try to make sense of the changes.

"Hi," she whispers softly, her voice faded from sleep. Lying against my chest, a little grin appears before she opens her eyes. I didn't have a doubt about staying, but if I had, the slate would be wiped clean.

This is why.

She is why.

She yawns but blinks and closes her eyes again, squeezing the hand she's holding between us. "I like you in my bed."

"I like you."

There's a pause long enough to make me wonder if she fell asleep again. But then she says, "Charming Harbor, never change."

"I'll change for you."

But I'm not entirely sure she heard me since her body grows heavier as her breathing evens. Then she whispers, "I don't need you to change who you are for me. I just need you." Closing my eyes again, I try to find the same deep sleep, but the smile plastered on my face might be the culprit keeping me awake. That's okay. I'm in no hurry to rush through the remaining hours I have with her before sunrise.

Despite my happiness, exhaustion sets in anyway, leaving me no choice but to give in and fall asleep.

20

_____

Lark

WE'VE ONLY BEEN DATING for a month, so how am I already accustomed to riding around in a six-figure car like I'm a princess? *When I met Harbor.*

"I need to study more," I say, resting my hand on top of his. I run my finger over the prominent veins that I find not only sexy but also safe—like his strength is on display.

He rubs the top of my thigh and gives it a little squeeze —equally sweet and possessive. We may have had a bumpy start, but sometimes life throws curveballs. I'm glad we committed to more with each other. It's been pure bliss ever since.

I'd know too. He's not the first guy I've dated, although there haven't been many . . . for good reason. But I've dated enough to know I've found something special in Harbor.

One of my favorite parts of dating him is that we talk about everything and nothing at all. There's no pressure to perform or be "on." Not every conversation has to be some great reveal about ourselves. Instead, it's been a journey of slow discovery. So much so that I wonder if this lifetime will ever be long enough to lose interest. It seems downright impossible when it comes to him.

Parking the car, he shrugs. "Okay, then we'll study more."

"No, *I* need to study more. You're a complete distraction."

He chuckles. "Maybe we should study in public places."

"Um, no. The last time we did that, you had me pinned to the Italian breads of the 17th Century section of the library with a hand over my mouth to muffle me."

Getting out of the car, he leans back in. "In my defense, we were shushed twice before you came on my hand."

He's so open about sex, like it's just a part of normal life. Guess he can be nonchalant about it since he's had it. His door closes, and then mine opens seconds later. I place my hand in his, and he brings me to him. *See?* Princess.

One arm comes around my waist as he leans in to kiss me but stops abruptly before impact. "We also made a killer loaf of bread that night."

"I felt obligated to check out at least one of the books we violated."

"You also came twice while it was baking."

"And that's why I need some time alone to study. I can't be coming all the time."

He tilts his head like the thought doesn't register. I've never felt better about myself, my body, or been in a better mood than when I'm with him. Does orgasming on the regular play a part in that? *Hell yes.* But it's also just the time I've spent with him. He always manages to make me smile.

Bending down to look me in the eyes, he says, "You say that like it's a bad thing."

"The problem is it's *too* good and causing my grades to

slip. I can't focus on anything else, and my applications are due soon. I haven't gotten everything together yet. Have you applied for med school?" You'd think I'd know this, but school is one of the last things we talk about when we're together.

He kisses me and then shuts the door, so we can head to class. He replies, "I'm working on it."

We reach the corner of the building where we usually say goodbye on days we go in different directions. "Maybe this will give you time to work on that. I don't want to be blamed for you missing deadlines.

"As long as you're not actually trying to get rid of me, I'll give you the time you need."

I fist his jacket and move in close. "And if I were trying to get rid of you?" I ask, raising an eyebrow and a smile I can't restrain.

Large hands go low around my hips and settle on my backside. "I'm not letting you get away that easy, Ms. Summerlin."

Giving him a quick kiss, I then straighten the backpack on my shoulders. "Good. Because I have no intention of letting you go either." Taking off slowly, I walk backward. "See you later, babe." I start the hike up the campus to the building for my first class of the day.

Harbor's still standing there when I look back. I smile to myself, imagining this must be what walking on cloud nine feels like. "Hey, Summerlin?"

I look back again before I get too far from him. Laughing, I reply, "What is it, Westcott?"

"How do you feel about dinner with my parents?"

Did he really just ask me where everyone in the vicinity can hear? *God, I hope so.* "Tell them I'd love to." I blow him a kiss and then turn back only to run into Amanda.

"I didn't take you guys," she starts, "for the whole make-a-scene, PDA type of couple. I figured you'd be more low-key."

We take a right through the quad, heading in the same direction. I'm still smiling like a fool. "If you haven't noticed, nothing about Harbor Westcott is low-key."

"Speaking of the Westcotts, I can't stop thinking about how much Harbor's changed since his cousin passed."

I do a double take from the swift change in direction of the conversation. "What do you mean?"

"Well," she says casually, "he used to come party down off Dobson with Lucas back when Dane first met Mia." She eyes me with a shrug. "You never came to those parties. Anyway, now Harbor just hangs out at home all the time. Our home, to be specific. Doesn't he have his own apartment?"

The words don't match the friendliness of her tone. "That's a lot to unpack, Amanda."

"Sorry, you're always with him, so we don't talk much anymore."

The change in mood blew in like the wind. I stop because now I feel bad because she's not entirely wrong. "Well, to address the apartment situation, yes, he still has it. Sometimes he's there, but most of the time, lately, at least, he's been staying with me at ours. I'm sorry if that bothers you. I didn't know you felt that way."

"I'm only bothered when I can't get into the bathroom when I want. And sometimes I feel like I'm intruding if you're in the living room eating together. But really, I'm just surprised you guys don't—" She finally notices I'm not next to her, and she turns back. "What are you doing?"

I walk forward but stop with a few feet between us. Still

confused by the comments, I hold on to the straps of my backpack for support. "I could ask the same of you?"

"What do you mean?" she asks of me this time. "I'm just saying that if I were you, I'd rather hang out in a big apartment with my boyfriend than with my roommate at our place in a tiny two-bedroom, one-bath. Guess that's just me."

Nothing about this feels good. In fact, it doesn't feel like us at all. We don't play dirty with each other, so I'm thrown off by what's really going on. Moving closer, I lower my voice since so many people are around. "Are you starting a fight with me?"

"Why would I want to fight with you?" She grips the straps of her bag, but her eyes never leave mine. We've been friends forever and can sometimes be a little blunt, so I'll give her the benefit of the doubt that she's just curious and at target practice taking aim at the first real relationship I've ever had and the only one that's mattered. "What's going on with you, Lark? Why are you defensive?"

"I'm not," I reply, my neck jerking back. Okay, maybe I am defensive, but how could I not after that accusation? It feels more like I'm protecting a relationship that came when I needed it most. I look at my watch. "I need to go, or I won't make it before the door is locked. Do you want to talk about this later?"

"Go." She playfully shoves me toward my building, like we weren't caught in the crossfire of our changing friendship. "There's nothing to talk about."

I start for my building but know we need to talk about this soon before it becomes a whole thing between us. It's never good to let things fester. "Let's hang out later. I can stop by the store and grab a pizza." I make the offer, but I still feel a little uneasy in the wake of the conversation we just had.

Her expression lifts, and she waves. "I'll bring the wine."

"See you at home tonight." Jogging to my building, me and another kid make it just before the door is closed. I find an empty desk on the far side of the classroom and swing my backpack to the floor. I don't have any classes with Harbor on Tuesdays or Thursdays, but I wish I did. But then again, maybe that's exactly what we need—us spending some time apart. *I don't know.* Amanda's gotten in my head.

How's it different from what I was suggesting to Harbor on the ride in today? I don't have to wonder because I know the intention. That wasn't about pushing Harbor away. It was about making sure I don't sabotage my future.

I love spending my days in his arms, kissing him, loving that man like he'll be the last I ever will. Surely, Amanda can see how happy he makes me. I dig out my laptop and start taking notes, but my thoughts keep veering back to what she said about the partying, and regarding the apartment. Did I detect an insinuation that he's keeping me away from it on purpose?

Why would he do that? He lives alone. There's no logical reason he would purposely be keeping me away. But just to overthink this even more, how is it that we've been dating for almost a month, and he hasn't invited me over, not once?

Let it go, Lark.

I didn't expect my day to derail before nine o'clock, but here I am with my thoughts and emotions nervously twisting in my belly. Have I been a bad friend to Amanda? To Dane? I haven't seen him since I worked with him two weeks ago. We don't get to hang out much anymore, not since he and Mia got back together and school reconvened.

I drop my head into my hands and rub my temples,

knowing I don't have the luxury to get sidetracked from my mission—getting into medical school. That must remain my top priority. I don't want to let my dad down now.

Before my last class at two, I text Harbor: *I'm going to see my dad after school, so I don't need a ride home. I'll walk from there. Love you.*

I hop into my seat and am settling in when he replies: *Love you.*

Class feels longer today, the minutes dragging until we're finally free. I stop at a water station to refill my bottle before trekking across campus and down a large hill. My thoughts are so scrambled today that I don't realize I forgot to put my music buds in my ears until I'm halfway to the shop.

Two streets over and six blocks down, I walk in through an open bay and search for my dad. Carrig is wiping his hands on towels when he sees me. "Oh, what brings you by, Lark?" He's only a year older than I am, but he's been learning to fix cars from my dad for years now. It's a dream of my dad's, and since he had a daughter with no interest whatsoever in cars, he transferred that attention to Carrig. Thank God.

Apparently, Carrig gets lots of visitors of the female persuasion from what my dad says, though. *Gripes about is more accurate.* They become quite the distraction to Carrig and my dad has to kick them out when they become a thorn in his side.

"Just looking for my dad. Is he around?" He points toward the office, which is in the direction I'm already heading. Peeking through the glass, I see him on the phone. I wave when he looks up and then drop my backpack behind the reception counter.

I only spin in the chair once before my dad comes

around the corner. "Good to see you, Pipsqueak. Is everything okay?"

I'd give him a hug, but not when he's in his mechanic's coveralls. I don't want to stain my college sweatshirt. "Everything's good." I lean against the counter. "You know I've been dating Harbor for almost a month now."

"It's getting serious?"

"It's been about a month. We hang out and get dinner together most nights." I keep things general, leaving out some of the details. The last thing my dad wants to hear about is the other stuff I do with Harbor.

If he found out about that, Harbor wouldn't survive the night, and I'd be headed to a convent. And we're not even Catholic.

He starts typing on the computer, his attention stolen away. "What does that mean? You celebrate," he says, glancing at me, "with a special dinner or something?"

Remembering that Harbor asked me this morning to have dinner with his parents, maybe that's what hitting a month means. I shrug. "Not sure. I haven't planned anything." I let a minute pass by, taking another spin in the chair, and then ask, "What do you think about Harbor coming over for Sunday dinner?" I keep it as casual as I can because my dad doesn't take well to disruptions in his routine. Resting his hands on the counter, he shifts his weight forward as he stares at me. I start to get nervous. Is it too soon, or will my dad always want it to be only the two of us? "We'll still watch the game, but we can talk beforehand . . . and stuff." God, I'm rambling.

"Okay."

He moves around me, walking toward the garage. He knows I'll follow. I've been following him around this shop my whole life, every day after school before I was old enough to stay at home alone, and then other times I'd come to do my homework at that very counter just to see him before dinner.

My dad hasn't only been my parent, but at different stages in my life, he's also been my best friend. Still is. I just can't talk to him about everything in my life like I could when I was little. I hop off the chair and cut through the doorway before the door closes behind me.

He's already ducked his head under the hood of a burgundy Camry when I reach him again. "Hand me the ratchet over there?" I scan the toolbox, grab the rotating tool, and set it in his waiting hand. "Thanks, Pip."

"As for Sunday, okay, he can come over? Or okay, you need to think about it?"

Lifting his head out from under the shadows of the hood, he says, "Bring him over. I'll make burgers."

I smile. "Thanks, Dad. You're the best."

He looks a little embarrassed but fixes his expression quick, so he appears indifferent about the compliment instead. "Don't thank me yet and tell him to bring a side dish."

21

Lark

EIGHT FIFTY-THREE, and still no sign of Amanda. I shove the pizza into the oven, too hungry to wait any longer. Even though it would be nice to have a glass of wine when it's done cooking, if for no other reason than to settle my anxiety regarding how my friend is acting, she was in charge of buying that, so there is none.

I sit in the living room with my laptop open, taking advantage of the time by going through application checklists. I scored well on the MCAT but was surprised not to receive any early offers of admission.

I'm told by my advisor not to worry. How is that even possible? Worrying is something I get straight A's in.

My phone screen lights up with a text message. I eagerly look down to see if it's from Amanda, but I'm not disappointed that Harbor sent it. *Do you want me to come over later? Or would you rather get together tomorrow?*

Sitting here realizing I've been stood up by my best friend, I text him: *What if we stay at your place tonight?*

He replies: *What time should I pick you up?*

Anyone trying to pull a fast one over on their girlfriend wouldn't invite them to the scene of the crime. Feeling vindicated, I type: *How's ten o'clock?*

Harbor: *See you then.*

The timer on the oven goes off and I return to the kitchen. As I'm pulling the pizza out of the oven, I decide I just need to go on with my night. Amanda clearly got a better offer. I settled back in on the couch and finish one piece just as I finish one of the applications.

My finger hovers over the "submit" button. It's normal to be nervous, but this feels like my entire future hangs in the balance. Technically, it does. I've worked hard for the past three-plus years, sacrificed having a life for having one in the future. There is no backup plan for if I don't get in or get in and don't get the scholarships to cover it.

I hit the button with my shaky finger and then flop back on the couch. There are no takebacks now. It's out there.

Six more to go.

I get through two more applications and three large slices of pizza when I hear the key sliding into the lock. The front door opens. Laughter enters before Amanda and Dane walk in together, and if I'm not mistaken, she wobbles on her ankles.

Not able to get her key free from the lock, she looks up and sees me. "Damn key always getting stuck. Does this happen to you?"

"Sometimes," I reply, much quieter than her volume.

"I'll get it out," Dane says, bumping her out of the way and bending down eye level with the lock as if that will somehow help. He glances at me. "Hi, Larky."

"Hi." I close my laptop and stand, collecting my belongings.

When I move into the kitchen to wash my plate, Amanda says, "You already ate? We just got here."

Since there's no bottle in sight, I'm thinking she and Dane shared the bottle of wine. And by the looks of them, they drank more than a bottle of wine tonight. *Did she forget about me?*

"It's almost ten. I'm cleaning up." I'm too pissed to play nice like nothing happened. I scrub the plate and rinse it, all while they stumble around eating the rest of the pizza.

With a mouthful, Dane falls against the counter beside me, and asks, "Why didn't you come out tonight?"

"I wasn't invited." I reach around him and grab the towel.

"Sure you were. You're always welcome."

I dry the plate and then move to put it up. "Excuse me," I say to my roommate, not bothering to even give her the courtesy of my eyes.

She slides to the right, enough for me to open the cabinet. "It was spur of the moment," she claims. "Dane had an extra ticket to see a band down at the Bend in the Road Bar."

He adds, "Mia couldn't make it. Last-minute appointment at the salon."

I actually don't care what they did. I care that my friend didn't respect our plans. It's not worth arguing with drunks, though, so I grab my laptop and phone and go to my bedroom. "What time is your boyfriend coming over?" she asks in a mocking tone before I can close the door to block them out. "I'm surprised he's not already here."

I close the door and start packing my stuff. I'll deal with her in a little while. I shove clothes into my book bag and then grab my makeup and other toiletries from the bathroom, stuffing it in there as well. Only five minutes until Harbor's supposed to be here and I'd rather spend them waiting at the curb than inside here with the two of them.

I walk past the kitchen where they're still eating and laughing as if they didn't purposely exclude me from going with them tonight. Although Dane seems to be under the impression that my best friend invited me.

He asks, "Where ya going?"

My eyes stare from him to her, and then I reply, "To my boyfriend's apartment."

"I didn't know you had a boyfriend." He speaks louder as if I can't hear them clear as day, "Since when?"

"Since a month ago." He's not been directly rude to me or anything, so I try not to be such a smart-ass to him. "Not many do know. We're taking our time without others inserting their opinions."

I walk out the door and am about to shut it behind me, but the key is still in the lock. *Drunks.* As much as I'm hurt by her actions and words, I still don't want anything bad to happen. I dip my head back in. "The key is still out here. Make sure to take the key out of the lock."

"I understand, *mother*," she replies in an annoying tone.

I stop in my tracks, leveling her with a dagger-filled glare.

First, she knows that was a dig because she knows the story about Liz. And secondly, I don't recognize her right now. This isn't my friend. This is someone who wants to hurt me.

Why?

What happened?

What is she not telling me?

Her anger regarding my relationship makes no sense.

My heart aches from the cut of her words. I blink back tears and raise my head in a sad attempt to stop myself from crying. When I walk outside, Harbor's already waiting for me. *For me.*

This man is here for me without question just like I am for him. That's never been more apparent than it is right now. He grins, and tonight, it's not so perfect, slightly lopsided in his smirk, but it's perfect to me.

He meets me on the path and takes my bag in one hand and my hand in his other. "Good day?"

I debate if I should lay my troubles on him the minute we're together again. He's so happy that I don't want to ruin his mood. He opens the car door and puts the bag in the back. I'm not always one for silence, so he looks at me and asks, "Everything okay?"

I bite the inside of my cheek. I have so much to be happy about, including finally going to his apartment tonight. I won't let her ruin this for me. Whatever she's upset about, we'll get to the bottom of it and work it out some other time.

I'll put on a happy face because Harbor deserves nothing less. "I'm good." I slip into the car.

When he gets in, he reaches over, resting his hand on my leg. "Hungry?"

"No. I had pizza earlier."

There's a hint of nervousness hanging in the air, his gaze volleying between me and the road. "I went to the store and got a few things. So if you're hungry—"

"You didn't have to do that."

"I wanted to. I don't have people over very often."

He starts driving again, always so careful when I'm in the car. I've been on dates when they didn't even care if I wore a seat belt. But here's Harbor barely driving the speed limit when I'm with him. I'm starting to believe it's another way he shows me how he cares about me. "Why is that?"

I'm answered with a shrug while he messes with the

heater at a stop sign. But my emotions aren't fully back in check after the fight with Amanda yet, and the warm fuzzies I get from being with Harbor can't cover the insecurities that have begun to shadow my patience tonight. I'm so conflicted, also not wanting to make him feel interrogated with no escape. "I've never seen the place. I don't even know where you live."

"Yeah." The shyest smile lies on his face, and he runs his thumb over his bottom lip. "I have no good excuse other than I didn't want my secret revealed."

"You have a secret?"

Rolling his palms over the steering wheel, he begins to laugh. "I have a feeling it won't surprise you."

Not sure what to think, I ask, "What won't surprise me?"

"I'm messy." One hand goes into the air as he laughs. "I spent an hour getting it clean again. Between me rarely being home lately and Noah hanging around more than usual, it was like a fucking bomb went off in there."

To say I'm relieved is an understatement. *He's messy* . . . That's all it is. Not some life-shattering news. I start laughing, mainly at myself for overthinking this. "I can be messy sometimes, too. My dad had to learn the skill of cleaning over the years. So I get it, especially with things like school and the applications getting in the way."

"Your brother stays with you?"

"Only when he wants to get laid." His gaze shoots to me. "I probably shouldn't have revealed that, but I'd rather spend the night with you than listen to him and some girl bang all night." He slows when the light turns yellow and then stops on red at the square downtown. "Between my apartment and the main house, he goes to mine. Not that he has much choice. My parents don't approve of one-night stands."

"Do any?" I laugh.

Chuckling, he replies, "Probably not." The light turns green, and he begins to drive again but glances at me quickly.

"My dad would flip if he caught me and some guy in bed."

"Some guy," he repeats as if the words don't sit right.

The image of him alone with "some girl" doesn't sit right with me either. I reach over and rub my hand over his leg. I move away from that thought. "Are you free to come over for Sunday dinner?"

"At your dad's house?"

"Yes. He's making burgers and said you need to bring a side dish, but I can cover that."

"No way. If he wants me to bring a side dish, I'm bringing it. I'm not starting off on the wrong foot with your dad."

"There's no starting off. You've already met him. Several times."

"But this is the first time we'll be hanging out. The game will be on, right?"

"He wouldn't have it any other way. It's the sound of my childhood."

At the next street, he takes a right and then another left. I don't ride my bike in this direction, which is opposite of where I live. Our little town has been growing steadily for the last decade, but I had no idea of the revolution happening on this side of town. "Who knew they were building low rises on the other side of campus?"

"I did since we deal with the noise every day. This is it."

I jerk my gaze forward in anticipation. It's a brand-new building, all right, but unlike the modern glass eyesore I expected, this building is designed in brick with black-framed windows and architectural detailing that could fool you into thinking it's older.

Harbor pulls into the garage and drives down the row until we reach the parking spots closest to the elevator. He parks but doesn't rush to get out. He doesn't seem himself, which makes me tense. Surely, a messy apartment can't be causing this.

We walk to the elevator holding hands, my backpack slung over his shoulder. His grasp is firm, his eyes forward, tempting me to laugh at how ridiculous the buildup of this apartment has become. When I lean against him, he automatically brings his arm around me. In his arms, the world doesn't feel so heavy. Fights with friends and stress from applications all disappear when I'm with him.

When we get in the elevator, he picks the fifth floor. "The penthouse?" I ask, my gaze shifting from the buttons to him before I catch a glimpse of myself in the reflected metal of the doors. Pressing my hair down, I slide my hand lower, hoping to calm the chaos.

"My parents bought it when Loch was ready to live in an apartment. Noah will probably move in next summer when he turns twenty-one. After he graduates, they'll save it for Marina. Of course that depends if she stays to attend Beacon U. to continue the tradition or breaks the mold."

Must be nice to have options like that. I catch myself before my thoughts turn sour. I can be jealous of how life seems to have no hurdles for him or his family, but how will that leave me? Alone and feeling like I judged him the way I would never want to be judged myself for barely scraping by. I'm grateful that I have a job that pays well enough for my priority to stay focused on school. "With four kids, it was probably a wise investment."

The doors open and we walk to the end of the hall, opposite of the other front door on the floor. He opens the door and waits with his back to it while I walk in. My mouth falls open, but I can't stop staring.

Now I understand why he was keeping it a secret.

22

Harbor

"ARE YOU FUCKING SERIOUS, NOAH?"

I slam the door, but it has a soft close mechanism, so I get no satisfaction from it. Lark is still standing in the entry like she's not sure what to do. I'm not sure what to do either, except I know I'm about to kick my little brothers' ass.

Noah stands, tossing his napkin to the table and stretching his arms in front of him like he's somehow going to stop me from coming for him full speed ahead. "Slow down, bro. Let me explain."

I don't know why I even entertain the idea, but I stand in the living room ready to tear him apart. The words rush from his mouth, "Trish and I showed up and noticed you weren't around." He glances at the couch and then at me again. "One thing led to another. The food was getting cold, so we decided to do you a favor."

My anger reaches my head, which feels like it's going to explode when I see the couch cushions are not how I left them. *Little fucker.*

The blonde still sitting at the table sets her fork down but stays seated. Since she doesn't appear to have any pants on, I understand why. *Fuck.*

I just wanted it to be special. I don't care about the food. I got it in case she was hungry. I care about everything else being ruined. The long-stemmed roses are all over the coffee table and floor by the couch instead of being in the box with the bow how I left them. *At least the other box is still wrapped.*

I turn back to catch a glimpse of Lark, who seems perfectly content to stay out of the fray. I do my best to apologize silently. This is not how tonight should have been. I wanted her to have romance without being over-the-top hearts and flowers. Lark's not that girl, but I got to thinking that maybe she never wanted it because she'd never received flowers from a guy before. I'm guessing no guy has allowed her to raise the bar of what she expects out of a boyfriend.

Trish asks, "You didn't do this for our date, Noah?"

My brother kneels beside her. I hadn't noticed he was only in his boxer briefs with a T-shirt thrown over him.

You know what? *Fuck this.* I go to Lark, cup her face, and whisper, "We can go to a hotel."

Clasping her hands around my wrists, she whispers, "We don't need to spend the money."

"Money doesn't matter."

Her body bristles, though she'd lie if I asked her. With her eyes set on mine, her gaze starts to distance herself. *Fuck. Fuck. Fuck.* Money is determined to mess with us—it not mattering in my life and mattering too much in hers.

She swallows, but it's heard under the murmurs of Noah trying to make this right with Trish.

It might be too late for me to do the same with my girlfriend. Lark's eyes leave mine, stretching over my shoulder.

When her gaze returns to me, she says, "We can hang out in your room or go back to mine." She doesn't sound upset, which is a relief.

Picking up her backpack, I lead her to my room, open the door, and set her bag inside. She walks in and now I'm the one who's swallowing hard. The blinds are already open when she crosses the room and stands in front of the large window that frames downtown Beacon. It's the same view from the living room, but it's much quieter in here.

"Let me deal with my brother, and I'll be back in."

"Don't be too hard on him, Harbor. I never needed any of that."

I told her I loved her a week after meeting her. I'd never said that to another girl I was dating. But I'd also never felt so cared for before by anyone other than my family. Her love, her care was different than all the other girls. I didn't hear about it. I felt it, making me fall fast and hard for Lark.

But hearing how she cares for my family, specifically the brother who is currently on my shit list, while sacrificing her needs . . . She might have just convinced me to fuck her as requested, like she's not a virgin. After that, I'll give her the world if she'll let me.

I kiss her and then close the door behind me.

My brother and Trish are in the other bedroom. I can hear their muffled voices and the sounds of an argument. When he walks out, fully dressed, I say, "I need to speak with you privately."

"We'll do it another time, Harbor."

"No, we're going to have this out now."

Rolling his eyes, he leans into the room, and tells her he'll be a minute. I walk to the window, trying to find the only place we can have this conversation that's not between the two bedrooms. Keeping my voice down, I say, "This is fucked up, Noah, and you know it," as soon as he reaches me.

He crosses his arms over his chest, matching mine. I expect an argument, but that's not what I get. "I'm sorry." He runs a hand through his hair as if you couldn't tell we were already brothers by our eyes and hair color. Give him a year or two and we'll also be the same size in height and build, or if the fucker is lucky, he'll be taller. "I wasn't thinking about you." He turns toward the bedroom as if to make sure Trish can't hear him. Lowering his voice, he adds, "I wasn't thinking at all."

Not more than a month ago, I was the same way, so Lark might be right. I shouldn't be too hard on him. He knows he screwed up my night, and I'm certain Trish isn't too impressed with how things played out.

"I'll apologize to your girlfriend if you'd like."

"She doesn't need you to. It's squashed between us, so it's over for her." I step closer and lower my voice this time, and say, "Look, you can use the apartment, but maybe not so . . . frequently. Lark and I are going to be here more often."

"Maybe it's time I get my own."

"Let's just get through this year. I'll be going to medical school, and it will be all yours."

He nods, but then holds out his hand. "Are we good?"

I take his hand, but then pull him against me to pat his back. "We're good."

As soon as we back away from each other, he says, "The roses were a nice touch. Trish loved them."

"Trish can have them. Make something up, like you had them delivered for her. After having her night ruined, she should have something nice come of it."

"Don't worry," he says, walking back to the other room. "Something came . . . of it."

I shake my head because this kid is too much. "You're such a fucker, Noah."

"That's why the girls love me." He opens the door and disappears into the bedroom.

That's my cue to return to my girlfriend. Not sure what Trish is to him, but I'm not sure it matters much tonight.

I open the door to find her still standing at the window. She looks back at me and then returns her gaze through the glass. "I didn't know our town was so pretty at night. How have I lived here my whole life and never seen an image of it from this elevation before?"

"This building has only been around for four years or so, and there aren't any high-rises, though not for long. One is being built next door."

"Soon we won't recognize Beacon at all." She sounds impressed with the view, but not so much about the changes to our town.

"It will be so different even after medical school." I shove my hands in my pockets and stay where I am, unsure how she feels about the situation we just encountered.

She angles toward the window again. "So will we."

"Is that something you think about?"

Glancing back over her shoulder, she smiles as if she knows I'm onto her. She likes routine but has a spontaneous side that she seems oblivious to. Guess I do know her better than she thinks. "All the time."

I go to her and wrap my arms around from behind. Dipping down to kiss her neck, I then whisper, "I think about you all the time."

"What about the future?" She turns in my arms, wrapping her arms around my neck. "What happens when it's time for us to go to medical school? You don't even talk about it? I have no idea where you're applying. Should we consider applying at some of the same schools? Or this, *us*, ends when fall comes next year?"

Her beautiful green eyes are deeper in color, caught up in the forest of her thoughts. Now that I've felt her love, her affection, and caring, I'm not capable of imagining my life without her. But I can't give her an answer that will appease. I can only tell her, "I'll go where you go."

Her body eases against mine, the response seeming to suffice. "Kiss me, babe."

The night felt ruined not ten minutes ago, but light shines in her eyes, giving me another opportunity. I kiss her, our tongues caressing as our hands find purchase against each other.

We move to the bed, but for a second, I still. Having sex was the intention but after all that's happened tonight, is it special?

She does a damn good job of sexually satisfying me without the headlining act. And from how she looks after I've gone down on her or fucked her with my fingers, I'd say were even.

It was supposed to be a romantic surprise. I wanted to make love to her. Well, I always want to do that, but tonight, it was supposed to be different, better than any expectation she might have. *Is that still possible?*

The tips of her fingers trace over my temple and then trail into my hair. Holding my face in her hands, she meets my gaze, and says, "Don't overthink this. All it needs to be is you and me. That's all I want."

I look at her once more but can't find a lie in her eyes. Leaning my head against hers, I close my eyes and breathe her in. "You and me." And then I kiss her so deep that her toes curl and her knees go weak.

23

Harbor

OUR BODIES ARE a frenzy of hands and clothes, bodies bumping together as if the words themselves unleashed the ravaging. The buttons of my shirt go flying and the fabric pushed from my shoulders. Her sweatshirt is tugged from her body, sending her hair flying.

My T-shirt is yanked up as I kick off my shoes. I take over and throw it across the room. Her tits are exposed before she starts on her leggings. I stop working on my jeans to give each one a deserved licking and then suck each nipple, caressing one with my tongue and then nipping the other. A gasp has her sucking in and then she narrows her eyes. "You're going to pay for that."

"I fucking hope so."

A devilish grin spreads across her face and reaches her eyes, and then we're racing each other to see who can get naked first. Her shoes come off and then her socks. The leggings are discarded as soon as my jeans hit the floor. I let her win because I'm a gentleman like that.

She's scrambling to the top of the bed, but that's not what I had in mind. I catch hold of her ankles before she can tuck them under the covers. "Not so fast, sweetheart." I pull her back to the edge of the mattress, and then rub over the underwear that's failing to restrain my hardening dick.

Lifting her chin with my fingers, I see a flash of excitement twinkle in her eyes. My girl has a dirty side, and I'm not upset about it. I take her hand to replace mine and then cover it to stroke my length together.

Her rapt attention is on our hands moving together, her chest rising and falling in rapid succession. Moving from her chin to her lips with my other hand, I run the rough tip of my finger over her soft and supple lips. "You've got me so hard. You ready for me to make you come?"

She licks her lips. "Yes." She gulps. "I'm ready."

"Tell me where you want to come. On my mouth, my fingers, or while riding me?" I press her harder against me, already craving a release.

Standing, she lifts to get as close as she can to eye level with me. She's a good three or four inches shy of my eyes, but she's still got my full attention. Grabbing my erection, she whispers, "Why bother with an appetizer when you're starving for the main course?"

Fuck me, that's it.

I grab her ass with both hands and squeeze, provoking a delighted squeal from her. "Get your ass up on that bed."

If I thought she was frenzied before . . .

She's tucked under the covers, looking like a sweet slice of heaven. I pull my boxer briefs down and slip out and onto the bed. Crawling over her, I kiss her once and then again just because I want to, and then ask, "How badly do you want me?"

"I want you so much. I think about it all the time."

I slip under the covers beside her. "Oh yeah, all the time?"

"Constantly."

"And what do you imagine when I'm taking you?" I run my fingers along the crease at the apex of her thighs, teasing around her lower lips.

Her breathing slows and her eyelids dip down as she struggles to hold them open. "You on top of me."

I climb over, wedging her butterflied legs wider, and settle between them. "Like this?"

"Yes."

"Am I making love to you or fucking you senseless?" Biting her bottom lip, she closes her eyes, and her breath staggers. She swallows and then licks her lips. Her hands are fisting the sheets, though I'd really like them touching me. When she doesn't answer, I kiss her again, and then whisper against her lips, "Be honest with me, baby."

"Fucking me senseless."

A smirk takes over, spreading so fucking hard, but I have no intention of hurting her—physically or otherwise. I kiss the corner of her mouth and slip my fingers straight into her heated entrance. "I promise to take care of every one of your fantasies. Tonight, for your first time, we are going to take it slow. And then I'm going to give you what you want and fuck you senseless."

"We can take it slow, but can we get started already?"

I chuckle and stretch to reach for the drawer of the nightstand. "So fucking demanding." Pulling out a condom, I drop it on her stomach, then flip to my back beside her and rest my head on a pillow. Tucking my hands behind my head, I grin. "You want to start, let's go."

She doesn't hesitate, as I knew she wouldn't. Taking the condom, she mounts me, straddling my legs, and rips open the package. She rolls the condom down like a professional. With a gleam in her eyes, she waggles her brows. "I learned from the movies."

"I'll admit I was curious."

When I'm all packaged up, she looks down at my dick, the good time she was having wiped away like a clean slate. "I'm nervous."

She's been bold. She's been vocal. But she hasn't done it yet, so I've had a feeling we should slow down a bit. I reach up and touch her cheeks, sliding my hand down over her collarbone and lower. Caressing her tit, I then sit up to kiss her. "It's okay. Just tell me how you're feeling."

Nodding, she says, "Tell me what to do."

She's a movie fanatic, so I know she's seen a sex scene or two, but this isn't a recreation of the act. The two of us are bonding for the first time. I take her hips and say, "I want you to lift up and go down at your own pace."

When she lifts, I position myself at her entrance. With her palms to my chest, she begins to lower. Her mouth falls open as her body stretches to fit around me, a verbal gasp and relief expended. Her mouth widens with every inch of me she takes. Panting, she pushes until she's fully seated, and then calms her breath.

Pride taking over her languid eyes is a sight to behold, the sound of her tender moans a musical melody. "You feel amazing, baby. So good, but are you okay?" I ask, still holding her hips, guiding her as she starts to find her rhythm.

"I'm good." Touching her belly, she says, "Full."

"Is it too much?"

"No," she says, finally smiling. "You feel incredible."

I rub my thumbs over the buds to ease any discomfort

she might be feeling. It's a good distraction if she's feeling any pain. "Find what feels good."

She slowly rocks back and forth, and with her palms pressed against me, she lifts to add to her pleasure. That's my girl, taking what she wants and what she needs. "You're doing so good. You feel . . ." Concerned for her, I haven't appreciated how tight she is wrapped around me. *Hot. Wet. Her body embracing mine.* "So fucking good, baby. Keep going."

I help her pick up her pace, and when I reach between to rub her clit, she bucks and slams back down on me. "That's it." Watching her tits bounce, her head falling back with her mouth open, our bodies slapping together, and the way her body is hell-bent on strangling an orgasm from me, I grab her hips, my fingers digging into her ass to encourage her to go faster. She does, and as her body starts to shift erratically, I begin to thrust, fucking her until she rolls over and I'm on top. My name is ripped from her lips, and her wet heat overwhelms me.

I fuck her through every tremor of her body's release. I fuck her as she chants my name like a prayer rolling off her tongue. I thrust and I fuck until I fall into the abyss of my own release.

Squeezing my eyes shut, I fight to remain in the aftermath of our connection.

"Harbor?"

Her whispers drag me back to reality, and I sink my weight down on top of her. I'm depleted of energy and floating in the high of finally having sex with her, but I open my eyes and look into her glassy greens. I push her hair away from her face, and kiss each of her pink cheeks. "That was amazing."

She's smiling while her hand pushes the hair from the

sweat on my forehead. "That was better than any fantasy I've had."

I move off her, and she takes a deep breath that wasn't possible when I was on top. I look at her, never seeing her more stunning than she is right now. "I'm glad to be of service." I take her hand and kiss each finger before holding it between us.

Our breaths finally even, and our hearts stop racing. Doodling on my chest, she asks, "How long do we have to wait before round two?"

"I love you so fucking much."

Her laughter brightens the room as she fills my life with more than I could have imagined. "I love you, babe." She sneaks into the bathroom as if we're going to get in trouble. It's an en suite, so I think we're safe. I still chuckle, though.

When she comes out, she says, "That's the nicest bathroom I've ever been in."

"It's yours to use whenever you want."

"Really? You might regret that offer." She jumps on the bed and slips her legs back under the covers, and I take my turn.

"Never. You could move in tomorrow, and I wouldn't have one doubt about you being here." The words came out as if it's not a real offer, but I mean it. It's just good to gauge the waters of her thoughts before any big lifestyle changes.

She's eyeing me as I walk to the bathroom. "You have a great ass," she says before I reach the doorway.

When I turn to give her the full view, I say, "Also yours anytime you want it."

"Bathrooms and your ass on tap?" She laughs, but it's full of giddiness. "You drive a hard bargain and other hard things, but I think I want to lie in this heavenly cloud of a mattress and just enjoy tonight for a little while. Is that okay?'

"More than okay." I close the door and clean up. When I'm finished in the bathroom, I say, "It's quiet out there."

"I haven't heard a thing." Sitting up, she asks, "Do you think they heard us?"

"The man in the moon heard you."

Flopping back on the bed, she sighs in horror. "So embarrassing."

I open the door and look out. The bedroom door across the living room is ajar, but there's no sound or sign of anyone else being here. "You're safe. They've already left."

"Excellent because I've been thinking about that kitchen island since we walked in."

I've created a monster.

24

Harbor

I CLEANED the apartment once Lark fell asleep.

She was exhausted. *Just how she should be.*

I was left wide awake with my thoughts clouding my better judgment. I shouldn't want her to move in after a month of being together, but I meant what I said about her being here, sharing my space, taking up more than her fair share of the closet, and coming home to her each day.

The dishes were put in the dishwasher, the roses were collected and put back in the box, and then tossed in the garbage chute down the hall. No way was my girl getting secondhand flowers.

When she wakes, I can't give her any of the things I bought, but I'll be here with coffee and ready for a third round since she got her second round wish just over an hour ago.

It could be like this for the rest of the year. Us, together, here, alone. Breakfast after I hit the gym or go for a run, then driving, riding, or walking to school together. It will be so easy for us to combine our lives since our schedules are similar.

A life with Lark isn't so foreign, but sharing the apartment could be nice. Noah wouldn't be happy since he'd have to find another place for his hookups, but that's the least of my concerns.

I leave my boxer briefs on when I return to the room since Lark fell asleep in another pair of mine. When I climb back into bed, time is creeping well into the morning hours. I lie next to her staring up at the ceiling. She closed the window shades, which is something I never do. I never worried before. There are no other buildings high enough to get a direct view into my room. Someone would really want to spy on me and need a telescope to make out anything I'm doing.

I still find comfort in the dark with her snuggled to my side. She gravitated over as soon as I was covered. I hold her, listening to her breathe, and hope she can calm my mind.

She keeps asking me about applying to medical school like I have to lift a finger. I don't. It's already taken care of. There's power in the Westcott name. I just don't know how to tell Lark that, along with the life of privilege I've led, the road ahead is paved in gold. It is what it is.

Rolling onto her back, she rests her arm across her forehead. "Are you awake, babe?" she whispers.

"Yeah," I say, keeping my voice fitting to the hour. Moving to face her, I can see her eyes are clenched closed. I reach over and rub her stomach. "Are you okay?"

I receive a nod, and then she squints her eyes and looks at me. "No, it hurts."

I sit upright. "What hurts?"

"My body." Staring at her, I roam her body as if I can find the pain source. She manages a slight smile. "Down there, Harbor."

"Ah. *Yeah* . . . About that, I should have given you some ibuprofen before bed." I flip the covers off and hurry into the bathroom. I'm popping the bottle open when she comes in behind me wearing my discarded T-shirt.

"Can I take a bath?"

"A bath?" I ask, looking back over my shoulder like I don't understand the meaning of the word. I've never taken one here before.

"I think the hot water will help."

"Sure. Let me get it going for you." I start the water, push the stopper in, and then reach into the cabinet to grab a towel for her. "You should probably sit, or will that hurt?" She's eyeing the hard lid of the toilet like it offended her. Setting the towel on top, I add, "This will help."

She sits down slowly, and asks, "What time is it?"

"Almost two."

Resting her head on the cabinet, she yawns. "Tomorrow is going to be rough."

"Maybe we should play hooky?"

Her head pops up. "I've never played hooky in my life, Harbor. I try to be cool like you, but I just can't get there."

I chuckle and hand her two pills. "You're the coolest woman I know. I'll be right back." Walking back into the kitchen, I pour a glass of water and return with it. She takes the pills while I check the temperature of the water. I don't know about taking a bath with no bubbles. I'm not a bath guy, but I'm pretty sure that Lark will want it to be like in the movies.

Remembering my mom once gave me a bottle that I

promptly buried at the back of the cabinet, I search for it. Success. I open the lid to smell it. "Does bubble bath go bad?"

"I wouldn't think so. Let me smell."

Her eyes widen, and she grins. "*Ooh*, I love eucalyptus and mint together." Teasing the hem of my shirt on her hip, she says, "Wanna join?"

I glance at the tub. "I don't think it's big enough for both of us." Taking the bubble bath, I start pouring it in.

She jumps up and grabs the bottle. "That's a lot, Harbor. Have you never taken a bath before?"

"Not since I was little."

Cutting off the water, she turns to me after setting the bottle on the counter. "Will you take one with me?" There's no way I can say no to her, especially since I'm the reason she needs a hot bath to help soothe her body. She presses against me, rubbing my shoulders. "Please."

I exhale and look at the bath again. "Okay. I guess I get in first." I grab two towels and set them on the towel rack above the tub, and then strip off my underwear. Stepping in the hot, soapy bath, I can admit that it feels good so far. I sit down and then spread my legs as wide as I can to make room for Lark.

She slips into my arms like a missing puzzle piece finding its home. Where I'm concerned, she is. I wrap my arms around her as she sinks deeper under the water. Her moan speaks right to my dick. I already know that's going to be a problem. She needs to heal, but it's going to be so fucking hard not to have sex now that we've opened those floodgates.

I might have overdone the bubbles because they're creeping over the sides of the tub. I'll clean the mess later once I get her back in bed and she falls asleep. Though I'm starting to wonder if she's falling asleep in here.

Her head rests on my chest, her breathing slow and even, and her eyes are closed. I kiss the side of her head and lean my head against the marble surround. Closing my eyes, I see how it would be so easy to fall asleep in here, even my mind is resting. As much as I like holding her wet and naked body, it's probably best if we don't stay too long.

There's no hiding I'm hard as a rock and pressed against her ass. Sinking my hands underwater, I explore her body— her inner thighs, stomach, the curve of her hips I dig so much, and her breasts. Her body is slick with soap and sexy as fuck.

I clamp down on my lip.

I cannot fuck her.

I cannot fuck her.

I cannot push into her pu—"Babe?" She sits up just enough to turn and look at me. "Your heart is racing." The movement of her ass over my erection makes it worse, causing words to escape me and my instincts to kick in. I start rocking underneath her, seeking relief. "Harbor?"

"This is fucking torture."

Her head jerks back as fast as her body does. Already half spun around to face me, shock overtakes her features. Her lips form an O that doesn't help the situation. I grab the sides of the tub and start to get out. She asks, "Taking a bath with me?"

I freeze. "What? No. The bath is good. Maybe I'll take more of them now, especially with you."

Her eyes go to my erection since it's pointing straight at her, and then she goes, "*Ohhhh*. That kind of torture." Grabbing my wrist, she says, "Come back, babe."

Debating between jacking off in the bedroom while she

finishes or maybe getting her to finish me off in here, I make the wiser decision. I slip back into the water and lean back. Rubbing my hand over my hair, I don't care that it gets wet. I just need to get this situation handled because sleep won't happen if I'm as hard as a rock all night.

She says, "Straighten your legs."

I don't have the will to fight her request or even question it. All the energy in my body has rushed to one member of it. I straighten my legs, and she straddles me. Grabbing her hips, I stop her from settling down. "I can't. I don't have a condom and water breaks it down anyway."

"As much as I'm curious how you know that information, we don't need a condom. I'm on the pill."

Holy.

Fuck.

How did I not know this?

All it would take is to pull her down, and I could be sinking into her bliss. It would be easy to take her offer, just go slow and make love instead of fuck. And the cleanup afterward would be a breeze. We could be back in bed in twenty minutes . . . okay, closer to ten because I know I won't last this time.

But when I look at her, I'm reminded of the pain she was in. I reach up and caress the side of her neck, staring into her eyes, knowing she's only doing this to please me.

It's so tempting to let her, too.

I sit up, and say, "You need to relax, baby. I know you're sore."

"But you'll be in pain if we don't."

I shouldn't laugh, but that's funny. "It's an annoyance, an irritation, even an ache, but I'm not injured." I push up again, and this time, take a towel and step out. Drying off, I tell her, "Sit back and relax. It will help you sleep."

"If you're sure—"

"I am." I move into the bedroom to give her privacy, hoping she'll stop worrying about me, and focus on her recovery. Because once she's good to go, there's no stopping us.

25

Lark

I LOST MY VIRGINITY.

Or did Harbor take it?

Either way, I'm no longer in the V-club, and I couldn't be happier I waited to give it to him. I couldn't have chosen a better person to spend my first . . . and second time with. My patience definitely paid off. *So did his.*

My friends complain about their first times, but you won't hear any complaints from me. My temperature is rising just thinking about last night. I feel so good, even if a little sore. But all highs have their lows. The person I would typically run to share my glorious news is not someone I'm currently speaking to. And that's messing with my happiness.

I could spend the next week ignoring Amanda or even make such a stink that she wouldn't want to even be in the same apartment as me, but fighting with my best friend bums me.

I start considering being the bigger person and reaching

out to her. Just feels like I'm always the one trying to make amends while she rides her high horse off into the sunset.

Deep down, I know that's not true. It's just how I'm feeling. I asked Harbor what he thought I should do this morning when I couldn't concentrate in class. He said, "Do whatever brings you peace."

It's good advice.

I text her: *Hi, will you be home after class?*

She replies: *Only long enough to change clothes. I have to work tonight.*

Be the bigger person, Lark. Choose peace. I type: *Can we talk while you get ready?*

There's a pause, and then she responds: *Okay.*

I'll take the okay and run with it. It's not a no. It's a yes. I reply: *See you then.*

I text Harbor right after: *I'm meeting Amanda after class to talk.*

Three dots wave across the screen and then his message pops up: *Good luck and text me later.*

I reply: *I will. Love you.*

His *I love you* comes swiftly after mine as if we were typing at the same time. I love being in love with him. Now if I can only get the rest of my life in order again . . .

AMANDA'S usually scuttling between the bathroom and her bedroom, but I find her putting on makeup by the window in the kitchen.

"Hi," I say, shutting the door behind and latching the bolt.

She glances over the handheld mirror she's holding, and

says, "Hey." But then she slowly lowers it and rests it on the counter. "Can I start since I don't have much time?"

"Sure." I set my backpack on the floor and strip off my jacket to hang it by the door.

As soon as I turn around, she rushes me, wrapping her arms around my neck and hugging me to her like she's grateful for the chance. "I'm so sorry, Lark."

I drop the walls around my heart that I built on my walk home and hug her as tightly as I can. "I'm sorry, too, Amanda."

She sniffles and leans back. "Why are you sorry? You did nothing wrong."

"I'm sorry we had a fight. I'm sorry for not having our girls' nights. I'm sorry for hurting your feelings." I start to pace but stop instead of wearing out the floor. "I hate to think that I caused you pain."

"I felt like you forgot me, like I wasn't important now that you found someone to replace me, like I wasn't your best friend anymore."

Leaning against the counter in the kitchen, I stretch my legs across to the peninsula and balance with my feet anchored there. She comes in and sits opposite from me, just like old times.

I say, "You have never been forgotten, and you haven't been replaced." We reach toward each other and hold hands in the middle. We wouldn't even be having this conversation if she weren't up for it. I'm grateful she's willing to nip this in the bud as soon as possible like I am. "You're still my best friend, Amanda."

"And you're still mine. I'm sorry for acting so awful toward you. I feel terrible." Her gaze dips to our hands, and she takes a breath. When she looks back up, she says, "I was jealous. You never go out, but somehow met a rich and gorgeous guy who cherishes you."

Rich isn't a quality of Harbor's, but I have a feeling most people quantify as nothing more than his financial situation. I'm either going to get upset or let her discover how great he is, and that money has nothing to do with it. The latter sounds like the path to peace.

She asks, "What time is it?"

"Five oh five."

Her legs drop, her feet landing on the floor. She leaves the kitchen and heads into her bedroom. "I can't be late, or I'll be fired. My manager has been on a rampage recently."

I follow her but stop and lean against the doorframe. "I'm glad we talked."

"Me too," she says. "I'm sorry about the apartment as well. I take it that's where you stayed last night."

Memories of last night send delicious shivers up my spine. "Last night was . . ." I bite my lip and then smile.

"Oh my God!" Her shriek startles me. "Lark Summerlin, did you have sex?"

So excited to be able to share with her, I shake my hips. "I finally had sex with Harbor."

She slams into me so hard that my back hits the frame when she hugs me. "I can't believe it. This is the best." But then she leans back suddenly and takes hold of my upper arms. "How are you?"

I finally feel free to fully embrace the change in me. "I feel . . ." I close my eyes the memory of how he kissed the side of my hip giving me tingles, and when he made me forget my name, I was only able to remember his as I called it out repeatedly. "I'm happy."

Her smile softens as she looks at me. "I'm so happy for you."

I start to giggle again. "I'm happy for me too." I take her hand and give it a little squeeze. "I'm also happy for us, Amanda, but I don't want to be blamed if you get fired, so shake a leg. You need to get going."

"Dane's giving me a ride."

"I bet Mia loves that," I say, sarcastically.

"Actually," she starts, bending down to slip on her sneakers. "She's been nice lately. Maybe she finally believes we're not in competition with her."

Crossing my arms over my chest, I hum. "That's interesting. Wonder why?"

"I'm not even bothering to try to figure her out. I'm just enjoying hanging out with Dane again."

I move when she cuts down the hallway and grabs her purse from the peninsula. "Has he said anything about Harbor?"

She's riffling through her bag but stops as if recalling a memory. "No. I don't think he knows you're dating him. I didn't say anything because you know how he feels about people from The Pointe." Swinging her bag over her shoulder, her arms go wide.

"Yeah, that's why I haven't told him." I hug her once more.

"It's going to be a hard conversation to have." Moving toward the door, she says, "Hey, what are you getting up to this weekend? Will I see you?"

"Probably not. I have to work two events tomorrow—a ladies who brunch and kids' afternoon tea—at the country club, naturally. You?"

"I work a double tomorrow, so I'll probably come home and crash."

Tucking some hair behind my ear, I lean against the counter. "We might cross paths. I'll be back to change for dinner. We're going out with Harbor's parents. First time," I singsong the last part.

"That's a big step."

"So was sex," I say, and do a little spin. "But look at me now."

"Gorgeous, *dah-ling*," she says in her best uppity accent. Opening the door, she stops to add, "I'm happy for you, Lark."

"Thanks."

The door closes. I don't rush for my room or text Harbor. I stand there a minute and look around. I'm so glad we made up and didn't drag it out, but change is still in the air. I can feel it.

"How did it go?" Harbor takes my overnight bag and loads it into the trunk next to my backpack. I have a feeling we'll be spending more time at the apartment now that we've christened it.

"All is well again." I smile, moving around the car to the passenger's side.

"Good. I know she's important to you. I'm glad the two of you could work through it." He starts the car and shifts into drive. Reaching over, he takes hold of my hand, brings it to his mouth, and kisses it. "I have bad news. My parents need to reschedule. My dad had to leave town for the city, something about Loch and his team calling a meeting in the morning."

I'm disappointed I won't get to have dinner with his mom and dad, but I get it. Stuff comes up. "Hope everything's all right."

"I'm sure it is or my mom would have told me. She sends her apologies."

"Tell her not to worry about it."

He rests our entwined hands on my lap. "I already did, so that means it's just the two of us tomorrow night. What about watching one of your favorite movies at my place? We can order dinner in."

My weekend just got so much better.

DANE EYES me like I did something wrong. "How'd you get here?"

"Hello to you, too," I reply with an edge of irritation that he's putting his bad mood on me. I pull a tray of mini chocolate croissants from the rack and prepare them for the oven.

"That's it?" he asks, leaning across the counter. "I waited at your house for like ten minutes."

Shifting the croissants so they're all angled the same way, I keep my eyes on the task at hand. "I appreciate that, but we didn't have a plan, Dane. I'm sorry that wires got crossed. I'll make sure to text you next time I need a ride."

"Oh, that's right. You have a boyfriend now, so you don't need friends." *Low blow.*

I look at him across the metal table and then rest my hands on the cold surface to help me keep my cool. "I do need friends. My friends are important to me. Amanda and I have worked out our differences, and we're moving forward. I didn't know you had such a problem with me having a life."

"When I get blown off, I do."

"Let's be clear here. You and I haven't hung out outside of work in a long time. Might even have been when you started dating Mia, so don't come at me like I'm the sole person to blame for the downfall."

Larry pushes through the door and comes to stand beside the rack. He looks at us and then says, "Get out there and start setting up the bar. Those ladies can drink."

Dane pushes through the door with attitude, leaving Larry and me standing there alone. He asks, "You good?"

"I'm good."

"Good." He walks toward the door and adds, "T-minus twenty minutes."

"I'll be ready for whatever life throws at me."

He pulls another tray from the rack and slides it to me. "That's great, but will the croissants be ready in time?'

"They'll be on the table at exactly eleven."

"Good."

I'm starting to think that's the only word he's capable of saying today. Let's just hope today's events go off without a hitch.

26

Lark

THE CONSERVATORY IS my favorite room in the country club. It's bright and airy, especially in summer when the flowers are blooming. I've been running mad trying to keep these ladies' mimosas on an endless tap, but now I need to refill their tea glasses since the food is about to be served.

I drift from one table to the next, overhearing things that aren't meant for outsiders. Most of it I don't even catch as my thoughts are still in bed with Harbor. We didn't have time this morning, but I'm still craving the feel of him inside me —the stretch, the fullness, the deepest of connections with him. I even crave the ache that reminded me of him the next day.

Two women sit alone off to one side, the other guests at the table currently floating around like butterflies visiting their friends.

"She's having to deal with her son's antics again," says a lady in an expensive pink suit. Everyone's clothes look way out of my budget, but hers is detailed with pearls that are probably real.

The other lady is demure in nature compared to the woman seated next to her. Dressed in all black, her deep brown hair has a distinctly defined streak of silver, and her face is commanded by overly arched, thin eyebrows. She says, "She's such a sweetheart and doesn't deserve this trouble."

I top off the iced tea glasses, weaving in and out of the tables at the *Ladies Who Lunch* crowd. I'm still clueless as to what exactly this club is about. All I hear is a bunch of snip-ing-with-a-smile comments and gossip spreading faster than a wildfire in heavy winds.

I've come to expect certain behavior from a few "ladies" I recognize from other events I've worked. And a few are always polite. Even now, they're not enjoying the gossip but talk more about fashion and traveling, their kids, and the gifts their husbands bought them.

"Delta has her hands full with the youngest male West-cott." I'm drawn to the conversation when I hear Harbor's mother's name and his last name. The woman picks the glass up just before I'm going to refill it and sips the remaining tea. Normally, that would be no big deal, but the way she eyes me over the crystal makes me think she did that on purpose. I roll my eyes. If it makes her happy to have us peons waiting on her, whatever. It's not worth expending my energy on trivial things.

I also don't mind hanging around a little longer to hear the rumors they're spreading about the Westcotts. I refill her gossiping cohort's glass, slowly, as she says, "My Tiffy says he's quite the playboy on campus."

"Did I mishear somewhere that Tiffy and he briefly dated?" She finally sets her glass back down on the white-clothed table, then clears her throat and coughs to get my attention. When I look at her, she taps the rim of the crystal.

When I first started working for Larry, those kinds of behaviors used to drive me bonkers. Over time, I've realized it's not personal. It's not about me at all. It's about how they feel about themselves. They're desperate to find someone "less than" so they can sit on their DIY pedestal to look down on.

"They did." She leans in and whispers, "Very briefly. He broke her heart after a few dates."

The snootier of the two doesn't bother to whisper at all when she says, "I overheard on the tennis courts that it was a one and done." Reaching out to her friend, she consoles her. "Poor Tiff."

The other lady still appears confused. "What does one and done mean?"

Snooty poos-poos her with a wave of her hand. "I have no idea, honey, but he's trouble like his older brother if you ask me. Something I do know is that Harbor Westcott has been sneaking around with some floozy downtown."

Floozy? My head jerks back. *Did they just call me a tramp? Or worse?*

"Ech." Disgust covers both of their faces as Tiff's mom leans back and adjusts her napkin. "He'll get the deviance out of his system and settle down soon enough."

My heart starts thumping in my chest as bile rises in my throat. Feeling sick, I notice my hands shake, and my head starts to spin as fast as my thoughts. I grab the chair to keep my balance, but my hand is slapped away.

"What are you doing?" Snooty is glaring at me. "Are you going to refill my glass, or do I need to get your manager?"

Still caught up in the insults, I'd forgotten the tea pitcher in my hand. I reach forward, listening to the ice shake against the metal. As if I'm nothing, they ignore me as I begin to break down.

Tiffy's mom says, "I hear he's going to be a doctor. His past deeds won't matter once he earns his PhD and finds a nice girl from Point Estates to marry."

"I've always said boys need to sow their seeds to become men. Better now than after they're married." They nod in unison.

I fill the glass, and just as I'm pulling myself together, Snooty says, "As for the girl, hopefully he doesn't get her pregnant. I hear she's a vile creature." Leaning in again, she whispers, "Likes to make a show of their *sexual* relationship."

The other woman gasps, throwing her hand over her heart. "Poor Delta."

"We can only hope he doesn't fall in love." *Too late, bitches.* "You remember how that whole thing worked out for the Jen—"

"Sh!" They share a look, a secret exchanged.

Shaking her head, she tsks and lowers her voice even more. "Her parents were heartbroken when she fell pregnant."

"Just awful. I'll tell you, though, if they didn't have so much money, the Westcotts would be run out of The Pointe because of those boys just like they were." *Who's they?* "I bet her husband cheats."

I clip the foot of her chair with my shoe, and the pitcher rattles in my hand. But I just about catch myself before I spill any tea, unlike what they've been doing. But sometimes an opportunity presents itself, and waiting for karma takes too long. The pitcher falls from my hand, hitting the floor, and splashes from the top opening . . . right onto to the bitch's skirt.

Not expecting it to work as well as it did, I gasp this time, throwing my hand over my mouth to hide my grin. They both lurch from their seats. Tiff's mom has tea splattered over her pale pink skirt. But the other woman is covered in the dark liquid. The perfectly coiffed streak she probably spent too much time taming into place is now wild and intermingling with the darker strands. Other than their screeches, the entire room is silent and watching, but no one makes any effort to help them.

Larry runs out of the kitchen, passing Dane, who's laughing his ass off. Larry asks, "What happened? What happened, ladies?"

Brushing her hair and streak aside, the woman's nose goes straight into the air. "This girl just spilled a pitcher of tea all over me." Her daggering eyes are intense, but I wear my anger like armor protecting me.

He yells for Dane to bring towels as he tries to help with the napkins that fell from their laps. She reaches down and grabs her handbag. "This bag costs more than your business, Larry. You're going to pay for it if it's ruined."

"I'm so sorry, Mrs. Bensimone." Larry scrambles to pat it dry but also glances at me. "Don't just stand there. Help." He keeps profusely apologizing, but I can't bring myself to do it. They're awful people and don't deserve an ounce of my respect.

The worst of the two women points and starts yelling at me. "Why are you standing there like an idiot? This bag is worth more than your life."

Through the chaos of the cleanup, I look at the turquoise bag, the one that's apparently worth more than my life. I can't be around these people. Not caring a damn anymore, I walk away.

Larry says, "Where are you going? Get back here."

I walk toward Dane, who's walking, not bothering to run, with his arms full of towels. Our eyes connect, and I may be wrong, but I detect a note of respect. Just as we pass each other, under his breath, he says, "Way to stick it to 'em." After our conversation earlier, I'll take it.

Untying my apron, I then push through the service door of the conservatory. Larry says, "You're fired," but his words are cut off when the door swings back. I pull my phone from the pocket and dump the apron on an empty rack in the kitchen, never breaking my stride as I head through the service entrance to the delivery area.

Remorse doesn't hit, and neither does fear.

I have a right to be treated with respect even if I screw up. And whether I technically screwed up remains to be seen. I take a deep breath. Although the days are chilly, there's still sunshine. I soak it in and start walking. It's only a handful of miles to the edge of town. I can take the trail sandwiched between the lake and the highway and use the walk to clear my head.

Wearing tights and still heated from offense, I'm not worried about getting cold.

By the third mile, I didn't take my work shoes into consideration. They're great when you're standing around all day, but they're not made for hiking. I come to a favored spot of daredevils, and others who just like a great view. I've been to Devil's Edge a few times over the years, but I've never gotten close enough to the edge to verify if the legends are true—do the gray walls of the cliff sparkle like diamonds in the sun?

Since I'll probably never be in a boat to know, I decide to rest closer to the edge and hope to find out.

With my legs dangling over the side of a jagged cliff, I take my shoes off and rub my feet. I should be more worried about paying my bills and how I'm going to get by. But the names I was called and the gossip about the Westcotts are still spinning in my mind. I can't believe those women. They're callous at best and hate-filled at worst.

Just awful.

My phone buzzes, so I pull it from the pocket of my short skirt to see a text from Harbor: *How's the country club crowd?*

I smile and then look out over the massive lake. I can barely make out the other side, giving me a sense of my size in this world. It's good to feel the greatness of nature. I wish Harbor was here with me to experience this.

I reply: *Truth? They're horrible people.*

Harbor texts: *I already knew that.*

Texting, I take a deep breath: *I guess you do.*

I pause with my fingers over the screen. It's not that I don't want to tell him what happened or how I quit. I just worry that I'll upset him over something he doesn't need to be bothered with. But with love comes honesty, so I type: *I quit today. Larry fired me. I'm not sure. Either way, I'm no longer employed.*

My phone rings.

Grinning, I answer, "You don't have to worry, Harbor. I'm fine. Maybe it hasn't set in yet, but I'll survive." The line crackles, and I dumbly look around like I can find the source of the bad connection.

He says, "That's a big deal, baby. Are you alright?"

"I'm okay. I really am." The sun is high in the sky, just gone noon, reflecting off the top of the water.

The day is warming up nicely, and the walk probably helped to get my blood flowing. Look at me handling being unemployed in such a healthy manner. He asks, "Where are you now?"

A shift causes my hose to snag. "Dammit." The run takes off the length of my leg, and I know these tights are goners.

"Lark, where are you?"

"I'm taking a break to rest at Devil's Edge."

There's a pause and then another crackle that has me checking the screen to make sure we're still connected. Then he asks, "Why are you there?" Like the phone, his tone has a gravel to it. "How did you get there?"

It has the hairs on the back of my neck rising from the seriousness. "I walked from the country club."

"Lark, Devil's Edge has been closed for the past two years." He sounds almost breathless as he moves about. The sound of a door squeals in the background. Knowing him, he'll rush to my rescue. Since my feet hurt, I wouldn't be upset.

I look around for signs but don't see any. "No, it's not. I'm sitting right here."

"Get to the road. Now." The shock of his demand has my breath stalled in my chest. "And don't go near the cliffs. Do you hear me, Lark?"

He makes me nervous, like it's life or death. I say, "Calm down, babe," but I still gather my legs onto the rock beside me and start to push away to get up.

"I'm on my way."

Not even a crackle is heard when the phone goes silent, so I bring it down to look at the screen again. This time the call is lost. Or did he hang up on me?

Rolling my eyes, I have no idea why he's so upset. Although scoring a ride back works to my benefit. It shouldn't take him long, maybe ten minutes max. I bend down to look at the run in my tights. *Damn.* These were my best ones, too.

I stand around and then lean against a tree, but my feet

still hurt even after slipping my shoes back on. I'm sure Harbor's hitting every red light, putting him in a worse mood than he already sounded like he was in. Not that Beacon has many lights, but I almost expected him to drive Cullen-style, pulling up with a skid.

I'm a little disappointed.

I laugh as I sit down with my legs dangling over the edge again. It's far more dangerous for me to stand on the side of the road than to lie here with my arms wide and eyes closed, basking in the blue sky and warmth of the day.

It's also more enjoyable.

"Lark!" Pebbles fly toward me as he runs in my direction.

Sitting up, I smile when I see Harbor running toward me, slowing when he gets close. "Hey there," I say, but then terror fills my insides when I get a better look at his face. I look over my shoulder to make sure nothing's there because it makes no sense why he looks like he just saw a ghost.

27

Lark

"DON'T MOVE," he says, his voice as grave as his skin.

I stay where I am, too afraid to take even a step. "Why?" I ask, my voice trembling.

His gaze keeps darting between me and the edge like someone's standing there. "You're scaring me, Harbor. What is it?" With my arms wide from my sides, I slowly turn my head to look behind me again. There's nothing there. Nothing but the rocks, the lake, and the sky.

The wind picks up, causing me to wobble in the breeze. "Whoa!" I overcorrect, making it worse and sending my right leg into the air. "Oh my God, Harbor!"

"Lark!" He lunges, just as I catch my balance right on the edge. His arms come around me, holding me so tight that I can't see around him.

I grip his shirt and try to regulate my breathing because my gut tells me something's wrong. His heart is pounding, and his silence is deafening. He barely moves, but I feel his mouth against my head, his breath warm compared to the air. He kisses me, and then whispers, "Don't. Move."

I don't either except for the hair on my head when the wind blows through the strands. I don't even breathe, waiting for him to tell me what to do. We stand there too long, not taking any steps away, so I ask, "Is it safe?"

His heart is beating in overdrive, so when he doesn't answer, I slowly turn to look up at his face. His gaze is locked in a standoff he's determined to win. I follow it over the cliff to a small ledge about ten feet below and suck in a harsh breath.

Before I have time to exhale, I'm swept into his arms. He carries me to a grassy area closer to the road and sets me down amongst the wildflowers that grow there. We're still holding on to each other. His grip doesn't loosen, and neither does mine.

Anguish contorts his handsome features, making him look almost unrecognizable. I reach up to caress his face, to ease the pain that's latched itself in his eyes. Tears flood my eyes as I try to comprehend what just happened. "Harbor . . ." There's no question or nothing to say. I just need to know he's still with me.

He closes his eyes and slowly releases a long breath while tilting his face to the sky. The breath he takes comes easier. Looking back at me, he runs his hand over my cheek. "Don't scare me like that again, baby." There's no anger in his tone, just concern and a dash of something unfamiliar.

We're far enough away to keep us safe, so I grin. "I'll do my best." I'm still unsure what I saw down there . . . I know, but I don't know if I'm right thinking about it, much less asking him.

"I need you to promise you'll never come back here, not ever, Lark. Can you do that?" Holding my shoulders, he tightens his grip with each insistence. "Will you do that for me?"

I wrap my hands around his wrists, still staring into his eyes that now reflect a watery surface. "I promise."

He nods as if that's enough for him. Taking my hand, we walk to the car in silence. The quiet between us used to be something I was okay with. Now, lately, it feels different. *We* are starting to feel different. *And I don't like it.*

The wind picks up, so we hurry and hop inside the car. Harbor doesn't rush to start it, but I'm ready to get out of here. I snap my seat belt and then sink against the seat. Closing my eyes, I wish this day away. It's been horrible, and it's not even two o'clock. "Can we go?" I ask, bordering on impatience.

He starts the car and shifts into gear. As soon as he pulls onto the road, I ask, "What just happened?"

Glancing at me quickly, he replies, "You got too close."

Maybe it's the tension between us, but the words hit me wrong. "To the cliff or to you?"

Emotion is lost in his eyes as he stares ahead at the road. Answered with silence again, I punch my fists against the seat beside my legs. "I'm too close to you, Harbor?" Staring right at him, I raise my voice when there's no reaction. "Too clingy? What is it?"

He swerves the car to the left, cutting across the other lane to a picnic area a little distance from the cliffs. I hold the door to keep from banging into it. Slamming on the brakes, he shoves the gear into the park, and gets out of the car. "Fuck!" he shouts as loud as he can, storming away from me with his fisted hands punching the air at his sides. "Fuck. Fuck. Fuck. *Fuck.*"

I've never seen him so angry. Even when I pushed his buttons early on, he never got mad, not like this. I sit in the car, not sure what to do. Do I let him process as he has requested in the past, or do I force him to address the issue?

Something I've learned about Harbor is that he says he needs time, but when I've asked, he still opens up like it wasn't time he needed but someone to be there for him.

I take a deep breath and open the car door. The anger I felt that caused him to pull over has subdued compared to before, and by the time I near Harbor, it's gone altogether. His back is to me, his arms crossed over his chest. I approach, not so quietly, thinking it's never a good idea to sneak up on someone, especially someone deep in thought as he appears to be.

Stopping to where I'm even with him, and our connection stretches between us, I whisper, "Harbor." There's no obligation to respond, just my heart speaking for me.

He looks at me.

I look at him, pleading with my eyes to understand what's happening. I don't see love in his eyes. I see defeat. It's then that I realize how temporary we may be. "Harbor?" I press this time, needing to hear his voice, needing him to hold me and tell me it will be all right. I just don't think he's capable of it after what happened on the cliffs.

What did happen back there?

He had turned away briefly, but then he looks over at me. "What were you thinking?" He stalks toward me, but I don't flinch like I did at one time. Not because he told me not to but because I know he won't hurt me. "You could have slipped like you fucking did. The rocks could have given way, the wind blowing in the wrong direction, anything. Anything could have sent you over that cliff."

"But it didn't." Then the image of what I saw on the ledge below comes back to me.

"You were lucky this time."

Crossing my arms over my chest, I snap back, "Guess you're going to have to share the title."

He spits in annoyance with a half smirk sitting on his face. "You want to know why I'm called lucky?"

My expression sours, and I roll my eyes. When they meet his again, I plant a hand on my hip. "Sure, I'll bite," I say, half-sarcastically and partly aggravated. "Why are you the lucky one, Harbor?"

"Because I survived Devil's Edge when my cousin didn't."

The ledge with chipped edges as if there'd been a recent rockfall.

The white paint faded from the sun, but clearly in the shape of a body.

The smirk is knocked right off my face, and my breath punched from my belly.

He sighs, looking down and pinching the bridge of his nose. When he looks back up, he says, "You didn't do your research."

"I didn't. I put my trust in you instead of the internet." I move closer to him, risking it all since we're close to a breaking point anyway. I can't hold back, not with him, not ever. He'll either be my closest ally or biggest enemy. There will never be middle ground for us. "Do you prefer I read about it online?"

"No."

"I'm damned if I do and damned if I don't. What do you want from me, Harbor?"

His hands are no longer clenched. The life that had left his eyes has returned, but the warmth that is usually there is remorse this time. "I love you, Lark."

"I know you do, but it isn't enough. I need answers."

He closes the gap, not leaving room for us to exist in a

purgatory of our making anymore. "Ask me anything, and I'll tell you, but don't make me confess like a criminal."

Tension has escaped his muscles, leaving him in surrender. I've been pushed to my limits as well, but I still won't hurt him. Not purposely. *The paint. The rockfall. The wind.* "Lucas slipped on the rocks? Is that how he died?"

"The truth?" he asks as if the concept is foreign to him.

I know it's not, so this is bad. "That's all we have left."

His gaze slides to the side of me and then returns with a renewed mission. "He slipped. That's what all the news articles will tell you. That's what my family knows. That's what I lived through. Him slipping and hitting the ledge."

I'm lost. It can't be that simple. Horrific, *yes.* An awful tragedy that Harbor survived. *Most definitely.* But something's not right, something I'm not privy to—a look, a secret, a lie in his eyes. I just have to know what to ask.

The question dawns on me. The only one that makes sense to ask. My hands start shaking, knowing this could change everything for him. His haunting words come back to me. "Ask me anything, and I'll tell you." My heart starts racing, afraid of the answer, but I ask anyway. "How did he die, Harbor?"

"Lucas didn't slip. He jumped."

The answer is harder to hear than I expected. Sickness coats my stomach as I realize the mistake I've made with my assumption. I throw my arms around him, hugging every part of him as if I'm the glue keeping him together. "You weren't keeping it from *me.* You were protecting *him.*"

I hold this man, his giant frame squeezed in my arms. When I finally let go, I step back to rest my palms on his chest. Harbor doesn't blink, and I'm not sure he's even breathing. He's just standing there, staring at me, so I whisper, "No one else knows, do they?"

He shakes his head.

I take a deep breath and tears fill my eyes again, thinking how seeing me on that same cliff brought back the worst day of his life. "Oh, Harbor, *babe*, I'm so sorry. I wouldn't have been there had I known. I'm sorry for putting you through that again." I lean my head against his chest, hoping, praying his arms wrap around me this time. Not for my comfort but for his, so he knows I'm here. "I'm not going anywhere. I'm not leaving you. I'm here. Right here with you."

Strong arms wrap around me, and I've never felt such relief and reward equally. He kisses my head, and then says, "The knot in my chest is gone."

The lies he carried . . .

The burden he bore . . .

The secrets he swore to uphold . . .

All weighed on him, and then his aunt tortured him some more.

I kiss his chest and then under his chin. His arms don't loosen until I wiggle enough to look up again. Searching his eyes, I return to what started it all, and ask, "Why are you the lucky one?"

"Because he tried to take me down with him."

My stomach drops, the revelation almost too much to handle. I might not have ever had the chance to love this man. I lift on my toes to kiss him, and then he kisses each of my cheeks where the tears stream down. He says, "You're only allowed to cry happy tears, remember?"

"They are happy. I'm happy you're here." We embrace again, but this time when we part, our hands stay together. The winds have changed, and the temperature has suddenly dropped. I think I've had enough of the cliffs today, maybe forever. Who cares if they're gray or shine like diamonds.

They almost stole him from me. I say, "I'm exhausted. Let's go home."

"Yours or mine?"

We start walking to the car. I think about his question, and only one thing comes to mind. "Wherever you are is home to me."

28

Harbor

IT HAPPENED SO FAST.

I went from spying on Lark in class to her being the part of my heart that makes it beat. One month?

That can't be right.

A lifetime can't explain what I feel for her. We're in too deep, emotions too heavy, the weight of gold, and a thousand love stories all in one.

She moves around the kitchen, putting a dash of this and a splash of that into the large pot on the stove. Since I was banned from assisting, I've watched her cook like a professional. She said her dad taught her how to cook. The meals aren't complicated, but they're good. "It smells incredible in here."

I think she also picked up a trick or two from working in the catering business.

We could've gone out. I could've treated her to the best meal in town to celebrate the occasion—our month-i-versary, as she calls it. She didn't want that.

She wanted to stay home.

She wanted me.

I refill her glass halfway. I've already learned she doesn't like the commitment of having to finish it. This is her second half glass, and I think tonight she'll finish the job.

I sit back down on the other side of the bar with my own glass of wine. I don't drink wine much, but I wanted to drink what she was having. I texted my mom for a recommendation. I know it's a good wine, but expensive, so I asked Lark to stay in the car when I ran in to buy it.

"I'm so hungry," she says, leaning against the other side of the island from me. She takes a sip and then licks her lips. Always a good sign that she likes it. Like the little wiggle dance she does when she's enjoying her food, she's so easy to read and so adorable.

"Can I ask you more questions?" she asks like that isn't already a question.

"It seems I'm an open book for you, so go right ahead."

"Are you sure? I don't want to ruin our night."

She doesn't see how much she's helped me. Not yet. I finally feel like I can breathe again. I feel light, like I did before . . . just before. The debt of gratitude I owe her is immense. I'll spend my days thanking her any way I can. "You can't ruin our night."

With each question she asks, I answer, my soul lifted from the hell where it's been living. But then just like she always does, she gets to the heart of the matter. "Why didn't you tell anyone?"

"I did, but my aunt called me a liar. She said the police report proved her son would never do that. And before my parents had a chance to arrive at the scene, she had police officers questioning my involvement as a suspect." I take a big gulp of wine. I thought about all the stuff a million times, but saying it out loud for the second time feels unnatural. "I know what happened. The only reason I survived is because I put on more muscle than he had that summer."

She looks at me lost in thought and hesitates to speak. I can almost see the words on the end of her tongue. But she moves to the pot and stirs, appearing to debate whether to ask.

"Anything, Lark. You can ask me anything." Though I keep my eyes on the wooden spoon as it takes another spin around the pot as a distraction.

She turns the knob, and then asks, "Do you know why he did it?"

"I know he'd been troubled for a long time. At one point, he wanted help. It was something we had talked about a few times." I spin the glass by the stem, but the memories are too strong to stay buried, and the conversations, confrontations we had come flooding back. "We had a big blowup that ended up in punches being thrown. I hit him first, but it was to stop him from getting in the car. He was high as fuck and just as drunk. Lucas knew just how to get me to react."

I gulp, ready for the good times to replace all the bad memories he left me with. "Don't get me wrong. I loved him as a brother. He had a way of twisting things on me, having me take the blame, so maybe what happened after his death was part of the pattern."

It took me more than a year to realize the day at Devil's Edge was a cry for help. Before that, I'd always considered it an attack."

She comes around and rubs my back. Resting her head on my shoulder, she whispers, "What caused his anger?"

"Probably the same thing that caused mine."

"Your aunt?"

Angling to the side, I kiss her forehead and then spin

around in the chair. Settling her on my lap, I run my hand over her thigh, admiring her pretty eyes. She sees me, the real me, and shines a light on the darkest parts of my life. "Lucas and I had grown apart. He was my best friend, but I didn't recognize him anymore. Weed can be fun occasionally, but he'd moved on from that, and I just wanted off that ride."

"What changed?"

"I was fighting with family, my grades had turned to shit, and I was borderline about to be kicked out of the University. Talks were happening." I scrub over my chin and the few days of growth shadowing my jawline. "The fun times weren't so fun anymore." Her hand replaces mine, but her soft touch is soothing.

"Your family cares about you, Harbor. They wouldn't be in talks if they didn't. I don't know them well, or at all, but I've been to enough events in The Pointe to know they're special. They're not like the others."

I take her hands between mine and look into her eyes. Stardust embodies her green eyes, the romantic heart seen so clearly in the coloring. She allows me to open my heart and pour my sorrows on her lap. I've been so fucking selfish, almost letting her day slip unnoticed. "Why did you quit your job?" I ask, brushing my fingertips over the exposed skin of her shoulder.

She shifts, and as if the pot called her name, she's drawn to it. Turning the knob off, she says, "I think it's ready."

I stand and come around to get the plates out of the cabinet. "And I think you're avoiding the question."

Stopping with the spoon in her hands, she seems to think about it, and then with what she was doing. "I think our night is full already. My problems can wait for another day."

I set the plates on the island and dig through the silverware drawer, trying not to put a spotlight on the issue but hoping she'll want to share. I feel better than I have forever. I want her to feel the same.

Lark starts plating the food like she's a real chef. It looks as good as it smells, so maybe she has another career in her if medical school doesn't pan out. Placing the peas in a perfect line with deft precision, she says, "I quit because one of the ladies at the brunch said her purse was worth more than my life." Standing up, she looks proud of her creation. "Voilà," she adds like what she just said prior isn't worth a second thought.

Sliding my arm around the small of her back, I kiss her cheek. "Looks amazing. You did good, baby."

She hugs me from the side. "Thanks, babe."

Handing her a knife and fork, she starts cutting into the chicken. I like that we stand in the kitchen eating together without the formality of a dinner production. Who are we fooling? No one. We don't have to. *This is us.* Casual homebodies. Someone who knew me back in my late teens would never recognize me these days. I like who I am with her.

I take a bite and moan in pleasure. The food is even better than it looks.

She makes a mean chicken dish, but I can admit that the woman has some quirks, like her acting as if the words of that lady don't affect her. They did at the time, considering she quit a job that she not only enjoyed but also needed to pay her bills. But maybe . . . maybe it doesn't. Maybe she knows her worth and what she means to the people who matter in her life.

Since she's not sharing more of her feelings, she's left me no choice. There's only one way to find out. I stab a piece of chicken, scoring a few peas as well, and drag them through the sauce, keeping my eyes down to act casual. "What kind of purse was it—*OW!*"

I catch her fist before it leaves my arm, and her other, and pull her to me. Still holding my little MMA fighter's wrists so she can't escape, I chuckle. "That was the weakest hit. It's like a fly throwing a punch. We need to get you pumping weights—"

"Okay, all right." She rolls her eyes but starts laughing. Still shaking her head, she says, "I didn't expect to hit a wall tonight."

"Neither did I, which is why I made the joke." I'm hoping it worked and she lets her guard down, opening up to me like I did with her. I release her wrists, and she stays.

Her smile softens as do the corners of her eyes. Reaching up, she runs her fingers over my lips and then lifts to give me a kiss. But then doesn't. With her mouth only a few millimeters from mine, she whispers, "The only joke around here is that you still think you're getting dessert after that."

She pushes off me, laughing as she returns to her plate and takes a bite. She's looking pleased as she can be with herself while I'm left scanning the kitchen for this sweet treat she speaks of before I realize she's referring to eating *her* cookie later.

Oh shit, I fucked up.

And she knows it by the smug smirk on her face. Nodding, she says, "Mm-hmm. Thought that might be something you'd want."

When she swallows, she takes a sip of wine, and then says, "I quit because I don't want to be around people like that. It's a job, but it's not worth my dignity."

"I'm proud of you."

"We'll see how proud you are when I'm some floozy kicked out of her apartment for not being able to pay rent."

Her fork clashes against the ceramic and then scrapes, piercing my ears.

I say, "First of all, what's a floozy? Secondly, you could always move in here."

Her mouth falls open, but when the shock wears off, she asks, "And have your parents pay my rent? Um, that's a kind offer, Harbor, but I don't think it's wise."

"I pay the rent. That's part of the deal to live here."

After a rapid succession of blinks, she says, "But how? You don't have job."

Setting my fork and knife down, I push the plate a few inches so I can rest my palms to the counter. "I have a monthly stipend. It covers the rent and my car."

"That's some allowance."

"Stipend," I correct. "There are expectations put in place. Rules we have to follow."

"Like?"

"Like keeping a certain GPA, not getting arrested or parking tickets."

Her fork hits her plate with a clatter. "You mean doing what you're supposed to do? Follow the law, make good grades, use good judgment, exist. You're telling me you get some ridiculous amount of money each month simply for existing?"

Normally, I'd get heated by her reactions, but I understand it this time. Staying calm, I reply, "I don't expect you to understand it. I'm just explaining how it is."

Maybe it was my tone, or not hiding my privilege, but she doesn't rattle off an angry list of how life is unfair. She looks at me, straight in the eyes, and says, "It was a turquoise Hermès bag."

She could have gone in a totally different direction with her reaction. But she chose *us* instead of our differences.

Lark

FROM THE LOWEST of the lows to floating on air, I can't say today started out as the best, but it ended that way.

Harbor turns off the TV after watching, or what it looked to be judging by his face—suffering, *Pretty Woman*, and we decided to call it a night. He sends me into the bedroom while he turns out the lights and checks the locks. I always feel safe in his arms, but I really enjoy how good it feels in his space.

I keep thinking about the offer he put on the table. Could *I* move in with him after such a short time of dating? Would it feel right not to contribute to the bills? My heart sings from the possibility of having to focus only on school. As much as that would be an amazing opportunity, I can't stop thinking about what happens when this school year ends.

It's not just the living arrangement that concerns me. *What will happen to our relationship?* Although we talked about it, I worry about the impact.

I open the door and flip on the light. Standing in the doorway, I look back over my shoulder to see him turning the lamp off. "What is that?" I ask, knowing he's not going to tell me, but it's fun to try.

"A present. You don't have to wait for me. You can open it."

I get closer, but only enough to admire the blue ribbon wrapped around the white box. "Why did you get me a gift?" I ask, loud enough for him to hear me in the living room.

"Because I wanted to."

Startled because he's right behind me, I playfully elbow him in the abs. "But I don't have anything for you."

"That's not the point of a gift." He lifts me and plants me right in front of the present. "Open it. It's not that big of a deal."

"Fine." It feels weird to get a gift out of nowhere, and I wish I had something to give him in return. "If it's not a big deal, just tell me what it is." I run my finger under the ribbon because it's too pretty to mess up. It's a fancy box like I've seen in the movies—one where the ribbon comes off the top—and not how people wrap presents in real life.

Harbor sits on the bed next to the box just as I lift the lid and move the tissue aside. I'm already smiling and glance his way. "You did not."

"See? No big deal."

"It's a big deal, babe. It's a big freakin' deal, and I love it."

I pull the shirt out of the box and hold it up in front of me. I can't resist. I toss it to him and pull my own shirt off over my head. Standing there without a bra or shirt on, Harbor says, "I would have given you this sooner if I'd known I would get to see those tits."

"Tits. It's so, I don't know. Vulgar."

Shrugging, I say, "I think it's direct." He reaches forward

and squeezes both at the same time. I stand in front of him and take my gift back, slipping the shirt over my head as he kneads anyway.

"That it is." But I don't know if I stand by that the way I used to or even vocalized. He never calls them tits in a crude way, but almost reverential. And what he's doing now feels so good that I consider leaving the jersey off a little longer just to let him continue.

But I'm too excited over this gift, and the fabric comes down. I run into the bathroom to take a look. From the bedroom, he asks, "How do you like it?"

"It fits perfectly." A little baggy so I can wear a shirt underneath when it gets cold, but it has a nice cut to follow the lines of my waist. I look at myself from every angle, smiling so much my cheeks start hurting. "How do I like it?" Admiring it a little longer in the mirror, I then turn to run into the bedroom and tackle him on the bed. Straddling him with my legs, I run my fingertips over the detailing of the team's name, the blue embroidered edges even nicer than I remember. "It's the best present I've ever got."

"Really?" There's a hint of surprise in the response.

I nod eagerly. "Really. Thank you. I absolutely love it." Anchoring my hands on either side of his head, I lower myself to kiss him. "What made you buy this for me?"

"You said you'd always wanted a Yankees jersey. No real fan can be without."

I won't disagree, but I also know this is officially the most expensive item of clothing I own. By the way his hands roam my body, I can tell I have him right where I want him. Squeezing my thighs with him between them is such sweet torture as I feel him growing harder by the second. "I should have warned you, babe."

"Warned me about what?"

"You're never getting this jersey off me again."

He balks in laughter. "Wanna bet?"

"What's the wager?"

Gripping my hips, he encourages me to rock on top of him. "If I get this shirt off you, you consider my earlier offer? Seriously consider it."

I already have, but I don't say anything because getting his hopes up and then saying no could put our relationship in jeopardy. "Okay. I'll agree to that, but what happens if I win? What's my prize?"

I run my tongue over my bottom lip, letting it linger in the corner for a few seconds simply because I know it drives him wild. He's mesmerized. I love that I've learned so much about him and what turns him on.

"I'll let you take my car on a joyride. Anywhere you want to go."

I loved driving his car the one time I did. The purr of the engine alone had me feeling powerful. I wouldn't mind it. "Hmm. I didn't expect the offer to be so tempting."

"Joyriding in my car is tempting, but living with me isn't? If I were a lesser man, I'd take offense."

"But you're not." I wiggle on top of his manhood just to prove a point. Holding out my hand, I say, "You got yourself a deal, Westcott."

We shake hands on it. It's an easy bet to accept with no real commitments attached. I was already considering the offer, so I'm halfway there. I'll still play along, though, to keep the fun going.

When I kiss him again, we roll over with our legs tangled together and arms wrapped around each other. With Harbor on top, the kiss deepens. He can look at me, and my body reacts, but when he moves against me, our bodies are already making love despite the clothes that cover us.

His hands slide under the jersey, finding my breasts again and squeezing to start but then teasing my nipples with his fingertips. The thin material of my yoga pants allows me to feel every inch of hardness underneath the denim. I take a deep breath, but the sensations are too intense, and I moan, not holding back.

Here, in his apartment, we get to be us. Loud, quiet, moaning, or talking until three o'clock in the morning. No one is around to tell us we're bothering them or keeping them up. It's us, doing what feels good.

Pushing up, Harbor hovers over me. As I search his eyes, his hands roam free over my body. He slows, then asks, "How are you feeling?"

"I'm ready to feel you inside me again."

"I can make that happen." We start to kiss, but he's quick to stop. "I've been thinking about what you said in the bath. Are you still open to it?"

I tick through the many things said, but only one stands out to me. "I'm on the pill—"

"How do you feel about not using a condom?"

"I just had sex for the first time. You felt amazing to me. I imagine the connection could be even better, so I'm open to it if you are."

"I was hoping you'd say that."

Our lips press together again, but then I stop him this time. "Babe?"

"Yeah?"

"Have you . . . *did you* . . ." I'm not sure how to say this without sounding jealous.

His hand caresses my cheek, and he whispers, "I've

never had sex without using a condom." *Why does this make me feel special?*

It shouldn't be a big deal, but it is. We start kissing again, and one thing leads to another. As usual, patience has left the building. I'm working on removing his jeans, and he's already managed to get my pants halfway down my legs. But the jersey's still on.

I'm winning.

But Harbor plays dirty, dipping his hand between my thighs and heading straight to the apex of my legs. As he massages circles over my clit, I move with the sway of his hand. Until his fingers find my entrance and dip in. He slowly drags them back out and over my belly and crosses my chest. Then he brings his fingers to his mouth and sucks them in.

The daring and erotic act is such a major turn-on. I hurry to remove his jeans and then his underwear, ready to slide down on top of him again and re-capture the electricity that leaves me feeling like a livewire buzzing in bliss.

He then runs a finger wet from his mouth over my lips and kisses me as if he's tasting me for the first time. "You taste as pure as an angel, like heaven on earth."

As he spreads my legs, his movements are rough, his touch filled with desperation and determination. He squeezes the outside of my thighs and runs a finger through my lips, then even farther down to touch my ass. Kisses are erratic as our bodies search for purchase. But I can't hold on because the desire is too strong. I reach between us and angle his penis toward my entrance. He thrusts into me, forcing out a gasp, and my grip on him tightens dramatically.

"Hold on to me," he says. "This isn't going to be gentle."

I've just grasped his shoulders when he starts thrusting.

It's hard and deep, the stretching and intensity of our connection that I craved returns. "God, yes. You feel so good." I dig my nails into the shoulders and then drag them down his back. As if that was the permission he needed, he starts fucking me like he'll never get another opportunity.

I hold him and use his body as leverage meeting him blow for blow, thrust for thrust. Sweat glistens on his forehead. His eyes are closed, clenched tight. The hold on my body is strong like I'm a rag doll. I don't mind and secretly crave it. I want him to take me, to use me how he needs because I'll do the same to him to chase my release.

The fire inside has been lit, the heat starting in my belly and spreading to my limbs. I move against him, with him, taking the fullness and fucking him like he's doing to me.

As we begin to lose control, I stop chasing and start racing toward the finish line. It doesn't take much, just a scrape of his nail over my clit, to send me spiraling. "Harbor."

One name escapes my tongue, and he's there, looking into my eyes as I fall to pieces. And I know, for certain, that nothing can tear us apart.

The stars shine before the dark sets in, and my body can finally rest. I don't let go of him, though, not until he's depleted and falling into peace with me.

His body rests on top of mine, and although it's harder to breathe under his weight, my arms tighten around him, never wanting to let him go. And I have my answer. "Jersey's still on, but you've just got yourself a new roommate."

30

Lark

"Don't tell my dad, okay?"

Harbor gives me a side-eye. "I wouldn't keep it from him for long. Omissions are considered lies."

"I know. I know." I tighten and loosen my fists before dragging my palms down the jeans over my thighs. My nerves are getting the best of me, and I have no idea why. Well, I have an idea . . . six-feet, two-inches of an idea currently digging out a side dish from the back seat. Needing to busy my hands, I ask, "Do you want me to carry the dish?"

"No." He shuts the door and steps onto the path. "I want him to know that I respect him. He told me to bring a side dish, so that's what I did." We start walking together though the path is too small to fit us next to each other. He waits for me to take the lead and then follows close behind.

"Are you nervous?" I ask, wishing I wasn't. My dad's not an intimidating guy, at least not to me, but he is overly protective of me. So who knows what he has planned.

"Should I be?" How is Harbor so calm?

"I am."

"Now you're making me nervous. Have any tips for me?" I take two steps up and turn around to face him. "Stick to beer, whatever game we're watching, the food, or me. Don't go venturing into other territory. That will just end in disaster."

"What about cars? We have cars in common."

"He doesn't like to talk shop, but he likes to talk about cars, in general. Maybe you can give him a ride in yours?"

"Or maybe I just give him the keys and let him go for a drive by himself?"

"It's worth a try." I run my fingers down his plaid button-up and then tap right over his heart. "Oh, and don't mention The Pointe Estates."

He tilts his head, his eyes staring through squinted lids. "So don't mention where I grew up? Gotcha."

"It's not about you, babe. It's about Liz. It's not worth treading into those choppy waters."

"Got it. No Pointe. No estates. Beer. Food. Sports. And you."

"Hey, you made a rhyme."

He chuckles. "Let's do this. I have plans for you later."

Turning around, I shake my ass as I take the last step. "Huh. Wonder if they'll clash with the plans I have for you." I glance over my shoulder and give him a little wink.

"Fuck, I hope so."

I open the screen door and reach for the knob on the front door. "Oh yeah, don't swear in front of him."

"Really? I didn't think your dad was—"

"Her dad was what?" Dad opens the door, pulling the knob out of my hand, and instantly silencing Harbor.

Harbor holds out the food. "I brought a side dish."

My dad grumbles, looking back and forth between the white baking dish and my boyfriend, and then turns around to go inside. "Better not be Brussels sprouts."

"There's bacon in them," Harbor replies, doing his best sales job. When I look back, a bead of sweat is forming on his hairline. He looks nervous. Now I'm not the only one. "Fuck," he says under his breath. Whispering, he says, "I knew I should have gone with the mac and cheese."

I take the dish from him and go inside the house, only pausing once Harbor is in the door, so I can say. "Don't worry. He'll eat them."

The familiar sound of grumbling is heard, but this time it's Harbor, not my dad. "This is starting off great," he says sarcastically.

Wishing I could hold it back, but I can't, so I laugh. "Come on. Let's go out back."

I leave the Brussels sprouts inside the oven. It's not on, but I'm hoping to keep them warm until we're ready to eat. In the back, I get my dad and Harbor settled in the nice chairs, each with a beer. They're content watching me rather than interacting with each other, so I try to instigate a conversation that will get them talking. I say, "Harbor gave me a Yankees jersey, a real one like they sell at the stadium shop."

My dad's eyes shift to Harbor. "What's the occasion?"

"No occasion," he replies. "I knew she always wanted one, so I thought I'd surprise her." *Oh crap.*

There are two ways to take that—as defense—he got me what my dad couldn't afford. Or offense—he got her something that she's always wanted. I have no idea how my dad will take it.

Gulping the beer, my dad lowers it right after. His gaze moves from me to Harbor when he says, "That's a nice gift."

I smile, proud of him for not making it something it's not. He gets up to flip the burgers, and I get another quick look at Harbor and give him a thumbs-up. Grinning, Harbor reaches over and takes my hand. Bringing it to his mouth, he kisses my palm.

The burgers get extra attention, and my dad lingers, which makes me think he's aware of us behind him.

Harbor then stands to help oversee the grill, and my dad starts talking to him about techniques, which appears to keep them not just occupied but bonding as well. I sneak inside to give them time to talk about whatever they need to get off their chests. For my dad, it's going to be questions regarding his intentions, some about his background, and his plans for the future.

I pour a glass of tea, choosing to be the designated driver tonight because I think Harbor will need the liquid courage more than me. The glass of tea reminds me of what that lady said to me. *Gross.* What a terrible human being.

I'm also reminded that I need to tell my dad. I'd hate for him to hear it from someone else. Who knows what version they'll tell. I return to the deck and sit on a stool. Harbor sits down, but he's still laughing. "Yeah, when they traded DeLeon, they lost the soul of the team."

"That's what I keep saying," my dad says, gripping his hands in front of him as he looks up at the sky in aggravation. "Such a shitty move."

Harbor shoots me a look, furrowing his eyebrow in question. I know what he's asking. John Summerlin swears worse than any sailor. I start laughing to myself because it's entertaining to innocently tease Harbor.

He reads me too well. That furrowed brow cocked up on the right side, and he says, "Totally fucked up."

My dad doesn't even blink, but Harbor mouths to me, "Paybacks are hell."

Fortunately, I'm saved by the bell . . . or, in this case, a text, which pulls my boyfriend's attention away from the trick I played on him.

My smile disappears when I see Harbor's expression wrinkle in concern. "What is it?" I ask.

"Nothing."

His response now catches my dad's attention. "You sure?"

With both Summerlins in your business, Harbor doesn't fight it. Looking at me, he replies, "My parents asked if we were free for dinner tonight. They're unexpectedly in town right now."

"Invite them over."

My gaze whips to my dad. I stay silent, trying to understand what just happened. Did my dad just invite the Westcotts, *of Beacon Pointe*, to our house for dinner? "Dad?"

He shrugs. "I threw plenty of meat on the grill." Ew, the sound of that is not tempting at all. "Invite them over," he says to Harbor, waving his arm in the air. It's clearly an invitation gesture, but it also feels a lot like what the fuck, let's do this.

I'm not sure how many beers my dad has drunk, but this is very unlike him. He looks sober. Glancing at Harbor, he, for some reason, doesn't look worried at all.

This is a horrible plan.

And just might be our undoing.

"They're coming over," Harbor says enthusiastically.

Crap.

I bolt from the stool and run to the living room. I leave the TV on since the game has started, but I turn down the volume. I fluff the pillows on the couch and drape the throw over the back of the couch. Taking the hem of my shirt, I run it over the dusty side table and am about to starfish the coffee table to wipe it down when my dad asks, "What are you doing, Lark?"

"Straightening."

"I straightened before you came over."

"Just a few missed spots."

"Are you embarrassed?" *Direct*. Leaving no wiggle room to fib.

"I'm not embarrassed of you or the house."

He sits down in his chair and rests forward, his eyes locked on mine. "Look, Pipsqueak, it's not the Ritz-Carlton or Beacon Pointe, but it's our home, and it's almost paid off. So you can run around here like your head was cut off and try to nitpick your way into a pretty picture, but your roots will always be here with me. Sports on Sundays. Your pink room from when that used to be your favorite color. And iced tea or a cold beer on the back patio. There's nothing to be ashamed of."

"Harbor grew up in The Pointe Estates." My dad's eyes are steady on mine, no crack in expression. "I'm not telling you to upset you. I'm telling you to prepare you. His parents still live there. It might even be the biggest property in the estates."

Harbor leans against the wall that divides the kitchen and asks, "Is that a problem?"

My dad stands, walking through the kitchen, and replies, "Not for me, but you two might want to have a conversation."

When he goes out back, Harbor and I are left standing there. The silence extends between us as we stare at each other. He finally says, "I need to ask you something, Lark, and I need you to be honest with me."

"I'm always honest with you."

He nods, looking down at the can of beer in his hand. He takes a deep breath and then looks up again. I'm not sure if it's his stance and how he fits right in here, the way disappointment and sincerity flickers through his eyes, or what it is, but a sense of devastation fills me.

Harbor stays where he is, and says, "I love you, Lark. More than anything I've ever loved before and have a feeling anything from here after. That's how strong I feel about you. Do you love me the same?" *Direct.* As if he learned from the best.

"I do." No hesitation. I speak from the heart. "I love you so much. That's what I fall back on anytime I struggle with the curveball thrown that day."

He chuckles softly as he comes to me and caresses the side of my neck. Leaning forward, he kisses my forehead and then leans back to meet my eyes. "Then we'll keep jumping these hurdles together."

The sentiment is sweet, but the words make me giggle. "I think we've reached our limit for sports analogies today."

He laughs a little harder this time. "We may have reached our limits for analogies, but I know something else that I could never tire of."

"Better say me, Westcott, or you're sleeping in the spare bedroom tonight."

"Technically, it's a part of you—Ow!" I wallop him in the arm.

"You deserved that." But he's right. I need to add weights to my routine.

I'm grabbed and pulled against him. I think so he can squeeze my ass. "You do have an incredible pussy—"

"Hello, Harbor."

"Oh shit," he mutters under his breath.

I don't want to turn around, but Harbor's hands have abandoned me, so I know my worst nightmare is about to come true.

"Hi, Mom. Dad."

I suck in a breath and put on my best smile, holding my head high. When I turn around, his mom smiles at me like I'm Santa Claus and I just made her Christmas. "Hello, Lark."

Harbor goes to the screen door and pushes it open for them. "How much of that did you hear?"

"More than a mother wants to."

Then the floor opens beneath my feet and ends my misery. I wish. Nope. Harbor still holds the title for the lucky one. I'm just the floozy whose face is beet red as I meet the man who carries my soul in his hands, my boyfriend's parents. With a smile still plastered on my face, I say, "I'm so glad to see you again."

31

Harbor

AFTER THE MOUNTAIN of a speed bump we ran over when my parents heard things never intended for their ears, it's been smooth cruising ever since.

I haven't seen my parents laugh so much in a long time. They're almost, dare I say, like regular people. People with lives that don't revolve around their kids and aren't stuck in suits in stuffy offices or running fundraising events.

Cooking dinner or running us to sports practice.

I don't recognize these imposters, but I'm not upset about seeing this side of them for the first time.

John, because that's what we're calling him now, cracks open another beer can and hands it to my mom. My gaze swings to Lark as I shake my head. She laughs, I think at me, but it could be seeing my mom drink beer from a can. That's a sight I never thought I'd see, so it's something we're experiencing together.

My mom turns the design to read the front of the can. "It's been a long time since I had one of these."

"How long?" I ask, thinking I might need another if this night continues like it is. Three's probably a good stopping point on a school night, plus we have a test in our first class tomorrow. I should probably review the test material, but I have a handy-dandy sexy study buddy to help me memorize the interior biomes of human anatomy. It's a refresher since I studied that in high school. I think I'll study the anatomy of a Lark tonight instead.

My mom looks up at the stars and then at my dad. "What was that dock party we went to sophomore year? Do you remember, Port?"

"Probably not if we were drinking these that night. I think we're going to need the kids to come pick us up to take us home." He pulls out his phone along with a pair of reading glasses. "I'll call Noah. Marina can ride with us, and Noah can drive the other car home."

I chuckle because they'd rather have a newly licensed sixteen-year-old drive them home than their wild child twenty-year-old son.

Lark's dad sits forward in the patio chair, and says, "You can always crash in the back bedroom, Lark's old room."

My mom waves him off. "No. No. We can't impose like that. It's no problem for the kids to come get us. It's only twenty minutes down the road."

She doesn't catch it, but I do. John stiffens and looks away, taking another swig of beer to cover up for whatever came over him. I imagine it's what Lark warned me about— don't mention the estates.

Turning her attention to Lark, she asks, "How long have you been with Larry's Catering?"

Like father, like daughter. Visibly tensing, she turns a cup of water around in her hands. "Two years, but as of yesterday, I'm a free agent again."

John's attention is caught, and he turns it on Lark. "What does that mean?"

"I quit yesterday, so I'll be looking for another job next week. I'm just taking a breather for a few days first."

Her dad's brows pinch together, and he shifts in his seat. "How are you going to pay rent? It's coming up quick."

"I have enough saved to cover the next month." She glances at me in her discomfort of the spotlight. I reach over and offer a hand, though she knows where I stand on the matter of where she lives. She takes my hand.

"And after that? You're dipping into your savings."

Lark's posture remains unchanged with no defensive pretenses. *That's my girl.* "Don't worry, Dad," she says, "I'll find another job."

My mom says, "If you'd like me to ask around—"

"I appreciate that, but it's not necessary." Her cheeks are flushed. Embarrassed is my least favorite hue on her. Post-orgasm is a different matter altogether.

Occasionally, I've caught my mom sneaking peeks at Lark. I can tell my mom approves of her. From Lark's welcoming way of speaking to everyone as if they're the most important person in the room to her intelligence, drive, and ambition to her kindness, she's easy to love.

I've been bucking against the system for so long that it feels good to finally have peace in my life, my parents' approval, and our family getting close again.

"Why did you quit?" my attorney father asks, but his voice is calm, even sympathetic. I don't love that he asked, but I don't think Lark needs me to save her, either.

I squeeze Lark's hand, and when she looks at me, she says, "I was working a brunch at the country club yesterday."

"The Ladies Who Lunch?" my mom asks. "I was

supposed to be there, but I was in Manhattan with a school event for Marina. Now I'm sorry I missed it."

"It was ugly," Lark says and then sighs. "I'm glad you weren't there."

"Tell them why, Lark," I say, keeping my voice low, though the others can hear me. "The details are important."

I'm shot a devil's glare. My dad asked the question, but somehow, *I'm the villain?*

Looking between her dad and my mom, she replies, "I spilled tea on one of their expensive purses."

"One of them was a bitch to Lark."

"Harbor," my dad says. His tone isn't irritated but more indifferent. "You shouldn't talk about people like that."

"She shouldn't have been a bitch."

John chuckles when he says, "I never much cared for pretenses. Although I do give people the benefit of the doubt—they're having a bad day or wrecked their car, which is something I see a lot of in my shop—kindness matters. When someone is rude to service workers, acting like they're above it all, they're not good people."

Wise words.

He's gruff, like Lark said, but he's honest, and you get what you get with him. I like that.

"It's not only how she acted," I start, trying to coax her into revealing the details. Tapping the toe of my shoe against the side of hers, I say, "Tell them what she said to you."

I can only imagine that she's hesitant to say bad things about anyone in my parents' social group, but I don't mind being the bad guy. "The lady told Lark that her turquoise bag was worth more than Lark's life."

"What?" My mom gasps. "That's horrible."

"That's what *I* think," Lark says. "Who would say that to

another person? To another human, much less someone serving you. It was an expensive bag, but do I mean so little to her that she values that more than a life?"

Leaning forward, John's eyes are wide. "No offense to our guests, but The Pointe is full of assholes."

Dad taps his can against John's drink. "Well said, John."

"It was a turquoise bag?" Mom asks.

Lark angles toward her and replies, "An *Hermès* bag. I recognize it from *Sex and the City*. They had a whole episode about the bag."

My mom stands and walks to the end of the deck, looking out over the yard. Port gets up and goes to her. "What is it?"

She rubs her hands over her arms like she's cold. "Betsy owns an Hermès. Turquoise specifically. She bought it on a trip a group of us took to London." A mischievous grin settles on her face, making me think there's more to the story. But then her expression sours. "She always makes a scene over that purse, once even demanding it have a seat in a sold-out event. Laila ended up standing the rest of the night just to shut Betsy up." The memory wrinkles my mom's face, but then she asks, "You spilled tea on it?"

When laughter bubbles up, my mom clamps her hand over her mouth. "I'm so sorry. I know this isn't a laughing matter. What she said to you was awful. I'm still shocked someone could say such horrid things to another person, but honestly, they're just not good people." My mom says the last part almost sheepishly as if she's done something wrong. Her better nature makes her feel guilty. She doesn't need that relationship dragging her down.

Dad looks at Lark again, his features tightening. "It's a shame you had to deal with that, but it doesn't surprise me to hear Betsy's involvement."

If the Bensimones try to fuck with my girl. *Not going to fucking happen.*

"They're not good people," he repeats after my mom. I think the beer is kicking in, but I still support my dad's honesty.

"That's the last straw with them."

John says, "This night took a turn I didn't see coming." He takes a swig from his can. "Nothing like betrayal to set things in motion."

We're all just staring at him, not only unsure of what he's referring to but also, I'm hoping he continues and gets the dirt out on the table. Lark's still staring at him when his eyes meet hers. I'm not sure what they exchange at that moment. Maybe it's something they've developed, a silent form of communication that only they share, but Lark suddenly says, "They were saying terrible things about your family. Mrs. Bensimone and the other lady." And then she downs her water.

The three of us remain silent, unsure how to comprehend what she just said, but John sits forward, resting his arms on his legs. "There's always more to the story."

I roll the admission around my mind to connect the dots. *"Terrible things about your family."* Her words finally make sense. "You dumped tea on her bag because of what she was saying about me."

"I dumped tea on *her* because of what she was saying about the Westcott family. The bag was just collateral damage."

Silence encircles us again until my mom says, "I don't think I want to know what was said, but . . ." She moves to sit by Lark. "She's always been a jealous bitch."

"Mom," I say, shocked but holy shit, that was awesome.

"Sorry, it slipped" She shrugs. "I'd like to thank you. You

don't owe my family anything, but knowing that someone stood up for us . . . Thank you."

"It's really not a—"

"It is," I say before she has a chance to undermine the good she's done. "You stood up for what was right when you had something to lose."

"It's only a loss if it meant something to you. It was a job. I can find another."

Rubbing Lark's arm, she adds, "I'd like to help however I can." My mom's a fixer. It's hard for her to sit and do nothing when there's an injustice. "I could call Larry—"

"No, really. Thank you, but I think my catering days are over. I enjoy cooking occasionally, but I don't love to work with food every day."

John stands, and I have a feeling the party will be over soon. "I've tried to get Lark to come work at the shop for years. I pay a fair wage, but it's always been something about working with her pops. Yada yada."

My mom asks, "Have you ever been into cars like your dad?"

She says, "I can usually get within the realm of make and model but forget it when it comes to engines or anything else. I was always stuck at the shop as a kid. I hung out by choice in middle school. It was the only way to really spend time with my dad. He worked all the time to make ends meet."

Laughter lightens the mood, and my mom singsongs, "Sounds like someone I know." My dad shrugs it off. Standing up, my mom dusts off her pants. "Well, if nothing else comes from this, and let's hope it lies where it landed, it's fair to say the Bensimones and Westcotts are going their separate ways."

"Thank fuck," I add with a humorless chuckle.

Shooting me a look that would crumple a weaker man, she waits for it. "Sorry." *And crumple me, apparently.*

Lark stands. "I'm getting more water. Does anyone else need anything?"

"I'll go with you," my mom says. "I think it's almost time for us to go anyway." They walk into the kitchen, but with the door open, I catch some of their conversation when it wafts outside. "Lovely night . . ."

"I'd love to have lunch when you have time . . ."

". . . Delicious burgers."

"Harbor says wonderful things about you . . ."

". . . I like that." Lark's smile is genuine, and her sincerity felt in all she does.

I love her—*unexpectedly and unabashedly.*

That my parents adore her means the world. It also means it might be easier when the time comes to tell them we're moving in together.

A sense of peace washes through me, and I finally feel settled in my skin. I've gotten past my reputation while building on the positive changes I've made. I would never use my girlfriend for my own benefit, but I can't stop thinking that Lark Summerlin might be my saving grace.

Holding up his phone, my dad announces, "The kids are here."

We all wander to the front of the house, not rushing out the door but lingering in the living room. My mom says, "What a spontaneous and entertaining night." She turns to John. "Thank you for having us in your home. It's lovely, and so were the burgers and beer. We had a great time."

I don't think John's used to getting that kind of gushing review, but he takes after his daughter when too much attention is paid to him. "It's nothing."

While Dad and John start talking about the shop and

him stopping by to check out the cars, my mom pulls Lark aside, and says, "It is such a pleasure to finally spend time with you. We'd love to have you and Harbor to our home the next time Loch is in town."

"I'd like that."

"Good, then it's settled. I'll send Harbor dates." Opening her arms, she and Lark embrace. Sometimes I worry that life is too good, that the bad has a place in my happiness. This is one of those times. Other than my siblings, everyone I care about and everyone who loves me is here in this room. And now they're always tied together as well.

Everyone wraps up their conversations and heads for the door, except my mom and me. I hug her, and say, "It was a good night."

She replies, "It was a good night. And Lark is so lovely. I'm happy for you, Harbor."

When I look over my shoulder at Lark, our gazes catch, and she smiles. It's not big or proud or even shy. It's delicate as if she's only smiling for me. "She really is. I'm a lucky guy."

"You are." My mom pats my cheek. "Take care of yourself, son. Love you."

"I love you, Mom."

My dad's arm comes around her back, and they move to the door. Mom stops, and says, "Oh, and the Brussels sprouts were delicious." *Polar opposite of John.*

I burst out laughing, knowing he wasn't happy with the side dish. "It's my mom's recipe." She smiles, but I hear John grumble about the sprouts.

Lark pats his back. "I'm proud of you for eating your vegetables, Dad. And you survived. Double win." *Then she cracks up.*

I've already mentally noted: *Don't make Brussels sprouts again.*

After we get my mom and dad on the road, we say goodbye to John and get in the car. That Lark's so sexy in the driver's seat is the only consolation prize for being a passenger in my own vehicle.

Snug in the driver's seat of my car, she rests back with the engine running and rolls her gaze to me. "Let's go home." She doesn't realize that it makes my heart clench and that all I hear is "let's go, home," as if, to her, the word home itself is my name.

These days, I've found my pride and joy might be more invested in the woman behind the wheel rather than the vehicle.

"I had a good time." She looks my way, but her gaze quickly returns to the road ahead. Silent questions darken her eyes as she pulls away from the curb. Her fingers tightening around the wheel whiten her knuckles, and her body somehow looks even smaller as if she's letting the voices inside her head win. "The Bensimones are a powerful family." Glancing at me, she asks, "Do I need to worry about repercussions aimed at my father or his shop?"

"I think they're safe."

"What about me?" Her voice is quiet, the sound of the road under the tires giving her solid competition.

I don't want to worry her since nothing may come of it, but there's an inkling of fear clawing toward the surface of my personal concern for her safety. I don't think they'd hurt her physically, but I'm not sure about emotional revenge. They tried to do me in. Reaching over, I hold her hand. "We're honest with each other, Lark." *Not a question.* Just stating facts.

"We are."

"So I won't lie to you about this. Everyone knows everyone's business in Beacon's Pointe. There's no escaping your past, and mistakes are used like weapons against you. I've learned this firsthand."

Her hand leaves my arm, and I instantly miss the connection and heat of her touch. She whispers, "There's no room for forgiveness?" She's been spared from these types of harsh realities. I'd love to have her hold on to her naïveté longer, but I don't think it's possible when dealing with these types of people.

"Stay out of the line of fire, and they'll find a new enemy." I bring her hand to my mouth and kiss it. "But whatever happens, I will also always fight for you, baby."

32

Lark

I'VE HEARD you can't have joy without having pain and that the two are irrevocably entwined. I never believed in that theory . . . until I met Harbor.

Joy and pain.

Harbor and me.

Forever intertwined.

Over the past two months, quiet moves have been made behind the scenes for us to live together. Not that I think Amanda is unaware. She'd have to be oblivious at this point. But we haven't said anything out loud.

I've made an effort to be in my apartment on the afternoons when I know she won't be rushing off to work, and we pick a night each week to spend together. Once I go to bed, secretly, it's torture not getting on my bike to ride home to Harbor.

But I stay to be a good friend so Amanda knows our friendship didn't end when I fell in love. Just as it didn't over the years during the fifty times she did. I don't say that to her, though. No use drudging up the past. I'm her best friend and stood by each time with open arms when those short-lived romances ended.

At just three months with Harbor, she could claim that I'm not in a better position than she was when they broke her heart. *She'd be wrong.* I may have found love when I wasn't even looking, but Harbor and I have built a foundation that only grows stronger with every hurdle we jump and day that passes.

But it's not a competition, so I can't imagine her not being thrilled for me.

I curl my legs under me on the couch and take a sip of wine. We've seen *You've Got Mail* a million times, but it never gets old. Since it's one of her favorites, I thought it would be great to use as a buffer for what I perceive she'll think is bad news.

She glances at me and then does a double take. "What?"

"I need to tell you something."

"You're pregnant."

My head tweaks on my neck. I didn't expect her to say that. "Why did you state that like it's a fact?"

"You're not pregnant?"

I roll my eyes and then narrow them. "So when it comes to me, the assumption is it's more shocking to not be pregnant?"

"Pretty much," she says, nodding profusely. "Dane even has a bet on it."

"I'm going to need more wine for this." I finish the glass and get up for a refill. I pull the bottle from the fridge. "Why are you two betting on me?"

"Well . . ." She hems, her eyes returning to the TV. Leaning forward, she pauses the movie, and then she haws before angling to face me. "Want to know the truth?"

That has to be one of the most annoying questions ever. "Why do people ask that? Who's telling others to lie to them?"

"I do. For instance, when I'm in a crowded bathroom and I'm feeling good, but I need a compliment to boost my courage before approaching some guy I think is cute, I'll ask how I look and tell them to lie to me." Apparently, this is common knowledge by how she speaks with such authority. "Drunk women huddled in the bathroom are the best boost a girl can get."

How did this conversation get so far off the rails? "Indeed, it's a very supportive community, but let's loop back to us. You know I'm on the pill so—"

"Accidents happen." She shrugs.

"Okay, sure. While that might be true, why is Dane betting against me?"

She kicks her feet up on the coffee table like our therapy session has begun. I'm just not sure who the patient is in the scenario. "Let's talk about why Dane's thinking you're pregnant, or soon to be," she says, eyeing me sideways, "is considered betting against you. Maybe he's impressed you scored a rich Pointe kid."

"For someone earning her minor in psychology, you sure do treat it like it's your major."

"In practicals, I've discovered that I'm really good at it. And I enjoy analyzing people. Tonight, you're the lucky one." *Lucky one . . .* I can't help but think of Harbor.

I fill the glass to the top because no half-full glasses for me tonight. "I don't know what to do with you."

"It's not me you have to worry about. It's the baby."

"Oh my God," I scoff and take large gulps of wine, but then I realize something. "See? I'm drinking, so obviously, I'm not pregnant."

"In some countries, wine is culturally accept—"

"I'm not pregnant, and I'm moving in with Harbor," I say, the words rushing out to end this loop of absurdity we're caught in. *And that ended it all right.*

She sets her glass on the coffee table and stands. "You're moving out?"

My throat thickens, making it harder to speak. "I, um," I say, gulping. "I haven't found a job, and our lease is up next month."

"You're moving out on me?"

Why'd she say it like that? My heart starts thumping, knowing hurting her is not my intention. "Well . . ." I say, starting slowly. "The lease is up—"

"You already said that, Lark." She comes to the other side of the peninsula. "You and Harbor are that serious?"

The question takes me aback. "Of course, we're that serious."

"But it's your first real relationship?"

"I've dated guys, Amanda. You act like I haven't. Because I didn't sleep my way through Beacon doesn't mean I'm naïve."

She laughs, but no humor is found in her eyes. "Is that what you think I've done?"

"No, it's an example of experiences, a comparison of what the expectation is for one against the other—"

"Stop it! Stop being book smart and shit. I may have slept with a few guys, but at least I didn't fall for their lies."

Lies?

I take an exasperated breath and slowly exhale. "Is this what we're doing? You're going to make up stuff about Harbor to put doubts in my head? For what? To keep me living here a few more months?" My arm flies up from my side. "I leave next summer for med school."

"*If* you get a scholarship."

I'm left speechless.

If. *If* . . . She says it like I've forgotten the deal, like I'm suddenly living in la-la land because I'm with Harbor. I swallow the hurt, and reply, "Yes. *If* I get a scholarship. Where do *you* stand with that? Hoping I don't so I can live here with you for however many years, or . . .?"

"Don't be ridiculous, Lark. You know I want you to get what you want."

"That's an odd way of saying I believe in you." I clear my throat and rub my lips together in thought. I'm lost on which direction to take this conversation. I decide I can't leave what she said unaddressed. "By trying to sabotage my relationship with Harbor by inferring he's being dishonest with me will only push me away from you. I don't want that. Please."

She pushes off the countertop and retrieves her phone from the table. Her fingers fly furiously across the screen, and then she tosses it to the couch.

Trying to keep my cool, I ask, "What are you doing?"

She shrugs and shoots her nose into the air. "Dane will be over in a minute."

"Why? He has nothing to do with this."

"Because you have Harbor to talk to, and I have Dane."

"I'm sure that goes over really well with Mia."

"It does, actually. We've become friends."

A shiver of betrayal runs up my spine. "Friends?" I ask, wide-eyed. "She called us whores because she couldn't grasp the concept that guys and girls can be friends without fucking."

Crossing her arms over her chest, she says, "Guess she figured it out."

Frustrated, I rub my brow. When I finally look up again,

I say, "I don't like fighting with you." Returning to the living room, I try to temper my emotions. "Forget about Dane and Mia. Let's not fight. Let's talk, just the two of us." We sit back in our respective spots on the sofa, but Amanda stares at the TV. The movie is paused on one of her favorite scenes. It's one of mine, too. I say, "I wasn't going to be able to commit to another lease because of med school."

"You could have signed a six-month lease. That would have given me more time to figure out what I'm doing after graduation."

"I could have. That was one option we've discussed in the past. The other was me moving home to save money before I leave for med school. It's been up in the air for more than a year. I'm just leaving a little sooner, but so you know, I'll still pay my share through the end of this lease."

With her arms crossed so tightly to her chest and her expression pinched, she appears to be an impenetrable fortress refusing to even listen. If I can't get through to her, explain my side, or come to an agreement, this is a waste of time. "Are you going to say anything?"

"I'm not sure what to say anymore. I miss the girl you used to be. You have no loyalty now." Her words slap me across the face, leaving me stunned. She pushes off the couch and walks down the hall, slamming her door behind her.

I sit there for a few seconds, not moving and unable to figure out what went wrong. I knew this wouldn't make her happy, but she was getting a paid apartment to herself. Our nights to hang out were still going to continue, but I guess I didn't even get the chance to tell her that.

I take my phone and text Harbor: *Can you pick me up?*

I won't stay here tonight. I'll walk if I must. I don't care how cold it is outside. I get up and go into my bedroom to take a mental picture of my stuff. That way, I can move forward and start planning what to do with all of it.

Harbor's text pops up: *Be right over.*

Some of my stuff will return to my dad's, and some I'll take with me to Harbor's . . . to *our* apartment. I've come to terms with the opportunity of saving money. He's convinced me that I don't owe him anything other than being his girlfriend, and even then, there aren't expectations attached to the living situation. I can get a job and pay half or take the money and put it into savings for next year.

"Hey, guys," Dane calls from the front door. I hear it close behind him and his footsteps coming down the short hall.

I'm folding clothes on the bed, a bunch of freshly washed but wrinkled T-shirts I forgot to get to the last time I was here when I say, "Hey, I'm in here."

He looks in, his eyes scanning the room. "Hear there's trouble over here."

"No trouble in here, but you might want to check on Amanda."

Holding up his phone, he replies, "She's been texting me." He leans against the wall just outside my door as if he's going to be there for a while. "Want to tell me your side?"

"I'm moving out." Keeping my eyes on the pile in front of me feels like I'm avoiding this conversation, but at this point, we're down to the facts.

"Because of a fight?"

"No. Because I'm ready to take the next step with my boyfriend."

"See? I think that's where the confusion starts. No offense, Lark," he says, drawing my eyes to him. "But you're thinking about you and acting on what you want. She's thinking about not only being left behind by you but where this leaves her in the long run."

I stop with a shirt in my hands, his words getting through my annoyance. "That actually makes a lot of sense."

His shoulders pop, and a smugness comes over him. "I don't have the fancy degrees like you two, but it's basic human psychology. Everyone is out for themselves."

I roll my eyes and start folding again. "I'm not out for myself. At the same time, I'm allowed to be happy. I'm allowed to grow up and move out. We weren't going to live together forever."

The creak of Amanda's door has me looking up at the hallway again. She says, "I thought we'd at least finish our senior year together. That doesn't sound so off-the-wall to me."

I can't blame her for assuming we'd continue living together. I honestly didn't know what I was going to do, but putting myself in her shoes, she's not leaving Beacon right after graduation. She doesn't know what she wants to do with the rest of her life.

I do.

Maybe some of these conversations never got below the surface because of assumptions, or maybe they were avoided, but neither of us can say that this wasn't coming. Moving in with Harbor might not have been on the bingo card, but I was always going to be leaving next summer.

Does it matter? *No.* None of it does now and won't get us closer to healing. I need to stop arguing and just move forward. I say, "It's not off-the-wall."

Dane backs up in the cramped space. "Wait a minute? You're moving *now*?"

I'd love to share my excitement and my nerves about this huge life move, but I'm thinking this isn't the time for that.

With the sound of his tone, it feels like they're doubling down on her original take. "I am. I'm moving in with my boyfriend."

"The mysterious rich kid I never get to meet?"

I reply, "Well, he's coming over, so you'll finally get to meet him." Amanda doesn't even blink at the news I'm leaving. She'll probably enjoy the reprieve.

"He better hurry because Mia's waiting in the truck." He says, "Come out here."

I pad into the living room behind Amanda. Dane stands by the door with his hand on the knob and looks at me. "You dropped a bomb on your friend and expect her not to be blown to pieces." Turning to Amanda, he adds, "The girl is in love. Maybe it will work out, or maybe it won't, but as friends, you'll be there for her, just like she's always there for you."

She's quick to say, "But—"

"No buts about it. The rich are all the same." He looks back at me now. "I hate to say it, but when you can have anything you want, what you have isn't so interesting. You need to be careful, Lark." Wrapping his arm around Amanda's shoulders, he keeps his gaze on me. "But if you aren't, we'll be here for you." Squeezing her, he adds, "Right, Amanda?"

She nods with the smallest of smiles on her face. "Right."

Okay, they're pulling on my heartstrings. "This is new for me, too. Please understand that I love him, and this is something I want to do."

"When I'm the voice of reason, you know we've hit the bottom of the barrel," he says. "If you love him, you should do it. Mia's going to be pissed if I take much longer, so make up and put the petty shit behind you."

Amanda looks at me at the same time I look at her. She's silent, but I can see remorse creeping into her eyes. I reach out and take her hand. "I'm sorry for not talking about this sooner and giving you more of a heads-up."

"Why did you wait?"

"Honestly, it was fun to dream with him in the beginning, but I needed to work some things out and wanted more time with him to make sure." That sounds bad and not what I mean at all. "Not that I have doubts about him. I doubted myself to know what was best for me and felt guilty for not renewing the lease with you. I was holding myself back."

"I get that, Lark. And it was bound to happen sooner or later, but I just thought I would be the one moving out on you."

Waffling my head, I say, "So did I, but maybe it's too soon to joke about it."

"I'm sorry." She wraps her arms around me. "Can we still have our weekly get-togethers?"

Wrapping my arms around her, I say, "I wouldn't have it any other way."

"That's my girls," Dane claims, grinning like a proud papa.

I slip on my boots, knowing Harbor will be here soon.

"Actually," Amanda says, knocking into him as she passes. "We're not your girls. Your girl is out in the truck waiting for you."

"Shit, that's right."

I grab my jacket and put it on. "Harbor is probably out there as well." When I reach for my scarf, I notice Dane's jovial nature vanishes and his eyes level on me.

"Harbor?" he spits.

"My boyfriend. You'll get to meet him on the way out."

I grab my phone and wallet, tucking them both into my pocket. With puppy eyes, I ask Amanda, "Do you mind cleaning up this week? I'll clean up next week, I promise."

Amanda moves toward the coffee table, and says, "No problem. I think I owe you a few anyway." She carries the plates into the kitchen. "And for the record, it's a shock to the system to me to hear the news, but I should have seen it coming. You guys are great together."

"Harbor Westcott from The Pointe?" Dane's still standing where we left him, but his entire body vibrates with anger.

Now I'm confused. And worried. I wrap my scarf around my neck, and ask, "You know Harbor?"

Anger turns his neck red, the coloring crawling upward. "I know him."

"What's wrong?" My phone buzzes in my pocket, so I pull it back out.

Just as I answer the call, Harbor says, "I'm here."

As if someone shot a starting pistol, Dane swings open the door and makes a run for the front. "I'm gonna fucking kill him."

33

Harbor

PARKED behind a truck I don't recognize, I get out of my car and head to the passenger side to wait for Lark. It's dark, but I can make out the silhouette of a woman sitting inside the rumbling old truck. The exhaust, which can't pass any state inspection, is about to kill me, so I walk up the slick path and call Lark to check on her. As soon as she picks up, I say, "I'm here."

The sounds of crashing causes me to duck until I realize it's inside the house. I run forward just as the main door flies open, and a man slips on the wet path.

I yell, "What the fuck?" moving out of his way.

"Motherfucker," he shouts, catching his balance. When he looks up, his rage is set on me. Unlike the truck, I know exactly who he is. Dane. "I told you to stay away from her."

Screaming pulls me toward the sound. I know Lark's voice and hear the terror. I run to get her, to protect her, to—
A locomotive slams into me from the side, taking me down. My eyes close on impact as I hit the ground. The mind plays

tricks when the body feels pain. My adrenaline kicks in before the pieces of what caused the impact come together. When the image is clear, I only see one thing—Dane.

My instincts have me shoving the weight of his body off me, rolling over, and throwing punches before my vision clears. When it does, my eyes lock on the target and my arms keep swinging. "Fucking asshole."

I'm grabbed from behind, my girl's voice filling my ears. "Please. Harbor. *Harbor.* Stop!" Pulling me, she doesn't make much headway. I punch the fucker in the face once more, busting something since he's now bleeding. "Harbor!"

I make the mistake of reacting to her calling my name and find myself on the receiving end of a hard-hitting uppercut.

The world slows as I fall backward, but when the darkness arrives to pummel me, images of Lucas come back. The fights we would get into for fun, the laughs we had though our faces hurt from being punched, and the fall . . . I land on my back, which forces my breath to halt in my chest.

The pain blunts in the cold air when I'm kicked in the side. Refusing to take another hit, I jump to my knees and then to my feet right after. If I've learned only one thing from my cousin, it was to never let them take you down with them.

Seeing Dane standing next to my heart as if he'll use her to shield himself, I'm sent into a rage and charge at him. I shove him so fucking hard that he flies before landing on his ass and skids across the soaking grass.

Lark flanks my side, grabbing hold of my arm. "Are you okay?" she asks, shifting in front of me. "Harbor?"

Still staring at Dane, I can't seem to figure out what started the fight.

She grabs my jaw, trying to force me to look at her. "Harbor?" Finally giving in to the demand, I briefly glance down but then look over her head as the girl from the truck runs to him.

Amanda stands in the middle, and asks, "What happened?"

Dane is on his feet, wiping his bloody mouth on his shirt. "*Mother* fuck." He stares at me and then stabs the air with his finger. "I told you to stay away from her. You just couldn't fucking listen, could you? You Pointe kids think you own everything, like you come slum it downtown and take a piss all over us, use our girls, and then toss them aside when you're bored."

"What the fuck are you talking about, Dane? I'm not using anyone, especially not Lark." My adrenaline continues to course through me. I shake my right fist, hoping to release some of it before it eats me alive.

Lark spins around, pressing her hands to my legs behind her. "What do you mean you told him I'm off-limits? There's so much wrong with that, Dane, that I almost don't know where to begin." She crosses her arms over her chest, shaking her head.

He's sniffling, still licking his wounds, like a cat dragging its paw across his sleeve. The girl with him shouts something about me being the asshole and my girlfriend a whore, but Lark's not fazed by her. She makes no move to give her the time of day.

Since Dane doesn't give her the courtesy of a response, Lark says, "You don't get to decide who I date. I know you act like my brother and have been there for me over the years, but I am a grown woman, so you need to back off."

His eyes pivot from mine to hers. "You're making a big fucking mistake." Patting his chest, he stares her down. "He's just like his cousin, Lark. I don't want you to find out the hard way. He's going to break your heart . . . Save yourself the trouble."

"It's *my* heart. That's the part you're forgetting. I appreciate the words of warning, but I know Harbor so much better than you do."

Dane says, "He'll prove me right one day. You'll see."

"Harbor has nothing to prove to you," she snaps. "He's already proven everything he needs to me."

"Talk to Terry," Dane says. "Talk to Amanda. She was there. She's your best friend. Would she lie to you? *No.* The rich pricks aren't strangers to our parties—"

"The parties that you told me I couldn't go to." Lark huffs.

"Yeah, those fucking parties because guys like him were cruising through to look for their next victims. Smoking our weed, stealing our booze."

Okay, that's it, fucker. "That's e-fucking-nough," I say. "I never used anyone, and there are no victims." I move forward, not scared to fight him until he tells the truth. Lark presses her body to me, fisting my coat as if I'll lunge at him if she doesn't try to stop me. "And don't talk about my cousin." Anger builds inside me, tensing me, so I get closer, ready to burn through my emotions with each punch to his face.

I hadn't noticed Lark moving with me as if she's attached. "He's not worth it," she says. "None of this is. Why are we even fighting?"

He says, "Their motives will always outwit your good intentions."

Sighing even louder, my girl's lost her patience. "All you are is one good quote. This isn't about the parties or your drugs. This is about you hating him for no other reason than his family is rich."

The girl with Dane smacks her gum, and then asks, "How rich?"

Losing it, Lark pushes off me and stomps to the path that divides us. "Mia, why are you with Dane?"

"He's supposed to be taking me to dinner." She rubs her stomach. "The baby and I are hungry."

Amanda throws her arms in the air. "Hold up. You're pregnant?"

Mia nods eagerly. "Two months."

Dane comes behind her and wraps his arms around her middle. "Surprise."

The five of us stand in complete silence. I'm not sure what Lark and Amanda are thinking or what I should be doing. My ribs hurt from the kick, probably bruised by his low fucking blow. No man with integrity kicks someone when they're down. But that kick is why his ass ended up on the ground.

Amanda asks, "Is it Dane's?"

"Amanda," Lark cautions.

But Mia grunts and stamps her feet. Whipping around, she grabs the front of Dane's shirt and shakes him. "I told you they wouldn't be supportive. I told you," she screams.

Nothing about this situation is good, but an even worse feeling settles in my stomach. I have nothing to protect Lark except myself. I'll do it. I'll do anything to keep her safe, but getting her out of here is best.

I take hold of Lark's hand and pull her back a few inches at first and then a couple of feet. I've seen a lot of fights over the years, but something in that girl's eyes is unhinged. No way do I want Lark anywhere near her line of fire.

Mia's still yelling about some guy named Steve she could have dated when I make intentional eye contact with

Amanda, silently warning her to get back. She doesn't hesitate and moves closer to the front door.

Screamer turns back, facing Amanda, and says, "It's his baby. Why would he give me this if it weren't his?" Tugging back the front of her coat, she reveals a hard-to-miss low-cut orange shirt that fits like a second skin. But it's not the coat we're all staring at. It's the pin she's wearing. "It's real diamonds," she hisses, "and more than you bitches will ever get."

I know what that is. I saw it once in the photo in Lark's bedroom. It's distinctive in shape, and though she glossed over it, she said it was stolen from her home. If I recognize it, Lark definitely does.

Fuck.

I catch hold of Lark's arms just as she pounces. "Where did you get that?" she shouts, swinging her arms like a wildcat.

Mia's startled and scuttles behind Dane like she needs protection. "He gave it to me."

Lark pivots, gaining ground by leveraging her boots against the same ground that has me sliding against my slick soles. "Give it back. Dane, give it back to me!"

My hold tightens as her anger grows. Amanda moves in, closer to Dane, and points at Lark. "That was her mother's."

Dane swings his arms behind him but glares at me as if I had something to do with it. *Fuck him.* "Shit, that sucks, doesn't it, Westcott?"

"Fuck you. I don't know what you're talking about, but I know you'd hurt your friend without a second thought."

Amanda's shaking her head. "Where's your loyalty, Dane? We've been there for you—"

"To the mother of my baby."

The words themselves appear to temper Lark, her body

losing the fight and weakening in my grip. When her arms fall to her side, I wrap my arms around her. She turns to me suddenly, tears breaking the dam of her lower lids, and her eyes desperate with pleading. "Please, Harbor. Help me get it back."

"You can't have it," Mia shouts, intent on dragging Lark back into this fight. "It's mine. Tell them, Dane."

This is probably the first time he thinks before he jumps into a fight. His eyes land on Lark, who's buried her head against my coat. I would make a move if it dried her tears and stopped her helpless cries. Amanda comes to her, hugging her from behind. Even encased in the love from both of us, her pain is palpable. But Dane still chooses to hurt her. "Some fucking friend you are," I spit at him.

"I'm sorry, Lark," Dane says. "But it was a good deal I couldn't pass up."

Through whimpering cries, she turns her head while still tucked in my arms. "Where did you buy it?"

He still doesn't answer, just standing there shaking his head like he's trapped between a soft and a hard place. He's not. He's making his choice known. He's not budging. He's not choosing his friend.

I almost can't blame him. I'd choose Lark if I were in the same situation. The difference is, I wouldn't give her something stolen.

I need to get her out of here before this escalates and gets worse, if that's even possible. It's pretty damn bad as it is. Kissing her head, I whisper, "We'll get it back. I promise. Let's just leave for now. We'll deal with it tomorrow."

Betrayal sinks into her beautiful features, forcing them to fall under the weight of her tears.

Something sets Dane off, stealing our attention, and he sends his girlfriend to wait in the truck for him. Mia's covering the diamond pin with her coat, hiding it from us as if Lark will steal it back if given a chance. *I'm not sure she wouldn't.*

As soon as she's gone, Dane says, "I'm sorry, Lark. You know I wouldn't hurt you—"

"You're hurting me. You're doing it right now. You attacked my boyfriend, and now Mia's wearing my . . . *Liz's* stolen brooch." Even in pain, she's holding on to more than she realizes, refusing to give her mom any access to her heart. Though, by how upset she is, she did a long time ago.

I let her go because I need to let her experience it. It's the only way she'll ever be able to package up that part of her life to manage it. She moves closer to him, her hands praying. "Please. Please give it back. I won't ask where you got it or how. I won't ask any questions at all. I just want it back."

"You can ask, but it's just a guy who used to hang around."

"Who?"

"Because you ask doesn't mean I can tell you."

Lark's hands fist at her sides, and I hear the deep breath she steals.

Dane continues, "It's better that way. Safer." He's staring at her, but I can see guilt beginning to riddle his eyes. *Good.* He should feel shitty for what he's doing to her. "Anyway, it's not like I asked where he got it. I didn't get it at the store in the mall or some shit like that. You just don't ask those kinds of questions when doing deals of that nature, especially when you know it's hot."

Each step she takes is tentative, but she still braves the journey. "Dane," she says, her voice so low it's hard to hear, but the tremble is caught on the end. "I'm begging you. I'll buy it from you. You can buy Mia something better, something . . . not stolen from one of your closest friends."

"Lark, I would," he says, glancing at the truck. "But she loves it. How can I take it from her now?"

"You just do." Her voice rises in the cool air, becoming hoarse.

I look around at the surrounding houses. Lights are on, but no one's come out to help or investigate. I'm kind of surprised the neighbors haven't called the cops yet.

"I can't," he states, his tone unwavering, unlike hers. "I'm not going to upset Mia when she's carrying my baby."

When Dane looks at me again, I see it, as expected all along. Any hope of him doing the right thing has already disappeared from his eyes. I knew he'd hurt her, but he doesn't matter. I'll take care of her. I'll make her feel so fucking loved that she won't need him or that brooch.

He spews, "I'm sure your boyfriend can buy something even better." As if he lacks a heart, he seems unable to see that it's not about money for Lark.

Tears rattle her shoulders. "It was my mom's."

Disappointed that he won't do this for her, I walk through the puddles that formed in the grass from an earlier storm and take her hand. She turns to me and buries her face against my chest. I say, "Be reasonable, man. You know what this means to her."

"It means just as much to Mia," he counters, ignoring that his friend is falling apart because of some selfish pride or something. I can't figure him out.

He won't sell it to Lark, so I know he won't sell it to me. There's no point in asking, at least not tonight when everyone's heated. Instead, I say, "You're such a fucking asshole."

"Back at ya."

Amanda steps in the middle of us. "Stop. This is too much." Facing Dane, she says, "Look at Lark. Look at your friend. Are you really doing this? You're going to keep it from her?"

"Don't get involved, Amanda."

"I'm involved because my best friend is involved, and I'll always have her back." She embraces Lark again. "This is your chance to do the right thing," she says. "if you're capable of it."

I think they can ask and beg all they want, but he's already decided. If he won't give it to her because of the sentimental value, then nothing will change his mind.

Lark looks up at me. "I want to go home."

Hearing her pain threaded through her tone, breaks me. I glare at him. "I'm starting to think you're the one who stole it, asshole."

Ignoring her altogether, he flips me the bird as he heads for the truck. "Fuck you." He stops before he steps into the street and taps his truck. "You want to know where I got it? Fine. I'll tell you, but remember, I tried to protect you, Lark."

"Protect me how? You're the one who's betraying me." She doesn't have enough anger to hold on to now that hope has been dangled like a carrot in front of her.

I hate that fucker for giving Lark hope when I know she'll only be disappointed. "This isn't over," I warn, a roar inside me itching to come out through my fists.

"Fine. You want to know how much it cost?" He looks me dead in the eyes, and a slimy grin appears. "A quarter bag and ten Oxy pills." His arms go out like he's getting the final laugh. "Your fucking cousin traded it for drugs." Dane lands his final blow, hitting me right in the gut.

34

Lark

"I don't understand."

Water pours on me, soaking my hair, my skin, all of me as steam billows in the air. Tears fall like the rain in the shower, blending in and streaming over me to the drain. It doesn't matter how wet my body is, I'm desperate to wash the betrayal of my friend down the drain. *I don't understand.*

I reach for the body wash, but I have no energy for such tasks. I should have taken a bath where I sunk under the water and disappeared. But Harbor needs my help, so I clean myself and wash my hair at his insistence. His theory is that showers always make you feel better. *I'm not convinced.*

I finish and dry off. With the towel wrapped around me, I hold the pieces together and open the door. Harbor's lying on the bed in his underwear. Resting with pillows under his head and shoulders, he has one leg bent while an ice pack covers some of his ribs on the other side of his body. His gaze goes from the TV to me, and he asks, "How was the shower?"

"Am I wrong for feeling like this?" I glance out the window to the lights beyond and then drop my head into my hand.

"How do you feel?"

"Lost." I look up at him, this incredible man, and confess what I should never say to him. "Empty, like I'm being left all over again. It makes me feel like I'm being ridiculous, petty, even though I don't care about the financial value."

"Come here." Propping himself up, he growls when moving and holds his side. I sit down carefully, not wanting to cause him more pain.

Rubbing my back, he runs his fingers lightly over my skin. He catches a drop of water I missed and brings it to his mouth, running it across his bottom lip. Although it seems impossible to think about anything else, my body reacts, sending a shiver over my skin and leaving goose bumps in its wake.

My nipples push against the soft fabric of the towel, so I tighten it as a wave of confusion comes over me. *How can I feel this attraction to him when I'm so emotionally drained?*

But as I let my gaze run over his body—the muscles creating hills and valleys, hard edges and sharp planes—I realize I feel so much *because* of him, not in spite of.

He drops the ice pack to the floor and then reaches for my hand tucked against the towel and my chest. His fingers are cold, but a warmth blooms in my chest and begins to spread. As he unwraps the towel like a present, exposing my body to the heated air and his craving gaze, I drop my eyes to my lap and gulp.

Pressing the palm of his hand to my skin, I suck in a staggered breath. "Look at me, Lark." I can't. It's not him but the conflicting emotions battling inside me. "Hey," he says, lifting my chin until my eyes reach his. "Don't ever look down, not ever. You hold your head up and demand respect."

"I don't know how to feel. It's too much and then nothing at all."

"Because you're thinking. How does your heart feel?"

He looks at me like he's the lucky one, but he's not the lucky one when it comes to us. *I am.* "Not as lost as my head."

Sliding his hand down my neck and resting it on my collarbone, he whispers, "How does your body feel?"

"Comforted by your touch," I whisper in return.

When his hand grazes over my skin and dips between my legs, he doesn't say anything. He slides through the slickness of my lips first, and then says, "Your body is feeling, experiencing, reacting. It's your head that's doing you in." He slides his finger up and down a few times and then rubs gently over my clit. "Just feel, baby. Relax your mind and listen to your body."

As if that was the permission I needed, I slowly grind against his hand in reaction. That will only be a temporary high. I need more of him, his hands on my body, and everything at the same time.

Lifting onto my knees, I allow the towel to fall from the bed. I bend over and kiss his ribs gently and then his mouth. "I don't want to hurt you."

He caresses my cheek and says, "I feel the same about you."

I don't doubt the love he has for me. I've been doubting myself. I refuse to do it anymore.

Stop thinking.

Just feel.

I crawl all the way onto the bed and move close and straddle him. He catches me by the hips before I'm seated on his lap, and says, "I think it might be better if I'm on top this time, considering this rib situation."

"Oh no." I lift and slip off him. "I'm sorry."

"It's okay, baby," he says, his voice deliciously dulcet. "I'm bruised, not broken."

The light from the bathroom trails across the room, catching us in the tail of it. I maneuver off him and lie down on the mattress instead. My body doesn't tremble despite having my emotions and weaknesses on display.

His eyes are hooded as if he's dreaming, and then he kisses me. Is that what I am? *A kiss and dream?* The rough of his fingertips awakens my skin as he grazes over my shoulder and down my arm, encircling what I imagine is where he really wants to be.

Harbor usually asks how I want to be pleasured. Not this time. *Just feel.* When he hovers over me and we kiss, a fire is unleashed between us. My legs spread, but he parts them even farther, roughly thumbing over my thighs.

His length is hard and ready to plunge, the sight of him in such a desirous stage causing my body to throb in eager anticipation. I pull him down by his shoulders, and our lips come together as our bodies reunite. He withdraws, and the emptiness instantly returns. "Don't tease, babe."

He teases his tip against my entrance. *Sexy bastard.*

And while his body taunts mine, the hunger in his eyes makes me think this might not be gentle. A hard thrust knocks my head into the padded headboard. Scrambling to find purchase, I fist the sheet with one hand and press the other over my head on the headboard.

Every thrust is more fuel for the fire, sending sparks shooting through my veins and my body coming alive. It's never less, always more—whether we fuck or make love or like now, both at the same time. He knows how to make me forget everything beyond the two of us.

His abs are taut as he moves over me, my whole body being touched, consumed, loved so deep that my insides clench to hinder the oncoming storm just to keep experiencing this sense of freedom I have with him. But it's too much . . . *he's too much.* When he pushes harder and moves faster, losing control on top of me, it's not ecstasy I see. It's love staring back at me.

Perfection.

Just as the winds of my release pick up, I grapple to hold his shoulders before the onslaught. It's too late. Too hard to hold on to that middle ground between the indulgence of the chase to the gratification of the release. I'm not ready to stop, but my body caves in, my back arching as a moan drifts from my lips. "Harbor," rips from my throat, stolen as I'm kissed.

My nails embed as he thrusts until he hits his release and then settles slowly on top of me. "Ow," he says, and then rolls carefully to the side.

Slowly catching my breath, I swallow to coat my dry throat, and then ask, "Are you okay?"

He chuckles. "That might be the first time I've ever been asked that after sex." Turning to look at me, a smile, though pained as he touches his side, he adds, "For the record, guys are always great after sex. Doesn't matter how busted up they are. It will still be the best fucking high they'll ever achieve if they're with the woman they love."

Despite his pain, he leans over and kisses my shoulder. "Like I am."

"Good to know." I grin and roll to my side to look at him. His hand is light to his side, but his jaw is starting to swell. I reach over and barely touch his face. "It's swelling."

He breathes a sigh, more annoyed than upset as he gets up. "That fucking uppercut he landed when I looked away. I'll put an ice pack on it."

"I'm sorry." I push up, resting my weight on a hand to the mattress.

Stopping on the edge of the bed, he looks back at me over his slumped shoulder. "Why are you sorry?" Genuine confusion is laced through his brows.

"Because you wouldn't be hurt if it weren't for me."

He turns away from me, scrubbing his face in his hands and then resting his arms forward on his legs. "You didn't cause that fight, Lark. He said what he said, but his grudge goes way back. We've crossed paths before. He didn't lie about Lucas and me combing his parties for girls. Hell," he says, looking back at me again. This time with a smirk. "We even stole his booze." He stands as slow as he can, his hand protectively covering his side. When he turns around, the grin is gone, and I already miss it. I look away as he says what he needs to get off his chest. "I'm damn sure not pleading a case. Facts are facts, but I'm telling you, no one in my past matters."

As much as I want Harbor not to focus on Dane and what he said, partly because it hurts to know I caused it, but also because I know Harbor would have blown it all off if it didn't affect him. "You don't have to justify your past to me." Rolling my head to the side, I ask, "Do you think I would believe him over you?"

"I don't know. I don't want to leave it to chance."

I slide out of bed and into his arms. "If I were ever forced to choose a side, I'm always choosing you, Harbor. Always. But you know that. So what's the real reason you're telling me?"

His head lowers, his gaze taken with it. Pressing his

temple against mine, he stays and inhales. The rough scruff on his face scratches against my soft cheek, and then I'm granted the warmth of his eyes again. "Because your so-called *friend* wants you to believe you're nothing but another Friday night fuck to me. You're not." Cupping my face, he kisses me and leans his forehead against mine. "You're the whole fucking universe. You're where time begins and ends and every moment in between."

I didn't know it was possible for a heart to soar, but I cover his hands, holding him so tight that he never lets me go, or I just might float away. "I love you," I whisper, though the words aren't adequate for how I feel about him.

Our heads straighten, but our eyes reestablish the connection as we stare into each other's gaze. He says, "I'll get your brooch back."

"How?"

"I don't know, but I'll figure it out." He kisses me and then whispers against my lips. "I promise you, Lark. One day, you'll have it back."

It's not what he says or even his tone. When his soul made a pact with mine, I knew he'd keep his promise.

35

Harbor

I COULD HAVE JUST CALLED the cops on Dane and Mia. They'd match it to the burglary report, arrest them for stolen property, and Lark would get her mom's jewelry back. All would be well again.

But it's not a simple situation. It's not strangers involved, but her close friend and the woman carrying his baby. I know she wants the brooch back, but I also know Lark would never want to ruin lives to get it. I'm not above it, but I think patience will be our ally.

I must convince him to give it back to her. I'll pay more than its street value since I know he can't pawn stolen goods. I'll do whatever it takes to make her whole again. I can't bring back her mom, but I can get back the only thing she has left of her.

After Amanda didn't answer at her place, I'm trying a different route. Might not be my best decision, but I'm desperate.

It's been years, three, maybe four since I've been to the

house on Dobson, but it appears abandoned—letters overflowing the mailbox and flyers hanging from the handle of
the screen door and littering the front porch. The land-
scaping and lawn are in need of a good trim. It's the broken
window and ripped curtain that doesn't sit right with me,
though. Lucas and I used to party here on occasion, but it
was late, usually after midnight. If I had seen it in the
daylight, I might not have come.

I don't mess with the rusting screen door. The sharp
metal pieces look ready to stab its next victim. I knock
beside the door on the rotting wood, hoping I don't break
right through. Stepping back, I leave space for whoever
answers the door, not wanting to crowd them.

The curtain inside is shifted to the right. Beady eyes peer
out at me and then to my car at the curb. "You a cop?"

"No. I used to come around back in the day. I'm
looking—"

"I don't care who you're lookin' for. Go away."

I dare to peer in, but he scurries behind the safety of the
door. "Is this Terry? Hey, I'm looking for Dane. You
remember him?"

There's rattling, like the sound of a cage, and then he
replies, "No, so fuck off."

I'll admit if this wasn't exactly like the start of most
horror movies, I'd probably stay and try a different tactic.
But no, I think I'm good. "Okay, cool, man. Thanks."

I walk on the stairs, wondering what the fuck I was
thinking. Not that I think he'd pull a weapon and shove me
in his cage, but I'm not feeling that lucky today. I get in my
car without incident and head to the restaurant near the
highway where Amanda works.

When I walk in, a few guys in trucker hats turn to stare,
not giving me an ounce of leeway to make myself more

comfortable. I look back to the right, where some families are sitting, and then to the left.

"Harbor?" Amanda's mouth twists, and she comes toward me from the right.

"Hey."

"What are you doing here? Is Lark okay?"

"She's . . ." I'm about to fill in with "good" or "fine" as expected, but I hesitate because she's getting by today after the emotional turmoil of the incident last night with Dane. But Amanda knows that, so I don't have to pretend. "She's been better. She's at the library tonight, studying."

Her expression softens in understanding. "She texted me earlier." She takes my elbow and pulls me off to the side out of the walkway. Taking a step back, she leans against a column and says, "I'm sorry, Harbor. Everything escalated so quickly."

"You didn't cause it, just like she didn't. There's history between Dane and me. He knew my cousin."

"Yeah, Lucas. I remember." Her gaze slides through the blinds and into the parking lot. "He used to talk about you. He'd actually brag about you, how good you were, always better than him. I wasn't around him much, but I heard him call you his ride or die."

"I was his ride. That's all."

The comment seems to catch her off guard by how she shifts and begins fidgeting with the pen in her hands. "So," she starts, rocking back on her heels. "What brings you by? I have a feeling it's not the god-awful three-day-old apple pie."

"So you don't recommend the pie?" I joke. "What do you recommend?"

"Eating somewhere else if you can, and I know you can."

"Noted." I chuckle. "Hey, *so* . . . I'm looking for Dane."

She cringes just a little, but it's noticeable. "Think that's wise?" Her gaze darts over my shoulder but then returns just as quickly.

She has customers waiting, so I pick up the pace, and say, "No, but if it helps me get the brooch back, I'll do it."

Leaning in, she whispers, "He's here, working in the back. He came in last week looking for more work because Larry's lost a few jobs since Lark walked out. So he came in and asked for a job." Looking around to make sure no one hears her, she adds, "I guess we know why now. Mia being pregnant."

"Oh, right. What are the chances I can get back there and speak with him?"

Checking the time on her phone, she says, "His break's coming shortly. If you hang out back, he'll be out there for a smoke." She grabs the pad out of her apron, and her smile tightens. "I need to get back to work."

"Thanks, Amanda. I appreciate it."

She gives me a nod and starts making rounds while I walk back out to my car. As she's advised, I pull my car around back and wait with my window down. As if she sent him herself, he pushes through the door and lights a smoke. Looking up, he comes stalking toward the car. "What the fuck are you doing here?"

I get out, not trusting him to treat my Maserati with the care she deserves. I raise my hands. "I come in peace, man."

He's got a busted-up black eye and looks like a split lip. The bruising on my ribs isn't as bad as it felt last night. My jaw still hurts, and he left his mark, so he should feel satisfied.

He says, "There is no peace to be found between us. We just need to stick to our sides of town." His shirt is covered in grime, jeans looking like they need a good wash. Dane could use a shave and a haircut probably, but I've seen him cleaned up and looking better at the catering gigs. Seems more is going on with him these days than his girlfriend getting pregnant.

"I love her, Dane. I love Lark more than anything. I can't stick to The Pointe when she was raised near downtown. Her dad still lives there. She does as well, at least for another month. We can't make this a territorial fight. Anyway, you're in The Pointe working sometimes."

He's sucking on the cigarette like it's a joint, not giving me an ounce of his attention as he stares at the highway. He coughs, then shoots me a look. "She's like a sister to me."

"Look, I can appreciate what you've done for her. You protected her from falling in with the wrong crowd."

"You, Westcott. You're a part of that crowd. You and Lucas were." He stabs his cigarette in the air toward me. "Why do you get to walk away like you're innocent, go to your fancy college, clean up or whatever the shit you did, and the little guy keeps getting stomped on?"

We both know why.

Money brings opportunity.

I scratch the back of my neck and look down, unsure what to say. I might not be able to bridge this gap with him, but maybe our common interest can. When I look up again, I say, "I don't know how hard you have it, so I won't pretend I understand. But this isn't about me. It's about Lark." I come a little closer, keeping him more than arm's length away. "You guys are from the same neighborhood, and from what she's told me, you grew up together from high school on. But that's all I know about your background because everything she's said was how good you've been to her and how you looked out for her and Amanda."

"She was sort of nerdy when we first met, always carrying

books around with her. She went through an awkward stage that I thought would stick. It would have been easier if it had. Once she turned seventeen, I had to throw down some ground rules with my friends. For her, I told her she wasn't allowed to date any of my crew. Most aren't doing any better than I am now. Lark was meant for bigger things than Beacon. Amanda, too, if she could stay focused."

"Lark's at the library right now."

He cracks up. "Good for her." There's something so genuine about the look in his eyes when Lark's or Amanda's names are brought up—a sincerity that I bet he doesn't reveal to many people.

Tossing the cigarette before he finishes it, he puffs his breath, then holds his hands behind his head. "I was keeping her away from guys like you and Lucas."

"You remember me like I was there with him those past few years. I wasn't. He sold his life for a quick fix. You never saw me doing any of that."

Dane stares at me. I can see he's not convinced by how his eyes are narrowed and he crosses his arms over his chest. "Maybe I threw you in the mix, not really paying attention. If I judged you wrong, I'm a big enough guy to apologize. Sorry."

It's not elaborate, but I'll accept it. "I need to clear my name because I don't want Lark paying for mistakes, especially if I didn't make them."

"You and your cousin look a lot alike."

"I can see that." I stretch out my hand. He looks between it and my eyes a few times and then takes it. We shake. "I appreciate the apology."

"I don't want to lose Lark's friendship. I need your help."

We step back again as a new line is drawn in the sand.

"You know what to do." Although I appreciate having my name cleared, that's not why I was looking for him. "That's why I'm here."

Sighing and shaking his head, he starts pacing. "I can't take it from her, man. I wish I could."

"You have a long history with Lark. You said it yourself that you don't want to lose her friendship, but you won't give her something that's rightfully hers to own. I bet you she's been there for you over the years like you have for her. I bet if you called her at any hour and needed something, she'd be there. Am I right?"

"You're right, but it doesn't change this situation."

"What will?" I'm not going to volley with him all night. I just wish he'd do the right thing to start with. "You know Lark. You know what it means to her. She deserves to have it back."

He pulls another cigarette from his pocket. It's bent as if he bummed it off someone. But he doesn't light it. He holds it between two fingers like the act itself is enough to settle his nerves.

When he checks his phone, I'm thinking we're on borrowed time. He finally says, "What would you have me do that doesn't fuck up my relationship with Mia?"

"If it's that volatile, it's already fucked up. But maybe . . ." Last resort. *Here goes.* "My cousin traded it for drugs. I'll trade you cash. What's it worth to you?"

"Priceless if it keeps the peace with Mia."

"Don't do this, Dane. You know what's right in this scenario. Lark loses if you choose wrong. I'll give you five thousand dollars."

"Fuck," he says, laughing and waving his arms in front of him. "Just like that, huh? Wish I'd been born a Pointe kid.

You know your cousin threw money around like it was endless and then his daddy cut him off."

Wait . . . I never heard this. "How would you know?"

"He and Ronnie hit a few houses back in the day when they needed a fix."

"Is that a fact?"

"Ask Ronnie. He's doin' time down in county."

I can't wrap my head around how bad it got for Lucas. Each new detail is a part of his life that I'm unfamiliar with when I thought I knew everything about him. The deeper I get into Lucas's history, the more I wish I didn't know.

"You didn't know they hit Lark's house? You didn't piece that together back then?"

"I was almost in as deep, dude. I wasn't investigating anything. He came to me and traded some goods I'd just gotten. Mia found it in a shoebox while clearing out the closet to put the crib."

"How did she know it was real?"

He shrugs, tucking the cigarette in his back pocket. "Girls know diamonds, I guess. Look, I need to go."

"You won't take the money?"

"It pains me because I could really use it, but we'll get by." He eyes me up and down, and then adds, "I get that you want to be the hero in Lark's story, but I can't rock the boat with Mia, especially when she's pregnant." He holds out his hand, and I know what it took for him to offer it to me, so I take it, and we shake again. "Sorry, man." His eyes dart behind me, and he says, "Sweet ride."

"No fucking way."

"Not even for Lark," he asks, fucking hopeful to make the trade.

"She'd never want me to do that."

"What do you want?"

Shaking my head, I reply, "It's in my parents' name. I just make the payments."

"Must be nice," he sings with a swagger to his step. "Must be nice."

Given one more minute, I would have been handing over the keys. But I know a car doesn't trade as easily as drugs do. *Fuck, I was close.* Lark would kill me, and I quite like seeing her every day.

He opens the door and looks back. His good mood is gone, replaced by the side I imagine Lark knows. "You're going to make sure she gets out of Beacon, right? You're her best chance."

"*She's* her best chance, but I'll make sure she does as a backup plan."

"Righteous."

I have the wildest thought. I run my hand through my hair, doubting I should even do this. The guy's causing Lark heartache on purpose. But maybe there's a way for him to change the direction of his life. Lark's heart is pure gold. I know she wouldn't be upset over what I'm about to do. "Hey, Dane." He looks back once more. I say, "If you're looking for more of a steady gig, I know a few guys who could probably use some help. Nothing big, but they have good benefits and offer a decent salary."

He stares at me, his face contorted like I might be pulling one over on him. "Why would you help me?"

I shrug. "You have a baby on the way, and because you're Lark's friend." I walk to my car. "Amanda has my number if you ever want the connections."

"Thanks."

I take one last look and then sink into my car. On the way to pick up Lark, I start thinking about this brooch. I think it's going to be chalked up to a lost cause. If he's not taking money, I don't have anything else to offer.

So other than stealing the brooch back from him, which has crossed my mind at one point, Lark may never have it in her possession again. As the messenger, I was not wanting to be the guy who breaks her heart.

I pull up out front, and she gets in. Leaning over, she kisses me all smiles like I didn't just fail my mission. "Hi," she says, strapping on her seat belt. "Did you get any texts recently?"

"Texts frommm . . ."

She shoves her phone in my face. "I got in, babe. I got into Yale Medical School. Did you hear back?"

I got the text weeks ago, but I didn't tell her because I wanted to see if she got in first. I'd already decided I'm going where she's going because I can't live without her. But what do I tell her? That I lied, that I only had to apply as a formality?

"I knew you could do it, baby." I lean over and kiss her. When we sit back, I start to drive us home.

She asks, "Is it normal not to receive the scholarship with the acceptance letter? I received both at the same time for Beacon."

"Maybe you get it when you commit?"

"Oh. Maybe you're right." She slides her finger up and down the screen, and then says, "Oh my God. I just committed to Yale." She's giggling in excitement when she adds, "I'm going to check emails just in case it comes in that way."

She's silent and staring out the window by the time I'm parking.

Her nerves are even eating away at *my* stomach. "Anything?"

"Still nothing." Her good mood has taken a turn for the worse. She chews on the inside of her cheek and gets out of the car without another word.

Trying to stay positive for her, I say, "I've heard sometimes people receive them later. Maybe it comes in a formal letter and not a text."

"I have a bad feeling about this." I reach over, taking her backpack and swinging it over my shoulder, and then take her hand as we walk toward the elevators. She stops suddenly, tears filling her eyes. "What if I don't get it?"

If I have my way, I'll give her the whole world and more like she gave me the universe. I wrap my arms around her and kiss the top of her head. "You will."

If I only knew then what I know now, I would have savored the kiss I placed on her head that day.

36

Harbor

FOUR MONTHS LATER . . .

I DIDN'T KNOW how to fix it . . . *to fix us.*

For months, Lark sat with the commitment letters from Yale and the four medical schools where she was accepted spread across the island for hours each night. Those nights turned into weeks and months. "Baylor's a great school," she says, looking at me over her laptop.

"Baylor is a great school,"

"But I don't want to be in Texas without you."

What? I shift on the couch and angle to face her. "Why would you be in Texas without me?"

"Because Yale is in New Haven and Grossman is in New York."

"I can go to Baylor with you. I'll go wherever you go." She's staring at me. I mean, she does that sometimes, but there's something more than lust in her eyes this time. There are questions. "What?" I ask, sitting forward.

"What do you mean what, Harbor? How would you go to Baylor? You didn't even apply."

"Well," I start . . . not sure how to break it to her. It's a secret I've kept hidden for a reason. Some days I'm still surprised that she hasn't called me on it. Makes me wonder if that's on purpose. She's a smart woman, but she conveniently avoids talking about my family's money and my access to it as much as possible.

I've overthought this for so long that I'm ready to rip off the bandage and just deal with it head-on. I know it will upset her. How can it not? Life's not fair. I've learned that the hard way. But I've never had to worry about finances. She's never asked me for a penny or a loan. But she's stressed about her future, and it's time for me to get involved.

"Well?" Her eyes are still on mine, the interest building in her expression when she tilts her head and starts chewing on the inside of her mouth. "How?" she presses again.

I blow out a long breath and then run my hand over my head. "We're together. We're together because we love each other—"

"Do I need to be nervous? That opener worries me."

"You don't need to be nervous. That's my point. I'll go wherever you go because I love you so much. This, you and me, we aren't temporary, baby. We're the real thing."

She sits up on the barstool at the island, and says, "I'd love to say I can go where you go, but that's just not true. I need a scholarship to cover my schooling. I'm confused, Harbor, because what you said is that you'll go to Baylor with me, but you didn't apply, so how are you going to school with me when you didn't even fill out the application?"

The best high from being accepted turned into the biggest disappointment each time she found out she didn't get the scholarships for her reach schools. I want this settled once and for good. "I'll help pay for your medical school."

She was rubbing her temple, but her hand stills. "What do you mean? You can't do that."

"I can do some." I stand and move to the other side of the island from her. "Baylor offered thirty percent. I can cover, *I don't know*, another thirty over four years, and then you'll get financial aid for the rest. Problem solved."

Blinking slowly, her tongue dips out to wet her lips, and then she closes her mouth again. "Hm."

"Hm?"

"I'm processing." That's fair. Then she raises her finger in the air. "How does that solve the problem? I would then owe you *and* the bank money."

"No."

"*No*?" she asks, her brows rising.

"No. I could give you the money."

"Um, double no." Shaking her head, she drops her gaze. "Absolutely not. Extra no. Whatever no gets through to you. No."

"*No*? Are you sure?"

"You're not giving me the money, Harbor. I'm not spending years of my life in debt to you. At least not financially. Sexually, even emotionally, I'm all in, running a tab. But you know how I feel about owing people and unpaid debts."

Remembering how she couldn't stand when I bought her coffee at TJ's, I know she hasn't changed. She got a job down at Moretti's to help pay rent. She can't just accept a damn gift without feeling guilty. It's both sweet and annoying because I have to predict how she'll react before I buy her anything. She adds, "I wasn't raised that way. There's so much more to it than the next four years, and then there's the residency. I'll be eighty before I can pay you back."

"What does it matter if we're still together?"

"If?" she says, the one word the only one she notes.

If she only knew how I'd give up everything just to be with her. I'd trade my life for hers if it meant making her dreams come true. Nothing else matters but us. I say, "When we're in our eighties *together*." I stare into her watery eyes. "I don't want you always worried about the next step. You'll never owe me money. I'll give it to you freely."

"Like you once said, no good deed goes unpunished, so we need to be ration—"

"No, we don't. We can be as irrational as we want to be. If being with you is the punishment, punish away." I come around to her and drag the tips of my fingers over her bare thigh. With her sleep shorts riding high, I reach the bend in her leg, tempted, even while having uncomfortable conversations, to slip sideways between her legs.

She takes my free hand and turns it over. Bending down, she kisses my palm. "I love being irrational with you, babe. We've done everything fast, thrown the odds out the window, and followed our hearts. But—"

I pull back and swing my arm away in frustration. "Fuck that. I don't give a fuck about playing by other people's rules. I have money. I have trust funds. Three actually and those don't include my parents' bank accounts. So no, I'll be as irrational as I want to be if it means we stay together."

Her mouth hangs open as her green eyes shine under the kitchen lights. The quicksand of my emotions starts sucking me under, so I back up, staring at her, knowing I just committed sins against her nature.

She laughs, which is a pleasant surprise, and says, "You have more money than sense. You know that, babe? I don't even know what to say to that. I can't wrap my head around blowing off reality to live in la-la land or in some unattainable fantasy world that gives freedom from worries, even for one day, much less for a longer period." She slides off the stool and comes to me. Wrapping her arms around my middle, she leans her head on my chest. Not long enough. Resting her chin there instead, she looks up at me. "Tell me what that freedom from worry feels like. I'm being genuine, Harbor. A part of becoming a doctor was the dream that I could taste that freedom one day. Is it worth it?"

I suddenly feel shitty for spending my days like I don't have a care in the world. I guess I don't, comparatively.

I have cares, but they're all wrapped up in her. I may not know much about how her world truly rotates, but I do know that time is slipping away from us, burying us under what happens next instead of living in the present. I'd never say anything, but the day she heard from Yale is the last day I remember feeling how we used to be . . . normal in our relationship, and it's all because of fucking money.

Always about money.

My fear, my true, deep-down, buried fear, is that I realize this plays out only one of two ways—she finds the money and we stay together, or she gives up her dream. If the latter happens, I don't know what will happen to our relationship.

"I will do anything to keep us together."

She presses herself against me as if she can't get close enough. I understand the craving. It's how I feel about her as well. Time is a ticking bomb, tricking us into thinking we'll find the money for her dream to come true. But I'm starting to worry we won't.

She whispers, "I can't take your money."

I already knew, but hearing her say it strikes a different chord. I kiss her head and hold her tight, knowing we're headed into the unknown.

Hours later, it's when she falls asleep in my arms, that I make up my mind. She won't approve, and she won't go along with it. I know what I must do.

MY DAD IS STILL STUCK in the conference room, so I wait in his office for my mom to arrive. She comes in, all smiles and arms spread wide for hugs. "It's good to see you, Harbor."

"You too, Mom." Lark and I spend time with our families, together and alone. She's taught me that no matter what, family is most important. I couldn't agree more.

My parents pulled me from my own misery. They told me I mattered. Even when the lies took over the truth, they gave me a chance to come back from the ashes. They loved me privately despite the sins they thought I'd committed and got me help. They loved me publicly and came to my defense when everyone else pointed the finger at me.

I don't want to disappoint them, but I'm worried I'm about to.

"No classes?" my mom asks, sitting in a chair next to mine and putting her bag on the floor.

"I have two hours on Thursdays at lunchtime."

"Ah." She starts to take off her coat and drapes it over the back of the chair. "It's starting to warm, but we're not quite there."

"No, we aren't."

She looks at me, her eyes seeing the concern in mine. "I hope you're okay."

"I am."

"And Lark?"

"She's good."

A soft smile appears. "That's good."

The door opens, and my dad comes in, grumbling. "I spend my days in meetings instead of litigating. I should have saved myself the money and gotten a business degree instead of going to law school." He stops to kiss my mom and then bring me in for a quick pat on the back. "How's everyone?" His eyes travel between the two of us. "Anything I need to be worried about?"

My mom replies, "Harbor called the meeting, so I'm in the dark just like you, Port." She turns to me. "What's going on?"

I don't know why my palms are sweating. I rub them over my jeans and just spit it out, "I need your help to send Lark to medical school."

My dad asks, "Okay, what does she need? A recommendation?"

My mom is quiet but curious, her voice soft when she asks, "I thought she got into the schools she wanted?"

"She did. That's the thing. Her hard work has paid off, but . . ." My dad sits forward, steepling his fingers. "She can't afford it. The scholarships didn't come through like she was expecting."

"Ah," my dad hums and sits back in his chair, turning his attention to Mom.

She asks, "We don't usually hold fundraising for a specific person, but more qualified applicants who apply. It could be very tricky to do something like that because we file as a nonprofit."

"It would be illegal, insider trading kind of thing, buddies helping buddies," my dad adds, his face pensive. "No, that won't work. We can't do that."

Feeling anxious, I sit forward. "I wasn't thinking of a fundraiser but more of a loan."

My mom's eyes widen. "A loan?" Then she starts to shake her head. "Harbor, that's not ever wise. We adore Lark, but she would be indebted to us for years. It could be twenty or even thirty or more."

My dad says, "No, I'm sorry. That's not possible."

"I was thinking the loan would be for me."

"No," my dad is swift in a reply. "You are not going to carry that burden. You do realize that I work so hard to make sure that my family is taken care of. We want each of you to launch into the world not only free of debt while supporting your dreams to help you soar in whatever you choose to do. We won't saddle you with that kind of debt when it's not yours to begin with."

"My dreams include her, and her dream is to be a doctor."

Touching my arm, my mom leans closer. "My charity can set up another scholarship. It won't cover medical school but can potentially give access to a thousand or upward of five thousand each year. I've been wanting to support students who choose to further their education. She would apply and be approved, but I think her being from Beacon and utilizing our wonderful local institution for undergrad will work in her favor."

"You're not listening to me." I stand and walk to the window to look out.

"We're here and listening, Harbor," my dad states. "The issue you've taken with us is that you're not happy with our decision. Did you think we would just say, here's three hundred thousand dollars to do as you please?"

Getting upset will get me nowhere with them, but I'm now on the defense. "You're not giving me money to do as I please, Dad. This is for Lark to follow her dreams."

"And she should follow them, but we can't bankroll them for her."

"I love her."

"Honey," my mom says, her shoulders falling as the conversation intensifies.

I walk the length of the office but stop, needing the space, and look back at them. I was unprepared for what I was asking and for their answer. This isn't a well-thought-out plan. It's me trying to save my relationship. "I realize what I'm asking is—"

"It's ludicrous, son."

"It's not. I'll do anything . . ." The desperate plea to my tone almost brings me to my knees, willing to beg, to do anything to help her so we can stay together. "I'll do anything to bring the light back into her eyes. She spends every day and all night looking for ways to supplement the aid. I don't want her in Texas simply because they made her the best offer. I want to wake to the melody of her laughter and see the smile I fell in love with back on her face."

My mom's breath shudders, and she wipes her index finger under her eyes. The tears are still in the corners when she stands and says, "Harbor, you're young, and you're having big emotions. We understand—"

"No, you don't," I say, anger tingeing my words. "I'm going to marry her. I swear to you I'm going to marry Lark one day, and then what will that debt mean? Nothing because I would have paid it off with one of my trust funds.

I'm just asking for access sooner to help us stay together in the meantime."

The room goes quiet, and my mom sits down. I return, gripping the back of the chair as silence extends and tension is thick in the air.

Taking a deep breath, I calmly say, "The closer we get to graduation, the more stress she's under. She's lost weight, and some days, I don't think she remembers to eat lunch. I know she wouldn't remember dinner if I weren't there to remind her." I drop my head down, unable to look them in the eyes as shame becomes my last resort. "I'm asking you, begging you, to please help."

The warmth of my mom's hand covers mine, and then she comes around and gives me a hug. I don't know what to make of it—her being my mom or will they tell me what I want to hear?

My dad rocks forward in his chair, and says, "I'm sorry, Harbor. You're conflating two different issues as if they're one and the same. Your love for Lark shouldn't change whether she attends medical school. If that's what your relationship is based on—"

"It's not."

Dad stands, his fingers pressed to the wood desktop. "You don't understand what you're asking of us. We won't pay for her school. There's nothing reasonable about asking us to do so either."

I raise my head, my stubborn side coming out. I have nothing to lose at this point. "You're saying no?"

"We are, honey," my mom replies softly, trying to temper our flaring moods.

"Then trade me. Mine for hers."

37

Lark

Two months later . . .

Harbor's been adjusting my graduation cords as if they needed to be.

They don't.

But I'm not going to say anything because I've become his sun and he, my moon. We can't stray far from each other's personal space before our gravitational pull brings us back into orbit.

I wouldn't have it any other way. That's why I'm going to New Haven with him. Yale awaits. We found a cute apartment just off campus, so we can walk to school together, and it's not a journey too far home when we stay late at night.

I'm so grateful that things worked out how they were supposed to. If I hadn't received that letter from Yale, telling me they took another look at my application during a holistic review, I wouldn't be making a new home with him.

Home . . . *Harbor.*

No apartment or house can be what he means to me, but I still look forward to our little haven together.

Straightening his graduation gown, I then put his tassel on the right side to make sure everything's perfect. Perfect is what our life has been. I shouldn't jinx it, but I won't discount the last nine months as anything less than magical. I lift and kiss him. "Are you ready?"

"As much as I ever will be."

Graduation has put my emotions through the wringer. Not only am I graduating from college, but I'm moving away from the only town I've ever known, from my dad and Amanda. The only saving grace is that my new adventure comes packaged with my soul mate onboard.

Something tells me Harbor must be going through the same because he's not quite been himself for a while. It's not personal to me. He treats me like a queen, but I wish I knew how to make him feel better, to get him excited about the move to New Haven.

He says, "I should get in line." When he takes my hand between us, it doesn't feel like he's holding it, but more that he's holding on to me. My heart clenches. He kisses me, and then says, "I'm proud of you."

"Thanks." He cups my face, not caring that we're in front of hundreds of people. He kisses me hard with intention, with promises, with all of him. "I love you, Lark. Remember that, okay?" He winks and gives me that sexy smirk that captivates my heart all over again.

"Okay." I swoon over this man so much. "I'm proud of you, too," I say, but he's too fast to tell him the same, disappearing into the buzzing crowd behind me.

Summerlin isn't that far from Westcott in the scheme of things, but it feels like a million miles away right now.

We're finally in a single file line when we feed into the gymnasium and take our seats. I look back to find him but don't want to make a scene by standing. I don't see him, so I turn back just as the ceremony begins.

We get through the first couple of speeches when I receive a text from my dad pinpointing where he's sitting with Amanda. I look for the scoreboard and then in the middle of the rows, spotting them because Amanda is waving furiously to get my attention. My dad just raised his hand from his lap, but he's grinning. Before I turn around, I scan the seats once more for Harbor. There are hundreds of graduates, but it shouldn't be this hard to find the most gorgeous man alive.

Yet it is.

Another failed attempt has my chest tightening. I pull out my phone and text him: *Where are you?*

I wait for a reply, knowing it's loud in here between the announcement of the graduate's names and the people cheering. But why wouldn't he feel it in his pocket?

Glancing back, I still can't figure out where he would even be sitting. How many rows? How far over? He's a big guy and hard to miss, but I'm missing him.

The "P" graduates are passing on the stage, receiving their diplomas when my phone finally vibrates. I scramble to see his text: *I'm picking up my paycheck after the ceremony, and then I'll go to your dad's for the party. Just a heads-up.*

Huh? *What paycheck?* I look at the name at the top of the messages—*Amanda.*

That makes more sense.

What the hell, though? I look back again, lifting on my hand to balance. Another scan and I still don't see him. My row is summoned to stand before I have a chance to text again. I walk down the aisle, searching row after row behind me.

The pit of my stomach grows heavy with worry. Something's not right. I need to see him. I need to see that Harbor was real and that this wasn't a dream. I'm about to detour back at the end of the row, but the professor herds us forward toward the side of the stage.

I pull my phone out and start texting Amanda: *Do you see Harbor?*

I send and then type: *Have you seen him at all since you've been here?*

Amanda finally replies: *Haven't seen him. You know my eyesight is crap. Maybe he's using the bathroom. Remember when I missed Taylor Swift because I had an irritable bowel as soon as we arrived at the stadium?*

As much as I'd love to travel down memory lane, I send another text: *Hard to forget your IB that night. Hey, do me a favor and look for the Westcotts. They should be here somewhere.*

The stage is only a few feet ahead when she replies: *I don't see his family, but I can't make everyone out.*

I'm told to shuffle forward to the base of the stairs. I tuck my phone into my pocket and then straighten the graduate robe over it. Holding my head high, I climb the stairs and wait until I hear, "Lark Summerlin."

I start walking, but my gaze drifts to the graduates at the back where the W names would sit. I hate that I make this about him. The moment is stolen after years of hard work. Face forward, Lark. I force myself into this moment right here and accept my diploma under cheers. I expected the loudest in the crowd to be my boyfriend, but it wasn't. It was my dad. I smile when I hear him, stop, pose, take the photo, and keep walking.

I gallop down the stairs and start back for my seat.

This gives me the best perspective to see the remaining graduates. I'm not the shortest person, but I feel it right now. Even on my tiptoes, I can't see the back left center rows.

Following my fellow graduates, I find my seat again and clasp my hands together on my lap to keep from fidgeting, or from checking my phone every five seconds. I'm surprised not to hear from him.

I'm not sure at what point I went numb, probably around X, but I watch the other graduates alphabetically after me until the last Z crosses that stage. Nothing makes sense, so when the caps are thrown, I'm rushing through the celebrating graduates. Caps are landing all around me, and people are hugging.

My name is called a few times by friends I've made over the years, but it's not said by the one person who I want to hear. By the time I reach the back of the chairs, I start turning, searching everywhere—the graduates, the stands, the families, the staff, the aisles, the rafters.

Harbor is gone.

Disappeared into thin air.

How?

Why?

Do I call 911?

What could have happened to make him miss his own graduation?

Was there a family emergency?

He wouldn't leave me without a good reason.

Could Amanda be right, and he got stuck in a bathroom?

I grab my phone but as soon as I start to call him with my shaking hands, I'm bumped, and it goes flying. "No. No. No. No. No." Dropping to my knees, I don't care how dirty the floor is or if I get trampled. I just need to find my phone and Harbor. I find it under a chair with a cracked screen, but it still works, so I call him again.

Holding it to my ear, I push through the revelers to find a place where I can hear. But my call goes to voicemail. "This doesn't make sense."

"What doesn't make sense?" I whip around to find my dad there. "Congratulations, Pipsqueak."

"Th-thanks," the word comes stuttering out as I try my hardest not to start crying.

My dad nods in sympathy. "Big day. Lots of emotions." He wraps his arm around my shoulders, and we start for the exit. "I'm really proud of you, Lark. The first in our family to graduate college, and now you're going to medical school—"

"Dad?" I stop, causing him to turn back.

His brow furrows as he shakes his head. Coming back to me, he asks, "What is it? What's wrong?"

"He's gone. There are no texts, no missed calls. Nothing. Harbor's gone."

"What do you mean Harbor's gone?"

Tears bubble over my lower lids as I point back at the stage. "Did you not notice they didn't call his name. He didn't walk the stage or claim his diploma."

"No," he says, "I dozed off after Amanda left. Just briefly." He sounds guilty when the last thing I care about is him sleeping through the last hour of a graduation ceremony.

"Dad, what if . . ." My tears multiply, falling down to the floor of the last place I saw him.

I'm brought into a hug, my dad holding me like he did when I was a little girl, stroking my hair, and promising that everything's going to be all right. But he can't keep that promise anymore.

My breath is jagged, but I collect it. "I have to find him. Will you help me?"

"On it."

Frantic, I start walking again, searching the crowded halls of the gymnasium, and my dad heads in the opposite direction. My gut already knows the answer, my head knowing this is pointless. He's not here. The beat of my heart, the breath of my soul has disappeared. *Just like him.*

When few people remain, my dad comes down the hall and says, "I checked every bathroom. He's not here, Pip. Still no contact?"

"No, none at all."

He tucks his hands in his pockets. "If you want my opinion, I don't think he's a missing person. I think he's just missing this event. It was kind of boring." He half smiles at me and rests his hand on my shoulder. "You were the highlight." The emptiness I feel is overwhelming, so much that even the kindest of gestures from my dad can't help me. "I think we should go, Lark."

I don't remember walking to the truck or getting in, strapping on my seat belt, or driving away from graduation. The mystery of Harbor's disappearance was the only thing on my mind. But when my dad got a text on the way to his house, my hands started to shake again. Anxious, I ask, "What is it?"

He pulls up to the curb and leaves the engine running. With his elbow anchored on the open window, he rubs his forehead. He exhales, caught in a conflict of his mind.

My heart starts racing, and I reach over to touch his arm. "Dad? Is it . . ." I can't say the words or his name, my thoughts running to the worst that could happen.

Dad gets out of the driver's seat and shuts the door. Leaning in the window, he says, "Go see the Westcotts." He taps the top of the cab and then turns to walk up the path.

"Why?" I call, leaning over from the other side of the truck.

"I don't know, Pip. It's best you talk to them."

The panic I feel inside worsens, but I don't rush to the driver's side and take off to The Pointe Estates. I sit on the passenger side, my mind going wild with what might be happening or already did. I'm not sure, but my heart tells me I'm not ready.

Taking a breath and then a longer one, I exhale and slide over the bench behind the steering wheel. I shift into gear and start the journey.

It's only twenty minutes if there's no traffic, but it's the longest drive of my life. I don't know how long it took, my mind reliving every detail of the last time I saw him and every word we spoke. *I love you, Lark. Remember that, okay?*

That's why they didn't call his name to accept a diploma.

This was planned all along.

That's why his parents weren't there.

He knew he was leaving.

That means . . .

He was leaving me.

38

Lark

I SHIFT the truck into park but stay, idling in the driveway of the Westcott estate. I'm not sure what I expected, but it wasn't seeing Harbor's car parked near the front door.

I feel sick.

That's something I never felt with Harbor before.

Nothing makes sense, so maybe he can unwind this mess and make it right again.

I look in the mirror and wipe away the makeup that's smeared under my eyes from crying. I can't touch up with my makeup bag at home, but does it matter? There's no way I'll be able to stop my tears from engulfing me with the two words I dread hearing—he's gone. I'm barely containing them now. Anyway, my makeup will probably be running again shortly.

I cut the engine and climb out of the cab, dropping from the high truck until my feet reach the ground. I don't lock it. *What's the point?* No one's going to steal it from this property. For that matter, I might as well leave the keys on the seat just in case I need a quick getaway. Not that I'm planning an escape, but something's gone terribly wrong, and I have a feeling I wasn't summoned out here to discuss my summer plans.

Wow, another thing that seems to be gone in an instant. Why were we making plans if he had no intention of following through? I'm so lost on what's happening and am ready to wake from this nightmare.

The door opens as soon as I take the first step to their front door. Marina's standing there with tears in her eyes as if she was the one who was left.

We've spent a little time together when Harbor and I would come over for dinner and celebrate over the holidays. But I wish we would have had more time to get to know each other. She's very poised for her age, intelligent, and is a great kid. By the time I reach the landing, she throws her arms around me and starts crying.

These aren't the tears from learning of a death or an accident. Those are black, with hope burned in the ashes. I can feel that flicker inside me, that little ember trying to persist and come to life. Harbor does that to me. He makes me feel nothing and everything all at once, fragmented, but hope still exists between us, our love burning through the tears of the brokenhearted.

I embrace his little sister like she's my own, soothing her. I find comfort that I'm not alone, that I'm not the only one who's been abandoned. But I realize his sister crying means I'll be the one crying again in a minute. "It's okay, Marina."

"He—"

"Marina," her dad says, his voice catching us off guard.

She takes a short breath, her eyes meeting mine so quickly that I don't have time to see what she already knows inside them. The coloring just about brings me to my knees, the same color that usually makes me weak in them when Harbor looks at me. She whispers, "I'm sorry," and then walks to her dad.

Like my dad did for me, hers holds her as she cries on his shoulder. Harbor's mom comes out and sees them. "Honey? Come here, Marina." She takes her hand and wraps her arms around her. Delta looks at me over her shoulder and says, "*Oh Lark . . .*"

Marina wipes her eyes and quietly moves through to the living room with her dad as I step up to the door.

Delta takes my hands, bringing me inside the house and then wrapping her arms around me so tight that for a moment, a moment so brief that it won't betray my dad, I wish she were Liz. *Is this what moms do?* They wrap you in a blanket of their arms when the world becomes too much to handle?

Her breath is shaky for someone who looks so composed . . . as if she's been dreading this visit as much as I am. She says, "I'm so sorry, Lark."

Reality hits hard with a boom kick to my heart.

Why is she sorry?

I start to push away, but she holds me tighter. "He loves you so much."

It's funny how the mind plays tricks on you, making you think that you'll live, that you're somehow strong enough to survive your heart being broken in two and your soul ripped from your body. *Tricks . . .*

The birds are singing, and the sky is so blue—my favorite shade or used to be—on the drive over. *Tricks . . .*

As my tears fall on the silk, I can't help but think her floral blouse was perfect for a springtime graduation, but here we are, crying on it instead. What an odd thing to notice. *Tricks . . .*

My eyes start to dry, but I'm left drained from the flooding emotions. I could cry for hours, but at this point, that's just my heart weeping.

"Let's get something to drink," Delta says, taking my hand and leading me into the kitchen. I see Noah and Marina outside at a table by the pool. Both look troubled. Noah with his slumped shoulders as he rests his head in his hands and Marina with her large sunglasses that may hide her crying eyes but not the red of her nose.

The only two missing are his dad and eldest brother, Loch. I've seen his dad, and I imagine Loch is around here somewhere. The Westcotts seem to be a family that comes together in an emergency.

Is that what this is?

An emergency?

A crisis to get through?

Did they gather when Lucas died? Or when Harbor was accused of letting him? Where were they when he shouldered the burden of that death to save his cousin's reputation? Or when his aunt leaned over a coffin to threaten him? To guilt him into living Lucas's life instead of his own?

I stand there with my heart lacking a beat in an empty shell of a body. Yet somehow my muscles are intact and tense. Every ounce of what remains of my being becomes protective, barricading me as if I'm standing among the enemies who betrayed me. Harbor would tell me otherwise, that they're operating on limited information.

But as I choose between sitting on a barstool or standing, I choose to stand with truths, *his secrets*, I shouldn't know.

Delta moves around the kitchen side, pulling various things from the cabinets. "You arrived sooner than I expected. I wanted to put out snacks. I'm sure you're starved after the long ceremony. What can I get you to drink?" she asks as if I'm whole before her and can stomach such things.

"Where's Harbor?"

There's no point in making small talk when we have the root of evil to contend with. *Lies. Cover-ups. Omissions.* They're all the same. I brace myself for which angle is chosen, though I know I'll never be prepared.

She pauses with a glass in her hand, the glass as visibly shaken as she is. "We should have tea. I think I have chamomile to help—"

"Do his dirty deed?"

She looks at me, her eyes a deeper blue. "Lark, I . . ." Delta sets the glass down and forgets about the snacks. Returning to the other side of the island, she says, "I don't agree with the decisions he's made."

"But you're going along with it, which is the same thing as supporting him."

"I . . ." Her gaze drifts to the outside, where the sight of her family gives her comfort. Wonder what that's like? Turning back to me, she says, "No, I'm not. I just thought you should be told in person."

My mind riffles through the words she's saying. I'm trying to make sense of them, but I can't come to a solid conclusion. "You're telling me what he didn't want to."

"Harbor's gone," she starts, looking down at her hands on the counter. She may be distracting herself from the pain by picking at a speck, but she's stronger than she's probably given credit for.

Me, on the other hand . . . Imagining the words playing in my head is not the same as hearing them come to life. He's gone. I grip the counter with both my hands and focus on my breathing.

Rushing around the counter, she comes to me and rubs my back.

"Don't touch me. You're not my m—*you're not my Liz.*"

Delta steps back, her hands raised as if she was burned. The comfort in her eyes is long gone and has been replaced with a myriad of emotions—hurt, fear, regret, empathy, tenderness—spinning in the centers like a merry-go-round. I have no idea where she'll land, but I back away from her, not needing her comfort when her son destroyed me.

When her eyes meet mine, she holds our eye contact, and I see she's settled on hurt. "Lark . . ." She starts strong, her tone much steadier than before. "I know you're hurt. We are too. We're also confused, but we've done what he asked us to. We'll do whatever we can to support him."

"Except believe him when he needed you most."

"What do you mean?"

I should carry this secret to the grave, but with Harbor gone, I'm feeling a lot like I have nothing left to lose. "Lucas . . ." And then I stop myself. "What am I doing?" I cover my mouth, horrified at who I am right now.

"I don't know. You're telling me about Harbor and Lucas." She rushes me, taking me by the wrists and holding them between us. "What do you know?" The words flow from her mouth in a panic. "Do you know what happened that day?"

Striking out in my pain to cause others the same isn't who I am. It's not who I want to be, either. "I shouldn't have said anything."

She searches my eyes and then begins to cry. Her hands lower, and she turns away from me. "He closed down, shut us out." Her sobs have her back wracking with sobs.

"I'm sorry," I say, feeling worse than I did when I arrived. "I shouldn't have done that to you."

Turning back to me, she says, "You didn't. It's just a reminder of how much pain he's been in, and we couldn't spare him from it. We tried, Lark. We got him help, let things go when he stepped out of line, and tempered our reactions for the longest time. From the car accident to when he came to us months ago about—" She stops abruptly and returns to the kitchen, snagging tissues from a box hidden beside the fridge.

Harbor and I were together at that time, so when she hands me a tissue, I ask, "What happened months ago?"

"That's why I texted your dad. I'm sorry for not coming to your party today. Under the circumstances, I thought it best to explain to your dad that you and I needed to talk. I wasn't sure if he'd like to drive you or if you'd come alone. Whether you'd come today or tomorrow. I just didn't know." She presses her hand to her head as if she's exhausted. "I'm sorry. I've been rude." She looks at me, and says, "Congratulations on graduating. We have a gift for you somewhere around here." She glances around like she left it here originally. "I . . ." Her mind suddenly seems to be elsewhere. She moves into the family room and sits on the edge of the sofa.

"What were you saying about Harbor and Lucas?"

Seeing this usually graceful and calm woman falling apart, I realize we may not be so far apart in our pain. With a shared interest in her son's well-being, I sit in a chair next to her. "Why did Harbor leave me?"

"He's doing what he believes is best for you."

I bristle from the words she dared to utter and then stand, needing space to help unfold my racing thoughts. "Why the elaborate plan? Why did he even show up today if he knew he'd be gone?" I pace the floor, asking everything that comes to mind. "Why not break up with me? Be honest, please. Tell me the truth. Do I mean so little to him that I don't even deserve a goodbye?"

"He loves you—"

"This doesn't feel like love. It feels like torture." The tears begin to well in the corners of my eyes, so I stop to dab them with the tissue.

"I'm sorry, Lark. He loves you more than you'll ever know."

When a lump forms in my throat, I'm convinced it's the remains of my heart trying to escape. "You're right. I *won't* know because he's gone. Where did he go anyway?"

She looks down and then dabs her eyes with a tissue as well. "I don't know."

"Why don't you know?"

Looking at me, she replies, "Because he knows I would tell you."

I wrap my arms around my middle, feeling guilt consuming me. I've been too hard on her. I can cry or even throw a fit, but it won't change that he left.

Delta's not the enemy but an ally to me. She's his mother, but Harbor knows she'd tell, so he didn't want to put her in an awkward position. Not that he succeeded, but he tried. *For her? For me?*

She leans forward as if she's sharing a secret of her own. "Harbor isn't my only wild child." Glancing through the windows, the slightest of smiles is seen when she watches Noah diving into the pool. When she turns back, she says, "But he considers himself a black sheep. What he hates about himself for being different, I adore. There's a quieter confidence." She grins like there's more to that story. "At least around me. I can't speak to his friends or those he's dated. I have a feeling some arrogance might play into his character when he's out in the world."

I think about the first time we met and how it wasn't arrogance but a sense of self that caught my eyes. He may have felt lost over the years—grieving not only his cousin's death but who he was before Lucas passed—but he was making strides to regain all he'd lost on the inside.

"It's not that which drew me to him. It was his character, his humor, the way he was always close to me, physically, and listened. He listened to me like someone who wasn't listening to himself. He understood the hole that Liz left. He didn't try to fill that, competing for the space would have been a useless endeavor. He just loved me enough that I didn't notice the absence of her anymore."

"May I ask who Liz is?"

I had been absently staring at a family photo on the mantel when I turn to look at her again. "Liz? Liz is my mom. But she left when I was two. Disappeared like Harbor."

"Liz Shaw? Elizabeth Shaw?" She slowly stands, staring at me like she's seen a ghost. Her eyes examine my face as if she's seeing another person altogether.

I turn away, the intensity of her stare feels too much for me to handle right now. *Shaw? Is that her name?* "I have no idea what her last name is . . . *was*. I don't know anything about her. I've never even seen my birth certificate." I waffle. "On purpose. She left me, so what was the point of investing my time in her?"

Delta is still staring, so I shift and say, "Please don't."

"I just can't believe . . ." Seemingly rattled, she moves toward the kitchen.

I ask, "You can't believe what?"

Turning back, she replies, "I can't believe you're her daughter."

"You knew her?"

She nods. "Liz was one of my school friends. She came over with her sweet daughter once." She looks at me in the same manner I was originally greeted—open arms and comforting. "I held you when you were little, and while we had tea and caught up on each other's lives, you and my son, who was just one year older, played together. I think I have a picture somewhere."

Is she saying I have a chance to find my mother? My feelings are conflicted. I never thought I could feel such immense emotions all in the same day. But here we are . . .

"I don't know where they are, but I'll look for them very soon for you."

"Thank you." I face the door and then tell her, "I think I need to go."

"It's been a lot today."

Walking to the door, she stays behind me. I open it and move outside, needing the reprieve from all things Harbor. "If you decide you can tell where or how he is, why he left, or anything that can bring some semblance of closure, I'd be very appreciative."

I start back to the truck, a million things crossing my mind. One that stands above all others is in the chaos of my boyfriend leaving me, I might have just found my mother.

39

Lark

Two months later . . .

WHILE MY DAD loaded the last box into the back of his truck and Amanda took photos around the house with my phone, I stood in the middle of my bedroom.

A stuffed bear that had seen better days.

The pink ruffled bedspread.

The photo of Liz and where the brooch used to be.

I run my finger over the top of my desk and then pick up the yearbook from where Harbor left it. Flipping through the pages, like he did that day, I find the picture that he didn't think was as bad as I once did. I close it when I feel a wave of emotion breaking on my heart's shoreline and put it back with the others where it belongs. I walk to the door, looking back once more, and smile before leaving and closing it behind me.

I've ghosted around Beacon for months now, hollow on

the inside, invisible and small as I can be, but here, working and minding my own business. Here, I can almost remember what it feels like to be real again. It was my refuge from the apartment, from life, from the memory of Harbor. Only a few surfaces bear his fingerprints, unlike my heart. I'm jealous. Or maybe it's regret. I'm not sure anymore. It's a mixture of emotions that I haven't sorted through yet. What's the point?

He's not here. *End of story.*

I cut through the living room and into the entry, snagging one of the hats my dad wears at the shop from the hook by the front door. It's his favorite. I slip it on, say, "Goodbye, house," blow it a kiss, and walk down the path to where the truck's parked at the curb.

"Nice hat." He doesn't ask for it back, already well aware of how sentimental I am.

I adjust it, preferring a slight curve to his straighter bill. "Thanks."

He opens the truck and leans on the door. "You ready, Pip?"

"As much as I ever will be." It's weird when Harbor's words return, coming from my mouth. I moved home the day after graduation, trying to rid my life of Harbor. I could toss the pillows and burn the sheets—Amanda's idea. I could donate every morsel of food to a bank to help others. But that wouldn't change the fact that he was there twenty-four hours earlier. I still smell his cologne in the air as a part of him remains just to torture me some more.

Facing the fact that his departure was planned, I found most of his belongings were gone before I walked across the stage that day. The furniture remained, and the cabinets were full of dishes. The towels were stacked as if prepared for the next tenant—Noah.

The Westcotts told me I could stay as long as I wanted. Noah even said the same. But why? Why stay in a space that feels like we never existed?

Since Amanda had moved into a studio a few blocks over from my dad at the beginning of the year, when I packed my stuff, barring a few things I couldn't find, I moved back into my childhood bedroom. It was comforting and easy to be here, to live with my dad and pretend Harbor was never part of my life, much less the largest part for a time.

But I was fooling myself into believing that he was found in objects—a chair he preferred over the couch, a coaster I insisted he use when watching TV, a lone sock found behind the couch. An empty side of the bed. A toothbrush left in a cup in the bathroom. There were reminders wherever I looked.

I left to save myself the misery only to find he's not just in the tangible things. He's everywhere. Still is on days when I'm more accepting of my fate. I see him in a box of cereal that he loved to eat a few hours after dinner. I feel him in the bath beneath me when I'm trying to escape all my memories with him. I'm haunted even outside on the patio when a breeze plays a cruel melody that sounds like the laughter we shared when we were happy.

Escaping was fruitless.

I endured instead.

That ache I once craved, the one I could feel the next day after he claimed every part of me, I now live with. Though it's changed from one of feeling full to barren emptiness. Maybe I'm not as ready as I said, but I have no choice. Harbor Westcott disappeared without a trace, at least in my life. His mom says he's f . . . she can't say it because she knows it's a lie. And that's not a lie she wants to tell me. Somehow through this nightmare, Delta and I have bonded.

We haven't spoken much over the summer, but enough to know she doesn't agree with whatever decision he made. Maybe she agrees with the reasoning . . . I get hints of that sometimes, but not him being gone or how he went about it. I don't get more than that. It's probably best that all I know is Harbor's alive, but he's not living.

That's of his own doing, so I have no sympathy for him.

"Here's your phone," Amanda says, jogging down the path. "I took lots of photos so home would always be with you." She snaps a pic of my dad, who's still grimacing long after she comes to stand next to me. Holding the phone above us, she says, "Fries before guys."

"Fries," I mumble and then laugh on the outside. I've learned I get fewer questions that way.

Amanda notices those things, but she's not going to say anything in front of my dad. She knows he's already worried. Add my move to New Haven into the fray, and well, I might just see John Summerlin, my gruff ole dad, shed a tear. We can't have that.

I hug Amanda. "It's only like four hours away. We can see each other whenever we want. I have the extra room waiting for you."

Her embrace tightens, her head coming to my shoulder. "I'll visit as soon as I get a car. I almost have enough saved." Her partying has slowed down, and she seems to have started taking school more seriously. She says I'm an inspiration.

I'm not. I just had nothing better to do than study.

"Love you."

She replies, "Love you, Lark." Pulling away, she crosses her arms over her chest and steps back on the curb. "I'm gonna go. I need to get my mom's car back to her. Text me when you get settled tonight."

"I will."

My dad gets in the truck. I look back at the house, snap one more photo, and then walk around to the other side. Just as I open the door, I hear backfiring. I look in that direction and see a familiar, beat-up Chevy pickup truck coming down the street. It's been a while since I've heard it and even longer since I've seen him.

My feelings haven't changed. When it came to friendship and loyalty, Dane didn't respect me enough to give me either. Him keeping the brooch was just too much for me to overcome last fall.

But ...

I don't know why I bother. I should get in the truck and go. I just can't. After all the years we've known each other, he may have betrayed me, but I don't have to carry this with me. I'll give him five minutes, whether he kept it because Mia just wanted it and wanted to hurt me or to hang on to her. Whatever the reason, I hope it keeps him warm at night.

I tuck my fingers into the pockets of my denim shorts, angling to get a look at him when he pulls up in front of the house. Dane takes his sweet time, long enough for me to check with my dad through the open window. "Do you mind waiting?"

"Are you sure you want to?"

This scene has played out in my mind so many times, but I'm blank of comebacks right now. *Of course.* "I'll be fine."

I move to the front of the truck, and he finally gets out and stands in front of his. "Hey," he says, his eyes darting from my dad to me. I didn't show up on his doorstep, so I don't feel I need to start this exchange. "I miss you, Lark."

"You chose not to have me in your life. Did you not think missing me would be a side effect?"

"I wasn't thinking clearly back then."

I nod, getting a good look at him. He's changed in a good way. Put on a little weight, got some sun. He looks healthier. Being a dad must suit him or being with Mia.

"Hey," he says as if we didn't just hit a wall with the last small talk. He shoves his hands in his back pockets as if I won't notice how nervous he is. I do. I see it in the way the heel of his boot bounces and how he keeps looking away, not able to hold eye contact. "Congratulations on graduating and getting into medical school. Do you think you'll come—"

"We're not going to do this, Dane." Tugging my hands free, I let them hang by my side. I listen as he moves in and out of different topics, trying to land on something that I might be open to exploring. *Not going to happen.* "I'm not."

"Do what?" This time his eyes stay steady on me.

"We're not going to stand here and act like we're friends anymore. We're not. You made that clear."

"But—"

"No buts," I say, shifting my weight to the other foot. "We always used to talk about loyalty. Where was yours?"

"I had no choice."

"You had no *good* choice," I snap. "But you had a choice, and you chose wrong."

"I did." He shakes his head. "I quit drugs. All of them. I don't drink much, but that's been harder to give up."

"I'm glad. You look healthier. It's noticeable. It's good for your family."

I sigh, my body feeling dragged down just talking to

him. "Look, Dane, my dad's waiting. I need to get going." I start for the door, ready to end this awkwardness between us.

"I came here to give this to you."

I turn back, my gaze dropping to his hand. The box fits in his hand. I know what it is, but I wonder if this is a trick. "What is it?"

"It's yours. It was yours all along."

My feet don't move from the spot, and I struggle to swallow around the lump in my throat. I look back at him and ask, "Why? Why now?"

"Besides stating the obvious, that I was wrong, someone did me a favor when they didn't have to."

"What did they do?"

He reaches forward, holding it in his hand. When I take the box, he says, "He helped me get a solid job with real growth potential."

"Growth potential," I say, a small smile coming along. Those are two words I never thought would come from Dane Brody's mouth. It's a nice change to hear him talk about a future. "Sounds very professional."

He shoves his hands in his pockets again. "I was an asshole to him. He didn't have to help me, especially after the shit I pulled, but he did and asked for nothing in return."

I hold up the box. "Then how does this factor in?"

He leaves me riddling through what he's shared, searching for the answer. Shame covers him as he looks down between us. "It felt right to get it back to you. I've wanted to since that night. I just didn't know how anymore."

"Like you just did." I hold it up.

"Guess it was simple all along. You know, Lark, people

love to kick you when you're down. I couldn't do him a favor, but I could do right by you."

I'm not sure what to make of the conversation. My feelings are a mixture of emotions. Maybe like Harbor liked to do, I need to process this meeting and see where I land on the other side of it. "Thanks for giving it back."

"You're welcome."

He turns to leave, but I ask, "How's the baby?"

Shrugging, he laughs, but there's no humor in it. "You'd have to ask Steve. Turns out, he became a father at the end of May."

I have to force my jaw to close. "Oh." I don't know what else to say. *He really did choose wrong.* He knows how I feel about Mia, how I always felt she was using him. He doesn't need me to say more when he's been through so much already.

He says, "Yeah. Pretty much sums it up." For the first time since he got here, his smile is genuine, and his shoulders appear lighter. It almost feels like old times. "I hear you're heading to Yale?"

"I am."

"Give 'em hell."

I grin, and then a little laugh comes out. "I always do." And then we exchange a shared look, one that says goodbye without giving it air.

He goes to his truck while I go to my dad's. Climbing into the cab, my dad raises an eyebrow as he eyes the box. "Is that what I think it is?"

I open the box and smile. Running my finger over the delicate diamonds, I turn it over to see that it looks as good as it ever did, and reply, "Yeah."

"Glad you got it back."

"Still no questions to ask?"

He starts the truck and then looks at me. "I promised I wouldn't. I'm good now that you have the brooch again."

"Me too." Dane's words come back to me. *"He didn't have to help me, especially after the shit I pulled."* Unfastening my seat belt, I say, "Stop the truck." I jump down to the street again, run to Dane's truck, and bang on the window.

He rolls it down. "What is it?"

"Was it Harbor? You said someone helped even after what you pulled. That sounds like Harbor." He doesn't blink. I nod, already knowing. I don't know why it matters, but this is the first tie to him I've had since he left.

Dane says, "He asked me not to tell anyone."

"I understand. I'm glad life is good."

"Thanks. Take care of yourself, Lark."

"I will." I run back to the truck as hope somehow sneaks in that this crumb might somehow turn into a whole loaf of bread. I have no idea why he would help Dane, but that he did, there's just something so pure about that gesture. And if it helped get my brooch back, I'm all for it.

I buckle back in, and my dad asks, "Still want to stop by the apartment?"

"Yes. I promised Delta I would. She says I left a box behind."

"Alrighty. Downtown it is." We almost reach the stop sign when I finally turn back to steal one last look at the house. My dad will always live there, so it won't be the last time I visit, but it won't ever be in the same way. I'm grown and starting my life.

Delta and Marina are standing by the curb when my dad parks just behind her Mercedes. "I'll only be a minute."

"I'll secure the box while you guys talk."

"Thanks, Dad." I get out and straighten my Beacon U T-shirt, always feeling underdressed around them. They would never say that. It's my own issue because they're always put together—Marina in a strapless green sundress and Delta in a floral dress with ties for straps that lace over her shoulder. I can only dream to one day look as pretty as they do.

Marina comes right for me and gives me a hug. "It's good to see you, Lark."

"You, too."

Delta and I embrace right after. I shove my hands in my back pockets, a little anxious since I don't know why they want to meet. I say, "My dad wants to get on the road."

"Yes, understandable," Delta says. "I wanted to give this to you." She pulls two photos from her purse. "I'm sorry it took so long. I knew I had a few photos but tracking them down proved the equivalent of climbing Mt. Everest. The good news? I found the photos. The other good news is our attic is clean and organized."

"Glad it helped." I take the photos, and ask, "What are they?" before turning them over. She doesn't need to answer. I know what both are just from seeing them. I know that one baby is me, and the toddler, I'd know those eyes anywhere. They hold the same depth they always did. Running the tip of my finger over the photo, I whisper, "Harbor." I don't mean to sound wistful, but I won't hide my feelings either. Some days I just don't have the energy.

I flip that photo behind the other of Li—my mom. I can pretend it's easier calling her by her name, but it never has been. That loss plagues me. And although I may never get answers, I believe in my heart that she left me because she had to, not choosing to. That's the difference between her and Harbor. He left because he wanted to.

"She's pretty," I say, glancing at Delta.

Leaning over and looking at the photo over my shoulder, she smiles. "She is."

"Do you know why she left? Do you remember by chance?"

"I don't. She wasn't around back then. I remember her visit being brief, but I never saw her again. She never called, and I had two boys at the time, and I was pregnant with Noah. I was tired—"

"It's okay. I understand. I appreciate the photos."

"My pleasure. I made a copy of both, but I wanted you to have the originals."

"Thank you." I look back at my dad in the truck and then at Delta and Marina again. "If this is the last time I see—"

"It won't be," Delta says so assuredly with a smile.

"Well, I guess I'll see you then." I turn around and head to the truck. It's tempting to hug them to tell them goodbye, but she's right. I can feel it deep down. We'll see each other again someday.

When I'm tucked in the truck again, I look at my dad. "I'm ready."

"Then let's go."

Unlike when we drove away from the house, I don't look back at the apartment or the town of Beacon. From now on, I'm only looking forward.

Two Years Later.

40

Harbor

THERE WASN'T A SHRED of my life that Lark Summerlin hadn't embedded. Not a second, a minute, or an hour. Not a day, a week, or a month. Not even a year. And I'm going on two without her.

The clothes I've washed too many times to still bear her scent, still do. Maybe it's my imagination. Maybe it's that we ended too soon. *I know we ended too soon.*

We ended by my own doing.

Do I regret forcing my parents' hand?

No.

It worked out for her exactly as planned. Though I can admit there were unforeseen flaws in that period of desperation. The main one being that I'm not her boyfriend anymore.

I chuckle, which is rare these days. Boyfriend and girlfriend will never encapsulate what we are ... *were* together.

Being Lark's boyfriend was in another lifetime. I wonder if I'd be her fiancé or even husband if I'd been allowed to stay. *Husband.* No way would I have not locked that relationship down if I had the chance. And she'd be my wife. *My wife.*

I fucking love the sound of that.

I drape my arm across my forehead, knowing I should get some sleep, but this night wasn't unique. This is how most of my nights into early mornings play out . . . my days as well. A perfectly executed agenda, covering the same topics in the same order every time. But still hoping I'll come to a better solution—one that puts Lark and me back together.

Mentally checking that off my list, I move to the next item on the agenda—regret. Regret is a wild card. Some days, I can acknowledge without the emotion attached, and others, those aren't my proudest moments. Tonight, I'll tackle that head-on.

I left.

Two words so small that even when they're together, they are still my biggest regret.

I had no choice.

I've justified the decision to leave a million times. I had to, as they say, throw myself on the sword to save what mattered most to Lark. I don't regret tricking her into medical school. I regret not figuring out a better way of going about it, a way where I would still be in her bed, in her heart, in her life.

The loss threatens to drag me under, so I push to surpass the emptiness I feel inside. But loss and I are on a first-name basis. Lucas and my life at that time. Lark and the life we were building together. I was lucky to survive my cousin, but I think I used up all my luck when it came to Lark.

Dragging my arm back down, I press the base of my palm against my chest in hopes of breaking up this knot that never seems to go away. For more than a year, I mistook it for a hole and tried to fill it. Somehow that made sense, but I guess it would behind the goggles of alcohol. After having been down that road years prior, I steered clear of drugs, but a laziness set in and booze complicated my perspective.

The knowledge of Lark living a life without me was too hard to bear. Didn't matter that I had chartered this course . . . I never thought I'd see her again, and if I did, she'd hate me anyway. I had nothing left to give, which means I had nothing left to lose.

I was kicked out of my apartment the day after I found a thong of hers mixed in with my freshly washed laundry. I had dumped everything straight from the box, not paying attention. I didn't take anything of hers, but finding them, smelling them, and not finding her scent did me in.

Guess the landlord didn't appreciate my design choices. He cited something about a broken table and a chair smashed into the walls of the LA studio I was renting. Some consider that art. I saw it as my anger personified. There was beauty in the destruction—the high I got and then afterward—but it wasn't satisfying. It didn't erase her from my memories or fix the pain I caused not only my heart but hers.

How could I make this right?

I could explain my thinking, that nothing else matters. *Only she matters to me.*

I've gotten good at making bad decisions. Self-fulfilling prophecy? *Maybe.* Shit ton of bad luck. *Definitely.* If I didn't lose her before, I would now.

Loss. It's a real bitch to deal with each day.

Rolling over, I grab the bottle of water from my nightstand and chug the rest of it down. Waking up before sunrise has become my ritual but not by choice. I toss it into the garbage in the bathroom and then walk into the living room of the apartment. I open the windows and the door to the balcony and let the breeze blow through. I still have an ounce of hope left that one day my soul will be cleansed and the good I do now will carry me home.

Home.

Lark.

They're not one and the same anymore, but my heart still tricks me into believing it some days. I make an espresso and then take a shower. I like the modern amenities tucked inside the ancient exterior of this apartment. At first, it appears worn down with cracks covering the surface and scars from the lack of attention. But at second glance, the beauty is still there. It's just buried under the years of the life around it. *I relate.*

I'm like a goddamn philosopher these days. It'd be nice to get out of my head for a while. I dry off and get dressed for a day at the office. Giving up Lucas's dream allowed me to finally focus on mine.

I had to come to the source to follow my dreams. That meant taking a chance and moving to Italy, the home of Maserati, Ferrari, and Lamborghini. If I want to compete with the big boys, I had to take a leap and invest time and money for this opportunity.

A bonus is that being in the city of Modena has given me an opportunity to slow down and pursue what I enjoy doing. I've learned everything I can about manufacturing Maserati vehicles, made connections, and was even offered a promotion and salary to stay that was hard to turn down. But I didn't come to Italy to stay forever. I came to get away. I came to learn. I came to find myself.

I know now.

I know who I am.

I know what I want.

And then I even spent time down in Maranello to learn about Ferrari, deciding my passion lies in the manufacturing and the design of these sexy cars. Not sure how a kid from Beacon Pointe weaseled his way into this industry, but it's started to heal me in ways I never expected. It hasn't fixed the knot, but I'm going to work on that as well.

I walk into the conference room, where I've earned a seat at the table, and share my vision. I'm low level in the company, but high enough to be taken seriously. The plan is laid out, and then I lay down my resignation.

As soon as I'm outside, I pull my phone from my pocket and call my mom. "I'm ready to come back."

She tries to temper her tone, but I hear the wave of excitement threaded through it. "We're ready to see you, honey."

It's been two long years since I've been home. Although I can't return to Lark since that door has closed, Beacon Pointe is calling.

ONE SUITCASE.

My entire life fits in one suitcase, and this stuff has no real value to me. I could have left it behind for the tenant and never thought twice about it.

Finely tailored suits.

Custom Italian shoes.

A laptop and a few souvenirs for my family.

Okay, so there are a few things of value but nothing I can't live without.

The trip is long, but not so bad when traveling first class. I walk outside the airport to see my brothers standing at the curb with a familiar car behind them. Noah says, "Harbor fucking Westcott is back in action and looking every bit the Italian model." I chuckle, leaving my suitcase on the sidewalk to give him a hug. "You're definitely going to be my wingman while you're in town." There's so much wrong, from the back in action to the wingman comment, but it's good to see him, so I'm not going to get into it at the airport.

We have time for those updates.

I pat him on the back, laughing. "Good to see you, Noah." I back up and punch his arm. "You got big."

"I was always big. You just got smaller." He clicks his tongue.

Chuckling, I shake my head. "Whatever helps you sleep at night, *little* brother."

Loch comes over, and we hug it out. He says, "Good to see you, Harbor."

"You, too. How's New York treating you?"

"I could use less stress, but someone has to do the heavy lifting for this family."

He's not wrong, but what does he want? A gold medal? He's packing millions in the bank, so I know it's not a bad payoff. I roll my hand in front of me and lower my head. "From the family, we thank you for your service."

"You always were a clown." He tosses the fob high in the air. I grab it and he says, "I assume you want to drive."

Is that even a question? "Do I want to drive? Fuck yeah, I do."

The Italian countryside has stunning scenery, but there's something about returning to your hometown. Maybe it's nostalgia or maybe the memories. In my case, I'm assuming the former, but nevertheless, it's good to be back in Beacon.

I'm not fully up the driveway when Marina opens the

door and waits on the landing. *Shit.* She doesn't look like a kid anymore. "When did our baby sister grow up?"

I glance at Loch as if he'll have the answers I'm seeking. He says, "I know. Last month, I had a talk with Dad. We were discussing if we need to get a shotgun."

Noah leans forward and says, "I kicked some guy's ass a few months back when I took her to a movie. He made some fucking lewd comment . . . Wonder how long it took the nurse to remove the popcorn from his nostrils."

"That's fucked up."

"So was he," Noah adds. I turn to look back at Noah, realizing he's dead fucking serious. "I fear for the first guy who breaks her heart."

"The first, but there will be more," Loch says, unbuckling his seat belt. "Guys are fuckers. Noah's going to end up in prison before Marina graduates from high school."

Noah laughs. "We've got two weeks. Want to wager?"

I pop the door open. "Nope."

Loch says, "It's not a wise bet to take." He gets out, and we walk to the door.

Marina comes running down the steps and throws herself into my arms. "I missed you so much."

"I missed you, too, kid."

She drops to her feet and plucks at the skirt of her dress. "Not such a kid anymore."

"Yeah. We'll talk about that another time."

"Huh?" She trails me up the steps. "Talk about what exactly?"

The sound of the trunk closing has me looking back. Noah has my suitcase, so I go inside the house. "Where are Mom and Dad?"

Marina wraps her arm around mine and rests her head against me. "Mom's probably out back. She cleans the pool to destress. She's been anxious all week and it finally came to a head this morning waiting for you. One leaf made its way into the pool, and she treated it like a national emergency. I think she just wants everything to be perfect for you."

"I don't need perfect." Wrapping my arm around my sister, I kiss her head. "I just need you guys. It's good to see you."

"You, too, Harbor." Her feet stop at the edge of the rug in the living room. I walked a few extra feet, my eyes on Mom through the windows, and then I glance back at Marina.

She says, "I think I'll give you guys some time together."

My sister's grown up without me. She used to be a clingy kid who would harass me into buying her sodas and stuff our mom didn't allow. My memories sneak back to the first time I met Lark at TJ's convenience store. I wouldn't have been in the right place at the right time if it weren't for my sister begging for a caffeine fix before we got back for the party that day.

Lark always believed in destiny and fate. I might hedge my bets on Marina.

I walk outside and say, "Hey, Mom."

She turns back, her face instantly turning a shade of pink as tears overwhelm her. Doesn't matter that her emotions get the better of her. My mom is beautiful, but her eyes lighting up when she sees me makes me happy I came back to Beacon.

I walk to her. She sets the skimmer down and opens her arms to me. She brings me into her fold and hugs me like she's been saving up to do this for years. I guess she has.

Her head drops against me, and I hear her sniffling. "I promised myself I wouldn't cry."

"It's okay." I hug her tight. "It's good to see you, Mom."

Seeming to collect herself by sniffling once more and wiping under her eyes, she raises her chin. "You look . . . you look so grown up, Harbor." I've changed on the inside, so maybe that's reflected on the exterior. She touches my cheek. "You're so handsome."

"I take after you guys."

My dad comes around the back corner of the pool house with a garden hose in his hands. "Where should we put the garden—Harbor. I didn't know you were home. Hold on."

He disappears again.

I turn to Mom and ask, "When did the two of you start taking care of the property yourselves?"

"We don't, but we've rediscovered our joy of being outdoors when the weather is nice and decided to take on a few projects to spend time together."

They're cute. If it keeps a marriage together, I'm all for it.

My dad returns hose-less this time. "I had to turn off the water." Embracing me fully, he doesn't give me a pat on the back. Just a genuine hug. "I'm glad to see you, Harbor."

"I'm glad to be here, Dad."

Stepping closer to mom, he holds her hand, and says, "We made lemonade. I'll go get it, and we can talk."

"Where are my parents, and what have you done with them?"

"Eh," my dad says, waving me off. "Figured you'd enjoy the lemon flavor after living in Italy. They're known for their lemons and limoncello." I like that he's sharing facts about where I've been. It's both entertaining and endearing.

Mom and I walk to the outdoor dining table and sit under the yellow umbrella. She reaches over and covers my hands with hers. "I'm just . . . the house feels right with you back in it."

I wondered if I would feel awkward or uncomfortable

being away from everyone for so long. That they all know the reason also played on my mind. What do they think of me? Did I lose respect? Or—

"Here we go."

My dad sits down, and my mom fills the glasses. I take a sip and then look around the estate. "I always loved it here. I missed it." Glancing back at them, I say, "I miss my family."

"We're just so happy," my mom says, a tentativeness in the back of her throat. "I worry—"

"You're happy but worried? What about?" I ask.

My dad rests his hand on her arm, and replies, "That you'll be leaving before we have a chance to spend some quality time together."

I think about Lark up in New Haven. Four hours and I could see her again. But should I is the question.

My mom says, "Thank you for always checking in." She's courteous enough to overlook the first few months after I left. It was probably the time when they were most worried. They should have been because I was a fucking mess.

After that, I refused to give up on this life. I didn't with Lucas, and I wasn't doing it now. "I feel good."

"You look good, son," my dad says. "Healthy. Happy. The life you've created is working for you. What brought you back?"

"I missed my family, so I learned what I needed to accomplish my goals and came back. To be upfront, I'll be home for a week, and then I'm heading to the city. I decided that would be the best place to start my business."

"So cars, huh?"

"High-end custom Italian cars," I clarify.

"I like cars," my mom says, "Maybe I should be your first customer."

"As much as I appreciate the support, Dad, we're talking

a million base price. I wouldn't let you spend your money like that."

He whistles. "Wow, that's impressive. I know there's a market for collectibles."

"I already have three orders. Once they're delivered in six months, those will hit the street and internet, and I'll get more orders."

"What's the maximum number of orders you can take at one time and still deliver?"

I like that my dad is not only holding me to the fire but pressing me to know my shit. I know it. "Twelve in production at one time with upward of thirty for the year in orders. Beyond that, I'll need to build my own factory instead of licensing rights and using other manufacturers."

My mom is wide-eyed. "Harbor, this is so impressive. You're building something from nothing from your own dreams."

"Yeah," I say, grinning. "I'm pretty proud of myself. This is not something I ever thought I could do two years ago. I was going to be a doctor."

"You would have been miserable," she says, reaching over again to touch my arm in comfort. "Your heart was never in it, but you seemed so focused that I didn't dare risk questioning you. I've learned from that. I now ask the necessary questions."

That we all have learned something from whatever I'm calling it these days—mistakes, crisis, life—will serve us better in not only our communication but moving forward to living our lives to the fullest.

Marina peeks out the back door, and asks, "Are we interrupting?" I can see her excitement to spend time with me. I feel the same about her and my brothers as well.

My dad says, "Come on out."

The three of them join us. It feels good to share some laughs and tell some stories, catching up and hearing about the basic things in their day like tests or a co-worker Loch finds distracting.

"One of the reasons I came back is that I need to tell you guys something," I say, not hesitant at all this time. "I'm not sure there's ever a good time to have this conversation, but it's time the truth came out."

Loch asks, "The truth about what?"

"Lucas's death and what happened to me the day he died."

My family is silent, eerily still. If I had a doubt, now would be the perfect time for one to sneak in. I don't, though. I can't live with this burden any longer. To truly live means to be honest with the people I care about, even at the expense of my cousin's life being tainted by his own actions.

I spend the next half-hour telling them every detail, from the drugs to the burglaries to our fight about a pact we made years earlier. It's not a pretty story and shines a light on the ugly life he was living. But it needed to be told. My soul would finally be freed from his for the first time since the day he died in my arms.

The shock and sadness were there, in their faces and their questions, but the tears that I'm here, that I'm back, that I was honest with them overshadows the rest. Once I reach the end, we stand and do a group hug, just like we did when I was little. And it's then that I realize I never lost them. My family loves me as much as I've always loved them. I just struggled to see it, to feel it to this extent, with my thoughts obscuring what was here all along.

Lying in bed after everyone has retired for the evening, I stare up at the ceiling with a smile on my face. As good as it feels to finally not be shouldering the pain of my secrets, I won't be whole until I fix my mistakes.

There's only one other person I need to make amends. And I have a feeling I'm two years too late, but that won't stop me from trying.

41

***

Lark

I STOP and look back over my shoulder.

As much as I like New Haven, I still feel the ghost of Harbor following me sometimes. We walked this way after we had signed the lease just to see how far the library was from the apartment. He insisted we live close since we'd be spending a lot of late nights there.

He knew.

He made that walk with me, planning the whole thing.

He was making sure *I'd* be safe.

I start walking again, but I can't shake the feeling. Why tonight? Why, after all these years, would he feel closer than he's ever been?

When I reach the doors, I turn around under the light and search the dark, the faces, the other students as they bustle around me. The beginning of the new year is always the busiest here. I prefer summer when so much of the Yale population has gone home. There are no waiting lists to check out books, and I can always find a table to sprawl my stuff out on.

By how many people are here tonight, I'll be lucky if I find a seat at all. Lucky . . . Luck was never one of my strengths. Medicine is, thank goodness. I score a seat near an outlet in the historical library, thinking maybe I am lucky. At least for the night.

It's a silent space, which I like best not only in the library but in life. I'm here to study, to learn, and to graduate, hopefully at or near the top of my class. Kids from Beacon proper, like me, rarely get the opportunity to leave. It's a great place to visit, but I have no intention of ever living there again.

I bury my head in my notes from class, books I borrowed from the restricted area, and the internet trying to piece this puzzle together. I have no idea why this isn't found all in one place. It's archaic that I must be physically in this building to find the information I need. Grumbling about it will get me nowhere, so I put my head down and keep going.

The next time I take a breath, I look up. I didn't notice the library had cleared out, leaving me with only a few others stuck like I am. I check the time. One hour until I need to move my stuff to the 24/7 room or go home before the library closes.

I twist to stretch my back, but a pain in my lumbar vertebrae has me pushing off the table to stand. I leave my area and wander the library. There's a fireplace at one end, but it's too early in the season to have a fire roaring. Looking up, I decide to look once more for a book I couldn't find earlier. Shelves full to the brim with colorful books covering everything a girl could dream of reading. Especially if she's into medicine like I am.

Taking the stairs, I climb to the second floor of the

reading room and walk the narrow aisle along the volumes until I reach the far end. Bending down, I turn my head sideways and run my gaze along the lower shelves and then higher, row by row, as my frustration grows. It has to be here. They showed it in the library at the desk earlier when I checked. I was sure it would be returned once the crowds left for the night.

Bending down in front of the next column of books, I hold the edge of the shelf for balance and start scanning.

"You look lost."

My body freezes other than my grip, which tightens its hold on the solid wood shelf. The voice shatters me, but I keep the broken pieces inside. I won't show weakness. I won't show I care. I won't—I look up to see Harbor watching over me.

The words have two meanings, but I'm not sure which one he's doing. I know because he's been watching over me since the day he left.

Paying my rent, not a day late, for two years.

A Visa gift card showing up like clockwork each month fully loaded with a thousand dollars.

Maybe I was being greedy to expect his love as well.

Despite how many times I told myself that I didn't need him, that I didn't love him anymore, I feel a beat inside my chest the second I see him again for the first time in years. Damn duplicitous heart.

I reply, "Aren't we all sometimes?" He offers me a hand, but I pull myself up, gripping a higher shelf just in case my knees weaken and become traitors as well.

There's no chuckle although I thought I was quite clever. Just that damn smile that always used to do me in, lying on his face. His face . . . God, I missed seeing it. I removed the photos from my phone the summer after he left. I packed away any reminders when I moved out. How can a face be so familiar that it's like I see it every day?

I guess I do. Even if I'm buried in books, papers, and tests, a memory of Harbor joins me at some point. Sometimes I spend time with him, and sometimes the visit is too short. It hurts all over again as if the wound is still fresh every time, though.

"I was," he says, his smile fading under the cover of sincerity.

Searching his features for the man I can hate again, I struggle to find him when he looks so much the same as when I loved him. Sure, he looks older, twenty-five versus twenty-three when he left. But only in that way that men age to become even more beautiful than they were.

It's almost annoying, considering I wouldn't have worn jeggings, a baggy sweatshirt, and dirty sneakers if I knew I would be seeing him . . . *or him see me.* My hair is bundled into a mess on top of my head, and I didn't bother with makeup—*Oh my God, snap out of it, Lark!*

"Well," I say, "I hope you found yourself wherever you've been." I walk around him and down the aisle toward the stairs.

"I did," he replies to my back.

I stop, not giving him a front-row seat to my emotions or even my expression. I start walking again, this time faster until I'm running down the stairs. I'm given a look by the librarian, so I slow down and pretend my body isn't ready to launch from my skin. Everything inside tells me to run, to get out of here as fast as I can. Not from fear but from the love that I just realized I still have for him.

Bastard.

I gather the notebooks and shove them in my bag before slamming my laptop closed and tucking it inside. Swinging it onto my shoulder, I collect the books and hurry back to the librarian. "Hi, I need to return these."

"Just leave them here."

"Thank you."

There's no sign of Harbor, and I don't know how to feel —do I want to see him again, to talk, to argue, to freaking kiss? Or is it best if he's gone?

Please let him be gone. I don't have time to figure out which emotion suits me best in this situation.

I push through the doors to see him waiting outside— hands in his pockets, a shier side of his earlier smile, but unfortunately, no less charming. His shoulders appear broader, but I'd have to be splayed across him to measure, and that's not going to happen . . . I don't think.

No.

It's not.

Why am I like this? What am I doing?

When I start walking in the direction of the apartment, he asks, "May I walk with you, Lark?"

"No." I keep walking. Despite how tempting it is to turn back and get one last look, his disappearance was child's play compared to this torture.

"Hey, Lark?"

"Leave me alone." I keep walking, too unsteady in my frame of mind to think rationally. That's what I need to think clearly around him, and I'm lacking all capabilities to reason.

The feeling of his presence earlier makes more sense now. He was freaking following me. *I knew it.* I felt him in the fall air, in the rustling of the leaves as a breeze blew through, and inside me, my intuition told me he was near. *The stalker.* It was cute back in Beacon. Here, on the streets of New Haven, it's not anymore.

As soon as I get into the apartment, I lock the door and the bolts, so basically do what I usually do. Toss my backpack to the table and head straight for the blinds to close them. Once the living room is secured, I close the blinds in both bedrooms as well.

Sitting on the edge of the bed, I hold out my shaking hands. Thank God I don't plan to be a surgeon. I sit on them, hoping that calms them down as I take several deep breaths.

For an organ that refused to cooperate the past two years, my heart is putting on quite the performance after seeing Harbor.

I missed dinner, opting to study instead, and the apple and salad I had for lunch has long worn off. My stomach growls, so I move into the kitchen and make a bowl of cereal. I never liked this cereal until it was around all the time when I lived with Harbor.

Sitting on the couch, I switch on the TV, hoping to switch off my mind. But even *Pretty Woman* can't turn my thoughts around when it finally sinks in that Harbor is out there.

He's here.

Somewhere.

Oh God, what have I done? I set the bowl on the coffee table and hurry for the door. But I stop and return to put the bowl on a coaster, and then make a run for him. I don't care that I'm in my socks or that I have to take the stairs. I take them anyway. I just need to get to him, to hear his side of the story. I push through the lobby and rush to the sidewalk.

Left.

Then right.

I look left again and then across the street. But there's no sign of him. How can that be? I threw two small hurdles his way, and he doesn't even try to jump them? Not even for me? Why'd he come back to New Haven, then?

Huffing a loud and exhaustive breath, I don't know if I feel defeated or deflated. *Both, actually.* When I turn around, I see his car parked down the street, and my feet stay, not willing to move despite my head's better judgment to do so.

He doesn't get out, but I see his silhouette in the driver's seat.

For a second, I smile, and my hand raises slightly from my side as if I'd seen a long-lost friend, before I catch myself and lower it again. I guess I have, his words playing back on a lowlights reel. *"You look lost."*

I am.

More than I realized until now.

I turn toward the door and open it. This time, I walk away *from* him.

Two Years Later.

42

Lark

"I THINK the blue dress is pretty, but the red reads sexy doctor alert."

"Amanda," I whisper, "my dad is in the next room. The last thing he wants to hear about is his daughter being sexy."

She stands from the bed, glancing from the door back to me. "He's going to hear about it eventually because you, my friend, are smokin' hot." She touches the tip of her finger to her ass and sizzles. "Pure fire."

I can't stop laughing. "You need to visit more often. You're good for my self-esteem." I give in to the fun and wiggle my hips. I look in the mirror, running my hands over my hips where the curve is more pronounced. My breasts are a little fuller. My hair, just below my shoulder blades, is longer than I've worn it since I was little.

The skintight dress doesn't allow me to hide any flaws. I could have slipped on shapewear to flatten my stomach, but I don't mind the natural shape. Amanda's right. I smile, staring back at not only the doctor I've become, but I do look like pure fire.

"You talked me into it. I'm going with the red." This is a nice departure from my usual uniform of a sweatshirt and leggings. I'm glad I splurged . . . well, bought it with one of the gift cards. Wearing this dress does make me feel sexy and a little bad under the good-girl graduation gown.

"Wise choice." Walking toward the bedroom door, she says, "We're heading over to the auditorium. I want a good seat so I can see."

"Don't stress about it. You see me all the time."

"Who says I was talking about seeing you? I'm going to be in a room full of doctors. I bet a few cuties are looking for a girlfriend."

I laugh as I go back into the bathroom for one last touch-up. "Geez, thanks," I tease. I lean in and then grab a washrag. Amanda said I needed to look the part of a doctor, but judging by how heavy she layered on the makeup, I think she's confusing nightclubbing with making hospital rounds. I tone it down just a little to find more of me under it all.

I slip on my heels, then dig through my small bag as I walk into the living room. "I can't fit much in here. Look, my phone and lip gloss. That's about it."

"Umm, Lark."

"What is it?" I dig my ID out of my wallet, then one of the gift cards I've been spoiled with the last four years, shoving them both in my crossbody purse. Maybe I shouldn't have come to rely on that money, but it served its purpose, which I assume was to make my life a little easier. I didn't need to get a job or skip buying a book that I needed to study. I've also saved half of the cards. One day, I'll give them back, fully loaded again.

If I'm not ever given the chance, I'll mail them to Harbor's parents, from whom I received the sweetest card and money order for five-hundred bucks to help me settle into the next stage of life. Marina added at the bottom—*or to take a vacation.*

I like her way of thinking. I could use a break, but my residency starts next week. No rest for the weary and I'm definitely weary.

When I realize Amanda still hasn't replied, I look up.

A large blue box with silver trim and gray ribbons stands upright on my table, blocking my view of her. "What is that?" I ask, clutching my purse with both hands.

From the couch, my dad says, "Just got delivered." He starts clicking through the TV stations like he's going to be here for a while. "Let me know when you're ready."

Amanda and I exchange a look, both of us blinking quickly for some reason. You'd think we'd never been around fancy boxes before . . . *okay*, we've been *around* them, but not so much received them.

There's no name across the box. Who would send me something that looks this expensive? I ask, "Who is it from?"

"I don't know." My friend touches the box like it might bite back. "There's a card."

I slip it from under the ribbon and open the small envelope. "I'm so fucking proud of you – H. H.? . . . *Oh shit.*" I cover my mouth and glance at my dad like I might get in trouble for swearing. "Sorry."

He laughs, knowing that's exactly what I did. "Not much I can say about it, Pip. You're a doctor now."

And twenty-six, but I'll always be his little girl.

Holding the card, I read it again. *And then again.*

My hands don't shake anymore when I think of Harbor, but my heart still races.

Amanda asks, "Who's H? . . . *Oh shit*." She covers her mouth when it dawns on her, then grabs my wrist like she's the one who needs support.

I never told her or my dad that I saw him one night, a couple of years back. I don't know why he came to see me in New Haven. Sometimes I spend hours lying in bed thinking about that night and if I had given him a chance to speak his mind. Not that I owe him a thing. I don't.

Not for the apartment.

Not for the gift cards.

Not for anything.

I didn't ask him to do any of it. He did it because he felt guilty for leaving. *Plain and simple.* So I'm not sure why he's giving a gift that, knowing him, is expensive, but there is no way in hell I'm keeping it. I look at Amanda, and say, "I thought you guys were going?"

"Not since this arrived. Are you going to open it?"

I'm already shaking my head when I reply, "No. I'm not. I'm going to send it back to him."

"Who are you sending it back to?" my dad asks, clicking off the TV. He stands and adjusts his waistband before walking to my side and giving me a quick hug.

"To the sender," I say, keeping it vague. I lift and kiss his cheek, hoping to distract him from the gift. "Thanks for driving in for the ceremony."

"I wouldn't miss it." He walks to the door, holding it open. "You ready, Amanda?"

She grabs her purse and over her shoulder to me, she says, "See you soon, *Doctor*."

"Yeah. Yeah," I say with a soft laugh, my eyes drifting back to the box. "See you soon."

My gaze dips back down to the card when I'm left alone

with it. It's not full of sweet nothings, but it packs a punch. *Harbor always did.*

When temptation grows, I warn myself, "Do not open it, Lark." Nothing good will come of opening a present from him, just like nothing good came from a relationship with him. Though I'm not sure how anything in such a pretty box could sour a mood, I remind myself there's a hell of a good chance it could affect me negatively, send my emotions spiraling, and ruin this graduation like he did the last one.

Throwing my hands up, I state, "Nope. I'm not doing it," and walk away to grab my cap and gown. I leave, locking the door behind me. It's the only way to keep me from tearing that box open.

I hurry across campus, filing in with the others flooding the auditorium. Once I find the other graduates, I take a deep breath to calm down. These heels are torture. Who thought rushing around a large campus would be a good idea? That would be me, guilty as charged. Too late to change my shoes now. Since the other graduates are milling around, I sneak into the bathroom to put on my cap and gown and fix my hair one last time.

The curls softened just as I hoped and the lighter strands that always appear with the warmer months have started to shine through my lighter brown hair. I smile, realizing I should have given Amanda more credit. My makeup is pretty in this lighting and makes the color of my green eyes pop.

From the dress to the makeup to the hair, and even to the stunning black shoes, I feel incredible, the best I've ever felt. Oddly, the most adult I've ever felt as well. Grown. I've grown so much over the past four years. I had to. The shock of Harbor exiting my life without notice gave me no room to back away from moving forward. I was already falling apart.

I would continue to shatter until nothing remained of me, or I would follow through with my dreams.

It doesn't matter that a part of me, a smaller part than I realized now when I'm looking back, went to medical school to spite him.

No. It only matters that I now have a prefix that I worked my butt off to earn. The M.D. at the end isn't shabby either. *Dr.* Lark Summerlin, *M.D.* I feel good, like the clouds are finally starting to clear.

When I return to the hall, I find my spot just as we start walking. I should be excited, but my intuition begs for attention. This is a huge achievement, my dream come true, so why can't I get this feeling of dread to subside? It's probably the pain from my last graduation still haunting me. I need to brush it off. This is my second chance and a greater achievement. *Enjoy it, Lark.*

I find my seat and resist the urge to look around. I spent most of my college ceremony searching for Harbor instead of listening to the speeches. I'm going to make a concerted effort to live here in the present this time. I just wish I could shake this odd feeling.

Not the dread.

The sense that Harbor is near, his eyes on me, grazing the length of my body, or that the butterflies in my stomach just awoke after years of hibernating. I should hate him. He wouldn't blame me. But instead, I find my thoughts of him, and what we used to be, have begun to mellow. That's only natural. The mind plays tricks like that to help one cope with reality.

He's thinking about me.

Still, after all these years.

Still, even after telling him to go away the last time he showed up here.

There's a small seed of satisfaction trying to bloom inside my belly from the knowledge that he's still thinking about me. At least the butterflies will have something to nibble on. If he weren't, there wouldn't be an ungodly expensive gift at my apartment still waiting for me to open.

Stop doing this. There's nothing to gain from this exercise. The one thing I never allowed myself to delve into was the idea of revenge. It was an easier road to take some nights in my head, but it wouldn't serve me well to travel it.

It wouldn't change what happened.

It would have only changed me.

Curiosity is killing more than the cat, so I finally look around. Amanda waves at me, and my dad sits a little straighter. I don't see anyone else I know. They're probably just parents of other graduates, so I breathe easier now.

The ceremony begins, and although my intentions were good to focus on the speakers, my mind drifts to what comes next instead. More change and bigger moves have been made with each stage of my life. And I move farther from my dad. I look back, stealing a glimpse of him before he notices.

He's always been a handsome man. He also doesn't lack attention from the women of Beacon. He may not be rich like those who reside in The Pointe Estates, but he has a busy mechanic shop and grills a mean meal. He never really dated because he put his energy into being there for me and supporting my journey every step of the way.

John Summerlin would never say it, but I know it breaks his heart that I'm settling in the city. He understands because he's my dad. One day, I'll make his sacrifices worth it. I don't know how, but I will. He deserves nothing less.

As for the residency in New York, I got the confirmation this week and scored a small studio a few blocks away from the hospital, subletting from a resident who didn't get a job offer. I have no intention of letting that happen to me.

Two hours later, I walk across the stage and am introduced as a doctor. I shake the dean's hand and then turn toward the audience knowing Amanda told me to pose for a photo. I grin under their cheers, embarrassment setting in from the attention.

I exit the stage and return to my seat. That feels relatively uneventful, and I'm not upset by it. I almost half expected to see Harbor seated in the audience, but there was no sign of him. I should be relieved, but my emotions are twisting, which leaves me more confused. I got what I wanted—a regular graduation ceremony.

I should be happy . . .

Everyone stands, filling the auditorium with cheers. I stand quickly and catch up to the reveling. *I did it. This was the dream, my goal.*

As the crowd disperses into the foyer and drains onto the surrounding sidewalks, I take off the robe because I'm feeling anxious and sit back down. Amanda and my dad are waiting on me outside, but my breath comes heavy in my chest as a myriad of feelings overwhelms me. I drop my head into my hands, closing my eyes, and just flow with the river of emotions inside me.

"Is it everything you ever hoped it would be?"

The dulcet tone that always fit night like a glove—seductive and deep.

His proximity wrapping around me like a blanket.

A warmth that seeps inside me that I know extends to the clarity of his brown eyes.

Harbor.

43

Lark

I DON'T MOVE A MUSCLE, not even taking a breath when I hear his voice.

Opening my eyes, I angle to look behind me. "Better."

Harbor smiles, the act coming so naturally, like we didn't crash and burn years prior. "I'm glad."

My breath starts to even, but I hate that it's in reaction to the comfort of him being here . . . *being near again.* "Why are you here, Harbor?"

"Because you weren't ready for me before."

"I'm not ready for you now." I stand as if I'm making a point. My thoughts are muddling, but I still push to say, "Being ready has nothing to do with you. You made your decision that I didn't matter enough to stay in your life."

His eyes unabashedly take me in from top to toes, and then he sits back, like he has the upper hand, sitting on his throne of confidence. *He doesn't.* I don't care how good he looks in a suit and tie or how his cowlick forms a wave of perfection just above his forehead. *Damn him.* Damn him to hell for momentarily distracting me from the pain he caused.

I yank the cap from my head and start down the row.

"I had to leave because you were *all* that mattered to me." I hate how calm he sounds, that confidence still ruling his tone.

Fury rushes my veins, and I fist my hands at my sides, the velvet cap getting the brunt of my anger. I turn back, throwing it on the chair with the gown. "You have some nerve saying that. Your memory has faded, but mine hasn't."

Leaning forward, he rests his arms on the chair in front of him. "What do you remember, Lark?"

"I remember you telling me how proud of me you were, kissing me like it was the last kiss we'd share." Tears collect in the corners of my eyes. Not from the pain I feel but from the anger that fills me. "You told me to remember you loved me always. You made me tell you I would. You drove us to New Haven, and we picked an apartment like we'd share it together. We made plans, Harbor." I lose steam, not seeing the point of revisiting memory lane. Exhaling, I whisper, "I remember you loved me."

I stare at him through the watery lens of my stubborn perspective, unable to understand what the point of this is. *Is he trying to win me back or close a chapter?*

"I still do."

I anchor my hand on my hip, shaking my head. "You can't."

After a quick shrug, he says, "What I can't do is help it."

"Try harder." I move down the row, and when I'm free from the surrounding chairs, I stop again. "Ugh!" He's infuriating. Spinning back, I ask, "Why did you leave? Where did you go?"

He comes closer, his steps slower as if we have all day to discuss the past. *I sure don't.* My mind is already balancing between my dad and friend who are waiting on me and this man who did so much damage that the aftershocks are still felt.

He says, "Los Angeles for a short time and then Italy for a couple of years. The last two, I've been around, traveling a lot for—"

"To process your feelings while I had to deal with mine?" I hate myself the second the words leave my mouth. I've never been one to choose the low road, but I also wasn't afforded the same emotional luxuries since he alone decided our fate.

This time he's staring at me, his expression lying in indifference. "I always did take too long for you." He slips his hand under the collar at his neck. "Seems I did this time as well." He walks past me, and says, "Congratulations, Doctor."

For graduating or for winning the argument?

I don't feel good either way. I wrap my arms over my stomach and then go back to grab the cap and gown I almost forgot. Why can't I just have a normal graduation?

I leave the building and search the sidewalk until I see Amanda and my dad waiting on a bench. I go to them, plastering on a fake smile, and ask, "Ready for lunch?"

They sit there, looking up at me like I've grown a third eye, and they don't know how to tell me. "What?" I ask.

Amanda says, "We didn't want to interrupt."

"I don't want to talk about that."

Standing up, my dad rubs my back. "Are you doing okay?"

"Fine," I snap, "never better."

"You sound *never better*." His eyes go wide like he's

signaling for Amanda to step in. *Just great.* They're now a tag team?

I hold out my hands to stop her from stepping in like I'm a delicate matter they need to handle. "I am." I start walking toward the apartment. "Let's drop this off, and we'll go eat."

"I think eating will help," Amanda says, keeping pace but staying a few feet behind me. "Food makes me feel better."

Better . . . this is not better than I hoped for. No, it's not better at all. *It's worse.* I'm tired of putting on a brave face for everyone, for pretending that a relationship I had at twenty-one isn't still defining my life four years later, and what ticks me off the most—I'm still in love with him. "Fuck!" I yell at the top of my lungs.

I close my eyes, but it's too late to stop the tears from coming. My dad comes around and wraps me in his blanketing arms. With me tucked under his shoulder, we walk the rest of the way to the apartment.

By the time I wash my face, the storm has blown over. I change into something more comfortable and go into the living room. "I'm ready. I'm so hungry." We move into the hallway, but I push back in and grab the large, unopened box.

"What are you doing with it?" Amanda asks.

"Getting rid of it."

"I'll take it if you're throwing it away."

I laugh. It's light but feels good to release. "I'm not throwing it away."

"What are you doing with it then?" She holds the lobby door open for me.

Returning to the sunshine, the day is warm, and the sky is blue. It feels a lot like a new beginning, so I can't have ghosts still haunting me. Standing on the sidewalk, I look down the street in both directions until I see *him* in his Maserati. "I'll be right back."

Marching right up to his car, I stand in front of it until he gets out. I move around and shove the box at him. "I don't want your gifts."

I expected a look of shock or dismay, something like I've seen in the movies I love, but he doesn't give me that. Instead, he takes the box and puts it in his back seat. With my arms crossed over my chest, I add, "I want nothing to do with you, Harbor."

"And why is that exactly?" he asks, so freaking innocently.

I roll my eyes. "Let me make this perfectly clear for you. You disappeared without a trace, leaving me without even the courtesy of an explanation. I still don't know why you needed to leave or if it was something I did—"

"You didn't do anything wrong."

"Yet you punished me as if I did." I scoff and look away. "God only knows why you left, but it took me visiting your mom for it to finally sink in." I glare right into his eyes. "You left me. You left me to fend for myself—"

"Don't twist it. I left so you didn't have to fend at all. Those four years were laid out perfectly for you. It was the perfect plan, and it worked."

Lost on this line of reasoning, I ask, "What worked?"

"You became a doctor."

"Oh my God, Harbor. Just stop." I throw my arms out in frustration. "Please stop with the riddles and nonsense. I'm a doctor because I earned my way into medical school and my scholarship. You don't get to take that away from me."

"I'm not. I wouldn't. It's your accomplishments that got you here, Lark. It truly is, but I'd like a chance to explain."

"No, you had that and blew it." I take a breath and exhale, lowering my voice. "Good—"

"Give me one more chance, baby." *And I thought I went low . . .*

I hate him for saying that name. Though, I'll be savoring the sound of him calling me baby for months and years to come.

Raising my finger, I'm about to tell him exactly how that will never happen. But I don't. I can't. I lower my finger because I still stupidly have feelings for this man. That's why I'm so affected by him. I can fight this attraction and reject any feelings that still exist for him, but that sounds like I'm being punished for his sins instead of the other way around.

There's no way destiny wants us together again. It's been proven time and time again. So why should I give him another chance? This isn't some movie. He's not coming to sweep me off my feet. This is real life. The damage has been done that's beyond repair.

And what if I did give him that chance?

I barely survived him the first time. I won't survive losing him twice, but the scars will deepen.

"Please, Lark. I know it's a lot to ask, but I'm asking anyway. Give me one more chance to make this right."

Nothing about this makes sense. Why aren't my fight-or-flight instincts kicking in? I'm not flighting or fighting. I'm leaning in, wondering if we spend some time together . . .

"Not today. I'm in no position in life to take . . ." I wave my hands in front of me. "This on, to take you on. If you want another chance, then you find me in a year, and I'll listen. That's all I can promise."

A wry grin spreads his cheeks, and he says, "And I can

promise you that you won't regret this decision. I'll see you in one year."

I lick my lips and raise my chin. "And if at that time, I never want to see you again, then you'll walk away, and that's it, right? No showing up unannounced or sending me gifts. No contact at all. Agreed?" I hold out my hand.

When he takes it, that chemistry we always shared ignites once more. "Agreed."

I pull my hand back and take one last look at him. "Okay, see you in a year."

"See you then."

A rogue thought comes to mind, so before I leave, I ask, "How will you find me?"

"Don't worry about that." He winks. "I have my ways."

That my panties still exist is a whole other issue after seeing his cockiness return.

I walk away, but turn back to say, "You sound like a stalker."

He shrugs. "What can I say? Some women bring it out in me."

Grimacing, I ask, "Women, as in plural? Not a good start."

"Woman. Only you, sweetheart."

I hate that I'm smiling, but ironically, I don't feel so much hate for him as I walk away. *Oh God, what have I done?*

One year later . . .

I don't know how many times I was told the pain from heartbreak would pass. It didn't, even when I foolishly believed it had. It would come roaring back into my life when I least expected it.

A plate of carbonara.

A silver Maserati parked on the street.

A bottle of soda like I once bought him at the convenience store.

Years later, I'm still living in misery.

The blind date sitting across from me isn't helping to prove my case otherwise. I ask, "So are the stocks up or down? And what does a bull market mean?" I've successfully kept Scott talking about his true love—*money*—through a round of cocktails. But now that we're ready to order, I'm having second thoughts about dating a stockbroker.

Do I even want to have dinner with him?

I mean, I've asked about him on purpose, to get to know him and see where his loyalties lie. In the last forty-five minutes, I've learned that they won't lie with the unlucky lady that ends up being his girlfriend. She'll be secondary to his passion for greed.

The server arrives tableside to take our order. I open my mouth, but then Scott says, "She'll have the house salad. That's a small, right?" I'm going to need a paper bag before I hyperventilate. *How dare he!* My face feels like I dipped it on the surface of the sun.

"Yes, sir," the server responds, his eyes shifting to me in concern as if he realizes I'm about to explode.

"Perfect."

Scott adds a lobster pasta dish for himself and then tells the server to hurry, citing a game on later that he wants to watch. *Is he kidding with me right now?* There's no punchline other than the mockery he's making of my appetite, so I think he's serious.

I excuse myself to the restroom and find the server to apologize. He says, "We get a lot of stockbrokers in here.

Trust me, honey, they're all the same. Get out now, and don't waste your time. Or that amazing dress."

The heat in my cheeks morphs from anger to flattery as I touch the soft pink fabric. "Thank you," I reply, looking down. "For both the advice and the compliment."

He taps me when I turn to go. "What did you want to eat?"

"I would order the carbonara, but it's not worth finishing this dinner with him."

"Agreed."

I use the restroom, taking my sweet time. Maybe Amanda can break away from writing her dissertation and meet me for a drink and a real dinner somewhere. Like he said, no point in wasting a good dress. She's been working hard at NYU for grad school and she's reached the finish line. I shoot her a text: *Free tonight?*

I reapply my lipstick and then look down just as her text comes in: *I can't. Sorry. I'll be free forever come next week. Rain check?*

After dropping my lipstick in my bag, I reply: *Next week it is. Good luck.*

I return to the table and start working on the second cocktail that's arrived. I'm going to need it to make it through this.

The salads are dropped off, and the server gives me a little insider's wink. Scott digs into his, stabbing a tomato like he's seeking revenge. I push my salad across the table for him.

"What are you doing?" he asks with his mouth full of food.

"You ordered two salads," I reply, feigning innocence. "Here's the second."

"No." His eyes narrow, his nostrils flaring. "I ordered *you* a salad."

"I didn't want a salad. I wanted pasta."

He balks. "A woman your age shouldn't be eating pasta."

"I'm twenty-six—"

"It'll go right to your hips."

I toss the napkin on the table. "And the problem is?"

The server swoops in, handing me a to-go bag. "I went ahead and put an order in for you. *To go and on the house.* And I threw in some bread because the bread's delicious, especially ours. There's also plasticware." Touching my arm, he sings, "Enjoy."

"Thank you. I most definitely will. Alone."

"That's what you'll be in New York City."

"Fuck you, Scott," I say his name with the same vigor he stabbed that innocent tomato. "I'd rather be alone with my pasta than shackled to an asshole like you." I leave, weaving through the tables toward the exit. The server high-fives me on the way out the door.

As soon as my heels hit the concrete, they stop right there.

Leaning against a newer version of the silver Maserati he used to have, Harbor is every bit Jake Ryan come to life. Adding his own spin, he runs the pad of his thumb across his bottom lip and glances down shyly. *Damn him.*

That I'm even standing upright at this point is a feat in and of itself. I grip the handles of the bag and lick my lips.

With his head still tilted down, he looks back up at me and raises his hand just enough to wave. "Hi." His voice reaches every nook and cranny of my body, bringing it to life again.

Smiling like a loon, I look down the sidewalk hoping to tame it, but there's no hope for that. When I turn back, feeding his ego, his smile is just as ridiculous as mine. He says, "Sorry I'm late."

Shifting my weight, I angle my hips and take an eager breath. "What took you so long?" I put our agreement out of my mind a long time ago, so even though I don't remember the exact date we saw each other last, he's right on time.

He opens the passenger door for me, and replies, "I took the scenic route."

44

Harbor

YEARS EARLIER, I told Lark we needed a redo. Our meeting wasn't one made of the stuff that filled the romance movies and books she loved. But I fucked up that redo back in New Haven. *Twice.*

This time, I'm not taking any chances. I won't fuck it up again. Too much time without her has passed. Every moment matters, so I'm not holding back anymore. If I've learned anything, it's that secrets are only meant to hold you back and make you despise the very thing you were protecting.

I reach the edge of the city and keep driving over the George Washington Bridge into New Jersey. Lark hasn't said a word since she got in the vehicle. I haven't felt the need to fill in the silence. I'm content with the trust she's given me that allows her to go wherever I choose.

It's tempting to reach over and hold her hand like we used to. I tighten my fingers around the steering wheel and try to keep my eyes forward. It's easier to face the future than stare at my past, wondering if we'll ever get back to where we once were in each other's lives.

There's no winning that battle. Lark has always been the most beautiful woman I've ever laid eyes on, so I steal a peek. The last light of the day shines through the windshield. It's bright, but she doesn't bother to shield her eyes. She embraces the light instead. Leaning forward, she closes her eyes and soaks in the rays.

I could stare at her for hours and find new captivations on every inch of her skin, but I drag my attention back to the road ahead, needing to stay focused on driving instead of the mesmerizing woman beside me.

Lark's features are more defined than when she was back in college. Her nose is a little sharper like her chin. Her skin is smooth, and I don't think I've ever seen a blemish on her. If there ever was a flaw, I never noticed. She used to wear her hair up most days. Now it's longer than it ever has been, shiny in the sunshine, and a thousand shades blending from blond to darker than my brown.

She looks incredible in that dress. It shows off the curves I used to spend nights traversing with my tongue. I thought I had better control of my cravings for her, but being inside the car with the rest of the world trapped outside, her sweet, floral scent wraps around me like a scarf. Her being this close to me again has unintended consequences that are out of my control.

I shift in my seat.

As if she senses my weakness for her, her eyes open, and her gaze slides over to me and down without apology. She says, "I have a feeling you weren't in the area."

I glance at her, catching sight of the gold centers where

the sun is as rapt as I am, finding peace within the greenest depths of Lark's eyes.

Death of me...

Closing my eyes briefly, I breathe, inhaling her into my lungs.

What a glorious death it will be.

I chuckle. "No, I wasn't in the neighborhood."

"I always knew you were a stalker." She grins, resting her head back on the seat. "I called it the first day we met."

She's right. "I'd been watching you since the first time I saw you." I grip the wheel like it can transfer the support I need to confess my sins. "You took my breath away. That had never happened before." I glance over at her again. "I knew you were special."

"I wasn't special because you noticed me, Harbor. I was special because I saw through your façade. I saw you."

I'm leveled by her words, and her insight hits me square in the heart. "You did see me. You're the first person who ever did. I meant to thank you for that." I volley my gaze between her and the road a few times. "After I left, I think I spent the first two years trying to become a man worthy of you again."

Her expression falls, but she doesn't give in and fights to keep the corners of her mouth even. "You were worthy the day we met, Harbor."

Hearing her tell me I'm worthy cuts deeper than a knife ever could. I know I did what I had to for her, but I still doubt how I went about it. I saw no other way. I scrub over my face and turn on the music.

We cover miles, but she's still riding along like we're on a pleasant Sunday drive. I finally reach our destination. I drive over gravel and park. Not making a move to get out, she asks, "Where are we?"

"Palisades Cliffs." I get out and come around, opening the door for her. When I offer my hand, she slips hers right in. The surge between us ushers us together when she stands, though our bodies barely touch. Looking at her, I tuck hair behind her ear as if I still have that right.

As if I hadn't, she turns back and grabs the bag out of the car. Carrying it with her, she walks to the end of the vehicle and turns back. "Hungry?"

I shut the door. "I can eat." We walk closer to the overlook, but I stop her. "You look fucking amazing, and those shoes ... *fuck me*, they're very ..." I gulp.

"You like?" She lifts a foot, teasing me.

"Yeah, I like. You could say that."

When she turns, I realize the view is almost gone for the night. We stand there, side by side, taking in as much as we can with the sun hiding under the tops of the distant hills. She turns to me. "I bet it's beautiful during the day."

"We'll have to return and find out."

She moves to a nearby park bench and starts unpacking the bag. When I sit next to her, she hands me a plastic fork. So I ask, "You're feeding me a doggie bag from a dinner you just had with another man?" *Gutsy, for sure.* Not that I care. I'll take anything she wants to share with me right now.

She's mid bite and starts laughing, and then covers her mouth. When she finally finishes chewing and swallows, she clears her throat. "It's a short story actually. It began when he ordered a salad for me and told me a woman of my age shouldn't be eating pasta."

"Does he want a fucking death wish?" I take a bite, remembering how she ate carbonara the first time we ate together.

"Right? That's what I thought."

"How did it end?"

"Well, when he ordered me a salad and told me I shouldn't be eating pasta, it was pretty much over right then."

"I'd say so." I'm about to take another bite, but ask, "So where did this come from?"

"The server was incredible. He saw what went down and made my order anyway, packed it to go, and I was gone."

"His loss."

"Your gain," she says, taking another bite.

It is my gain. She is. He's a fool for fucking up, but I get it. We all do now and then, yet there's no coming back from what he did and said. I wonder if I have a better chance.

We eat a few more bites before she says, "I wish I had brought some water."

"I have some." I get up and pop the trunk. Pushing the flannel blanket to the side, I open the flap to the basket and pull two bottles of water from it.

I'm about to close the trunk when she asks, "What's this?" I watch as her gaze darts around the trunk, and I'm quickly found guilty right after. She runs her fingers over the hand of the basket. "You brought a picnic for us?"

Busted. I run my hand over my hair. "Well, yes."

"Why are we eating cold pasta then?"

"Because you love that dish."

She sets the bag in the trunk with the pasta dish tucked back inside. "It's not Moretti's." She remembers. I don't know why that gives me hope, but it does. Moving to the back rear of the car, she leans her hip against it. Her gaze lengthens toward the road as a car passes by.

When she turns back to me, she says, "I'm starting to realize that it wasn't the pasta I loved back then. Maybe it was the company."

That's when I know in my heart that we aren't too far gone. This is the chance I never thought I'd get.

She digs into the basket and pulls a bottle out. "You brought wine. Can I have a glass?"

Over the next hour, our conversation has started to flow like it used to, without any pain clouding it. I stick to water since I have a long drive back, but I pour her a second glass. She has her knees tucked to her chest after discarding the heels while drinking the first glass.

"Lark?" She turns to look. I say, "I'd like to tell you the rest of the story of my cousin's death, if that's all right."

Her lips have parted, and she leans forward, rubbing my shoulder. "Are you sure?"

"I shouldn't have kept it in." I swallow harder. Despite being open with my family a few years back, it's not something I often talk about. "It controlled my life for too long. I told my family everything, and releasing the lies changed my life. I wish I had been strong enough to tell you when we were together. To trust you instead of trying to protect you from it."

"You never should have had to bear that burden." She nods and takes another sip of the wine. "I'm here and listening. Whatever you say is safe with me."

I know . . . *I knew* all along. "Back when Lucas and I were fifteen, we were smoking weed and drinking, dabbling in a few heavier things. While under the influence of probably all of those things, we made a blood pact. If I go, you go. It was dumb and had no real meaning behind it. Best friends making vows they had no intention of carrying out just to see if the other was that loyal. I mean, it was right after he said if I smoke, you smoke. If you drink, I drink. If I go, you go. Meaningless in the scheme of things, but especially when you're high as a fucking kite."

Lark's body has stilled beside me. Her glass is now next to her on the bench, and she's staring out like she can still see the Hudson. When her mouth opens, I think she's going to ask a question. I wish she would, but she doesn't. She takes my hand instead and holds it on her lap.

Needing to get this story off my chest, I say, "I told you we weren't hanging out much those last couple of years. I wasn't into the same scene, but I remember when he showed up at my house. He seemed sober enough. Dragged me from the pool to go check out the cliffs at Devil's Edge." I exhale as the memory comes back. "I was glad to see him. It had been too long. I'd been holing up in my room, so I went along. He drove us out there and ran so fast from the car that I thought he was about to jump. Fuck." I scrape my nails over my scalp to redirect the pain threatening to over-whelm me.

Lark whispers, "It must have been terrifying."

It's not a word I would use often, but she nailed how I felt back then. "He was starting to bounce, anxiety getting the better of him. He was erratic and kept grabbing my shirt, wanting me to listen. I was listening, man. I was listening." I glance at her again, and this time, her eyes meet mine. "He brought up the pact."

"Harbor . . ." I can't tell if it's a cry of sympathy or a warning to stop.

"I'm sorry. I can stop."

"No. I don't want you to. It just hurts to know you carried this secret all on your own." She takes my hand and brings it to her mouth. When she presses her lips to the top of it, I close my eyes and savor everything about it, about her, at this moment. I may not get another.

"Lucas was convinced that day was the day we needed to hold each other accountable for the pact. He was determined to make me keep my promise." My knee is bouncing. I wish it were daylight so I had something steady to set my eyes on. Fisting and releasing, stretching my fingers, I fist again and repeat as anxiety rebuilds from that day. "He just kept swearing that I swore my life that night, grabbing my hand to show me the scar."

A tear rolls down Lark's cheek. I reach to wipe it away for her, but then I pause. She gives my hand a little squeeze and the green light. I gently catch the tear and hold it to my lips, tasting her for the first time in what feels like forever. The tears she cries for me give me strength, knowing she still cares. "He went to the edge and told me he didn't want to live this life anymore. When I went to stop him, he grabbed my shirt to take me with him."

With a gasp, she jumps to her feet and throws her arms around me. "That's horrible, babe." The wine spills, but neither of us cares. As I pull her onto my lap, this woman I never stopped loving, I know what saved that day and again years later. *She did.*

Her tears seep through my shirt, but she doesn't hold back, just like the name she called me. We're bonded more than she used to think. We always will be.

I hold her tightly to me, and say, "He jumped, but I fell. My life was inexplicably tied to his that day. He hit his head, not clearing the cliff, and I fell on my back fifteen feet below Devil's Edge, landing on a ledge." I exhale and set her back on the bench. As much as I want to hold her again, I need space to work this out not just in my head but also around me.

I say, "I broke a leg and most of my ribs on one side, but I held Lucas in my arms until he died. It wasn't long, probably ten minutes, but I was stuck there for hours praying I'd be saved."

Swear on My Life

"I'm sorry, Harbor. I'm so sorry you went through that."

Seeing her in her bare feet against the gravel, I stop and scoop her into my arms. "Did you not feel the pain under your feet?"

"How could I when your pain was so much greater?"

Sighing, I'm so torn up that I'm not sure how to feel. She has me feeling like a superhero flying back into her life, into her arms again, but I'm not a fool. This story takes a toll when I relive the words that tell the story. *Is she just feeling sorry for me?*

I carry her to the car and set her in the seat. Kneeling beside her, I say, "Don't do that. Don't compare our pain. Yours matters to me just as much, if not more, than any I've experienced."

She caresses my cheek. "How did you survive?"

"I was there, but my phone had fallen out of my pocket. Lucas didn't have one on him. So I waited. For hours, I waited. At different points, I was fading in and out of consciousness. I knew that wasn't a good sign, so I focused all my energy on one thing."

"What was it?"

I drag the pads of my thumbs over the apples of her cheeks and wipe away the tears and makeup that's run down her face. "A bird."

"A bird?"

"Yeah. This little bird was perched high in a tree that overhung the cliffs and lake." I'm glad she smiles. I say, "I listened to that bird, tuned into its melody as it sang. I remember that bird being there, singing to keep me awake, until I was rescued."

"How did they find you?"

"My car. I'd run so fast to stop Lucas that I'd left my door open. A passerby called it in, and the police and paramedics came." I smile. "That bird kept me alive."

She smiles, her hands resting on my knees. "It sounds like it. What kind of bird was it?"

"It was a lark."

45

Harbor

HER EYES SOFTEN at the outside corners as she stares into my eyes. God, I miss lying in bed next to her, talking into the early hours of the morning, sometimes until the sun sneaked in and shined a light on the golden flecks of her eyes.

She still has the most captivating eyes I've ever seen in a kaleidoscope of greens and golds.

Angling, she dips her legs out of the car again. Lark leans forward and cups my face. We move closer, so close until her forehead is against mine.

It wasn't just the late-night talks I missed. I miss *her*. I miss the smell of her bubble bath still lingering in the bathroom after she got out. I miss the elastics she'd use to twist her hair on top of her head. I'd find them everywhere, from a blue one in the crack of the couch to a pink one in the fridge once, and a handful on her nightstand. I miss her claiming one of the nightstands as her own. I miss her claiming me as her own. I miss her so fucking much.

I close my eyes, not from fear that this will be the last time I'm close to her, but the opposite. This feels like a new beginning. An acceptance of who we were and who we are in the present.

She whispers, "I don't know what to say."

"You don't have to say anything at all. I didn't know your name the first time I laid eyes on you. I didn't even know it a month later when you bought the soda at TJ's—"

"And you called me sweet cheeks." She smiles for me, and my whole world tilts on its axis.

I'm worn down, the trauma of that day years ago exhausting me in ways that may take a lifetime to recover. But I will recover. I know that now. I caress her cheek feeling I'm earning the right back, even if at a slower pace than I like. "And you called me babe."

She nods with a sweet smile arranged on her beautiful face. "I remember when I told you my name and the way you looked at me . . ." She takes a shaky breath. "No one's ever looked at me the way that you do. Even now, after the years, the pain, the crushed hearts, the lost souls, you still look at me like I'm everything."

"You are. To me, you always will be." The weight of the words holds all my truths inside them. "I'm sorry I hurt you, Lark."

With one hand still firmly pressed to my cheek, she slides her other down my neck. Looking into my eyes, she says, "I wish you hadn't."

"It's my biggest regret."

When she tears her eyes away from me and takes a breath as if she's gasping for air, the point of the knife prods this fucking useless organ in my chest. It's an unpaid passenger on every journey I make.

She nods slowly and then closes her eyes briefly. "I

didn't expect you to keep your promise." Her eyes glance to me and then away again. "But you're here, Harbor, and I'm . . ."

"You're what? You can tell me anything."

Seeming to catch herself, she sits up and then tucks her legs back inside the vehicle just as tears overflow her lower lids. Looking down at her fingers twisting in her lap, she shakes her head. "I can't do this again, Harbor."

"What is this?" I ask, hearing the lengthening distance in her voice. Looking at me, she hesitates, then licks her lips as if the words are already there, but she doesn't want to say them out loud. As much as I don't want to hear a rejection, I still care what she has to say. "You can tell me, Lark."

Her gaze slides up until our eyes meet again. "If I'm not careful," she whispers, "I'll fall in love again."

I kneel before her again. "You say that as if it's the worst possible outcome."

"This isn't a fairy tale, Harbor. You don't get to barge into my life and sweep me off my feet. That ship has sailed."

I stand and turn, looking around as if I'll find an answer in the dark that surrounds us. The knife slides in without resistance, straight to the heart of who I am, deflating any hope I carried of reigniting our flame.

With my hands on my head, I pace away from the car, wishing I could make her see how much I care. Money never impressed Lark Summerlin. Character does, and she believes I lack integrity. *Would she feel differently if she knew the truth?* Standing ten feet away or so to give her all the space she needs to see me, *all of me*, I ask, "Are you open to the possibility?"

"You don't know what you're asking."

"I know better than I ever did. I know who I am, even if you can't see it."

"It doesn't matter what I see. You're still asking me to throw caution to the wind and trust you again." She rubs her forehead, seemingly troubled by raising her voice. When she looks up again, her eyes are focused on me. "I did that once, and it didn't end well for me."

"You're a doctor. It ended exactly how it should have."

"I would have chosen you if I had been given a choice." Tears roll down her cheeks, and she reaches for the door. I stand, knowing I'm not changing her mind, at least not tonight. "I realized years ago that you weren't the knight in shining armor, but my story's villain." Her gaze crawls back to mine, and through a shaky breath, she says, "I'm sorry for everything you've gone through, for the evil that forced you into a corner. I'm glad you've fought to live your life to the fullest again. But maybe . . . maybe that's the only happy ending we can hope for us."

When she holds the door even tighter, I stand so she closes it. But then she reopens it, and says, "I forgot my shoes."

I look at the park bench and see the glass, the wine bottle, and her shoes still there. "I'll get them."

The door closes as soon as I walk away. I don't take offense. Pushing me away and blocking me out are her defense mechanisms. What I think or feel doesn't matter. I care too much to push her beyond her comfort level. I pick up the shoes and the glass, dumping the remaining drops to the ground, then grab the bottle.

I felt the beginning not the end. My mind is reeling as much as my heart. This isn't our end. I would feel it.

After I load the stuff in the trunk, I get in the car and hand her the shoes. "Thank you," she says quietly as if she's being intrusive. *It's bullshit that she sounds small.* She should never be anything less than the incredible person she is.

"A year ago," I say, starting the engine. "I asked for another chance. You gave that to me without question tonight. I want to thank you for this opportunity."

Her chin lifts as she angles my way. "You're welcome."

I back out of the overlook parking spot. "I'll get you back to the city." Now she eyes me, her lips twisted to one side as she bites the inside of her cheek. I continue, "I'm sure you have a busy day tomorrow."

"I do, actually."

I pull back onto the road, knowing I have one hour, not for me to change her mind, but for her to do it. Convincing someone to love you is only a temporary trick. The real magic is when they believe it themselves. Then it's genuine.

Keeping the music low in the background, I ask, "Why did you apply for your residency in New York?"

Planting her elbow on the door, she rests her head in her hand and tightens her expression as if she might be onto me. But then she says, "It's easier to disappear here and live life on your own terms."

"Why do you want to disappear?"

"I don't need a lot to make me happy. A great bagel, solid friendships, and family. I'm within a few hours, if not closer, to all those things." She smiles, easing back against the leather seat. "I'm also a people watcher. I like the city, the vibe, the busyness of it all. Everyone has somewhere to be. It's nice to sit in the chaos without getting sucked into it."

Her smile is enough of a reward to soothe the angst twisting inside. I go on to ask, "Do you believe that people can change?"

"Oh, um . . ." She glances at me, appearing surprised at the question by how she readjusts, and her brows rise. "I believe people will change when it feels right to do so. For some, it might take a lifetime to realize they need to. Others change in the moment."

"What about forgiveness?" I ask, silently pleading that she can give me a reason to hold on to hope.

"Am I being interrogated?"

"No. I just want to hear your thoughts."

"What about forgiveness?" she repeats the question as she mulls her answer. There's no sigh of defensiveness, but I'm still glad she can speak her mind. "Forgiveness takes time."

As much as I hate to admit it, we still have a few hurdles to jump, so I understand what she means. "I don't know if I'll ever be able to forgive my aunt for the guilt she put on me and the lies she made me tell about my cousin."

"I understand. I'd struggle with that as well."

I still don't understand my aunt's motives. To protect a reputation he'd already jaded? To destroy me in her grief? I'll probably never have the answers. I'm not upset that she's been removed from mine and my family's lives.

As for Lark, I want to know everything she believes. I ask, "What about love?"

"What about love?"

"Do you think it's meant for everyone, even the damned and damaged?"

That she hasn't shied away from answering any of my questions is a good sign. She's engaging as well as enchanting. She replies, "I think even the most injured hearts have the capacity for love. It comes through forgiveness, but if the person can find the strength, they can move on. Not everyone can."

"Can you?" *God, I hope so.*

"I hope so." Her gaze extends through the windshield as she adds, "My dad didn't."

The knot that had been eased years ago upon my return to the States rolls across my chest, picking up everything I had left untouched—the truth of her scholarship, why I left, and even the way I found her at the restaurant earlier tonight. The details could make things worse or bring us together, but I won't take the gamble. Not with her. Not with this chance. "Why not?"

"He couldn't forgive my mom. He's spent his life hurt to the bone." She turns to look at me, a hand covering her mouth under wider eyes, like the similarity just struck her. "I don't want to live the rest of my life trapped by the pain of the past."

"I would never want that for you."

Her hand lowers, and there's the smallest of knowing smiles along with a roll of her eyes. "I bet."

"I *will* bet. I'll bet destiny hasn't played her hand when it comes to us." Okay, resorting to what I know she believes in might be considered shady, but what's the point of having inside information if you don't use it?

Her smile blooms, and I'm not fucking upset about it. "How much?"

"How much what?"

"How much are you wagering on destiny?" I love seeing a mischievous gleam in her eyes. *She's invested.* How much remains to be seen.

"Everything."

"Everything?" She sits upright. "The car and the answers you've never given? The—"

"The house, the condo, my heart," I say, sneaking that in.

Renewed energy flows through the car as the weight of earlier finally dissipates.

She asks, "How will we know if we win or lose?"

"Guess we'll just have to wait to find out." The city looms

in the distance, and by the time we're crossing the Wash-ington Bridge again, dread sets in. I'm not ready to say goodbye or good night to her.

I hear her swallow, making me believe she feels the same.

I know her address, though I've never been in the area. Still, this is about what she wants, so I ask, "Where would you like me to drop you off?"

"You can drive me home. Thank you."

I'm inventing scenarios to justify why she'd give up that information so easily to me—like her not wanting to walk in those heels or it being dark—she says, "I trust you, Harbor. You have always looked out for me. I know you never hurt me on purpose. I can see that now. You left me to protect me. Maybe one day you'll trust me enough to tell me why."

Lark's always been so damn smart, but her heart reads me so well. She's not asking me, so I nod, knowing one day I will.

After she directs me to her neighborhood, I can't say I'm impressed. It's fine, but I'd prefer her somewhere with more security, like a lobby and a doorman, some barrier between her and the street. But that's not my place, and I won't make her feel bad or worry about something that she can't help.

I stop at the curb, get out, and come around to help her. She's steady already when she takes my hand. I'm not sure I am being this close to her.

She says, "How did you know where I was tonight?"

"I followed you from the hospital." I watch her carefully, waiting for her reaction.

Her eyes glance at the car behind her. "How in the world did I miss a silver Maserati following me?" She doesn't sound bothered in the least. She sighs dreamily as her hand touches my chest. "I'm glad you found me. It's been a good night, even with the bumps in the road." She pulls her hand back quickly as if it had gone rogue and was fraternizing with the enemy. Exhaling with a little coo, she moves around me and heads for the door to her building.

I close the door and turn around to watch her, to make sure she gets in safely. She punches in a code on the keypad and then opens the door. I don't know where we stand or where we're leaving this, but I have to try. *Again.* Not just for me, but because I don't want her living the rest of her life trapped in pain from the past either.

This is it.

My last chance.

"Hey, Lark?"

Shouldering the door open, she turns back. "Yes, Harbor?" She can say all she wants to about not wanting to metaphorically open the door to me again, but I hear that threadbare hope hanging on for dear life in her voice.

"Are you free Saturday night?"

Her gaze goes sideways along with her hip. She can put on the show like she doesn't want to go, but her heart does. I can feel it. She just needs to get out of her head. "I don't think that's a good idea."

"Really?" I ask, surprise rising inside. "I think it's a fucking great idea." I walk around my car and open the driver's door. Leaning on top of the hood, I say, "Is five good for you?"

"Harbor?" She plants her hand on her hip. "What are you doing?"

"Giving us the redo we deserve."

46

Lark

I DELETED Harbor Westcott from my life a long time ago.

His number.

Our photos.

And as many memories as I could purge over the years, though the bin in the back of my mind is overflowing because I refuse to empty it.

The truth is that I didn't want any hint of him seeping into the life I had after him. Then why did I beg Margaret to trade shifts with me on Saturday—me taking her morning—so I could be ready at five for him? Why did I try on the same red dress that had Harbor readjusting his pants at graduation last year? But more importantly, why am I texting his sister to get his phone number to ask if said red dress is appropriate?

Ugh!

Marina replies: *It's the same number he's always had.*

I type: *I deleted it back in Beacon.*

Three dots do the wave thing and then her next message pops up: *Harsh.*

Me: *No, not harsh. What he did to me was harsh.*

Marina: *Not if you knew why he did it...*

I stare at the screen and read the message again and over again. She knows why he left me? Has she known all along?

Marina's his little sister, his only sister. I know they were close, so I assume they still are, but she and I were close for a time as well. I miss her. She was like the little sis I never had. I remember going to their house in The Pointe after graduation and her crying on my shoulder because he left. We were in this together. *So I thought.*

Harbor used to say she couldn't keep a secret. Well, she's done a fine job of keeping this one. I call her immediately.

"Hello," she answers like she doesn't have a care in the world while I'm over here panicking.

"Why did Harbor leave?" I pluck the dress away from my skin, not wanting to nervously sweat on it.

"I don't think it's my place to tell you, Lark. I'm sorry."

Exhaling from the wind of hope being knocked out of me, I then ask, "But you knew why all along?"

"No . . . I found out when he returned."

"Tell me something, anything, Marina, about why he left me?"

"He didn't leave you." She pauses, and then I hear her mom calling her name in the background. "One minute, Mom," she yells, holding the phone away from her mouth.

She's going in circles and not getting to the point. I'm seeing a pattern with the Westcotts.

"I'm back. You still there, Lark?"

"Yes?" I cling to her voice, holding my phone tighter and needing anything that will help me put this nightmare behind me once and for all.

"I don't think I'm supposed to say anything, but I'm not sure Harbor ever will." Is it wrong that I'm silently praying she shares what she knows with me?

My mind speeds through every reaction he'll have once he hears she told me. I'm okay dealing with the consequences because I've never wanted to hear something more in my life. "Please tell me."

I hear her blow out a deep breath, and then she says, "Don't tell him I told you, though, okay?"

"Okay . . . Hey, how did you know we're talking again?"

"You asked for his phone number, so I figured talking was involved somewhere in that equation."

"*Ah*. That makes sense." Am I ready to finally hear the truth? *Damn right, I am.* "Now tell me."

"What?"

"Marina."

"I was kidding," she says, laughing. "Settle down. Aren't you supposed to be the adult between the two of us, Doctor?"

I burst out laughing. I miss her and her humor. And she's right. I take a deep breath, shaking my restlessness out by waving my hands, and then say, "I'm good. Let's go."

"Harbor traded his education for yours."

"Wh—" I must have misheard. "What did you say?"

She repeats herself, but I still can't wrap my head around what she means. My head spins through hundreds of scenarios, but I still can't make sense of it. How would his education have been traded for mine?

What did he do? I need to sit, but I lie down on the bed, setting the phone next to my ear. My head hurts, but my heart is aching.

"Lark, are you still there?"

I turn just enough to say, "Kind of," in the direction of the phone.

"I know, it's a lot."

"It *is* a lot." Pulling the phone closer, I turn on the speaker. "I don't understand how he sacrificed himself for me. Tell me again, slower this time."

"Harbor . . . talked my parents . . . into paying," she says, overenunciating every word like we don't speak the same language. "For your medical school . . . instead of his."

I sit up, take it off speaker, and hold the phone to my ear again. "I hear what you're saying, but that's just not true, Marina. Your parents didn't pay for my education. I got a full scholarship from Yale for medical school. I still have the letter."

"I don't know the details, Lark. I just know that's what went down. I remember them having a big fight months before he left. I found out later that's what caused it."

I just can't make sense of this, and the shuffling on the other end of the line keeps distracting me. She says, "I need to run, but it's good to hear from you."

"You, too. Let's talk soon. I want to hear about everything going on in your life."

"You've got yourself a deal."

When we hang up, I pace the floor a few rounds because I can't stop thinking about what she said. I shouldn't give it a second thought, but it makes no sense. Why would she be under that impression? Weaving around the bed, I kneel in front of the two-drawer filing cabinet I use as a nightstand.

Flipping through the bottom drawer, I find the Yale file and the letter tucked inside. When I read it, though, nothing jumps out as odd. It's even on official letterhead with a seal from the financial department.

I set it down on my small desk by the window and take

my dress off, not wanting to wrinkle it. I hang it back up and slip on my Yale School of Medicine sweatshirt, sit down at the desk, and pull up the department's webpage. Locating the number, I call and ask to whom I speak with regarding the scholarship. The lady on the other end transfers my call to a man who sounds ready to call it a day, telling me he'll look into it and send me an email in response.

Why am I nervous?

I'm a doctor. It doesn't matter now. What will they do, tell me they made a mistake and force me to pay hundreds of thousands of dollars back? I exhale, thinking it's wise not to get worked up over imaginary scenarios. I might not have been nervous before, but I am now.

Pretending this is a normal Thursday night isn't working, though. Even though I don't expect to get an email back, the week's almost over. What if I don't get the answers? What answer am I looking for?

My thoughts are jumbled, unsure of what to think. I keep refreshing my email account every few minutes, hoping to solve this mystery. I call it a night just after ten and go to bed.

I'm good at keeping the world outside my shifts. Being present can mean life or death. But I check my emails on my break and then at lunch. When I'm home and finally settling in with a bowl of tomato-basil soup and a grilled cheese, I start a movie, determined not to waste another night on this email business. Not even ten minutes later, my email pings, and I dive from my desk across the bed to where I left my laptop.

"Dammit." *Spam.* "This is ridiculous. I got the scholarship and went to school. End of story. Harbor doesn't get to steal the credit from—" I stop, remembering something he once said. *"Those four years were laid out perfectly for you. It was the perfect plan, and it worked."*

It worked.

What worked?

What was the plan?

My laptop pings again. I roll my eyes and go to close it down for the night, annoyed that it owns my complete attention. But the word *Yale* in the sender's name catches my eye. I bend down and click to open the email. I scan it so quickly that I need to reread it just to make sure I understand. "Blah, blah, blah . . . your scholarship was made in donation . . . by the Safe Haven Trust managed by Westcott Law Firm . . . Those are the only details we can share as part of the agreement. Blah, blah, blah . . ."

Westcott Law Firm.

Safe Haven Trust.

Safe Haven . . .

"Harbor."

47

Lark

I've put this dress on and taken it off three times. Why am I going? What am I doing? Why do I want him to think I'm sexy? My appearance shouldn't matter.

I take the dress off and slip on a pair of fitted jeans. And since the Yankees are playing today, I dig out my jersey from the dresser and slip it on over my head.

But what if we're going to a nice restaurant?

Harbor said this is a do-over, which we also need to discuss. He did keep his promise. He came back to me just like he said he would.

As I angle in front of the bathroom mirror, the debate wages on. I bet he scored reservations at the hottest place in the city and plans to wine and dine me.

I'm not opposed to this scenario, especially since I now know what he did for me. Though I still don't know why.

Screw it. Red dress it is, and I'll wear the shoes he loved on me earlier in the week. I get dressed, grab my clutch, and then hurry to the street to wait, but as soon as

I swing the door open, he's already there. I don't think he's a sight I'll ever get used to. "How long have you been here?"

"Not long." I won't complain that I don't have to wait on him. It's actually sweet that he showed up early. He opens the door, and adds, "You look beautiful."

"Thanks," I say, blushing like I'm twenty-one and standing with him in that convenience store all over again. I don't regret the red dress.

Traffic isn't bad, but we're not getting anywhere fast either, so I beat around the bush, and ask, "Do you live in the city?"

A grin crosses his expression. "I do. I live in Tribeca." I don't know why this comes as such a shock, but it's weird to think of him dwelling in the same town as me, yet we're not together. Our lives felt so intertwined at one time that it feels unnatural not to know he lived here as well.

"Do you have a parking garage for your car? You seem to prefer to drive."

"The building has a garage, and I have a reserved spot, a view of the city, and—"

"More than one room?"

His eyes stay on the road ahead. "Yes, more than one room."

Taking the opportunity to look at him, really look at him, I see him in a new light. He's handsome, too handsome to stare at for too long. I say, "I live in a studio near the hospital."

"How's that?"

"Good. Easy to maintain, which is good considering the number of hours I work."

He nods, and then asks, "You work a lot?"

"I work a lot."

He glances over. "How do you balance your social life with work?"

I start laughing. "I don't. I traded a shift and went in this morning at four o'clock to be here with you thirteen hours later."

He rests his arm between us, his hand so close but seemingly just out of reach. It feels wrong for some reason. Too far from me. "You didn't have to do that, Lark. We can work around your schedule."

I want to touch him, for him to touch me, to feel whole again.

"I wanted to." I rest my arm next to his on the console. *Casually* . . . I'm thinking I'm not as slick as I thought because his gaze slides over our arms, lingering a few seconds, and then reaches my eyes.

Under the light of new information, I see him differently. The anger I clung to like a life preserver to save me, to give me something that made sense when he left, has disappeared overnight. "Thank you."

Yale didn't give me a scholarship. He did. Well, his parents, but he made the sacrifice. *What did I do?* I wallowed in the pain of my loss, not thinking he had any repercussions.

So much more makes sense now. The last time we were together, he shared so much with me about the tragedy of him and his cousin, the details I was always too afraid to ask because I wanted to avoid upsetting him. It brought up the pain of him leaving, not loving me enough to stay as well.

But I was wrong.

He left because he loved me. That was the only conclusion he came to, but I still need to hear him tell me. I thought that was why he asked for another chance a year ago.

It's harder for me to remember the pain I was in when his intentions were good, generous, and because he loved me. He wouldn't have done it otherwise. I just wish he would have trusted me enough to tell me back then. So much time has been wasted. *And for what?*

I slink my hand under his and look at him. He faces me with questions rising in his eyes but doesn't dare tempt fate in the opposite direction we're heading. His fingers fold together with mine, and though his eyes are forward on the road again, he's smiling like he just won the lottery.

Since I'm in unfamiliar territory—emotionally and in Manhattan—I ask, "Where are you taking me?"

"To where I live. I thought it was only fair since I know where you live."

I can't wait to see where he lives. I don't know enough about him these days to even have a prediction, but it doesn't go unnoticed that he's including me in all parts of his life—past and present.

Also, I've already duly noted that we're in Tribeca, so he's fancy just like he was back in college. *Some things never change.*

He pulls into a garage and then parks. Looking at me, he says, "I thought this would go differently." He glances at our hands, twisting them and bringing them to his mouth, and kissing the top of mine.

"How did you see it?"

"I thought there'd be more animosity." He releases my hand and turns off the car. When he comes around to my side to open the door, I slip my hand in his again and step out to stand before him. "Last time didn't go as planned. I upset you."

"I was still hurt." I should be more nervous than I am, but I know what I'm doing, and it feels right.

"You're not hurt anymore?"

I'm no longer scared to fall in love with him. I'm scared of losing him again. "I am hurt, Harbor, but I'm seeing things in a whole new way."

"What changed?" He holds my hand, and we walk together to the elevator.

"Everything."

We get in the elevator, and though I can see from the way his expression isn't eased that he still has questions, he's patient, willing to let them unfold naturally.

The doors open, and we walk down a hall. "I kind of expected you to live in a penthouse."

He holds up a key card pulled from his pocket, and we gain entrance to the apartment. Shouldering it open, he says, "Hopefully, it doesn't disappoint."

I walk in, and my breath catches. My hand is against my chest as I take in a view of what feels like the entire city. Harbor guides me forward by the lower back and then shuts the door. "House sweet house."

It's a gorgeous space—like a loft in the sky. It's old New York in style with brick walls, warm wood cabinetry in the small kitchen, and matching floors that look to have seen some history. The leather couch looks cozy with a blanket draped over one side and a fireplace facing it. Other than barstools parked at the island, there's a brass and glass dining table that seats six. It's right out of *Architectural Digest*, and that's not even mentioning the terrace. "It's sweet indeed, but the phrase is home sweet home."

He leads me toward the large terrace. "A *place* could never be my home."

I set my clutch down on the island, standing in the middle of the space. That's when I spy a door leading to a bedroom. "Why not?"

Reaching over his shoulder to rub the back of his neck, he locks his eyes on mine. There's a shared pause between us, causing my breath to slow. Then, as if he's freed from a spell, he signals outside. "I have a surprise for you."

"Really?" I ask with a surge of giddiness rolling up my spine.

"It wouldn't be a surprise if I told you. Come on. Let me show you." He moves to a button on the far brick wall of the space. With the push of a button, the glass that covers most of the length slides on a track, bringing the outside in and us outside. He walks onto the terrace and then disappears around the corner. I follow him, not sure what to expect, which seems to be a running theme with him.

Around the corner is a table draped in white linens, votive candle holders, napkins, and silverware. Off to the side, a brass cart with wine and a chilling bottle of champagne stands next to a decanter of what I assume to be whiskey by the amber color. The lower shelf houses dishes and glasses of varying sizes. I can assume they were protected from the wind until we arrived. There's only a gentle breeze tonight, and the weather is perfect. It's a great reminder of how perfect Harbor always was as well.

"This is magical. Better than any restaurant, and we get to share it alone instead of with half of New York."

He's grinning like he just won a hometown game, and says, "I'm glad you like it. I hoped you would." He walks to the cart. "Can I make you a drink?"

"I'll have what you're having."

He pulls two lowball glasses and drops ice from a bucket inside while I wander the expansive terrace. Beyond being in Tribeca, this place alone probably costs a fortune. I stand at the far edge near an arranged seating area and look across the city as far as I can see. "Incredible."

"I could say the same."

I turn to find him standing with two drinks in his hands, and his eyes already set on me. I swallow hard, feeling his gaze reach the deep recesses of my body and weaken my knees like he used to.

He hands me the glass, then taps his against mine. "To—"

"Us," I say.

"To us." He dips his head, and then we sip with our eyes locked together. He then holds his hand out, and says, "You up for cooking?"

"We're making dinner?"

"I thought it might be fun."

I take his hand as we walk back inside. "Thought you didn't cook?"

"I don't much, but I learned a few dishes while in Italy." We reach the kitchen, and I see ingredients bundled in the corner of the counter.

I don't recognize the brands, and they're all in Italian. "You're going to make pasta for me?"

"It's the food of love. What else would I make for you?"

I melt into a puddle right here beside him, not sure I'll ever recover from his charm. The last guy ordered me a salad. Harbor wants to feed me carbs. I made the right decision. He gets a pot of water boiling and turns on the TV. "The Yankees game is starting. Do you mind the background noise?"

He knows the way to my heart. "Do I mind the best sport ever played being on? That would be a no." I bump up against his side. "Since when did you become a Yankees fan?"

"I'm a big fan of yours, if you haven't noticed, and since

you love the Yankees, I can make the sacrifice and cheer them on."

He's doing everything right, so right to make me swoon. I want to give in to him, to drop all walls and start fresh. I can see that he's changed physically with the five years that have passed, but internally, he's lived a lifetime. I'm so drawn to him, attracted to him body and soul, but we need to get the issues on the table to deal with first.

During the bottom of the second inning, I've been put in charge of chopping tomatoes and onions. He toasts garlic and pine nuts, and we add the onions into the pan while the water boils. Lemon slices are added in, then a layer of white wine. While the pan simmers, we stand in the living room, my shoes long discarded, watching the game, telling stories from the years the other missed, and laughing.

It's light with him. Fun. So much feels good that I'm afraid to ruin it.

Still sipping the drink, I finish it and then head to the terrace on a commercial break with him for refills. While he fills the glasses, I ask, "What did you do instead of going to medical school?"

The question doesn't seem to faze him. "You know about LA and Italy. I created a business plan and partnered with Italian luxury carmakers and brands to make custom sports cars."

"Cars?" I grin. "You always loved your Maserati."

He hands back my glass, and says, "I found a niche market for those who love cars more than I do. I've been here in the city for the past two years, growing the company."

Looking around, I add, "It seems you have found success with it." I grip the top of the chair nearby and tilt my head. "I had no doubt you'd find success in anything you tried."

"Thanks. I could say the same for you. Look at what you've achieved. Everything you dreamed."

"Not everything, but one of the biggest."

"What else do you dream about, Lark?" The sun hasn't even set, but I'm feeling a little tipsy.

I have a feeling it's more the company than the whiskey. "Sharing my life with someone special. How about you?"

He exhales, the warmth of his eyes coating me. "Do you still believe in destiny?"

My breathing deepens, and I take a sip to distract myself from how he affects me. "I still believe."

"I met my soul mate at twenty-two," he says, his eyes searching mine. "If I were to ever share my life again, it will only be with you."

I've become acquainted with the racing of my heart around him, but this time, it halts entirely. He closes the distance between us, setting his drink on the table, coming so near when he dips his head toward my ear. Sliding his arm around my waist, he whispers, "No apartment, city, or place could ever replace the home I found in you." Then he adds, "Breathe, baby."

I suck in a breath just as he leans back. Our bodies are still pressed together, his arm still holding me tight. We tilt our heads enough to see each other's eyes. I'm breathing, but barely as he steals it all over again. I whisper, "What do we do about that?"

He smirks and gives me a wink. "Fuck fate and make our own rules from now on."

I kiss him before he has the chance to kiss me. Wrapping my arms around his neck like a life preserver, I hold on to him like anger once held on to me. Unrelenting. I kiss him until our bodies mold together and our tongues touch, and then begin a slow and seductive tango.

The stove is turned off, and clothes fall to the floor as we pass the TV during the third inning and work our way into the bedroom. We kiss in a frenzy of hands and knees, legs and arms—feeling, connecting, admiring—falling to the bed and back into each other.

We make love with the shades wide open and no covers to hide any part of us. He stares into my eyes the first time he pushes in and dips his head when fully seated. A pause as if he can't catch his breath extends, and then he lifts, pushing my hair back from my face. "I never stopped loving you, Lark."

His words sink into my heart, and I feel their raw honesty. It's then that I also realize that no matter how much I thought I hated him, I only felt that strongly because I loved him so much. I still do. So much. "I love you," I reply, not worried about saying it first or too soon. I tell him how I feel, refusing to waste any more time on grudges and missed opportunities. I won't give air to the pains of the past and mistakes we both made. I caress his face and kiss him. "I love you, Harbor. I always will."

HAPPINESS IS WRITTEN all over Harbor's face.

A grin so genuine that it makes my heart ache in the best of ways.

His eyes are bright and wide on the game, but he's stealing glimpses of me like he can't believe I'm here.

And his hand has kept a constant connection with me since we sat down on the couch.

Cozy in a pair of his boxer shorts and an old Beacon U T-shirt, my legs are cuddled under the blanket as I take the last bite of pasta. "That recipe will get you laid," I say, only partly teasing.

He chuckles, rubbing my leg. "Good to know."

We've spent years apart, but it doesn't feel that way. I feel twenty-one with him again, our whole lives still ahead of us. I'm grateful we rediscovered our love when we did.

When a commercial comes on, I finally tackle the issue on the tip of my tongue all night. "Did you pay for my medical school?"

"What?" His brows pinch, and he does a double take. "Who told you that?"

"Why do you think someone told me that? Does it matter? Is it true?" His eyes shift away from me, but this time, I crawl across the couch and plant myself on his lap. With my arms around him, I kiss him once again, and then say, "Your parents paid, but I know you made it happen. Safe Haven Trust . . ." I watch his reaction as guilt settles into his eyes. "*Harbor.* Very clever, by the way."

His hand slides over my hip, holding me as if we spend every night like this, like time had no hold on us at all. He whispers, "How long have you known?"

"A few days." I glance at his lips, a sudden wave of comfort washing over me, and the urge to kiss him growing again. "I don't know how you pulled that off, Harbor, but for my own peace of mind, will you tell me how you did it?"

The game comes on again, but he mutes it. Rubbing circles over my hip, he says, "I asked my parents to give you the money they had set aside for me."

"Why?"

"Because I knew I wouldn't be able to live with the thought of you not achieving your dream."

"But you traded your future for mine. You shouldn't have done that."

"That's why I left." He slides his hand up my arm and over my shoulder, coming to rest on the side of my neck. "You would have never let me."

As I see the pain in his eyes as he tells me the truth, mine begin to water. "Not if I had a say."

"I know. When my parents agreed, I made sure all the pieces were in place—"

His words come back again, and I say, "It was the perfect plan, and it worked." Silence seeps in as we look into each other's eyes. "Was the pain worth it to be here now?"

"Yes," he answers with no doubt in his eyes. "Your happiness means more than anything else to me. If I can play a part in it, I'll do it all over again."

"I want to be with you, but . . ." I kiss him and then rest my head on his shoulder. "I need you to promise me you'll never leave me again, Harbor."

Grazing his hand over my cheek, he says, "I'm never leaving you again, baby."

48

Lark

THREE MONTHS LATER ...

HARBOR MOVED my stuff into the apartment the week after we had sex ... *I mean*, after we got back together. *But the sex was pretty damn amazing.* Still is.

I also realized my love for him had never truly faded. It had only been hidden by stormy clouds. It's so easy to love Harbor—then and now—but loving him in the aftermath of the storm we survived, our love has grown even deeper than I thought possible.

There are no benefits to living in the past when there's so much happiness to be found in the here, the now, and in the future together. But sometimes, life still throws a curveball ...

The cute two-room plus terrace apartment he owns just so happens to sit on top of a three-thousand-square-foot penthouse he also owns. I found out that our apartment is an addition he built onto the rooftop deck.

We have plenty of time to move downstairs and eventually start a family. We're still young and want to enjoy this stage of our lives. I ideally want to get through my residency as well, but my priorities are shifting enough to think about starting a family with him.

Harbor's still just as busy building his company as I have been with my shifts, so there's a lot to consider before diving into the next stage. Bonus, I love watching him work. Watching him in action is a glorious sight to behold. He didn't just tap into a market. He tapped into his passion, and I couldn't be more proud of him.

So although it's a stunning apartment and a very *Pride and Prejudice* ending for a fairy tale, I prefer our love nest for the two of us—the soft as a cloud bed and the large terrace where he set up a movie screen for us to watch the Yankees kick ass all season. There's just something about being in close quarters filled with our love.

How could I not be wildly in love with him? Harbor gave up everything for me. He doesn't see it that way, though, and he once said, "I got a life in exchange, the one I wanted, instead of my cousin's." My heart is full knowing he's pursuing his dreams and I get to bear witness.

Despite the hurdles we've covered, the next obstacle shows up in the form of an invitation. There's no return address to give me insight before opening. Just a handwritten letter without postage left with security downstairs in the lobby.

I flip it over several times like I might get a hint because it's so odd and kind of unsettling that it was hand-delivered. Setting it down, I wait for Harbor to come home.

Not an hour later, I hear the alarm's quick beat pattern

from the bath, and call out, "I'm in here."

It takes him a minute to make his way back to the bathroom. Harbor may be wealthy beyond reason, but his habits would fit a simpler life. He likes routine. Don't get me wrong, though, because he has a fantastic spontaneous streak. Once my schedule became more predictable, we could plan our time together better. We go out at least once or twice a week, especially if it's to meet with his clients and their significant others. But most nights we prefer to eat here, cook together, or if it's been a day, *which happens*, order in.

He's been known to surprise me with a quick trip here and there. What's the point of having all that money if you never enjoy it? When I'm in my own practice, I plan to surprise him in return.

With my head rested back and my eyes closed, I can see him dropping his keys in the bowl by the door, setting any packages we received on the island, and then stripping off his suit jacket as he works his way to the bedroom.

I open my eyes just as he leans against the doorway, unbuttoning his sleeves and rolling them up. *This man . . .* He's like the gift that keeps giving. I ask, "How was your day?"

"Better now that I'm seeing you." He comes over to bend down and kiss me. "How was yours?"

"Indulgent. I never know what to do on my days off, so I stayed in bed most of the day. I caught up on sleep, did a little reading, and watched a movie. Uneventful."

"Sounds full." He then asks, "What's the letter on the counter?"

"I don't know. I was waiting for you to get home to open it."

He crosses his arms over his chest and leans his bicep on

the doorframe. "Why?"

"Just wanted you here. Do you want to grab it?"

"Drink?" he asks once he disappears into the room again.

"Wine works. There's an open bottle in the fridge." I lie back, but my bubbles are starting to dissipate, and the hot water is now only warm. I won't be in much longer at this rate.

He returns, setting the glass on the small table next to the tub, and then asks, "Want me to open it since you're wet?"

"Yes, please." I take the glass and a large sip. It's weird that this feels different. We get invitations all the time, but this doesn't feel like a charity or event to attend. It's personal.

He pulls a flat card from the envelope and scans it, glances at me, and then exhales. Rubbing his hand over his head, he looks back at me, and says, "If you weren't already sitting down—"

"What is it? Who's it from?"

"Liz."

The glass bangs against the side of the tub in my rush to sit up. "My mom?" I ask, knowing exactly who Liz is.

Turning the card to face me, he points at the signature. "Elizabeth Shaw."

I squint to read it from across the bathroom. "What does it say?"

Reading over it again, he replies, "She's inviting you to dinner."

"When? Where?" I set the glass down and grab a towel when I stand.

Harbor's gaze travels from my knees to my eyes and then returns to the card. Though a mischievous glint appears when he sneaks another look at me. "You're very distracting."

I roll my eyes because I can say the same about him, and have, many times. He offers me a hand when I step out of the tub. With the towel wrapped around me, I lean against him and read the card for myself.

"I didn't even know if she was alive." I wander into the bedroom to get dressed. "This is a lot to process."

"There's no request to reply. She's telling you where she'll be and at what time, but it's up to you what you choose to do with that information."

"I have until Friday night to decide."

"Three days."

"Three days to decide if I want to see the woman who abandoned me or move on with my life."

Three days to decide if I put a bow on that part of my life by not going.

Three days to get the closure I've wanted since she walked out the door.

Three days that will change the rest of my life forever.

Three days to decide . . .

I look back once more at Harbor.

He mouths, "You got this," from the car before he pulls away from the restaurant.

I can do this.

It's no big deal. Just meeting your mother for the first time since she left you.

No biggie at all.

I picked comfort over trying to impress anyone. Wearing dark jeans and a jacket over a tank top, I look down at my penny loafers, suddenly feeling underdressed for this restaurant. *Too late now.*

I walk up to the woman behind the podium, and say, "Hi, I'm meeting someone here for dinner."

Without looking at me, the host asks, "Name on the reservation?"

"Elizabeth Shaw."

She grins, but I don't sense any sincerity in it. By how busy she is, I won't take it personally. Leading me through the tables to a back room filled with even more tables, I see Liz before we get close. It would be hard not to recognize an older version of myself.

Is it weird to think she's pretty? Is that a compliment in disguise for myself? Anxiety has my feelings reeling along with my mind. The host says, "Here you are."

Liz looks up from her phone and then quickly stands. Looking at me probably how I'm staring at her. Her hair is medium brown in color and falls just below her shoulders. It's straight, not like mine that has my father's wave to it. Her eyes match though but hold more gold than green in them. I say, "Hello."

Dressed in fitted black pants and a white blouse, she looks younger than her age, maybe early forties. Until now, I'd almost forgotten that she was so young when she had me.

She sets her phone down, and then says, "Lark, it's . . . it's such a pleasure to see you again." Though she makes it sound like we've met more recently, I don't consider that to be accurate since I was a toddler. But I do find relief from her appearing as nervous as I am. Signaling to the chair across from her, she smiles. "Please. Sit."

Pulling the seat out, I sit down and hang my purse from the top of the chair. We sit across from each other a moment before she says, "Thank you for coming. I didn't think you would."

"I didn't know if I would. Not until a few hours ago."

She swallows, and it makes me self-conscious when I do. I take the glass of water already on the table and sip. She asks, "Would you like a drink? I'm having wine, hoping to settle my nerves." She laughs anxiously.

Call me soft, but my heart feels for her and me trying to reconnect after a horrible situation. "It's nice to see you, too. Why did you . . . why now?"

"My parents passed away a few years ago, and I realized that life is too short to not be there for those you love."

The shock of learning that both my grandparents have passed away, that they're gone without the option of ever having a reunion is disconcerting. I take the napkin from the table and twist it in my lap. "I'm sorry for your loss."

"I'm sorry for yours," she replies. Leaning forward, she says, "They had a lot of regrets."

"Most people do on their deathbeds." I don't mean to sound cold, but I'm more confused than ever as to why I'm here. "I'm sorry."

"No, it's understandable. That's why I waited to reach out to you. It's hard to empathize with someone when they've been hurt by you."

I start to release and feel more myself. "It's not hard. I'm a doctor. I do it every day."

Her smile is tight, but she nods. She releases a long breath just as the server arrives to take our drink orders. I order wine, thinking she's probably right. Maybe it will help me drop my guard so I can enjoy this meeting instead of it being a confrontation. But also because I keep thinking about how she confessed that she loves me, even if it was indirectly.

"I'm so proud of you, Lark. You've accomplished so much that I wonder if it would have been the same if I had been there."

"We'll never know, but I'm starting to realize that living in the past won't move the needle forward. I have questions, and I'm hoping you'll be willing to answer at least some of them. I'll give you that same opportunity, and then when we leave, we can decide what happens from here. How does that sound?"

"I'd like that very much. Would you like to go first?"

The wineglasses and a bottle are set on the table. After the server pours the wine, we order appetizers. I'm not sure if we'll make it to dinner, so this feels like less of an obligation. The alcohol helps. I've asked so much of her, but I've still been dancing around what I want to know most. So I take another heavier sip, and ask, "Why did you leave?"

"I've been trying to figure that out myself for twenty-five years. The reasons made sense in the beginning, but then time passed, and it felt too late to turn back. Does that make sense?"

"No, it doesn't. I was your daughter. You had a man who worshipped at your feet. You left us. You left us for what? Why?"

It's the first time tonight that tears begin to well in her eyes. And because I feel this surge of overwhelming emotion from just voicing that question, I take my napkin and dab the corners of my eyes.

She dabs her own eyes, and then says, "My parents cared more about status than my happiness back then. I loved your dad so much, but they cut me off when I refused to stop dating him. They cut me out of their lives entirely. I had no money. I had nothing more than a high school diploma and eyes full of stars when John and I fell in love. Then I had a baby—you. I don't think you'll be surprised to hear you were unplanned, but we never had a doubt about starting our family. It just came a little sooner than expected."

Briefly looking across the room, she turns her attention to the wineglass and takes another sip. "It's a hard lesson to learn that money matters when you're surviving off love. If I found a penny, I'd pick it up because we needed it. We had nothing back then, and your dad was trying to buy his garage. It wasn't going to happen. He would have been turned down for the loan." She's nodding as if she's attempting to convince herself.

"How would leaving me get him the shop?"

"It wasn't as easy as you make it sound. There were offers and threats. My parents wanted to leave Beacon Pointe to remove me from the situation."

Jabbing my fingers into my chest, I say, "I was the situation."

"This is what I meant by being too late to turn back. The deal was that John would get the loan he needed if I left him." She pauses, looking down and wiping her eyes again.

"Okay, I understand what a hard position that would be, but he would have made it work without a loan. Why did you leave me?"

"Because they threatened to get custody and take you from us. If I left, at least John would have you. I figured one parent was better than none." She toys with her napkin and then adds, "I made the biggest mistake in my life leaving the two of you, but please realize at twenty-one, I thought it was the only option I had. I believed them."

"Yet you kept them in your life."

"No," she says, shaking her head. "Not for a lot of those years." Pressing her palms on the tablecloth, she sinks in her seat just a little "I promise you, Lark, I did what I thought would be best for the two of you. I've lived in hell since the day I walked away."

"Why are rich people so evil?"

Dipping my head down, I know that's not true. The Westcotts are some of the most generous people I've ever known. And Harbor, my Harbor, is always worrying about others. It seems there are just a few bad seeds.

"I'm sorry," she says. "I don't expect you to forgive me, but I hope that we can start working toward having a relationship."

"A relationship?" I'm not sure how to feel about that. I think it's because I didn't expect her to take responsibility like she has. She was young, made a bad decision that sounds like she's spent her life regretting.

How many more years do we have to suffer? Medically speaking, resentment wreaks havoc on your mental and physical health. Personally, it's hard not to feel something when it's clear Liz is in so much pain. There's still so much to work through, but what if . . . what if we tried to work through it together? The best gift we can give ourselves is the option to try to move forward.

I reply, "I think I'm ready to start from here, from today and this meeting."

Her smile is the widest I've seen. "I appreciate that so much. Thank you."

She reaches down and pulls a large white envelope from her bag. Patting it, she says, "I'd like to continue this anytime you're available and up for it. "I know this is hard, but I would like to ask if we can see each other again?"

It is draining, but I can feel the possibility of coming to peace with her. I have to focus on that aspect. "I'd like that."

She smiles at me. "Thank you. Let me give you my

number."

We exchange information and then turn to leave, but I stop and go to her. "May I hug you?"

"I'd love that." She wraps her arms around me, making my heart hurt just a little. This is what it would have felt like had I grown up around her and gotten mom hugs. They're pretty great.

She hands me the envelope. "I want you to have this."

"Okay." I take it and tuck it under my arm.

She says, "I always loved you. I never stopped." I smile, feeling a little more whole, and think, that's all I ever wanted to know. "Goodbye, Lark."

"Goodbye, Mom."

Seeing Harbor already waiting on the sidewalk, I rush into his arms, fully embracing him. Liz and John didn't get their happy ending, but I won't lose mine.

He wraps himself around me, holding me tight and kissing my head.

He was right.

This is home. Like he once said, the place doesn't matter. *Home is found in him.*

We get in the car and start back for the apartment. He asks, "How'd it go?"

"I think it was better than I expected."

"That's good." He glances over and then rests his hand on my leg. "But I'm not surprised. You're amazing." Always my biggest fan. *The charmer.*

I rest my hand on his, loving the warmth. "Thanks, babe." I take a deep breath, smiling as joy takes hold of me. I was loved. This is all the little girl inside me ever wanted to hear. Feeling content, I rest back in the chaos of traffic and smile. "For the first time in my life, I now know she loved me."

EPILOGUE

Harbor

Three months later . . .

My life didn't begin and end with Lark Summerlin. It froze in time because of her.

Room 156.
    Row 14.
    Seat 20.

Lark wasn't the type I usually dated back in high school or college, but she was the girl I fell hopelessly, madly in love with the moment I laid eyes on her. I still remember every detail about her.

Strands of hair loose that had escaped the elastic.

The way her eyes narrowed when she was trying to concentrate.

There was no doubt that she was there to learn.

I never thought I stood a chance after purposely

bumping into her. Busy digging in her backpack, she never looked up. Sometimes I wonder what would have happened if she had. Would I have done anything differently if we had met under those circumstances?

No.

The past six months have been a blur. Honestly, I can't tell you a fucking thing we've been up to since most of that time was spent in bed. Just how we like it. Sure, we bought season tickets to the Yankees and went to games last summer.

Liz and Lark's connection appears to be growing stronger each time they see each other. I'm glad they're rebuilding their relationship. If I had to bet on them, I think they'll heal most of their wounds. They both want to, they say, so that's a positive sign.

When it comes to Lark and me, just being upfront, but our lives are pretty much sex, sleep, eat, work, repeat the rest of the time. And neither of us would have it any other way. I can't imagine my life without her.

And I don't plan to. *Not ever.*

That bird saved me that day on the ledge. *Lark saved me years later.* She didn't just give me the time of day. She gave me the time of her life and made my life worth living. I'll never stop thanking her for that opportunity.

It's been a long day, and the apartment is quiet when I enter. Without the lamp on in the bedroom, the only light is dusk sneaking in through the edges of the curtains. I wish I could see more of my beauty, but I know my eyes will soon adjust. Dealing with ego-driven clients all day is exhausting, but when I see Lark with her hands tucked behind her back and completely naked on the bed, I'm fully energized again. She smirks, knowing exactly what she's doing. *The siren.*

Lark's eyes roam over my body, settling on my dick for a

few extra seconds before challenging me when she locks onto my gaze. She asks, "*Hard* day?"

"Getting harder by the second." I grab her by the ankles and pull her to me. Hovering over her, I kiss her lips and tease her nipples before stripping my dress shirt and pants from my body. Seems only fair to finish and get fully naked like she is, so I do.

"Do you have dinner plans?" She bites her lower lip.

I rub the inside of her thighs and then drop to my knees, kissing them and spreading her legs apart. I kiss the soft skin and head higher, draping her legs over my shoulders. I run the tip of my nose along the bend of her leg and then inhale, closing my eyes.

She's intoxicating, but our physical connection will never match the depth of the love I feel for her. I can survive anything knowing she'll be waiting for me on the other side. She's wholly captivated my soul, but she's also squirming for attention, so I reply, "I do. I have plans for you, Dr. Summerlin."

Dipping down, I make love to her with my mouth and then to her body, staring into those gorgeous green eyes of hers until neither of us can keep them open. Our releases hit hard, and we fall apart in each other's arms.

Not forty-five minutes later, she moans in pleasure . . . beside me as she takes another bite of the blueberry pancakes we ordered. She reaches for a cup of orange juice and takes a sip as soon as she swallows her food. "I realized today," she starts, "that I don't exercise anymore."

Chuckling, I say, "You get enough at home."

"And I'm on my feet all day at work." She takes a breath and leans back against the wall, wrapping one arm over her stomach. After setting the OJ down, she laughs lightly. "This is my love language right here. Feeding me carbs with a big helping of you, babe."

She's adorable.

After dragging her food through the syrup at the bottom of the tray, she then eats it. "Why does breakfast in bed make everything taste so much better?"

I finish my bacon and start back on my scrambled eggs. "Maybe it's the company and not the food."

"The company is pretty delicious." Leaning over, she kisses my shoulder.

I'm tempted to kiss her syrupy lips. I'm craving her—*all of her*—again, but I resist even though she's looking at me like she might prefer I have her for dessert. The woman's insatiable.

Orange juice.

Food.

Syrupy fingers . . . mmm.

Fuck. That doesn't help take my mind off my dick and how delectable she looks next to me. But then she asks, "You know what I could go for?"

Fuck it. Who am I trying to impress? I can't resist her. I kiss her until the containers are forgotten and fall off the bed. I kiss her hard and then fuck her until she only remembers my name.

In the shower, she says, "I was going to say some home-made beans and franks, but the sex was better." We fall into laughter and then start kissing. One thing always leads to another with her. When it comes to Lark, I'm the insatiable one.

After shutting off the lights and checking the locks, I settle back in bed next to her. She's close to a deeper sleep, so I move to her and wrap my arm around her. I love this woman with all my heart. Yep, I'm the lucky one all right.

Closing my eyes, I breathe in the tranquility she brings, then quickly fall asleep wrapped around her.

I'm woken by the sound of pacing in the bedroom. Opening one eye and then the other, I find Lark near the window. "Hey," I ask, my voice raspy with sleep. "What's going on?"

She points across the room, and asks, "That's what I'm wondering? What is that still doing in your possession?"

"What?" I twist to see a box in the dark near the bathroom. "What is it?"

"That's what I'm wondering."

I sigh and rub my eyes. Sitting up, I see the time—3:45 AM—and then slide my gaze lower across the room. From what I can make out, she's in a pair of boxer shorts and a tank top. "Are you going to make me get out of bed?"

She bends to pick it up and then comes to sit next to me. "Ah," I add. "That."

"Yes, that."

"I thought you were going to tell me you're pregnant or something."

I earn a smile, although slight, for that. "You'd love that, wouldn't you?" she asks, her tone softening along with her annoyance.

Reaching over, I caress her cheek with the back of my fingers. "I wouldn't be opposed to it."

Leaning over, she gives me a kiss. "I love you." She props back up. "Now, tell me why you still have this box, babe. I thought this was long gone. You know I never want to be anything like a Bensimone." Her nickname for bitch is quite entertaining, especially since the country club revoked the Bensimones' lifetime membership, and my mom booted her from the fundraising organization she runs.

I chuckle. "You should have just opened it back at graduation."

"You know I don't like ridiculously expensive gifts. What's the point in spending so much on something that you need a security guard when using it?" I adore her big heart and how superficial stuff doesn't matter, but it also makes it hard to buy her presents sometimes.

Rubbing her leg, I reply, "Not sure if you remember, but I sell ridiculously expensive cars as gifts all the time. Those cars paid for the penthouse and our little addition up here."

Her shoulders round, and she sighs this time. "You know what I mean."

"I do, but open it, baby. I might surprise you in a good way."

"You always surprise me in a good way." She takes the end of the ribbons and pulls. "I'm nervous. It's not a turquoise bag, is it? I'd hate that gift."

"I thought of that, just to hear you laugh, but no, it's not turquoise." She stops and shoots me a glare. I chuckle harder. "It's not a bag at all. Happy?"

"Okay, I'm happy," she says, seeming to calm. She lifts the lid and sets it aside on the bed. "Another box?" She glances up and then pulls it out to give a little shake. "It has weight to it. What is it?"

I don't have a nervous bone in my body. This is something I wanted to give her years prior, but the middle of the night works as well. "Just open it."

She lifts the flaps on the box, removes the tissue, and then stops, covers her mouth, and starts crying. I wrap my arms around her and pull her to my chest. "It's not that big of a deal." I kiss her head.

Sitting up, she says, "Creating a scholarship in my name for kids who might never get the opportunity to follow their dreams is a *very* big deal." She kisses me. "And the best present you could ever give me." She caresses my cheek. "What an incredible graduation present. Thank you, babe." She kisses me again. I'll take as many as she's willing to give.

"You started this years ago, and I didn't even know."

"I wanted a gift that kept giving, so I cashed out one of my trust funds. The scholarship is fully funded for the next twenty years. And you've already had two Beacon graduates pursue higher education because of you."

Though tears still glisten on her cheeks, she grins. "Because of you."

This time I kiss her, rolling her gently onto her back. Staring into her eyes, I ask, "Will you marry me, Lark?"

"Thought you'd never ask." She pulls me down to kiss her this time, and when our lips eventually part, she says, "A thousand times yes."

My wife is stunning in a white, strapless dress with a skirt that just barely catches in the wind. The brooch was her *something old* that she wore in her hair. It was a nice touch, especially since her mom was there. But for me, the little yellow ribbon she wore pinned to the garter—in her words, "to honor the bird that saved me"—cemented what I knew all along. *I'm still the lucky one.*

"*You* are the Lark that saved me, baby."

John walked her down the aisle in the backyard of my parents' home. The ceremony wasn't big, just the people who matter—my family, her dad, Amanda, and a few others who touched our lives along the way. Even Dane stopped by as an invited guest. He shook my hand and wanted to thank me for changing his life.

I take no credit for that.

He changed the course of his life when he made amends with the people he hurt. Living with a clear conscience makes life so much sweeter.

My aunt wasn't invited. I know it's healthier to forgive her in the long run, but I'm not there yet.

But something Lark said to me more recently stuck. *"There have been more than enough broken hearts in this lifetime."* After checking with her dad, she invited Liz.

And she showed up.

I leave her and John chatting at the buffet to find my bride near the garden just before sunset. "Need a breather?" I ask, wrapping my arms around her.

"No. Just wanted to stand back and take it all in. I used to work these events, and now, here I am hosting one." She smiles. "It's pretty surreal."

Lark hasn't changed from the girl I met, but I have. *For the better.* Because if I learned anything along this journey to the altar, it's that all we used to be doesn't matter. It's who we are now that counts. When she helped me escape my past, I discovered who I had always wanted to be. In business—*my own boss.* In my personal life—*her husband.*

Now I've achieved both.

I hold out my elbow, and she wraps her arm around it. "Are you ready to spend the next eighty years together?"

"Only eighty?" She laughs and bumps into me. "I've been thinking."

"About?"

"I think forever sounds better. What do you think?"

"Sounds perfect to me, Doctor."

YOU MIGHT ALSO ENJOY

<u>**Recommendations**</u> - Three books I think you'll enjoy reading after *Swear on My Life*. All are stand-alones that will grab your heart and carry it through the story.

**Turn the page to read a sample of Best I Ever Had

Read in Kindle Unlimited and Listen in Audio

Best I Ever Had - You will be on the edge of your seat with your heart on the line as two soul mates fight for the future stolen from them.
   READ NOW
   We Were Once - When one time isn't enough, comes a sweep you off your feet second chance romance. Free in Kindle Unlimited.
   READ NOW
   Everest - I let her slip through my fingers once. I won't make that mistake twice. Secrets broke us apart. Can a second chance bring us back together?

READ NOW

BEST I EVER HAD

They came without warning—
the storm and the man.
One day, I'll look back and realize they were one and the
same.

PROLOGUE

No halo is hanging over her chestnut-colored hair, and she's paler than most of the sun-worshiping girls at the party. She blends into the background. Not much about her outfit stands out—corduroy miniskirt, sunset-orange tights, ankle boots, and a burgundy top caught at the waist. No one else seems to notice her.

Except me

. . . And Troy Hogan.

But seeing the way he wraps his arm around her neck, I'd say they're already well-acquainted. That's too bad.

For him.

She may be dating him tonight, but we haven't met yet.

CHAPTER 1

Cooper Reed Haywood

FIVE MONTHS Later

I'VE NEVER BELIEVED in omens or signs, but I've been given several in the past hour.

The lights of Bean There coffee shop shine like a beacon through the heavy pelts of rain. I make a mad dash for the door, swinging it open with more force than necessary in my rush to get inside. No one appears bothered when the bell above the door rings, but I get two quick glances from over the tops of laptops near the counter.

And then they carry on minding their own business.

"Seat yourself," chimes a voice from behind a swinging door. The porthole window gives me a glimpse of the brunette bustling in the back.

I score a table by the window and, as luck would have it, an outlet. My laptop doesn't have enough juice to last the hours needed to write my paper. When my building lost power and the generator didn't kick in, I went to the library. The horde of over-caffeinated and procrastinating students pouring out of the doors told me I'd have no luck in there.

After rubbing my hair dry with the hood of my jacket, I unpack my bag to prepare for the long night ahead. As this coffee shop is on the opposite side of town from where I live and farther from Atterton University's campus than I generally travel for a hot brew, this is my first visit. But it's decent in here, low key with a kind of old-school hideaway vibe to it —lamps instead of bright overhead lights, scuffed wood floors that have seen better days, and jazz playing in the background.

Apparently, I'm the only one not privy to this secret. Every table, though they're small, is occupied. Bags on the floor, laptops open, the unflattering glow of LED white lights reflecting across faces half-hidden by their screens.

Little plates with muffins and coffee cups fill the tables to the point I'm starting to think these people are taking up residency instead of just being here for the evening. That or the staff is slacking. Since I'm not seeing anyone other than the girl in the back, I'm thinking that might be more the case.

When I reach down to plug my laptop in, I hear, "The storm rolled in without warning."

I turn back to see golden-centered hazel eyes peering down at me and a smile that momentarily makes me think sunshine has broken through the rain. But those sunset-orange tights give the brunette beauty away as images of a party last summer come flashing back.

Not sure why I glance down at her ring finger. *Habit, I guess.*

I've been called a player a time or ten, but I've only ever set out to break apart one relationship.

Hers.

Wonder if it worked. "Hi," I say.

Her smile widens. "Hi." When she glances out the window, I'm given a quick chance to study her. *Again.*

It's not been a year since I last saw her, not even quite five months, but she looks a little different. Other than the telltale sign of a small green apron signifying that she works here, the strings are pulled tight around a curvy little waist I wouldn't mind exploring sometime, and her hair is longer with lighter-colored strands blended in.

High cheekbones highlight those pretty hazel eyes and long lashes, but I'm drawn to the natural pink pucker of her lips as she studies the weather outside. Most girls choose cherry gloss, but her mouth is matte. It makes me curious what she tastes like.

A black suede skirt instead of corduroy and the same boots she wore at my party. But that's not the difference I'm sensing. I can't quite put my finger on it.

She shifts to look back at me. "I was saying the storm came out of nowhere."

"The weather app predicted it, but no one expects a summer storm like this in December."

"Not without snow along with it, but the fifties won't get us there. And technically, that'd be a winter storm then."

"I hate snow."

Her smile remains as bright as her eyes. "I don't mind it so much."

"Yeah?" This time, I grin. "What is it about snow that you don't mind so much?"

She slips into the seat across from me without an invitation. I like that about her. Leaning forward as if she's revealing a secret, she replies, "I think it's more the images it conjures. A Baileys Irish Cream hot chocolate by a roaring fire. Curled up in a big, cushy chair reading a book while snow falls outside. Christmas morning and presents under the tree."

"Sounds perfect."

"To me, too." She stands. "Can I get you something to drink and eat?"

I look toward the display cabinet under the counter. Nothing appeals to me, so I eye the chalkboard menu on the wall. "What's your soup today?"

"Tomato basil. It's really good and even better with a grilled cheese." She pushes some hair behind her ear, revealing a name tag pinned to her green apron.

"You know how to upsell," I say, getting a good look at the name that I never got when I first saw her. "Story. That's a—"

"Unique. Weird. Strange name. I get that all the time." She shrugs and laughs to herself. "I could be describing my mom the same way."

Our eyes lock together, and I say, "Beautiful. I was going to say beautiful."

"Oh." Cringing, she seems to lose some of the composure she was holding on to seconds prior. *Ah, fuck.* She blushes, and I know I'm done for. "Um, that's very nice of you to say. Thank you."

"You're welcome, Story."

"Don't go wearing it out now."

God, I'd love to wear it out.

Her laughter dances around us, keeping smiles on both our faces. She's utterly breathtaking. "What's your name?" she asks.

"Story?" Some guy calls out to her from across the café, redirecting her attention to him.

"Be right there, Lou." She turns back to me but thumbs

over her shoulder. "Louis. He's a handful around finals." Snapping a pen and pad from her apron, she asks, "The soup and sandwich?"

"How can I resist?"

"Good choice." With a wink, she walks away but backs up and returns. "And to drink?"

"Coffee. Black is good."

I don't expect a smile in return for my order, but I get one anyway. She's easy to admire. *Pretty, like her name.* It's not one thing specifically, but how her features work together with the heart shape of her face that makes her so appealing. She taps my table with her pen. "I'll be back."

"Hope so."

She backs away, still looking at me, but then runs into the chair of another patron. "Oh, sorry."

The guy has no patience for her and grumbles something under his breath that makes me want to teach him some manners with a punch to the face. I let it go this time, though, and get back to why I'm here in the first place.

"I'm right here," Story says tableside.

"What?"

She drags her free hand under the mug for effect. "Your coffee."

"Oh, that." I rub the side of my neck. "Right. The coffee."

Setting it down, she says, "I didn't mean to sneak up on you."

"Sometimes life does that."

"When you least expect it," we say in unison and then break into laughter.

She rests a hand on the opposite chair and tilts her head like she plans to stay awhile. I can't say I'd be upset by it. I'd rather spend time with her than work on this fucking paper.

"I use that quote all the time, and no one ever knows what I'm talking about," she says.

"Maybe we were the only two who saw the film?"

"Could be." Her eyes widen and capture the shine from a nearby lamp. "There *was* only one other person in the theater when I watched it at the Pantheon."

"Two o'clock showing?"

"Yes," she replies, her smile growing by the second. "Did you know it only played for one day?"

Snapping my fingers, I then point. "The girl with the pickle?"

She bursts out laughing before she quietens and looks around. No one dares to give Story a dirty look. Me, on the other hand, I get three. They're just jealous.

"I feel like I'm owed a secret of yours since you know one of my dirty little ones."

"I have a strong suspicion you're not the only one who eats pickles during a movie."

"True. They do keep the jar right there on the counter. Oh, crap!" She dashes across the shop, pushing through to the back. "Dammit!" Her voice reaches all the way to my table in the front.

I start to wonder if I should offer assistance, but just as I stand, she pushes through the door and heads my way with a plate in her hands. "Everything okay?" I ask.

"It's all good. I burned one grilled cheese to smithereens because I left it too close to the fire on the grill." She sets the plate down with a bowl balanced on top. "Fortunately for you, that was my dinner and not yours."

Looking at the plate and then back at her, I offer, "We can share?" I gesture to the other chair again, my paper now on the back burner near the fire, ready to fail me for ignoring it.

"No, that's yours."

"I don't mind." Picking up one-half of the cut sandwich, I dunk it in the soup. "Chef recommended." I take a bite, letting the creamy soup meld with the cheesy bread. I haven't had a grilled cheese in a long time. I'd forgotten how good they are. The chill from the rain has worn off, but the soup and sandwich warm me on the inside. "It's really good."

Her hand covers her belly, and she looks around as if others are eavesdropping. "My stomach just growled."

I push the plate closer to her. "Take the other half."

"I—"

"I insist."

She bobbles her head in debate and then sits. "Well, since you insist." Picking up the other half, she dips a corner into the soup, then devours a big bite. "Little known fact about the coffee shop. We only make this meal on stormy days. I've pleaded to management to keep it on the menu, but the owner insists it tastes so good because we crave it."

"Absence makes the stomach grow fonder."

"Something like that." She takes another bite and monitors the other patrons. Everyone's too involved in their work to care about her taking a break with me.

When we finish our halves, she moves the bowl to my side of the table. "I appreciate the snack. Now eat your soup." Pushing up, she adds, "I need to get back to work."

Glancing at my laptop, I say, "I guess I should, too."

"I'll leave you to it." She backs away and adds, "Thanks for sharing. The food's on me."

I'm sure she means something entirely different than the images populating my brain. I finish the soup, then dig into my paper. The professor crossed a line when she threatened me with an F. So what if I skipped some classes and forgot about a few assignments? I aced the tests, and I'll be golden when I finish this paper.

If only something more interesting didn't hold my attention. It's when I'm watching her flutter around the shop that I realize that, unlike the party, she doesn't blend in here at all despite the dark-colored clothes.

No, Story is just the book I want to read.

But if memory serves me right, and it always does, she had a boyfriend back in August.

Fuck.

Troy Hogan.

He and I have had more than our fair share of encounters. None went well for him. The thing is, Story was never in attendance. *Did they break up?*

Catching her eyeing me, I grin. She smiles from behind the counter like I didn't just bust her and keeps staring at me. I don't mind those hazel eyes on me, but I can't figure her out.

When that Lou character calls her over again, I check her out. Five-three. Five-four max. Hair kissing the middle of her back. Even through the heavier material of the clothes, I can tell she's got a rockin' little body. She doesn't come off as the type of girl to hide her curves. She just has the confidence to wear what she likes.

Passing by, she drops off a glass of water and swipes the empty plate and bowl. I'd forgotten about the coffee since I only ordered it so I wouldn't get kicked out of the place. I take a sip of it even though it's cooled. I really need to focus, and maybe the caffeine can help.

I stick in my earbuds, turn on a white noise track, and start where I left off in my research. I'm not sure how long I've been working, but when I sit up to stretch, I notice half the place has emptied out.

Story hops off the counter and comes over with a water pitcher. As she tops off my glass, she says, "I never did get your name."

I've thought about this girl over the past five months, wondering what ever happened to her. I'd see Hogan and look for her to pop out of his beatdown truck. That never happened. But here she is as if something bigger just played their hand, and we've hit the jackpot. I hold my hand out. "Cooper."

She slips her hand in mine, and when we shake, she says, "It's nice to meet you, Cooper."

"The pleasure's all mine." Our hands fall apart. Since I was never one to beat around the bush, I ask, "Are you seeing anyone?"

To continue reading Best I Ever Had, Click Here.

Now available in ebook, paperback, and audiobook.

THANK YOU

You are amazing.

I appreciate my readers so much. I know you have a million+ choices when you reach for your next read. Thank you for choosing mine.

Brittni Van, Content Editing, Overbooked Author Services
Jenny Sims, Copy Editing at Editing4Indies
Kristen Johnson, Proofreader
Michele Ficht, Beta Reader,
Andrea Johnston, Beta Reader
Cover Design: RBA Designs
Photographer: Christian Oita
Model: Michael Yerger

My team is truly the best. I can't thank each of you enough. Your support and patience with me is noticed and so appreciated. I love you and cherish you endlessly,

Suzie

Love always to my world - my family <3

FOLLOW ME

To keep up to date with her writing and more, visit S.L. Scott's website: **www.slscottauthor.com**

To receive the newsletter about all of her publishing adventures, free books, giveaways, steals and more:

https://geni.us/intheknow

Follow me on TikTok: https://geni.us/SLTikTok
Follow on IG: https://geni.us/IGSLS
Follow on Bookbub: https://geni.us/SLScottBB